How Love Came to Professor Guildea & Other Uncanny Tales

ROBERT HICHENS

Introduction by S.T. Joshi

Stark House Press • Eureka California

HOW LOVE CAME TO PROFESSOR GUILDEA
AND OTHER UNCANNY TALES

Published by Stark House Press
1315 H Street
Eureka, CA 95501, USA
griffinskye3@sbcglobal.net
www.starkhousepress.com

"How Love Came to Professor Guildea" and "The Lady and the Beggar" from *Tongues of Conscience* (originally published and copyright © 1900 by Methuen & Company, London, and Frederick A. Stokes, New York).

"The Collaborators" from *The Folly of Eustace and Other Stories* (originally published and copyright © 1896 by D. Appleton, New York).

"A Tribute of Souls" and "The Man Who Intervened" from *Bye-Ways* (originally published and copyright © 1897 by D. Appleton, New York).

"The Spinster" from *The Black Spaniel and Other Stories* (originally published by Methuen & Company, London, 1905, and Frederick A. Stokes, New York, 1905; copyright © 1905 by Robert Hichens).

"The Lost Faith" from *Snake-Bite and Other Stories* (originally published and copyright © 1919 by Cassell and Company, London).

"Introduction" copyright 2023 © by S. T. Joshi

This edition copyright © 2023 by Stark House Press. All rights reserved under International and Pan-American Copyright Conventions.

ISBN: 979-8-88601-051-0

Book design by Mark Shepard, shepgraphics.com
Proofreading by Bill Kelly
Cover art by C. B. Williams

PUBLISHER'S NOTE
This is a work of fiction. Names, characters, places and incidents are either the products of the author's imagination or used fictionally, and any resemblance to actual persons, living or dead, events or locales, is entirely coincidental. Without limiting the rights under copyright reserved above, no part of this publication may be reproduced, stored, or introduced into a retrieval system or transmitted in any form or by any means (electronic, mechanical, photocopying, recording or otherwise) without the prior written permission of both the copyright owner and the above publisher of the book.

First Stark House Press Edition: March 2023

How Love Came to Professor Guildea and Other Uncanny Tales

How Love Came to Professor Guildea: Professor Guildea is an extremely unsentimental man—he doesn't need nor want anyone's affection. He has his work, and that is enough. Until one evening when he sees a figure in the park, and crosses the street to investigate. No one is there, and yet Guildea is convinced that someone follows him back into his house… a strange presence with a curious and very irritating attraction to him.

A Tribute of Souls: Alistair Ralston, the young Laird of Carlounie, has a feeble soul matched to his pinched and pallid body. But his desires are Gargantuan, as is his hate for those more fortunate. And so one day he takes a book of magical incantations into the woods and makes a pact with the grey traveller: three souls to Satan in exchange for a renewed body. He is brought back to Carlounie in a fever. When he recovers, he is a new man—powerful, driven. It is time to use this power…

The Lost Faith: Olivia has known most of her life that she has the power to heal. It all comes down to faith. After she heals young Fernol West—victim of a head injury—her fame spreads to England, where she and Fernol are hosted by the noted eccentric, Lord Sandring. When Olivia meets Sir Hector and is asked to cure his skeptical sister of her blinding headaches, her real test of faith begins.

Enter the mysterious realm of Robert Hichens. These three stories and four more weird tales of the unexpected—await you…

Contents

Introduction 7
How Love Came to Professor Guildea 12
The Collaborators 51
The Man Who Intervened 68
A Tribute of Souls 83
The Spinster 124
The Lady and the Beggar 134
The Lost Faith 148
Bibliography 249

Introduction

By S. T. Joshi

At the turn of the twentieth century, British author Robert Hichens (1864–1950) established himself as one of the most dynamic fiction writers in the English-speaking world. His first four short story collections—*The Folly of Eustace and Other Stories* (1896), *Bye-ways* (1897), *Tongues of Conscience* (1900), and *The Black Spaniel and Other Stories* (1905)—contained tales ranging from brief vignettes to substantial novellas. More relevantly, they featured an array of material that simultaneously explored the weirdness inherent in such supernatural motifs as the ghost, the revenant, and psychic possession, but also in the more problematical aspects of human personality. This selection of Hichens's stories presents a sampling from these collections—as well as one later story—that fully justifies their branding as "uncanny."

Hichens saw strangeness everywhere, but particularly in the manner in which human beings deal with the varied, complex, and at times torturous circumstances of life. Most of the stories in this volume are ones in which characters are faced with a crucial, life-altering decision—and how these characters, as well as those around them, respond is at the heart of the stories. Consider "The Spinster." A noblewoman, Lady Inley, eschewing female solidarity, expresses disdain for the elderly, unmarried woman of the title:

> "Miss Bassett is, or was, one of those funny old spinsters who always look the same and always ridiculous. Dry twigs, you know. One size all the way down. Very little hair, and no emotions. If it weren't for the sake of cats, one would wonder why such people are born. But they're always cat-lovers. I suppose that's why they're so often called old cats."

This passage is emblematic of the venerable critical dictum that sentiments expressed by a fictional character should not be unthinkingly attributed to the author. Hichens himself may indeed (in accordance with the Anglo-American culture of his time) have had an exaggerated sense of the biological, social, and cultural distinctions between men and women, as elements in other stories attest; but it turns out that the spinster in question—along with her cat, who plays an expectedly central role in the narrative—is very different from Lady Inley's scornful description; and that is the very thing that saves the noblewoman's life.

If "The Spinster" is the tale of a crime averted, "The Collaborators" hints at a hideous crime that has covertly been committed. The two authors who decide to collaborate on a novel that they hope will make their reputations (and a good deal of money) could not be more different. Andrew Trenchard is one who "possessed little sense of humour, but immense sense of evil and tragedy and sorrow." His colleague, Jack Henley, is brash, optimistic, and always ready to latch on to an opportunity to advance himself. The novel they write—although it is mostly the work of Trenchard—is a grim one about a man who tries to wean a woman off of her addiction to morphine but then succumbs to it himself. But what is the ending to be? Trenchard argues that the logic of the story requires a tragic denouement. Henley finds that prospect so repulsive that he begs off the project; but he tells his collaborator, "You will finish the book. I feel that; I know it." This is a tale of life imitating art, to the detriment of all concerned.

The basic thrust of these two stories is in a sense mingled in "The Man Who Intervened," where a parson, Anthony Endover, attempts to prevent his friend Sergius Blake from killing a rival over what that rival did to a woman friend, Olga Mayne. The mores of the time prevented Hichens from speaking in anything but euphemisms over how that rival "ruined" Olga, but some sexual irregularity is implied. The climax of the story justifies Sergius's remark that "No man or woman ever understands another—really." This is a motto that could be applied to Hichens's work generally.

The three tales in this volume that are explicitly supernatural are among his greatest. "A Tribute of Souls" was written in collaboration with Frederic Hamilton (1856–1928), a nobleman and Conservative politician who was editor of the *Pall Mall Magazine* from 1896 to 1900; the story appeared there in two parts in the August and September 1897 issues. This expansive and cumulatively powerful novella tells of a morally and physically weak man in Scotland, Alistair Ralston, who yearns to be strong and handsome ("I knew myself, and I longed to be other than I was"). He encounters a "grey traveller" on his estate, who tells him that he needs to bring "three souls to Satan" in order to secure his wishes. After a brief but serious illness, he finds that he is indeed an imposing physical and mental specimen, and he goes about systematically corrupting the souls of those around him: Dr. Wedderburn, a pious physician whose simple Christian faith he destroys; Kate Walters, his former nurse; and her ex-fiancé, Hugh Fraser, whom he injures by taking Kate away from him.

The story is, manifestly, a variation of the "Satan-tempting-humanity" motif—a point emphasized by Alistair's reading of Goethe's *Faust* in the early parts of the narrative. Is that "grey traveller" Mephistopheles or some other devil, or perhaps Satan himself? Who can say? But Hichens has several clever twists up his sleeve, and the end result is very different from what Alistair had hoped for.

"The Lady and the Beggar" is perhaps the slightest tale in this volume, but its etching of the cold, heartless Mrs. Errington—who has only scorn for those less fortunate than herself—is memorable. Why, then, did she specify in her will that most of her substantial assets be given to the poor? Her encounter with a beggar must have had something to do with it—and she comes to believe that that beggar is something more than the dissolute wretch she takes him to be.

It is impossible to discuss "How Love Came to Professor Guildea"—one of the transcendent weird tales in literature—in brief compass. Who but Hichens could have devised the improbable scenario whereby a hard-hearted professor is haunted by the ghost of a woman *who loves him?* This is just about the most hideous fate that could be imagined for a man who found no time "for love, either of humanity in general or of an individual." In a sense, this story links up with "The Lady and the Beggar" in suggesting that it is the protagonist's guilt or unease over some past action that brings down the supernatural manifestation upon him or her. This is the sort of scenario in which Hichens finds a wealth of human torment and misery, and it is the slow, meticulous accumulation of details—both supernatural and emotional—that allows all the characters in his tales to gain the fully rounded humanity that brings them to life. And it is this same attention to detail—as, for example, in "Professor Guildea," when the ghost is first suspected by the bizarre actions of a parrot—that creates the uncanny realism of the supernatural events Hichens etches so subtly and delicately. The author requires the expansiveness of the novelette to convey the richness of his weird scenarios, and some of them attain a cumulative power that creates that rarest fusion in literature—the fusion of horror and pathos.

"The Lost Faith" was written quite a bit later than the other stories in this book, first appearing in *Snake-Bite and Other Stories* (1919). This short novel is a tapestry of conflicting human actions and emotions, all revolving around a tangentially supernatural idea—that of faith healing. When the young American faith healer Olivia Traill comes to

England, she is met with withering scorn and skepticism by the press and the medical fraternity. But her apparent cure of the crippling headaches of a Miss Burnington makes us wonder whether her healing—based on explicitly Christian principles—is valid. When Miss Burnington's brother, the distinguished soldier General Sir Hector Burnington, unexpectedly takes ill, all the characters in the tale—now including Fernol West, whom Olivia had cured of his severe depression in America—become enmeshed in a grim nexus of crime, horror, and tragedy.

Once again, Goethe plays a minor but key role in the narrative. The German writer is quoted as saying, "In Faith everything depends on the fact of believing." Fernol is of course utterly under Olivia's spell and fully believes in her abilities. Olivia herself—sensitively depicted as humble, endowed with a simple but firm faith in her powers, and utterly devoid of charlatanism—becomes gradually less certain that she is a healer at all, and it is this "lost faith" that engenders the dramatic denouement. This story may be only on the borderland of the weird, but it is "uncanny" in the fullest sense, and its careful portrayal of all the central figures in the text is a tribute to the literary skill Hichens gained from an early age and utilized throughout his long career.

Robert Hichens is a writer whose work, strange or otherwise, cries out for resurrection. *Tongues of Conscience*—which contains "How Love Came to Professor Guildea," "The Lady and the Beggar," and several other lengthy tales of the supernatural—is one of the pillars of the weird fiction of its time; a dozen or more tales he wrote over the decades are a testament to his pervasive interest in the genre; and the short novel *The Dweller on the Threshold* (1911) is an exemplary adaptation of the motif of psychic transference. We owe it to ourselves to explore the rich treasure-house of literary work that he left behind.

—December 2022

....

S. T. Joshi is a freelance writer and editor. He has prepared comprehensive editions of H. P. Lovecraft's collected fiction, essays, poetry, and letters, including an annotated edition of *The Case of Charles Dexter Ward* (2010). He is the author of *The Weird Tale* (1990), *The Modern Weird Tale* (2001), *I Am Providence: The Life and Times of H. P. Lovecraft* (2010), and *Unutterable Horror: A History of Supernatural Fiction* (2012), and has edited the anthology *American Supernatural Tales* (2007).

How Love Came to Professor Guildea & Other Uncanny Tales

ROBERT HICHENS

How Love Came to Professor Guildea

I

Dull people often wondered how it came about that Father Murchison and Professor Frederic Guildea were intimate friends. The one was all faith, the other all scepticism. The nature of the Father was based on love. He viewed the world with an almost childlike tenderness above his long, black cassock; and his mild, yet perfectly fearless, blue eyes seemed always to be watching the goodness that exists in humanity, and rejoicing at what they saw. The Professor, on the other hand, had a hard face like a hatchet, tipped with an aggressive black goatee beard. His eyes were quick, piercing and irreverent. The lines about his small, thin-lipped mouth were almost cruel. His voice was harsh and dry, sometimes, when he grew energetic, almost soprano. It fired off words with a sharp and clipping utterance. His habitual manner was one of distrust and investigation. It was impossible to suppose that, in his busy life, he found any time for love, either of humanity in general or of an individual.

Yet his days were spent in scientific investigations which conferred immense benefits upon the world.

Both men were celibates. Father Murchison was a member of an Anglican order which forbade him to marry. Professor Guildea had a poor opinion of most things, but especially of women. He had formerly held a post as lecturer at Birmingham. But when his fame as a discoverer grew he removed to London. There, at a lecture he gave in the East End, he first met Father Murchison. They spoke a few words. Perhaps the bright intelligence of the priest appealed to the man of science, who was inclined, as a rule, to regard the clergy with some contempt. Perhaps the transparent sincerity of this devotee, full of common sense, attracted him. As he was leaving the hall he abruptly asked the Father to call on him at his house in Hyde Park Place. And the Father, who seldom went into the West End, except to preach, accepted the invitation.

"When will you come?" said Guildea.

He was folding up the blue paper on which his notes were written in a tiny, clear hand. The leaves rustled drily in accompaniment to his sharp, dry voice.

"On Sunday week I am preaching in the evening at St. Saviour's, not far off," said the Father.

"I don't go to church."

"No," said the Father, without any accent of surprise or condemnation.

"Come to supper afterwards?"

"Thank you. I will."

"What time will you come?"

The Father smiled.

"As soon as I have finished my sermon. The service is at six-thirty."

"About eight then, I suppose. Don't make the sermon too long. My number in Hyde Park Place is a hundred. Good-night to you."

He snapped an elastic band round his papers and strode off without shaking hands.

On the appointed Sunday, Father Murchison preached to a densely crowded congregation at St. Saviour's. The subject of his sermon was sympathy, and the comparative uselessness of man in the world unless he can learn to love his neighbour as himself. The sermon was rather long, and when the preacher, in his flowing black cloak, and his hard, round hat, with a straight brim over which hung the ends of a black cord, made his way towards the Professor's house, the hands of the illuminated clock disc at the Marble Arch pointed to twenty minutes past eight.

The Father hurried on, pushing his way through the crowd of standing soldiers, chattering women and giggling street boys in their Sunday best. It was a warm April night, and, when he reached number 100, Hyde Park Place, he found the Professor bareheaded on his doorstep, gazing out towards the Park railings, and enjoying the soft, moist air, in front of his lighted passage.

"Ha, a long sermon!" he exclaimed. "Come in."

"I fear it was," said the Father, obeying the invitation. "I am that dangerous thing—an extempore preacher."

"More attractive to speak without notes, if you can do it. Hang your hat and coat—oh, cloak—here. We'll have supper at once. This is the dining room."

He opened a door on the right and they entered a long, narrow room, with a gold paper and a black ceiling, from which hung an electric lamp with a gold-coloured shade. In the room stood a small oval table with covers laid for two. The Professor rang the bell. Then he said,

"People seem to talk better at an oval table than at a square one."

"Really. Is that so?"

"Well, I've had precisely the same party twice, once at a square table, once at an oval table. The first dinner was a dull failure, the second a brilliant success. Sit down, won't you?"

"How d'you account for the difference?" said the Father, sitting down, and pulling the tail of his cassock well under him.

"H'm. I know how you'd account for it."

"Indeed. How then?"

"At an oval table, since there are no corners, the chain of human sympathy—the electric current, is much more complete. Eh! Let me give you some soup."

"Thank you."

The Father took it, and, as he did so, turned his beaming blue eyes on his host. Then he smiled.

"What!" he said, in his pleasant, light tenor voice. "You do go to church sometimes, then?"

"To-night is the first time for ages. And, mind you, I was tremendously bored."

The Father still smiled, and his blue eyes gently twinkled.

"Dear, dear!" he said, "what a pity!"

"But not by the sermon," Guildea added. "I don't pay a compliment. I state a fact. The sermon didn't bore me. If it had, I should have said so, or said nothing."

"And which would you have done?"

The Professor smiled almost genially.

"Don't know," he said. "What wine d'you drink?"

"None, thank you. I'm a teetotaller. In my profession and *milieu* it is necessary to be one. Yes, I will have some soda water. I think you would have done the first."

"Very likely, and very wrongly. You wouldn't have minded much."

"I don't think I should."

They were intimate already. The Father felt most pleasantly at home under the black ceiling. He drank some soda water and seemed to enjoy it more than the Professor enjoyed his claret.

"You smile at the theory of the chain of human sympathy, I see," said the Father. "Then what is your explanation of the failure of your square party with corners, the success of your oval party without them?"

"Probably on the first occasion the wit of the assembly had a chill on his liver, while on the second he was in perfect health. Yet, you see, I stick to the oval table."

"And that means—"

"Very little. By the way, your omission of any allusion to the notorious part liver plays in love was a serious one to-night."

"Your omission of any desire for close human sympathy in your life is a more serious one."

"How can you be sure I have no such desire?"

"I divine it. Your look, your manner, tell me it is so. You were disagreeing with my sermon all the time I was preaching. Weren't you?"

"Part of the time."

The servant changed the plates. He was a middle-aged, blond, thin man, with a stony white face, pale, prominent eyes, and an accomplished manner of service. When he had left the room the Professor continued, "Your remarks interested me, but I thought them exaggerated."

"For instance?"

"Let me play the egoist for a moment. I spend most of my time in hard work, very hard work. The results of this work, you will allow, benefit humanity."

"Enormously," assented the Father, thinking of more than one of Guildea's discoveries.

"And the benefit conferred by this work, undertaken merely for its own sake, is just as great as if it were undertaken because I loved my fellow man and sentimentally desired to see him more comfortable than he is at present. I'm as useful precisely in my present condition of—in my present non-affectional condition—as I should be if I were as full of gush as the sentimentalists who want to get murderers out of prison, or to put a premium on tyranny—like Tolstoi—by preventing the punishment of tyrants."

"One may do great harm with affection; great good without it. Yes, that is true. Even *le bon motif* is not everything, I know. Still I contend that, given your powers, you would be far more useful in the world with sympathy, affection for your kind, added to them than as you are. I believe even that you would do still more splendid work."

The Professor poured himself out another glass of claret.

"You noticed my butler?" he said.

"I did."

"He's a perfect servant. He makes me perfectly comfortable. Yet he has no feeling of liking for me. I treat him civilly. I pay him well. But I never think about him, or concern myself with him as a human being. I know nothing of his character except what I read of it in his last master's letter. There are, you may say, no truly human relations between us. You would affirm that his work would be better done if I had made him personally like me as man—of any class—can like man—of any other class?"

"I should, decidedly."

"I contend that he couldn't do his work better than he does it at present."

"But if any crisis occurred?"

"What?"

"Any crisis, change in your condition. If you needed his help, not only as a man and a butler, but as a man and a brother? He'd fail you then, probably. You would never get from your servant that finest service which can only be prompted by an honest affection."

"You have finished?"

"Quite."

"Let us go upstairs then. Yes, those are good prints. I picked them up in Birmingham when I was living there. This is my workroom."

They came into a double room lined entirely with books, and brilliantly, rather hardly, lit by electricity. The windows at one end looked on to the Park, at the other on to the garden of a neighbouring house. The door by which they entered was concealed from the inner and smaller room by the jutting wall of the outer room, in which stood a huge writing table loaded with letters, pamphlets and manuscripts. Between the two windows of the inner room was a cage in which a large, grey parrot was clambering, using both beak and claws to assist him in his slow and meditative peregrinations.

"You have a pet," said the Father, surprised.

"I possess a parrot," the Professor answered, drily, "I got him for a purpose when I was making a study of the imitative powers of birds, and I have never got rid of him. A cigar?"

"Thank you."

They sat down. Father Murchison glanced at the parrot. It had paused in its journey, and, clinging to the bars of its cage, was regarding them with attentive round eyes that looked deliberately intelligent, but by no means sympathetic. He looked away from it to Guildea, who was smoking, with his head thrown back, his sharp, pointed chin, on which the small black beard bristled, upturned. He was moving his under lip up and down rapidly. This action caused the beard to stir and look peculiarly aggressive. The Father suddenly chuckled softly.

"Why's that?" cried Guildea, letting his chin drop down on his breast and looking at his guest sharply.

"I was thinking it would have to be a crisis indeed that could make you cling to your butler's affection for assistance."

Guildea smiled too.

"You're right. It would. Here he comes."

The man entered with coffee. He offered it gently, and retired like a shadow retreating on a wall.

"Splendid, inhuman fellow," remarked Guildea.

"I prefer the East End lad who does my errands in Bird Street," said the Father. "I know all his worries. He knows some of mine. We are friends. He's more noisy than your man. He even breathes hard when he is specially solicitous, but he would do more for me than put the coals on my fire, or black my square-toed boots."

"Men are differently made. To me the watchful eye of affection would be abominable."

"What about that bird?"

The Father pointed to the parrot. It had got up on its perch and, with one foot uplifted in an impressive, almost benedictory, manner, was gazing steadily at the Professor.

"That's the watchful eye of imitation, with a mind at the back of it, desirous of reproducing the peculiarities of others. No, I thought your sermon to-night very fresh, very clever. But I have no wish for affection. Reasonable liking, of course, one desires," he tugged sharply at his beard, as if to warn himself against sentimentality—"but anything more would be most irksome, and would push me, I feel sure, towards cruelty. It would also hamper one's work."

"I don't think so."

"The sort of work I do. I shall continue to benefit the world without loving it, and it will continue to accept the benefits without loving me. That's all as it should be."

He drank his coffee. Then he added, rather aggressively:

"I have neither time nor inclination for sentimentality."

When Guildea let Father Murchison out, he followed the Father on to the doorstep and stood there for a moment. The Father glanced across the damp road into the Park.

"I see you've got a gate just opposite you," he said idly.

"Yes. I often slip across for a stroll to clear my brain. Good-night to you. Come again someday."

"With pleasure. Good-night."

The Priest strode away, leaving Guildea standing on the step.

Father Murchison came many times again to number one hundred Hyde Park Place. He had a feeling of liking for most men and women whom he knew, and of tenderness for all, whether he knew them or not, but he grew to have a special sentiment towards Guildea. Strangely enough, it was a sentiment of pity. He pitied this hardworking, eminently successful man of big brain and bold heart, who never seemed depressed, who never wanted assistance, who never complained of the twisted skein of life or faltered in his progress along its way. The Father pitied Guildea, in fact, because Guildea wanted so little. He had told him so, for the intercourse of the two men, from the beginning, had been singularly frank.

One evening, when they were talking together, the Father happened to speak of one of the oddities of life, the fact that those who do not want things often get them, while those who seek them vehemently are disappointed in their search.

"Then I ought to have affection poured upon me," said Guildea, smiling rather grimly. "For I hate it."

"Perhaps someday you will."

"I hope not, most sincerely."

Father Murchison said nothing for a moment. He was drawing together the ends of the broad band round his cassock. When he spoke he seemed to be answering someone.

"Yes," he said slowly, "yes, that *is* my feeling—pity."

"For whom?" said the Professor.

Then, suddenly, he understood. He did not say that he understood, but Father Murchison felt, and saw, that it was quite unnecessary to answer his friend's question. So Guildea, strangely enough, found himself closely acquainted with a man—his opposite in all ways—who pitied him.

The fact that he did not mind this, and scarcely ever thought about it, shows perhaps as clearly as anything could the peculiar indifference of his nature.

II

One Autumn evening, a year and a half after Father Murchison and the Professor had first met, the Father called in Hyde Park Place and enquired of the blond and stony butler—his name was Pitting—whether his master was at home.

"Yes, sir," replied Pitting. "Will you please come this way?"

He moved noiselessly up the rather narrow stairs, followed by the Father, tenderly opened the library door, and in his soft, cold voice, announced:

"Father Murchison."

Guildea was sitting in an armchair, before a small fire. His thin, long-fingered hands lay outstretched upon his knees, his head was sunk down on his chest. He appeared to be pondering deeply. Pitting very slightly raised his voice.

"Father Murchison to see you, sir," he repeated.

The Professor jumped up rather suddenly and turned sharply round as the Father came in.

"Oh," he said. "It's you, is it? Glad to see you. Come to the fire."

The Father glanced at him and thought him looking unusually

fatigued.

"You don't look well to-night," the Father said.

"No?"

"You must be working too hard. That lecture you are going to give in Paris is bothering you?"

"Not a bit. It's all arranged. I could deliver it to you at this moment verbatim. Well, sit down."

The Father did so, and Guildea sank once more into his chair and stared hard into the fire without another word. He seemed to be thinking profoundly. His friend did not interrupt him, but quietly lit a pipe and began to smoke reflectively. The eyes of Guildea were fixed upon the fire. The Father glanced about the room, at the walls of soberly bound books, at the crowded writing table, at the windows, before which hung heavy, dark-blue curtains of old brocade, at the cage, which stood between them. A green baize covering was thrown over it. The Father wondered why. He had never seen Napoleon—so the parrot was named—covered up at night before. While he was looking at the baize, Guildea suddenly jerked up his head, and, taking his hands from his knees and clasping them, said abruptly:

"D'you think I'm an attractive man?"

Father Murchison jumped. Such a question coming from such a man astounded him.

"Bless me!" he ejaculated. "What makes you ask? Do you mean attractive to the opposite sex?"

"That's what I don't know," said the Professor gloomily, and staring again into the fire. "That's what I don't know."

The Father grew more astonished.

"Don't know!" he exclaimed.

And he laid down his pipe.

"Let's say—d'you think I'm attractive, that there's anything about me which might draw a—a human being, or an animal, irresistibly to me?"

"Whether you desired it or not?"

"Exactly—or—no, let us say definitely—if I did not desire it."

Father Murchison pursed up his rather full, cherubic lips, and little wrinkles appeared about the corners of his blue eyes.

"There might be, of course," he said, after a pause. "Human nature is weak, engagingly weak, Guildea. And you're inclined to flout it. I could understand a certain class of lady—the lion-hunting, the intellectual lady, seeking you. Your reputation, your great name—"

"Yes, yes," Guildea interrupted, rather irritably—"I know all that, I know."

He twisted his long hands together, bending the palms outwards till his thin, pointed fingers cracked. His forehead was wrinkled in a frown.

"I imagine," he said—he stopped and coughed drily, almost shrilly—"I imagine it would be very disagreeable to be liked, to be run after—that is the usual expression, isn't it—by anything one objected to."

And now he half turned in his chair, crossed his legs one over the other, and looked at his guest with an unusual, almost piercing interrogation.

"Anything?" said the Father.

"Well—well, anyone. I imagine nothing could be more unpleasant."

"To you—no," answered the Father. "But—forgive me, Guildea, I cannot conceive you permitting such intrusion. You don't encourage adoration."

Guildea nodded his head gloomily.

"I don't," he said, "I don't. That's just it. That's the curious part of it, that I—"

He broke off deliberately, got up and stretched.

"I'll have a pipe, too," he said.

He went over to the mantelpiece, got his pipe, filled it and lighted it. As he held the match to the tobacco, bending forward with an enquiring expression, his eyes fell upon the green baize that covered Napoleon's cage. He threw the match into the grate, and puffed at the pipe as he walked forward to the cage. When he reached it he put out his hand, took hold of the baize and began to pull it away. Then suddenly he pushed it back over the cage.

"No," he said, as if to himself, "no."

He returned rather hastily to the fire and threw himself once more into his armchair.

"You're wondering," he said to Father Murchison. "So am I. I don't know at all what to make of it. I'll just tell you the facts and you must tell me what you think of them. The night before last, after a day of hard work—but no harder than usual—I went to the front door to get a breath of air. You know I often do that."

"Yes, I found you on the doorstep when I first came here."

"Just so. I didn't put on hat or coat. I just stood on the step as I was. My mind, I remember, was still full of my work. It was rather a dark night, not very dark. The hour was about eleven, or a quarter past. I was staring at the Park, and presently I found that my eyes were directed towards somebody who was sitting, back to me, on one of the benches. I saw the person—if it was a person—through the railings."

"If it was a person!" said the Father. "What do you mean by that?"

"Wait a minute. I say that because it was too dark for me to know. I merely saw some blackish object on the bench, rising into view above the level of the back of the seat. I couldn't say it was man, woman or child. But something there was, and I found that I was looking at it."

"I understand."

"Gradually, I also found that my thoughts were becoming fixed upon this thing or person. I began to wonder, first, what it was doing there; next, what it was thinking; lastly, what it was like."

"Some poor creature without a home, I suppose," said the Father.

"I said that to myself. Still, I was taken with an extraordinary interest about this object, so great an interest that I got my hat and crossed the road to go into the Park. As you know, there's an entrance almost opposite to my house. Well, Murchison, I crossed the road, passed through the gate in the railings, went up to the seat, and found that there was—nothing on it."

"Were you looking at it as you walked?"

"Part of the time. But I removed my eyes from it just as I passed through the gate, because there was a row going on a little way off, and I turned for an instant in that direction. When I saw that the seat was vacant I was seized by a most absurd sensation of disappointment, almost of anger. I stopped and looked about me to see if anything was moving away, but I could see nothing. It was a cold night and misty, and there were few people about. Feeling, as I say, foolishly and unnaturally disappointed, I retraced my steps to this house. When I got here I discovered that during my short absence I had left the hall door open— half open."

"Rather imprudent in London."

"Yes. I had no idea, of course, that I had done so, till I got back. However, I was only away three minutes or so."

"Yes."

"It was not likely that anybody had gone in."

"I suppose not."

"Was it?"

"Why do you ask me that, Guildea?"

"Well, well!"

"Besides, if anybody had gone in on your return you'd have caught him, surely."

Guildea coughed again. The Father, surprised, could not fail to recognise that he was nervous and that his nervousness was affecting him physically.

"I must have caught cold that night," he said, as if he had read his friend's thought and hastened to contradict it. Then he went on:

"I entered the hall, or passage, rather."

He paused again. His uneasiness was becoming very apparent.

"And you did catch somebody?" said the Father.

Guildea cleared his throat.

"That's just it," he said, "now we come to it. I'm not imaginative, as you know."

"You certainly are not."

"No, but hardly had I stepped into the passage before I felt certain that somebody had got into the house during my absence. I felt convinced of it, and not only that, I also felt convinced that the intruder was the very person I had dimly seen sitting upon the seat in the Park. What d'you say to that?"

"I begin to think you are imaginative."

"H'm! It seemed to me that the person—the occupant of the seat—and I, had simultaneously formed the project of interviewing each other, had simultaneously set out to put that project into execution. I became so certain of this that I walked hastily upstairs into this room, expecting to find the visitor awaiting me. But there was no one. I then came down again and went into the dining room. No one. I was actually astonished. Isn't that odd?"

"Very," said the Father, quite gravely.

The Professor's chill and gloomy manner, and uncomfortable, constrained appearance kept away the humour that might well have lurked round the steps of such a discourse.

"I went upstairs again," he continued, "sat down and thought the matter over. I resolved to forget it, and took up a book. I might perhaps have been able to read, but suddenly I thought I noticed—"

He stopped abruptly. Father Murchison observed that he was staring towards the green baize that covered the parrot's cage.

"But that's nothing," he said. "Enough that I couldn't read. I resolved to explore the house. You know how small it is, how easily one can go all over it. I went all over it. I went into every room without exception. To the servants, who were having supper, I made some excuse. They were surprised at my advent, no doubt."

"And Pitting?"

"Oh, he got up politely when I came in, stood while I was there, but never said a word. I muttered 'don't disturb yourselves,' or something of the sort, and came out. Murchison, I found nobody new in the house—yet I returned to this room entirely convinced that somebody had entered while I was in the Park."

"And gone out again before you came back?"

"No, had stayed, and was still in the house."

"But, my dear Guildea," began the Father, now in great astonishment. "Surely—"

"I know what you want to say—what I should want to say in your place. Now, do wait. I am also convinced that this visitor has not left the house and is at this moment in it."

He spoke with evident sincerity, with extreme gravity. Father Murchison looked him full in the face, and met his quick, keen eyes.

"No," he said, as if in reply to an uttered question: "I'm perfectly sane, I assure you. The whole matter seems almost as incredible to me as it must to you. But, as you know, I never quarrel with facts, however strange. I merely try to examine into them thoroughly. I have already consulted a doctor and been pronounced in perfect bodily health."

He paused, as if expecting the Father to say something.

"Go on, Guildea," he said, "you haven't finished."

"No. I felt that night positive that somebody had entered the house, and remained in it, and my conviction grew. I went to bed as usual, and, contrary to my expectation, slept as well as I generally do. Yet directly I woke up yesterday morning I knew that my household had been increased by one."

"May I interrupt you for one moment? How did you know it?"

"By my mental sensation. I can only say that I was perfectly conscious of a new presence within my house, close to me."

"How very strange," said the Father. "And you feel absolutely certain that you are not overworked? Your brain does not feel tired? Your head is quite clear?"

"Quite. I was never better. When I came down to breakfast that morning I looked sharply into Pitting's face. He was as coldly placid and inexpressive as usual. It was evident to me that his mind was in no way distressed. After breakfast I sat down to work, all the time ceaselessly conscious of the fact of this intruder upon my privacy. Nevertheless, I laboured for several hours, waiting for any development that might occur to clear away the mysterious obscurity of this event. I lunched. About half-past two I was obliged to go out to attend a lecture. I therefore, took my coat and hat, opened my door, and stepped on to the pavement. I was instantly aware that I was no longer intruded upon, and this although I was now in the street, surrounded by people. Consequently, I felt certain that the thing in my house must be thinking of me, perhaps even spying upon me."

"Wait a moment," interrupted the Father. "What was your sensation? Was it one of fear?"

"Oh, dear no. I was entirely puzzled—as I am now—and keenly interested, but not in any way alarmed. I delivered my lecture with my usual ease and returned home in the evening. On entering the house again I was perfectly conscious that the intruder was still there. Last night I dined alone and spent the hours after dinner in reading a scientific work in which I was deeply interested. While I read, however, I never for one moment lost the knowledge that some mind—very attentive to me—was within hail of mine. I will say more than this—the sensation constantly increased, and, by the time I got up to go to bed, I had come to a very strange conclusion."

"What? What was it?"

"That whoever—or whatever—had entered my house during my short absence in the Park was more than interested in me."

"More than interested in you?"

"Was fond, or was becoming fond, of me."

"Oh!" exclaimed the Father. "Now I understand why you asked me just now whether I thought there was anything about you that might draw a human being or an animal irresistibly to you."

"Precisely. Since I came to this conclusion, Murchison, I will confess that my feeling of strong curiosity has become tinged with another feeling."

"Of fear?"

"No, of dislike, of irritation. No—not fear, not fear."

As Guildea repeated unnecessarily this asseveration he looked again towards the parrot's cage.

"What is there to be afraid of in such a matter?" he added. "I'm not a child to tremble before bogies."

In saying the last words he raised his voice sharply; then he walked quickly to the cage, and, with an abrupt movement, pulled the baize covering from it. Napoleon was disclosed, apparently dozing upon his perch with his head held slightly on one side. As the light reached him, he moved, ruffled the feathers about his neck, blinked his eyes, and began slowly to sidle to and fro, thrusting his head forward and drawing it back with an air of complacent, though rather unmeaning, energy. Guildea stood by the cage, looking at him closely, and indeed with an attention that was so intense as to be remarkable, almost unnatural.

"How absurd these birds are!" he said at length, coming back to the fire.

"You have no more to tell me?" asked the Father.

"No. I am still aware of the presence of something in my house. I am still conscious of its close attention to me. I am still irritated, seriously annoyed—I confess it—by that attention."

"You say you are aware of the presence of something at this moment?"

"At this moment—yes."

"Do you mean in this room, with us, now?"

"I should say so—at any rate, quite near us."

Again he glanced quickly, almost suspiciously, towards the cage of the parrot. The bird was sitting still on its perch now. Its head was bent down and cocked sideways, and it appeared to be listening attentively to something.

"That bird will have the intonations of my voice more correctly than ever by to-morrow morning," said the Father, watching Guildea closely with his mild blue eyes. "And it has always imitated me very cleverly."

The Professor started slightly.

"Yes," he said. "Yes, no doubt. Well, what do you make of this affair?"

"Nothing at all. It is absolutely inexplicable. I can speak quite frankly to you, I feel sure."

"Of course. That's why I have told you the whole thing."

"I think you must be overworked, over-strained, without knowing it."

"And that the doctor was mistaken when he said I was all right?"

"Yes."

Guildea knocked his pipe out against the chimney piece.

"It may be so," he said, "I will not be so unreasonable as to deny the possibility, although I feel as well as I ever did in my life. What do you advise then?"

"A week of complete rest away from London, in good air."

"The usual prescription. I'll take it. I'll go to-morrow to Westgate and leave Napoleon to keep house in my absence."

For some reason, which he could not explain to himself, the pleasure which Father Murchison felt in hearing the first part of his friend's final remark was lessened, was almost destroyed, by the last sentence.

He walked towards the City that night, deep in thought, remembering and carefully considering the first interview he had with Guildea in the latter's house a year and a half before.

On the following morning Guildea left London.

III

Father Murchison was so busy a man that he had little time for brooding over the affairs of others. During Guildea's week at the sea, however, the Father thought about him a great deal, with much wonder and some dismay. The dismay was soon banished, for the mild-eyed priest was quick to discern weakness in himself, quicker still to drive it forth as a most undesirable inmate of the soul. But the wonder remained. It was destined to a crescendo. Guildea had left London on a Thursday. On a Thursday he returned, having previously sent a note to Father Murchison to mention that he was leaving Westgate at a certain time. When his train ran in to Victoria Station, at five o'clock in the evening, he was surprised to see the cloaked figure of his friend standing upon the grey platform behind a line of porters.

"What, Murchison!" he said. "You here! Have you seceded from your order that you are taking this holiday?"

They shook hands.

"No," said the Father. "It happened that I had to be in this neighbourhood to-day, visiting a sick person. So I thought I would meet you."

"And see if I were still a sick person, eh?"

The Professor glanced at him kindly, but with a dry little laugh.

"Are you?" replied the Father gently, looking at him with interest. "No, I think not. You appear very well."

The sea air had, in fact, put some brownish red into Guildea's always thin cheeks. His keen eyes were shining with life and energy, and he walked forward in his loose grey suit and fluttering overcoat with a vigour that was noticeable, carrying easily in his left hand his well-filled Gladstone bag.

The Father felt completely reassured.

"I never saw you look better," he said.

"I never was better. Have you an hour to spare?"

"Two."

"Good. I'll send my bag up by cab, and we'll walk across the Park to my house and have a cup of tea there. What d'you say?"

"I shall enjoy it."

They walked out of the station yard, past the flower girls and newspaper sellers towards Grosvenor Place.

"And you have had a pleasant time?" the Father said.

"Pleasant enough, and lonely. I left my companion behind me in the passage at Number 100, you know."

"And you'll not find him there now, I feel sure."

"H'm!" ejaculated Guildea. "What a precious weakling you think me, Murchison."

As he spoke he strode forward more quickly, as if moved to emphasise his sensation of bodily vigour.

"A weakling—no. But anyone who uses his brain as persistently as you do yours must require an occasional holiday."

"And I required one very badly, eh?"

"You required one, I believe."

"Well, I've had it. And now we'll see."

The evening was closing in rapidly. They crossed the road at Hyde Park Corner, and entered the Park, in which were a number of people going home from work; men in corduroy trousers, caked with dried mud, and carrying tin cans slung over their shoulders, and flat panniers, in which lay their tools. Some of the younger ones talked loudly or whistled shrilly as they walked.

"Until the evening," murmured Father Murchison to himself.

"What?" asked Guildea.

"I was only quoting the last words of the text, which seems written upon life, especially upon the life of pleasure: 'Man goeth forth to his work, and to his labour.'"

"Ah, those fellows are not half bad fellows to have in an audience. There were a lot of them at the lecture I gave when I first met you, I remember. One of them tried to heckle me. He had a red beard. Chaps with red beards are always hecklers. I laid him low on that occasion. Well, Murchison, and now we're going to see."

"What?"

"Whether my companion has departed."

"Tell me—do you feel any expectation of—well—of again thinking something is there?"

"How carefully you choose language. No, I merely wonder."

"You have no apprehension?"

"Not a scrap. But I confess to feeling curious."

"Then the sea air hasn't taught you to recognise that the whole thing came from overstrain."

"No," said Guildea, very drily.

He walked on in silence for a minute. Then he added:

"You thought it would?"

"I certainly thought it might."

"Make me realise that I had a sickly, morbid, rotten imagination—heh? Come now, Murchison, why not say frankly that you packed me off to Westgate to get rid of what you considered an acute form of hysteria?"

The Father was quite unmoved by this attack.

"Come now, Guildea," he retorted, "what did you expect me to think? I saw no indication of hysteria in you. I never have. One would suppose you the last man likely to have such a malady. But which is more natural—for me to believe in your hysteria or in the truth of such a story as you told me?"

"You have me there. No, I mustn't complain. Well, there's no hysteria about me now, at any rate."

"And no stranger in your house, I hope."

Father Murchison spoke the last words with earnest gravity, dropping the half-bantering tone—which they had both assumed.

"You take the matter very seriously, I believe," said Guildea, also speaking more gravely.

"How else can I take it? You wouldn't have me laugh at it when you tell it me seriously?"

"No. If we find my visitor still in the house, I may even call upon you to exorcise it. But first I must do one thing."

"And that is?"

"Prove to you, as well as to myself, that it is still there."

"That might be difficult," said the Father, considerably surprised by Guildea's matter-of-fact tone.

"I don't know. If it has remained in my house I think I can find a means. And I shall not be at all surprised if it is still there—despite the Westgate air."

In saying the last words the Professor relapsed into his former tone of dry chaff. The Father could not quite make up his mind whether Guildea was feeling unusually grave or unusually gay. As the two men drew near to Hyde Park Place their conversation died away and they walked forward silently in the gathering darkness.

"Here we are!" said Guildea at last.

He thrust his key into the door, opened it and let Father Murchison into the passage, following him closely and banging the door.

"Here we are!" he repeated in a louder voice.

The electric light was turned on in anticipation of his arrival. He stood still and looked round.

"We'll have some tea at once," he said. "Ah, Pitting!"

The pale butler, who had heard the door bang, moved gently forward from the top of the stairs that led to the kitchen, greeted his master respectfully, took his coat and Father Murchison's cloak, and hung them on two pegs against the wall.

"All's right, Pitting? All's as usual?" said Guildea.

"Quite so, sir."

"Bring us up some tea to the library."

"Yes, sir."

Pitting retreated. Guildea waited till he had disappeared, then opened the dining room door, put his head into the room and kept it there for a moment, standing perfectly still. Presently he drew back into the passage, shut the door, and said,

"Let's go upstairs."

Father Murchison looked at him enquiringly, but made no remark. They ascended the stairs and came into the library. Guildea glanced rather sharply round. A fire was burning on the hearth. The blue curtains were drawn. The bright gleam of the strong electric light fell on the long rows of books, on the writing table—very orderly in consequence of Guildea's holiday—and on the uncovered cage of the parrot. Guildea went up to the cage. Napoleon was sitting humped up on his perch with his feathers ruffled. His long toes, which looked as if they were covered with crocodile skin, clung to the bar. His round and blinking eyes were filmy, like old eyes. Guildea stared at the bird very hard, and then clucked with his tongue against his teeth. Napoleon shook himself, lifted one foot, extended his toes, sidled along the perch to the bars nearest to the Professor and thrust his head against them. Guildea scratched it with his forefinger two or three times, still gazing attentively at the parrot; then he returned to the fire just as Pitting entered with the tea-tray.

Father Murchison was already sitting in an armchair on one side of the fire. Guildea took another chair and began to pour out tea, as Pitting left the room closing the door gently behind him. The Father sipped his tea, found it hot and set the cup down on a little table at his side.

"You're fond of that parrot, aren't you?" he asked his friend.

"Not particularly. It's interesting to study sometimes. The parrot mind and nature are peculiar."

"How long have you had him?"

"About four years. I nearly got rid of him just before I made your acquaintance. I'm very glad now I kept him."

"Are you? Why is that?"

"I shall probably tell you in a day or two."

The Father took his cup again. He did not press Guildea for an immediate explanation, but when they had both finished their tea he said:

"Well, has the sea air had the desired effect?"

"No," said Guildea.

The Father brushed some crumbs from the front of his cassock and sat up higher in his chair.

"Your visitor is still here?" he asked, and his blue eyes became almost ungentle and piercing as he gazed at his friend.

"Yes," answered Guildea, calmly.

"How do you know it, when did you know it—when you looked into the dining room just now?"

"No. Not until I came into this room. It welcomed me here."

"Welcomed you! In what way?"

"Simply by being here, by making me feel that it is here, as I might feel that a man was if I came into the room when it was dark."

He spoke quietly, with perfect composure in his usual dry manner.

"Very well," the Father said, "I shall not try to contend against your sensation, or to explain it away. Naturally, I am in amazement."

"So am I. Never has anything in my life surprised me so much. Murchison, of course I cannot expect you to believe more than that I honestly suppose—imagine, if you like—that there is some intruder here, of what kind I am totally unaware. I cannot expect you to believe that there really is anything. If you were in my place, I in yours, I should certainly consider you the victim of some nervous delusion. I could not do otherwise. But—wait. Don't condemn me as a hysteria patient, or as a madman, for two or three days. I feel convinced that—unless I am indeed unwell, a mental invalid, which I don't think is possible—I shall be able very shortly to give you some proof that there is a newcomer in my house."

"You don't tell me what kind of proof?"

"Not yet. Things must go a little farther first. But, perhaps even to-morrow I may be able to explain myself more fully. In the meanwhile, I'll say this, that if, eventually, I can't bring any kind of proof that I'm not dreaming I'll let you take me to any doctor you like, and I'll resolutely try to adopt your present view—that I'm suffering from an absurd delusion. That is your view of course?"

Father Murchison was silent for a moment. Then he said, rather doubtfully:

"It ought to be."

"But isn't it?" asked Guildea, surprised.

"Well, you know, your manner is enormously convincing. Still, of course, I doubt. How can I do otherwise? The whole thing must be fancy."

The Father spoke as if he were trying to recoil from a mental position he was being forced to take up.

"It must be fancy," he repeated.

"I'll convince you by more than my manner, or I'll not try to convince you at all," said Guildea.

When they parted that evening, he said,

"I'll write to you in a day or two probably. I think the proof I am going to give you has been accumulating during my absence. But I shall soon know."

Father Murchison was extremely puzzled as he sat on the top of the omnibus going homeward.

IV

In two days' time he received a note from Guildea asking him to call, if possible, the same evening. This he was unable to do as he had an engagement to fulfil at some East End gathering. The following day was Sunday. He wrote saying he would come on the Monday, and got a wire shortly afterwards: "Yes, Monday come to dinner seven-thirty Guildea." At half-past seven he stood on the doorstep of Number 100.

Pitting let him in.

"Is the Professor quite well, Pitting?" the Father enquired as he took off his cloak.

"I believe so, sir. He has not made any complaint," the butler formally replied. "Will you come upstairs, sir?"

Guildea met them at the door of the library. He was very pale and sombre, and shook hands carelessly with his friend.

"Give us dinner," he said to Pitting.

As the butler retired, Guildea shut the door rather cautiously. Father Murchison had never before seen him look so disturbed.

"You're worried, Guildea," the Father said. "Seriously worried."

"Yes, I am. This business is beginning to tell on me a good deal."

"Your belief in the presence of something here continues then?"

"Oh, dear, yes. There's no sort of doubt about the matter. The night I went across the road into the Park something got into the house, though what the devil it is I can't yet find out. But now, before we go down to dinner, I'll just tell you something about that proof I promised you. You remember?"

"Naturally."

"Can't you imagine what it might be."

Father Murchison moved his head to express a negative reply.

"Look about the room," said Guildea. "What do you see?"

The Father glanced round the room, slowly and carefully.

"Nothing unusual. You do not mean to tell me there is any appearance of—"

"Oh, no, no, there's no conventional, white-robed, cloud-like figure. Bless my soul, no! I haven't fallen so low as that."

He spoke with considerable irritation.

"Look again."

Father Murchison looked at him, turned in the direction of his fixed eyes and saw the grey parrot clambering in its cage, slowly and persistently.

"What?" he said, quickly. "Will the proof come from there?"

The Professor nodded.

"I believe so," he said. "Now let's go down to dinner. I want some food badly."

They descended to the dining room. While they ate and Pitting waited upon them, the Professor talked about birds, their habits, their curiosities, their fears and their powers of imitation. He had evidently studied this subject with the thoroughness that was characteristic of him in all that he did.

"Parrots," he said presently, "are extraordinarily observant. It is a pity that their means of reproducing what they see are so limited. If it were not so, I have little doubt that their echo of gesture would be as remarkable as their echo of voice often is."

"But hands are missing."

"Yes. They do many things with their heads, however. I once knew an old woman near Goring on the Thames. She was afflicted with the palsy. She held her head perpetually sideways and it trembled, moving from right to left. Her sailor son brought her home a parrot from one of his voyages. It used to reproduce the old woman's palsied movement of the head exactly. Those grey parrots are always on the watch."

Guildea said the last sentence slowly and deliberately, glancing sharply over his wine at Father Murchison, and, when he had spoken it, a sudden light of comprehension dawned in the Priest's mind. He opened his lips to make a swift remark. Guildea turned his bright eyes towards Pitting, who at the moment was tenderly bearing a cheese meringue from the lift that connected the dining room with the lower regions. The Father closed his lips again. But presently, when the butler had placed some apples on the table, had meticulously arranged the decanters, brushed away the crumbs and evaporated, he said, quickly,

"I begin to understand. You think Napoleon is aware of the intruder?"

"I know it. He has been watching my visitant ever since the night of that visitant's arrival."

Another flash of light came to the Priest.

"That was why you covered him with green baize one evening?"

"Exactly. An act of cowardice. His behaviour was beginning to grate upon my nerves."

Guildea pursed up his thin lips and drew his brows down, giving to his face a look of sudden pain.

"But now I intend to follow his investigations," he added, straightening his features. "The week I wasted at Westgate was not wasted by him in London, I can assure you. Have an apple."

"No, thank you; no, thank you."

The Father repeated the words without knowing that he did so. Guildea pushed away his glass.

"Let us come upstairs, then."

"No, thank you," reiterated the Father.

"Eh?"

"What am I saying?" exclaimed the Father, getting up. "I was thinking over this extraordinary affair."

"Ah, you're beginning to forget the hysteria theory?"

They walked out into the passage.

"Well, you are so very practical about the whole matter."

"Why not? Here's something very strange and abnormal come into my life. What should I do but investigate it closely and calmly?"

"What, indeed?"

The Father began to feel rather bewildered, under a sort of compulsion which seemed laid upon him to give earnest attention to a matter that ought to strike him—so he felt—as entirely absurd. When they came into the library his eyes immediately turned, with profound curiosity, towards the parrot's cage. A slight smile curled the Professor's lips. He recognised the effect he was producing upon his friend. The Father saw the smile.

"Oh, I'm not won over yet," he said in answer to it.

"I know. Perhaps you may be before the evening is over. Here comes the coffee. After we have drunk it we'll proceed to our experiment. Leave the coffee, Pitting, and don't disturb us again."

"No, sir."

"I won't have it black to-night," said the Father, "plenty of milk, please. I don't want my nerves played upon."

"Suppose we don't take coffee at all?" said Guildea. "If we do you may trot out the theory that we are not in a perfectly normal condition. I know you, Murchison, devout Priest and devout sceptic."

The Father laughed and pushed away his cup.

"Very well, then. No coffee."

"One cigarette, and then to business."

The grey blue smoke curled up.

"What are we going to do?" said the Father.

He was sitting bolt upright as if ready for action. Indeed there was no suggestion of repose in the attitudes of either of the men.

"Hide ourselves, and watch Napoleon. By the way—that reminds me."

He got up, went to a corner of the room, picked up a piece of green baize and threw it over the cage.

"I'll pull that off when we are hidden."

"And tell me first if you have had any manifestation of this supposed presence during the last few days?"

"Merely an increasingly intense sensation of something here, perpetually watching me, perpetually attending to all my doings."

"Do you feel that it follows you about?"

"Not always. It was in this room when you arrived. It is here now—I feel. But, in going down to dinner, we seemed to get away from it. The conclusion is that it remained here. Don't let us talk about it just now."

They spoke of other things till their cigarettes were finished. Then, as they threw away the smouldering ends, Guildea said,

"Now, Murchison, for the sake of this experiment, I suggest that we should conceal ourselves behind the curtains on either side of the cage, so that the bird's attention may not be drawn towards us and so distracted from that which we want to know more about. I will pull away the green baize when we are hidden. Keep perfectly still, watch the bird's proceedings, and tell me afterwards how you feel about them, how you explain them. Tread softly."

The Father obeyed, and they stole towards the curtains that fell before the two windows. The Father concealed himself behind those on the left of the cage, the Professor behind those on the right. The latter, as soon as they were hidden, stretched out his arm, drew the baize down from the cage, and let it fall on the floor.

The parrot, which had evidently fallen asleep in the warm darkness, moved on its perch as the light shone upon it, ruffled the feathers round its throat, and lifted first one foot and then the other. It turned its head round on its supple, and apparently elastic, neck, and, diving its beak into the down upon its back, made some searching investigations with, as it seemed, a satisfactory result, for it soon lifted its head again, glanced around its cage, and began to address itself to a nut which had been fixed between the bars for its refreshment. With its curved beak it felt and tapped the nut, at first gently, then with severity. Finally it plucked the nut from the bars, seized it with its rough, grey toes, and, holding it down firmly on the perch, cracked it and pecked out its contents, scattering some on the floor of the cage and letting the fractured shell fall into the China bath that was fixed against the bars. This accomplished, the bird paused meditatively, extended one leg backwards, and went through an elaborate process of wing-stretching that made it look as if it were lopsided and deformed. With its head reversed, it again applied itself to a subtle and exhaustive search among the feathers of its wing. This time its investigation seemed interminable, and Father Murchison had time to realise the absurdity of the whole position, and to wonder why he had lent himself to it. Yet he did not find his sense of humour laughing at it. On the contrary, he was smitten by a sudden gust of horror. When he was talking to his friend and watching him, the Professor's manner, generally so calm, even so prosaic, vouched for the truth of his story and the well-adjusted balance of his mind. But when he was hidden this was not so. And Father Murchison, standing behind his curtain, with his eyes upon the unconcerned Napoleon, began to whisper to himself the word—madness, with a quickening sensation of pity and of dread.

The parrot sharply contracted one wing, ruffled the feathers around its throat again, then extended its other leg backwards, and proceeded to the cleaning of its other wing. In the still room the dry sound of the feathers being spread was distinctly audible. Father Murchison saw the blue curtains behind which Guildea stood tremble slightly, as if a breath of wind had come through the window they shrouded. The clock in the far room chimed, and a coal dropped into the grate, making a noise like dead leaves stirring abruptly on hard ground. And again a gust of pity and of dread swept over the Father. It seemed to him that he had behaved very foolishly, if not wrongly, in encouraging what must surely be the strange dementia of his friend. He ought to have declined to lend himself to a proceeding that, ludicrous, even childish in itself, might well be dangerous in the encouragement it gave to a diseased expectation. Napoleon's protruding leg, extended wing and twisted neck, his busy and unconscious devotion to the arrangement of his person, his evident sensation of complete loneliness, most comfortable solitude, brought home with vehemence to the Father the undignified buffoonery of his conduct; the more piteous buffoonery of his friend. He seized the curtains with his hands and was about to thrust them aside and issue forth when an abrupt movement of the parrot stopped him. The bird, as if sharply attracted by something, paused in its pecking, and, with its head still bent backward and twisted sideways on its neck, seemed to listen intently. Its round eye looked glistening and strained like the eye of a disturbed pigeon. Contracting its wing, it lifted its head and sat for a moment erect on its perch, shifting its feet mechanically up and down, as if a dawning excitement produced in it an uncontrollable desire of movement. Then it thrust its head forward in the direction of the further room and remained perfectly still. Its attitude so strongly suggested the concentration of its attention on something immediately before it that Father Murchison instinctively stared about the room, half expecting to see Pitting advance softly, having entered through the hidden door. He did not come, and there was no sound in the chamber. Nevertheless, the parrot was obviously getting excited and increasingly attentive. It bent its head lower and lower, stretching out its neck until, almost falling from the perch, it half extended its wings, raising them slightly from its back, as if about to take flight, and fluttering them rapidly up and down. It continued this fluttering movement for what seemed to the Father an immense time. At length, raising its wings as far as possible, it dropped them slowly and deliberately down to its back, caught hold of the edge of its bath with its beak, hoisted itself on to the floor of the cage, waddled to the bars, thrust its head against them, and stood quite still in the exact attitude it always assumed when its head was being scratched by the Professor. So complete was the suggestion of this delight conveyed by the bird that Father Murchison felt as if he saw a white finger gently pushed among the soft feathers of its head, and he was seized by a most strong conviction that something, unseen by him but seen and welcomed by Napoleon, stood immediately before the cage.

The parrot presently withdrew its head, as if the coaxing finger had been lifted from it, and its pronounced air of acute physical enjoyment faded into one of marked attention and alert curiosity. Pulling itself up by the bars it climbed again upon its perch, sidled to the left side of the cage, and began apparently to watch something with profound interest. It bowed its head oddly, paused for a moment, then bowed its head again. Father Murchison found himself conceiving—from this elaborate movement of the head—a distinct idea of a personality. The bird's proceedings suggested extreme sentimentality combined with that sort of weak determination which is often the most persistent. Such weak determination is a very common attribute of persons who are partially idiotic. Father Murchison was moved to think of these poor creatures who will often, so strangely and unreasonably, attach themselves with persistence to those who love them least. Like many priests, he had had some experience of them, for the amorous idiot is peculiarly sensitive to the attraction of preachers. This bowing movement of the parrot recalled to his memory a terrible, pale woman who for a time haunted all churches in which he ministered, who was perpetually endeavouring to catch his eye, and who always bent her head with an obsequious and cunningly conscious smile when she did so. The parrot went on bowing, making a short pause between each genuflection, as if it waited for a signal to be given that called into play its imitative faculty.

"Yes, yes, it's imitating an idiot," Father Murchison caught himself saying as he watched.

And he looked again about the room, but saw nothing; except the furniture, the dancing fire, and the serried ranks of the books. Presently the parrot ceased from bowing, and assumed the concentrated and stretched attitude of one listening very keenly. He opened his beak, showing his black tongue, shut it, then opened it again. The Father thought he was going to speak, but he remained silent, although it was obvious that he was trying to bring out something. He bowed again two or three times, paused, and then, again opening his beak, made some remark. The Father could not distinguish any words, but the voice was sickly and disagreeable, a cooing and, at the same time, querulous voice, like a woman's, he thought. And he put his ear nearer to the curtain, listening with almost feverish attention. The bowing was resumed, but this time Napoleon added to it a sidling movement, affectionate and affected, like the movement of a silly and eager thing, nestling up to someone, or giving someone a gentle and furtive nudge. Again the Father thought of that terrible, pale woman who had haunted churches. Several times he had come upon her waiting for him after evening services. Once she had hung her head smiling, had lolled out her tongue and pushed against him sideways in the dark. He remembered how his flesh had shrunk from the poor thing, the sick loathing of her that he could not banish by remembering that her mind was all astray. The parrot paused, listened, opened his beak, and again said something in the same dove-like, amorous voice, full of sickly suggestion and yet hard, even dangerous, in its intonation. A loathsome voice, the Father thought it. But this time, although he heard the voice more distinctly than before, he could not make up his mind whether it was like a woman's voice or a man's—or perhaps a child's. It seemed to be a human voice, and yet oddly sexless. In order to resolve his doubt he withdrew into the darkness of the curtains, ceased to watch Napoleon and simply listened with keen attention, striving to forget that he was listening to a bird, and to imagine that he was overhearing a human being in conversation. After two or three minutes' silence the voice spoke again, and at some length, apparently repeating several times an affectionate series of ejaculations with a cooing emphasis that was unutterably mawkish and offensive. The sickliness of the voice, its falling intonations and its strange indelicacy, combined with a die-away softness and meretricious refinement, made the Father's flesh creep. Yet he could not distinguish any words, nor could he decide on the voice's sex or age. One thing alone he was certain of as he stood still in the darkness—that such a sound could only proceed from something peculiarly loathsome, could only express a personality unendurably abominable to him, if not to everybody. The voice presently failed, in a sort of husky gasp, and there was a prolonged silence. It was broken by the Professor, who suddenly pulled away the curtains that hid the Father and said to him:

"Come out now, and look."

The Father came into the light, blinking, glanced towards the cage, and saw Napoleon poised motionless on one foot with his head under his wing. He appeared to be asleep. The Professor was pale, and his mobile lips were drawn into an expression of supreme disgust.

"Faugh!" he said.

He walked to the windows of the further room, pulled aside the curtains and pushed the glass up, letting in the air. The bare trees were visible in the grey gloom outside. Guildea leaned out for a minute drawing the night air into his lungs. Presently he turned round to the Father, and exclaimed abruptly,

"Pestilent! Isn't it?"

"Yes—most pestilent."

"Ever hear anything like it?"

"Not exactly."

"Nor I. It gives me nausea, Murchison, absolute physical nausea."

He closed the window and walked uneasily about the room.

"What d'you make of it?" he asked, over his shoulder.

"How d'you mean exactly?"

"Is it man's, woman's, or child's voice?"

"I can't tell, I can't make up my mind."

"Nor I."

"Have you heard it often?"

"Yes, since I returned from Westgate. There are never any words that I can distinguish. What a voice!"

He spat into the fire.

"Forgive me," he said, throwing himself down in a chair. "It turns my stomach—literally."

"And mine," said the Father, truly.

"The worst of it is," continued Guildea, with a high, nervous accent, "that there's no brain with it, none at all—only the cunning of idiotcy."

The Father started at this exact expression of his own conviction by another.

"Why d'you start like that?" asked Guildea, with a quick suspicion which showed the unnatural condition of his nerves.

"Well, the very same idea had occurred to me."

"What?"

"That I was listening to the voice of something idiotic."

"Ah! That's the devil of it, you know, to a man like me. I could fight against brain—but this!"

He sprang up again, poked the fire violently, then stood on the hearthrug with his back to it, and his hands thrust into the high pockets of his trousers.

"That's the voice of the thing that's got into my house," he said. "Pleasant, isn't it?"

And now there was really horror in his eyes, and in his voice.

"I must get it out," he exclaimed. "I must get it out. But how?" He tugged at his short black beard with a quivering hand.

"How?" he continued. "For what is it? Where is it?"

"You feel it's here—now?"

"Undoubtedly. But I couldn't tell you in what part of the room."

He stared about, glancing rapidly at everything.

"Then you consider yourself haunted?" said Father Murchison.

He, too, was much moved and disturbed, although he was not conscious of the presence of anything near them in the room.

"I have never believed in any nonsense of that kind, as you know," Guildea answered. "I simply state a fact which I cannot understand, and which is beginning to be very painful to me. There is something here. But whereas most so-called hauntings have been described to me as inimical, what I am conscious of is that I am admired, loved, desired. This is distinctly horrible to me, Murchison, distinctly horrible."

Father Murchison suddenly remembered the first evening he had spent with Guildea, and the latter's expression almost of disgust, at the idea of receiving warm affection from anyone. In the light of that long ago conversation the present event seemed supremely strange, and almost like a punishment for an offence committed by the Professor against humanity. But, looking up at his friend's twitching face, the Father resolved not to be caught in the net of his hideous belief.

"There can be nothing here," he said. "It's impossible."

"What does that bird imitate, then?"

"The voice of someone who has been here."

"Within the last week then. For it never spoke like that before, and mind, I noticed that it was watching and striving to imitate something before I went away, since the night that I went into the Park, only since then."

"Somebody with a voice like that must have been here while you were away," Father Murchison repeated, with a gentle obstinacy.

"I'll soon find out."

Guildea pressed the bell. Pitting stole in almost immediately.

"Pitting," said the Professor, speaking in a high, sharp voice, "did anyone come into this room during my absence at the sea?"

"Certainly not, sir, except the maids—and me, sir."

"Not a soul? You are certain?"

"Perfectly certain, sir."

The cold voice of the butler sounded surprised, almost resentful. The Professor flung out his hand towards the cage.

"Has the bird been here the whole time?"

"Yes, sir."

"He was not moved, taken elsewhere, even for a moment?"

Pitting's pale face began to look almost expressive, and his lips were pursed.

"Certainly not, sir."

"Thank you. That will do."

The butler retired, moving with a sort of ostentatious rectitude. When he had reached the door, and was just going out, his master called,

"Wait a minute, Pitting."

The butler paused. Guildea bit his lips, tugged at his beard uneasily two or three times, and then said,

"Have you noticed—er—the parrot talking lately in a—a very peculiar, very disagreeable voice?"

"Yes, sir—a soft voice like, sir."

"Ha! Since when?"

"Since you went away, sir. He's always at it."

"Exactly. Well, and what did you think of it?"

"Beg pardon, sir?"

"What do you think about his talking in this voice?"

"Oh, that it's only his play, sir."

"I see. That's all, Pitting."

The butler disappeared and closed the door noiselessly behind him. Guildea turned his eyes on his friend.

"There, you see!" he ejaculated.

"It's certainly very odd," said the Father. "Very odd indeed. You are certain you have no maid who talks at all like that?"

"My dear Murchison! Would you keep a servant with such a voice about you for two days?"

"No."

"My housemaid has been with me for five years, my cook for seven. You've heard Pitting speak. The three of them make up my entire household. A parrot never speaks in a voice it has not heard. Where has it heard that voice?"

"But we hear nothing?"

"No. Nor do we see anything. But it does. It feels something too. Didn't you observe it presenting its head to be scratched?"

"Certainly it seemed to be doing so."

"It was doing so."

Father Murchison said nothing. He was full of increasing discomfort that almost amounted to apprehension.

"Are you convinced?" said Guildea, rather irritably.

"No. The whole matter is very strange. But till I hear, see, or feel—as you do—the presence of something, I cannot believe."

"You mean that you will not?"

"Perhaps. Well, it is time I went."

Guildea did not try to detain him, but said, as he let him out, "Do me a favour, come again to-morrow night."

The Father had an engagement. He hesitated, looked into the Professor's face and said,

"I will. At nine I'll be with you. Good-night."

When he was on the pavement he felt relieved. He turned round, saw Guildea stepping into his passage, and shivered.

V

Father Murchison walked all the way home to Bird Street that night. He required exercise after the strange and disagreeable evening he had spent, an evening upon which he looked back already as a man looks back upon a nightmare. In his ears, as he walked, sounded the gentle and intolerable voice. Even the memory of it caused him physical discomfort. He tried to put it from him, and to consider the whole matter calmly. The Professor had offered his proof that there was some strange presence in his house. Could any reasonable man accept such proof? Father Murchison told himself that no reasonable man could accept it. The parrot's proceedings were, no doubt, extraordinary. The bird had succeeded in producing an extraordinary illusion of an invisible presence in the room. But that there really was such a presence the Father insisted on denying to himself. The devoutly religious, those who believe implicitly in the miracles recorded in the Bible, and who regulate their lives by the messages they suppose themselves to receive directly from the Great Ruler of a hidden World, are seldom inclined to accept any notion of supernatural intrusion into the affairs of daily life. They put it from them with anxious determination. They regard it fixedly as hocus-pocus, childish if not wicked.

Father Murchison inclined to the normal view of the devoted churchman. He was determined to incline to it. He could not—so he now told himself—accept the idea that his friend was being supernaturally punished for his lack of humanity, his deficiency in affection, by being obliged to endure the love of some horrible thing, which could not be seen, heard, or handled. Nevertheless, retribution did certainly seem to wait upon Guildea's condition. That which he had unnaturally dreaded and shrunk from in his thought he seemed to be now forced unnaturally to suffer. The Father prayed for his friend that night before the little, humble altar in the barely furnished, cell-like chamber where he slept.

On the following evening, when he called in Hyde Park Place, the door was opened by the housemaid, and Father Murchison mounted the stairs, wondering what had become of Pitting. He was met at the library door by Guildea and was painfully struck by the alteration in his appearance. His face was ashen in hue, and there were lines beneath his eyes. The eyes themselves looked excited and horribly forlorn. His hair and dress were disordered and his lips twitched continually, as if he were shaken by some acute nervous apprehension.

"What has become of Pitting?" asked the Father, grasping Guildea's hot and feverish hand.

"He has left my service."

"Left your service!" exclaimed the Father in utter amazement.

"Yes, this afternoon."

"May one ask why?"

"I'm going to tell you. It's all part and parcel of this—this most odious business. You remember once discussing the relations men ought to have with their servants?"

"Ah!" cried the Father, with a flash of inspiration. "The crisis has occurred?"

"Exactly," said the Professor, with a bitter smile. "The crisis has occurred. I called upon Pitting to be a man and a brother. He responded by declining the invitation. I upbraided him. He gave me warning. I paid him his wages and told him he could go at once. And he has gone. What are you looking at me like that for?"

"I didn't know," said Father Murchison, hastily dropping his eyes, and looking away. "Why," he added. "Napoleon is gone too."

"I sold him to-day to one of those shops in Shaftesbury Avenue."

"Why?"

"He sickened me with his abominable imitation of—his intercourse with—well, you know what he was at last night. Besides, I have no further need of his proof to tell me I am not dreaming. And, being convinced as I now am, that all I have thought to have happened has actually happened, I care very little about convincing others. Forgive me for saying so, Murchison, but I am now certain that my anxiety to make you believe in the presence of something here really arose from some faint doubt on that subject—within myself. All doubt has now vanished."

"Tell me why."

"I will."

Both men were standing by the fire. They continued to stand while Guildea went on,

"Last night I felt it."

"What?" cried the Father.

"I say that last night, as I was going upstairs to bed, I felt something accompanying me and nestling up against me."

"How horrible!" exclaimed the Father, involuntarily.

Guildea smiled drearily.

"I will not deny the horror of it. I cannot, since I was compelled to call on Pitting for assistance."

"But—tell me—what was it, at least what did it seem to be?"

"It seemed to be a human being. It seemed, I say; and what I mean exactly is that the effect upon me was rather that of human contact than of anything else. But I could see nothing, hear nothing. Only, three times, I felt this gentle, but determined, push against me, as if to coax me and to attract my attention. The first time it happened I was on the landing outside this room, with my foot on the first stair. I will confess to you, Murchison, that I bounded upstairs like one pursued. That is the shameful truth. Just as I was about to enter my bedroom, however, I felt the thing entering with me, and, as I have said, squeezing, with loathsome, sickening tenderness, against my side. Then—"

He paused, turned towards the fire and leaned his head on his arm. The Father was greatly moved by the strange helplessness and despair of the attitude. He laid his hand affectionately on Guildea's shoulder.

"Then?"

Guildea lifted his head. He looked painfully abashed.

"Then, Murchison, I am ashamed to say I broke down, suddenly, unaccountably, in a way I should have thought wholly impossible to me. I struck out with my hands to thrust the thing away. It pressed more closely to me. The pressure, the contact became unbearable to me. I shouted out for Pitting. I—I believe I must have cried—'Help.'"

"He came, of course?"

"Yes, with his usual soft, unemotional quiet. His calm—its opposition to my excitement of disgust and horror—must, I suppose, have irritated me. I was not myself, no, no!"

He stopped abruptly. Then—

"But I need hardly tell you that," he added, with most piteous irony.

"And what did you say to Pitting?"

"I said that he should have been quicker. He begged my pardon. His cold voice really maddened me, and I burst out into some foolish, contemptible diatribe, called him a machine, taunted him, then—as I felt that loathsome thing nestling once more to me—begged him to assist me, to stay with me, not to leave me alone—I meant in the company of my tormentor. Whether he was frightened, or whether he was angry at my unjust and violent manner and speech a moment before, I don't know. In any case he answered that he was engaged as a butler, and not to sit up all night with people. I suspect he thought I had taken too much to drink. No doubt that was it. I believe I swore at him as a coward—I! This morning he said he wished to leave my service. I gave him a month's wages, a good character as a butler, and sent him off at once."

"But the night? How did you pass it?"

"I sat up all night."

"Where? In your bedroom?"

"Yes—with the door open—to let it go."

"You felt that it stayed?"

"It never left me for a moment, but it did not touch me again. When it was light I took a bath, lay down for a little while, but did not close my eyes. After breakfast I had the explanation with Pitting and paid him. Then I came up here. My nerves were in a very shattered condition. Well, I sat down, tried to write, to think. But the silence was broken in the most abominable manner."

"How?"

"By the murmur of that appalling voice, that voice of a love-sick idiot, sickly but determined. Ugh!"

He shuddered in every limb. Then he pulled himself together, assumed, with a self-conscious effort, his most determined, most aggressive, manner, and added:

"I couldn't stand that. I had come to the end of my tether; so I sprang up, ordered a cab to be called, seized the cage and drove with it to a bird shop in Shaftesbury Avenue. There I sold the parrot for a trifle. I think, Murchison, that I must have been nearly mad then, for, as I came out of the wretched shop, and stood for an instant on the pavement among the cages of rabbits, guinea-pigs, and puppy dogs, I laughed aloud. I felt as if a load was lifted from my shoulders, as if in selling that voice I had sold the cursed thing that torments me. But when I got back to the house it was here. It's here now. I suppose it will always be here."

He shuffled his feet on the rug in front of the fire.

"What on earth am I to do?" he said. "I'm ashamed of myself, Murchison, but—but I suppose there are things in the world that certain men simply can't endure. Well, I can't endure this, and there's an end of the matter."

He ceased. The Father was silent. In presence of this extraordinary distress he did not know what to say. He recognised the uselessness of attempting to comfort Guildea, and he sat with his eyes turned, almost moodily, to the ground. And while he sat there he tried to give himself to the influences within the room, to feel all that was within it. He even, half-unconsciously, tried to force his imagination to play tricks with him. But he remained totally unaware of any third person with them. At length he said,

"Guildea, I cannot pretend to doubt the reality of your misery here. You must go away, and at once. When is your Paris lecture?"

"Next week. In nine days from now."

"Go to Paris to-morrow then, you say you have never had any consciousness that this—this thing pursued you beyond your own front door!"

"Never—hitherto."

"Go to-morrow morning. Stay away till after your lecture. And then let us see if the affair is at an end. Hope, my dear friend, hope."

He had stood up. Now he clasped the Professor's hand.

"See all your friends in Paris. Seek distractions. I would ask you also to seek—other help."

He said the last words with a gentle, earnest gravity and simplicity that touched Guildea, who returned his handclasp almost warmly.

"I'll go," he said. "I'll catch the ten o'clock train, and to-night I'll sleep at a hotel, at the Grosvenor—that's close to the station. It will be more convenient for the train."

As Father Murchison went home that night he kept thinking of that sentence: "It will be more convenient for the train." The weakness in Guildea that had prompted its utterance appalled him.

VI

No letter came to Father Murchison from the Professor during the next few days, and this silence reassured him, for it seemed to betoken that all was well. The day of the lecture dawned, and passed. On the following morning, the Father eagerly opened the *Times*, and scanned its pages to see if there were any report of the great meeting of scientific men which Guildea had addressed. He glanced up and down the columns with anxious eyes, then suddenly his hands stiffened as they held the sheets. He had come upon the following paragraph:

"We regret to announce that Professor Frederic Guildea was suddenly seized with severe illness yesterday evening while addressing a scientific meeting in Paris. It was observed that he looked very pale and nervous when he rose to his feet. Nevertheless, he spoke in French fluently for about a quarter of an hour. Then he appeared to become uneasy. He faltered and glanced about like a man apprehensive, or in severe distress. He even stopped once or twice, and seemed unable to go on, to remember what he wished to say. But, pulling himself together with an obvious effort, he continued to address the audience. Suddenly, however, he paused again, edged furtively along the platform, as if pursued by something which he feared, struck out with his hands, uttered a loud, harsh cry and fainted. The sensation in the hall was indescribable. People rose from their seats. Women screamed, and, for a moment, there was a veritable panic. It is feared that the Professor's mind must have temporarily given way owing to overwork. We understand that he will return to England as soon as possible, and we sincerely hope that necessary rest and quiet will soon have the desired effect, and that he will be completely restored to health and enabled to prosecute further the investigations which have already so benefited the world."

The Father dropped the paper, hurried out into Bird Street, sent a wire of enquiry to Paris, and received the same day the following reply: "Returning to-morrow. Please call evening. Guildea." On that evening the Father called in Hyde Park Place, was at once admitted, and found Guildea sitting by the fire in the library, ghastly pale, with a heavy rug over his knees. He looked like a man emaciated by a long and severe illness, and in his wide-open eyes there was an expression of fixed horror. The Father started at the sight of him, and could scarcely refrain from crying out. He was beginning to express his sympathy when Guildea stopped him with a trembling gesture.

"I know all that," Guildea said, "I know. This Paris affair—" He faltered and stopped.

"You ought never to have gone," said the Father. "I was wrong. I ought not to have advised your going. You were not fit."

"I was perfectly fit," he answered, with the irritability of sickness. "But I was—I was accompanied by that abominable thing."

He glanced hastily round him, shifted his chair and pulled the rug higher over his knees. The Father wondered why he was thus wrapped up. For the fire was bright and red and the night was not very cold.

"I was accompanied to Paris," he continued, pressing his upper teeth upon his lower lip.

He paused again, obviously striving to control himself. But the effort was vain. There was no resistance in the man. He writhed in his chair and suddenly burst forth in a tone of hopeless lamentation.

"Murchison, this being, thing—whatever it is—no longer leaves me even for a moment. It will not stay here unless I am here, for it loves me, persistently, idiotically. It accompanied me to Paris, stayed with me there, pursued me to the lecture hall, pressed against me, caressed me while I was speaking. It has returned with me here. It is here now,"—he uttered a sharp cry—"now, as I sit here with you. It is nestling up to me, fawning upon me, touching my hands. Man, man, can't you feel that it is here?"

"No," the Father answered truly.

"I try to protect myself from its loathsome contact," Guildea continued, with fierce excitement, clutching the thick rug with both hands. "But nothing is of any avail against it. Nothing. What is it? What can it be? Why should it have come to me that night?"

"Perhaps as a punishment," said the Father, with a quick softness.

"For what?"

"You hated affection. You put human feelings aside with contempt. You had, you desired to have, no love for anyone. Nor did you desire to receive any love from anything. Perhaps this is a punishment."

Guildea stared into his face.

"D'you believe that?" he cried.

"I don't know," said the Father. "But it may be so. Try to endure it, even to welcome it. Possibly then the persecution will cease."

"I know it means me no harm," Guildea exclaimed, "it seeks me out of affection. It was led to me by some amazing attraction which I exercise over it ignorantly. I know that. But to a man of my nature that is the ghastly part of the matter. If it would hate me, I could bear it. If it would attack me, if it would try to do me some dreadful harm, I should become a man again. I should be braced to fight against it. But this gentleness, this abominable solicitude, this brainless worship of an idiot, persistent, sickly, horribly physical, I cannot endure. What does it want of me? What would it demand of me? It nestles to me. It leans against me. I feel its touch, like the touch of a feather, trembling about my heart, as if it sought to number my pulsations, to find out the inmost secrets of my impulses and desires. No privacy is left to me." He sprang up excitedly. "I cannot withdraw," he cried, "I cannot be alone, untouched, unworshipped, unwatched for even one-half second. Murchison, I am dying of this, I am dying."

He sank down again in his chair, staring apprehensively on all sides, with the passion of some blind man, deluded in the belief that by his furious and continued effort he will attain sight. The Father knew well that he sought to pierce the veil of the invisible, and have knowledge of the thing that loved him.

"Guildea," the Father said, with insistent earnestness, "try to endure this—do more—try to give this thing what it seeks."

"But it seeks my love."

"Learn to give it your love and it may go, having received what it came for."

"T'sh! You talk as a priest. Suffer your persecutors. Do good to them that despitefully use you. You talk as a priest."

"As a friend I spoke naturally, indeed, right out of my heart. The idea suddenly came to me that all this—truth or seeming, it doesn't matter which—may be some strange form of lesson. I have had lessons—painful ones. I shall have many more. If you could welcome—"

"I can't! I can't!" Guildea cried fiercely. "Hatred! I can give it that—always that, nothing but that—hatred, hatred."

He raised his voice, glared into the emptiness of the room, and repeated, "Hatred!"

As he spoke the waxen pallor of his cheeks increased, until he looked like a corpse with living eyes. The Father feared that he was going to collapse and faint, but suddenly he raised himself upon his chair and said, in a high and keen voice, full of suppressed excitement:

"Murchison, Murchison!"

"Yes. What is it?"

An amazing ecstasy shone in Guildea's eyes.

"It wants to leave me," he cried. "It wants to go! Don't lose a moment! Let it out! The window—the window!"

The Father, wondering, went to the near window, drew aside the curtains and pushed it open. The branches of the trees in the garden creaked drily in the light wind. Guildea leaned forward on the arms of his chair. There was silence for a moment. Then Guildea, speaking in a rapid whisper, said,

"No, no. Open this door—open the hall door. I feel—I feel that it will return the way it came. Make haste—ah, go!"

The Father obeyed—to soothe him, hurried to the door and opened it wide. Then he glanced back at Guildea. He was standing up, bent forward. His eyes were glaring with eager expectation, and, as the Father turned, he made a furious gesture towards the passage with his thin hands.

The Father hastened out and down the stairs. As he descended in the twilight he fancied he heard a slight cry from the room behind him, but he did not pause. He flung the hall door open, standing back against the wall. After waiting a moment—to satisfy Guildea, he was about to close the door again, and had his hand on it, when he was attracted irresistibly to look forth towards the park. The night was lit by a young moon, and, gazing through the railings, his eyes fell upon a bench beyond them.

Upon this bench something was sitting, huddled together very strangely.

The Father remembered instantly Guildea's description of that former night, that night of Advent, and a sensation of horror-stricken curiosity stole through him.

Was there then really something that had indeed come to the Professor? And had it finished its work, fulfilled its desire and gone back to its former existence?

The Father hesitated a moment in the doorway. Then he stepped out resolutely and crossed the road, keeping his eyes fixed upon this black or dark object that leaned so strangely upon the bench. He could not tell yet what it was like, but he fancied it was unlike anything with which his eyes were acquainted. He reached the opposite path, and was about to pass through the gate in the railings, when his arm was brusquely grasped. He started, turned round, and saw a policeman eyeing him suspiciously.

"What are you up to?" said the policeman.

The Father was suddenly aware that he had no hat upon his head, and that his appearance, as he stole forward in his cassock, with his eyes intently fixed upon the bench in the Park, was probably unusual enough to excite suspicion.

"It's all right, policeman," he answered, quickly, thrusting some money into the constable's hand.

Then, breaking from him, the Father hurried towards the bench, bitterly vexed at the interruption. When he reached it nothing was there. Guildea's experience had been almost exactly repeated and, filled with unreasonable disappointment, the Father returned to the house, entered it, shut the door and hastened up the narrow stairway into the library.

On the hearthrug, close to the fire, he found Guildea lying with his head lolled against the armchair from which he had recently risen. There was a shocking expression of terror on his convulsed face. On examining him the Father found that he was dead.

The doctor, who was called in, said that the cause of death was failure of the heart.

When Father Murchison was told this, he murmured:

"Failure of the heart! It was that then!"

He turned to the doctor and said:

"Could it have been prevented?"

The doctor drew on his gloves and answered:

"Possibly, if it had been taken in time. Weakness of the heart requires a great deal of care. The Professor was too much absorbed in his work.

He should have lived very differently."

The Father nodded.

"Yes, yes," he said, sadly.

The Collaborators

I

"Why shouldn't we collaborate?" said Henley in his most matter-of-fact way, as Big Ben gave voice to the midnight hour. "Everybody does it nowadays. Two heads may be really better than one, although I seldom believe in the truth of accepted sayings. Your head is a deuced good one, Andrew; but—now don't get angry—you are too excitable and too intense to be left quite to yourself, even in book-writing, much less in the ordinary affairs of life. I think you were born to collaborate, and to collaborate with me. You can give me everything I lack, and I can give you a little of the sense of humour, and act as a drag upon the wheel."

"None of the new humour, Jack; that shall never appear in a book with my name attached to it. Dickens I can tolerate. He is occasionally felicitous. The story of 'The Dying Clown,' for instance, crude as it is it has a certain grim tragedy about it. But the new humour came from the pit, and should go—to the *Sporting Times*."

"Now, don't get excited. The book is not in proof yet—perhaps never will be. You need not be afraid. My humour will probably be old enough. But what do you say to the idea?"

Andrew Trenchard sat for a while in silent consideration. His legs were stretched out, and his slippered feet rested on the edge of the brass fender. A nimbus of smoke surrounded his swarthy features, his shock of black hair, his large, rather morose, dark eyes. He was a man of about twenty-five, with an almost horribly intelligent face, so observant that he tried people, so acute that he frightened them. His intellect was never for a moment at rest, unless in sleep. He devoured himself with his own emotions, and others with his analysis of theirs. His mind was always crouching to spring, except when it was springing. He lived an irregular life, and all horrors had a subtle fascination for him. As Henley had remarked, he possessed little sense of humour, but immense sense of evil and tragedy and sorrow. He seldom found time to calmly regard the drama of life from the front. He was always at the stage door, sending in his card, and requesting admittance behind the scenes. What was on the surface only interested him in so far as it indicated what was beneath, and in all mental matters his normal procedure was that of the disguised detective. Stupid people disliked him. Clever people distrusted him while they admired him. The mediocre suggested that he was liable to go off his head, and the profound predicted for him fame, tempered by suicide.

Most people considered him interesting, and a few were sincerely attached to him. Among these last was Henley, who had been his friend at Oxford, and had taken rooms in the same house with him in Smith's Square, Westminster. Both the young men were journalists. Henley, who, as he had acknowledged, possessed a keen sense of humour, and was not so much ashamed of it as he ought to have been, wrote—very occasionally—for *Punch*, and more often for *Fun*, was dramatic critic of a lively society paper, and "did" the books—in a sarcastic vein—for a very unmuzzled "weekly," that was libellous by profession and truthful by oversight. Trenchard, on the other hand, wrote a good deal of very condensed fiction, and generally placed it; contributed brilliant fugitive articles to various papers and magazines, and was generally spoken of by the inner circle of the craft as "a rising man," and a man to be afraid of. Henley was full of common sense, only moderately introspective, facile, and vivacious. He might be trusted to tincture a book with the popular element, and yet not to spoil it; for his literary sense was keen, despite his jocular leaning toward the new humour. He lacked imagination; but his descriptive powers were racy, and he knew instinctively what was likely to take, and what would be caviare to the general.

Trenchard, as he considered the proposition now made to him, realized that Henley might supply much that he lacked in any book that was written with a view to popular success. There could be no doubt of it.

"But we should quarrel inevitably and doggedly," he said at last. "If I cannot hold myself in, still less can I be held in. We should tear one another in pieces. When I write, I feel that what I write must be, however crude, however improper or horrible it may seem. You would want to hold me back."

"My dear boy, I should more than want to—I should do it. In collaboration, no man can be a law unto himself. That must be distinctly understood before we begin. I don't wish to force the proposition on you. Only we are both ambitious devils. We are both poor. We are both determined to try a book. Have we more chance of succeeding if we try one together? I believe so. You have the imagination, the grip, the stern power to evolve the story, to make it seem inevitable, to force it step by step on its way. I can lighten that way. I can plant a few flowers—they shall not be peonies, I promise you—on the roadside. And I can, and, what is more, will, check you when you wish to make the story impossibly horrible or fantastic to the verge of the insane. Now, you needn't be angry. This book, if we write it, has got to be a good book, and yet a book that will bring grist to the mill. That is understood."

Andrew's great eyes flashed in the lamplight.

"The mill," he said. "Sometimes I feel inclined to let it stop working. Who would care if one wheel ceased to turn? There are so many others."

"Ah, that's the sort of thing I shall cut out of the book!" cried Henley, turning the soda water into his whisky with a cheerful swish.

"We will be powerful, but never morbid; tragic, if you like, but not without hope. We need not aspire too much; but we will not look at the stones in the road all the time. And the dunghills, in which those weird fowl, the pessimistic realists, love to rake, we will sedulously avoid. Cheer up, old fellow, and be thankful that you possess a corrective in me."

Trenchard's face lightened in a rare smile as, with a half-sigh, he said: "I believe you are right, and that I need a collaborator, an opposite, who is yet in sympathy with me. Yes; either of us might fail alone; together we should succeed."

"*Will* succeed, my boy!"

"But not by pandering to the popular taste," added Andrew in his most sombre tones, and with a curl of his thin, delicately-moulded lips. "I shall never consent to that."

"We will not call it pandering. But we must hit the taste of the day, or we shall look a couple of fools."

"People are always supposed to look fools when, for once, they are not fools," said Andrew.

"Possibly. But now our bargain is made. Strike hands upon it. Henceforth we are collaborators as well as friends."

Andrew extended his long, thin, feverish hand, and, as Henley held it for a moment, he started at the intense, vivid, abnormal personality its grasp seemed to reveal. To collaborate with Trenchard was to collaborate with a human volcano.

"And now for the germ of our book," he said, as the clock struck one. "Where shall we find it?"

Trenchard leaned forward in his chair, with his hands pressed upon the arms.

"Listen, and I will give it you," he said.

And, almost until the dawn and the wakening of the slumbering city, Henley sat and listened, and forgot that his pipe was smoked out, and that his feet were cold. Trenchard had strange powers, and could enthral as he could also repel.

"It is a weird idea, and it is very powerful," Henley said at last. "But you stop short at the critical moment. Have you not devised a *dénouement?*"

"Not yet. That is where the collaboration will come in. You must help me. We must talk it over. I am in doubt."

He got up and passed his hands nervously through his thick hair.

"My doubt has kept me awake so many nights!" he said, and his voice was rather husky and worn.

Henley looked at him almost compassionately.

"How intensely you live in your fancies!"

"My fancies?" said Andrew, with a sudden harsh accent, and darting a glance of curious watchfulness upon his friend. "My— Yes, yes. Perhaps I do. Perhaps I try to. Some people have souls that must escape from their environment, their miserable life-envelope, or faint. Many of us labour and produce merely to create an atmosphere in which we ourselves may breathe for a while and be happy. Damn this London, and this lodging, and this buying bread with words! I must create for myself an atmosphere. I must be always getting away from what is, even if I go lower, lower. Ah! Well—but the *dénouement*. Give me your impressions."

Henley meditated for a while. Then he said; "Let us leave it. Let us get to work; and in time, as the story progresses, it will seem inevitable. We shall see it in front of us, and we shall not be able to avoid it. Let us get to work"—he glanced at his watch and laughed—"or, rather, let us get to bed. It is past four. This way madness lies. When we collaborate, we will write in the morning. Our book shall be a book of the dawn, and not of the darkness, despite its sombre theme."

"No, no; it must be a book of the darkness."

"Of the darkness, then, but written in the dawn. Your tragedy tempered by my trust in human nature, and the power that causes things to right themselves. Good-night, old boy."

"Good-night."

When Henley had left the room, Trenchard sat for a moment with his head sunk low on his breast and his eyes half closed. Then, with a jerk, he gained his feet, went to the door, opened it, and looked forth on the deserted landing. He listened, and heard Henley moving to and fro in his bedroom. Then he shut the door, took off his smoking-coat, and bared his left arm. There was a tiny blue mark on it.

"What will the *dénouement* be?" he whispered to himself, as he felt in his waistcoat pocket with a trembling hand.

II

The book was moving onward by slow degrees and with a great deal of discussion.

In those days Henley and Trenchard lived much with sported oaks. They were battling for fame. They were doing all they knew. Literary gatherings missed them. First nights knew them no more. The grim intensity that was always characteristic of Trenchard seemed in some degree communicated to Henley. He began to more fully understand what the creating for one's self of an atmosphere meant. The story he and his friend were fashioning fastened upon him like some strange, determined shadow from the realms of real life, gripped him more and more closely, held him for long spells of time in a new and desolate world. For the book so far was a deepening tragedy, and although, at times, Henley strove to resist the paramount influence which the genius of Trenchard began to exercise over him, he found himself comparatively impotent, unable to shed gleams of popular light upon the darkness of the pages. The power of the tale was undoubted. Henley felt that it was a big thing that they two were doing; but would it be a popular thing— a money-making thing? That was the question. He sometimes wished with all his heart they had chosen a different subject to work their combined talent upon. The germ of the work seemed only capable of tragic treatment, if the book were to be artistic. Their hero was a man of strong intellect, of physical beauty, full at first of the joy of life, chivalrous, a believer in the innate goodness of human nature. Believing in goodness, he believed also ardently in influence. In fact, he was a worshipper of influence, and his main passion was to seize upon the personalities of others, and impose his own personality upon them. He loved to make men and women see with his eyes and hear with his ears, adopt his theories as truth, take his judgment for their own. All that he thought *was*—to him. He never doubted himself, therefore he could not bear that those around him should not think with him, act towards men and women as he acted, face life as he faced it. Yet he was too subtle ever to be dogmatic. He never shouted in the marketplace. He led those with whom he came in contact as adroitly as if he had been evil, and to the influence of others he was as adamant.

Events brought into his life a woman, complex, subtle too, with a naturally noble character and fine understanding, a woman who, like so many women, might have been anything, and was far worse than nothing—a hopeless, helpless slave, the victim of the morphia habit, which had gradually degraded her, driven her through sloughs of immorality, wrecked a professional career which at one time had been almost great, shattered her constitution, though not all her still curious beauty, and ruined her, to all intents and purposes, body and soul. The man and the woman met, and in a flash the man saw what she had been, what she might have been, what, perhaps, in spite of all, she still was, somewhere, somehow. In her horrible degradation, in her dense despair, she fascinated him. He could only see the fire bursting out of the swamp. He could only feel on his cheek the breath of the spring in the darkness of the charnel house. He knew that she gave to him his great lifework. Her monstrous habit he simply could not comprehend. It was altogether as fantastic to him as absolute virtue sometimes seems to absolute vice. He looked upon it, and felt as little kinship with it as a saint might feel with a vampire. To him it was merely a hideous and extraordinary growth, which had fastened like a cancer upon a beautiful and wonderful body, and which must be cut out. He was profoundly interested.

He loved the woman. Seeing her governed entirely by a vice, he made the very common mistake of believing her to have a weak personality, easily falling, perhaps for that very reason as easily lifted to her feet. He resolved to save her, to devote all his powers, all his subtlety, all his intellect, all his strong force of will, to weaning this woman from her fatal habit. She was a married woman, long ago left, to kill herself if she would, by the husband whose happiness she had wrecked. He took her to live with him. For her sake he defied the world, and set himself to do angel's work when people believed him at the devil's. He resolved to wrap her, to envelop her in his influence, to enclose her in his strong personality. Here, at last, was a grand, a noble opportunity for the legitimate exercise of his master passion. He was confident of victory.

But his faith in himself was misplaced. This woman, whom he thought so weak, was yet stronger than he. Although he could not influence her, he began to find that she could influence him. At first he struggled with her vice, which he could not understand. He thought himself merely horrified at it; then he began to lose the horror in wonder at its power. Its virility, as it were, fascinated him just a little. A vice so overwhelmingly strong seemed to him at length almost glorious, almost God-like. There was a sort of humanity about it. Yes, it was like a being who lived and who conquered.

The woman loved him, and he tried to win her from it; but her passion for it was greater than her passion for him, greater than had been her original passion for purity, for health, for success, for homage, for all lovely and happiness-making things. Her passion for it was so great that it roused the man's curiosity at last; it made him hold his breath, and stand in awe, and desire furtively to try just once for himself what its dominion was like, to test its power as one may test the power of an electric battery. He dared not do this openly, for fear the fact of his doing so might drive the woman still farther on the downward path. So in secret he tasted the fascinations of her vice, once—and again—and yet again. But still he struggled for her while he was ceasing to struggle for himself. Still he combated for her the foe who was conquering him. Very strange, very terrible was his position in that London house with her, isolated from the world. For his friends had dropped him. Even those who were not scandalized at his relations with this woman had ceased to come near him. They found him blind and deaf to the ordinary interests of life. He never went out anywhere, unless occasionally with her to some theatre. He never invited anyone to come and see him. At first the woman absorbed all his interest, all his powers of love—and then at last the woman and her vice, which was becoming his too. By degrees he sank lower and lower, but he never told the woman the truth, and he still urged her to give up her horrible habit, which now he loved. And she laughed in his face, and asked him if a human creature who had discovered a new life would be likely to give it up. "A new death," he murmured, and then, looking in a mirror near to him, saw his lips curved in the thin, pale smile of the hypocrite.

So far the two young men had written. They worked hard, but their industry was occasionally interrupted by the unaccountable laziness of Andrew, who, after toiling with unremitting fury for some days, and scarcely getting up from his desk, would disappear, and perhaps not return for several nights. Henley remonstrated with him, but in vain.

"But what do you do, my dear fellow?" he asked. "What becomes of you?"

"I go away to think out what is coming. The environment I seek helps me," answered Andrew, with a curious, gleaming smile. "I return full of fresh copy."

This was true enough. He generally mysteriously departed when the book was beginning to flag, and on his reappearance he always set to work with new vigour and confidence.

"It seems to me," Henley said, "that it will be your book after all, not mine. It is your plot, and when I think things over I find that every detail is yours. You insisted on the house where the man and the woman hid themselves being on the Chelsea Embankment. You invented the woman, her character, her appearance. You named her Olive Beauchamp."

"Olive Beauchamp," Andrew repeated, with a strange lingering over the two words, which he pronounced in a very curious voice that trembled, as if with some keen emotion, love or hate. "Yes; I named her as you say."

"Then, as the man in the play remarks, 'Where do I come in?'" Henley asked, half laughing, half vexed. "Upon my word, I shall have some compunction in putting my name below yours on the title page when the book is published, if it ever is."

Andrew's lips twitched once or twice uneasily. Then he said, "You need not have any such compunction. The greatest chapter will probably be written by you."

"Which chapter do you mean?"

"That which winds the story up—that which brings the whole thing to its legitimate conclusion. You must write the *dénouement*."

"I doubt if I could. And then we have not even now decided what it is to be."

"We need not bother about that yet. It will come. Fate will decide it for us."

"What do you mean, Andrew? How curiously you talk about the book sometimes—so precisely as if it were true!"

Trenchard smiled again, struck a match, and lit his pipe.

"It seems true to me—when I am writing it," he answered. "I have been writing it these last two days and nights when I have been away, and now I can go forward, if you agree to the new development which I suggest."

It was night. He had been absent for some days, and had just returned. Henley, meanwhile, had been raging because the book had come to a complete standstill. He himself could do nothing at it, since they had reached a deadlock, and had not talked over any new scenes, or mutually decided upon the turn events were now to take. He felt rather cross and sore.

"*You* can go forward," he said: "yes, after your holiday. You might at least tell me when you are going."

"I never know myself," Andrew said rather sadly.

He was looking very white and worn, and his eyes were heavy.

"But I have thought some fresh material out. My idea is this: The man now becomes such a complete slave to the morphia habit that concealment of the fact is scarcely possible. And, indeed, he ceases to desire to conceal it from the woman. The next scene will be an immensely powerful one—that in which he tells her the truth."

"You do not think it would be more natural if she found it out against his will? It seems to me that what he had concealed so long he would try to hide forever."

"No," Andrew said emphatically; "that would not be so."

"But—"

"Look here," the other interrupted, with some obvious irritability; "let me tell you what I have conceived, and raise any objections afterwards if you wish to raise them. He would tell her the truth himself. He would almost glory in doing so. That is the nature of the man. We have depicted his pride in his own powers, his temptation, his struggle—his fall, as it would be called—"

"As it would be called."

"Well, well!—his fall, then. And now comes the moment when his fall is complete. He bends the neck finally beneath his tyrant, and then he goes to the woman and he tells her the truth."

"But explain matters a little more. Do you mean that he is glad, and tells almost with triumph; or that he is appalled, and tells her with horror?"

"Ah! That is where the power of the scene lies. He is appalled. He is like a man plunged at last into hell without hope of future redemption. He tells her the truth with horror."

"And she?"

"It is she who triumphs. Look here: it will be like this."

Andrew leaned forward across the table that stood between their two worn armchairs. His thin, feverish-looking hands, with the fingers strongly twisted together, rested upon it. His dark eyes glittered with excitement.

"It will be like this. It is evening—a dark, dull evening, like the day before yesterday, closing in early, throttling the afternoon prematurely, as it were. A drizzling rain falls softly, drenching everything—the sodden leaves of the trees on the Embankment, the road, which is heavy with clinging yellow mud, the stone coping of the wall that skirts the river.

"And the river heaves along. Its gray, dirty waves are beaten up by a light, chilly wind, and chase the black barges with a puny, fretful, sinister fury, falling back from their dark, wet sides with a hiss of baffled hatred. Yes, it is dreary weather.

"Do you know, Henley, as I know, the strange, subtle influence of certain kinds of weather? There are days on which I could do great deeds merely because of the way the sun is shining. There are days, there are evenings, when I could commit crimes merely because of the way the wind is whispering, the river is sighing, the dingy night is clustering around me. There can be an angel in the weather, or there can be a devil. On this evening I am describing there is a devil in the night!

"The lights twinkle through the drizzling rain, and they are blurred, as bright eyes are blurred, and made dull and ugly, by tears. Two or three cabs roll slowly by the houses on the Embankment. A few people hurry past along the slippery, shining pavement. But as the night closes in there is little life outside those tall, gaunt houses that are so near the river! And in one of those houses the man comes down to the woman to tell her the truth.

"There is a devil in the weather that night, as I said, and that devil whispers to the man, and tells him that it is now his struggle must end finally, and the new era of unresisted yielding to the vice begin. In the sinister darkness, in the diminutive, drenching mist of rain, he speaks, and the man listens, and bows his head and answers 'yes!' It is over. He has fallen finally. He is resolved, with a strange, dull obstinacy that gives him a strange, dull pleasure—do you see?—to go down to the room below, and tell the woman that she has conquered him—that his power of will is a reed which can be crushed—that henceforth there shall be two victims instead of one. He goes down."

Andrew paused a moment. His lips were twitching again. He looked terribly excited. Henley listened in silence. He had lost all wish to interrupt.

"He goes down into the room below where the woman is, with her dark hair, and her dead-white face, and her extraordinary eyes—large, luminous, sometimes dull and without expression, sometimes dilated, and with an unnatural life staring out of them. She is on the sofa near the fire. He sits down beside her. His head falls into his hands, and at first he is silent. He is thinking how he will tell her. She puts her soft, dry hand on his, and she says: 'I am very tired to-night. Do not begin your evening sermon. Let me have it to-morrow. How you must love me to be so persistent! and how you must love me to be so stupid as to think that your power of will can break the power of such a habit as mine!'

"Then he draws his hand away from hers, and he lifts his head from his hands, and he tells her the truth. She leans back against a cushion staring at him in silence, devouring him with her eyes, which have become very bright and eager and searching. Presently he stops.

"'Go on,' she says, 'go on. Tell me more. Tell me all you feel. Tell me how the habit stole upon you, and came to you again and again, and stayed with you. Tell me how you first liked it, and then loved it, and how it was something to you, and then much, and then everything. Go on! go on!'

"And he catches her excitement. He conceals nothing from her. All the hideous, terrible, mental processes he has been through, he details to her, at first almost gloating over his own degradation. He even exaggerates, as a man exaggerates in telling a story to an eager auditor.

He is carried away by her strange fury of listening. He lays bare his soul; he exposes its wounds; he sears them with red-hot irons for her to see. And then at last all is told. He can think of no more details. He has even embellished the abominable truth. So he is silent, and he looks at her."

"And what does she do?" asked Henley, with a catch in his voice as he spoke. Undoubtedly in relating a fictitious narrative Andrew had a quite abnormal power of making it appear true and real.

"She looks at him, and then she bursts out laughing. Her eyes shine with triumph. She is glad; she is joyous with the joy of a lost soul when it sees that other souls are irrevocably lost too; she laughs, and she says nothing."

"And the man?"

Andrew's eyes suddenly dilated. He leaned forward and laid his hand on Henley's arm.

"Ah, the man! that is my great idea. As she laughs his heart is changed. His love for her suddenly dies. Its place is taken by hatred. He realizes then, for the first time, while he hears her laugh, what she has done to him. He knows that she has ruined him, and that she is proud of it—that she is rejoicing in having won him to destruction. He sees that his perdition is merely a feather in her cap. He hates her. Oh, how he hates her!—hates her!"

The expression on Andrew's face became terrible as he spoke—cruel, malignant, almost fiendish. Henley turned cold, and shook off his hand abruptly.

"That is horrible!" he said. "I object to that. The book will be one of unrelieved gloom."

"The book!" said Andrew.

"Yes. You behave really as if the story were true, as if everything in it were ordained—inevitable."

"It seems so to me; it is so. What must be, must be. If you are afraid of tragedy, you ought never to have joined me in starting upon such a story. Even what has never happened must be made to seem actual to be successful. The art of fiction is to imitate truth with absolute fidelity, not to travesty it. In such circumstances the man's love would be changed to hatred."

"Yes, if the woman's demeanour were such as you have described. But why should she be so callous? I do not think that is natural."

"You do not know the woman," began Andrew harshly. Then he stopped speaking abruptly, and a violent flush swept over his face.

"I know her as well as you do, my dear fellow," rejoined Henley, laughing. "How you manage to live in your dreams! You certainly do create an atmosphere for yourself with a vengeance, and for me too. I believe you have an abnormal quantity of electricity concealed about you somewhere, and sometimes you give me a shock and carry me out of myself. If this is collaboration, it is really a farce. From the very first you have had things all your own way. You have talked me over to your view upon every single occasion; but now I am going to strike. I object to the conduct you have devised for Olive. It will alienate all sympathy from her; it is the behaviour of a devil."

"It is the behaviour of a woman," said Andrew, with a cold cynicism that seemed to cut like a knife.

"How can you tell? How can you judge of women so surely?"

"I study all strange phenomena, women among the rest."

"Have you ever met an Olive Beauchamp, then, in real life?" said Henley.

The question was put more than half in jest; but Trenchard received it with a heavy frown.

"Don't let us quarrel about the matter," he said, "I can only tell you this; and mind, Jack, I mean it. It is my unalterable resolve. Either the story must proceed upon the lines that I have indicated, or I cannot go on with it at all. It would be impossible for me to write it differently."

"And this is collaboration, is it?" exclaimed the other, trying to force a laugh, though even his good nature could scarcely stand Trenchard's trampling demeanour.

"I can't help it. I cannot be inartistic and untrue to Nature even for the sake of a friend."

"Thank you. Well, I have no desire to ruin your work, Andrew; but it is really useless for this farce to continue. Do what you like, and let us make no further pretence of collaborating. I cannot act as a drag upon such a wheel as yours. I will not any longer be a dead weight upon you. Our temperaments evidently unfit us to be fellow-workers; and I feel that your strength and power are so undeniable that you may, perhaps, be able to carry this weary tragedy through, and by sheer force make it palatable to the public. I will protest no more; I will only cease any longer to pretend to have a finger in this literary pie."

Andrew's morose expression passed away like a cloud. He got up and laid his hand upon Henley's shoulder.

"You make me feel what a beast I am," he said. "But I can't help it. I was made so. Do forgive me, Jack. I have taken the bit between my teeth, I know. But—this story seems to me no fiction; it is a piece of life, as real to me as those stars I see through the window-pane are real to me—as my own emotions are real to me. Jack, this book has seized me. Believe me, if it is written as I wish, it will make an impression upon the world that will be great. The mind of the world is given to me like a sheet of blank paper. I will write upon it with my heart's blood. But"—and here his manner became strangely impressive, and his sombre, heavy eyes gazed deeply into the eyes of his friend—"remember this! You will finish this book. I feel that; I know it. I cannot tell you why. But so it is ordained. Let me write as far as I can, Jack, and let me write as I will. But do not let us quarrel. The book is ours, not mine. And—don't—don't take away your friendship from me."

The last words were said with an outburst of emotion that was almost feminine in intensity. Henley felt deeply moved, for, as a rule, Andrew's manner was not specially affectionate, or even agreeable.

"It is all right, old fellow," he said, in the embarrassed English manner which often covers so much that might with advantage be occasionally revealed. "Go on in your own way. I believe you are a genius, and I am only trying to clip the wings that may carry you through the skies. Go on in your own way, and consult me only when you feel inclined."

Andrew took his hand and pressed it in silence.

III

It was some three weeks after this that one afternoon Trenchard laid down his pen at the conclusion of a chapter, and, getting up, thrust his hands into his pockets and walked to the window.

The look-out was rather dreary. A gray sky leaned over the great, barrack-like church that gives an ecclesiastical flavour to Smith's Square. A few dirty sparrows fluttered above the gray pavement—feverish, unresting birds, Trenchard named them silently, as he watched their meaningless activity, their jerky, ostentatious deportment, with lacklustre, yet excited, eyes. How gray everything looked, tame, colourless, indifferent! The light was beginning to fade stealthily out of things. The gray church was gradually becoming shadowy. The flying forms of the hurrying sparrows disappeared in the weary abysses of the air and sky. The sitting room in Smith's Square was nearly dark now. Henley had gone out to a *matinée* at one of the theatres, so Trenchard was alone. He struck a match presently, lit a candle, carried it over to his writing table, and began to examine the littered sheets he had just been writing. The book was nearing its end. The tragedy was narrowing to a point. Trenchard read the last paragraph which he had written:

"He hardly knew that he lived, except during those many hours when, plunged in dreams, he allowed, nay, forced, life to leave him for a while. He had sunk to depths below even those which Olive had reached. And the thought that she was ever so little above him haunted him like a spectre impelling him to some mysterious deed. When he was not dreaming, he was dwelling upon this idea which had taken his soul captive. It seemed to be shaping itself towards an act. Thought was the anteroom through which he passed to the hall where Fate was sitting, ready to give him audience. He traversed this anteroom, which seemed lined with fantastic and terrible pictures, at first with lagging footfalls. But at length he laid his hand upon the door that divided him from Fate."

And when he had read the final words he gathered the loose sheets together with his long, thin fingers, and placed them one on the top of the other in a neat pile. He put them into a drawer which contained other unfinished manuscripts, shut the drawer, locked it, and carried the key to Henley's room. There he scribbled some words on a bit of notepaper, wrapped the key in it, and inclosed it in an envelope on which he wrote Henley's name. Then he put on his overcoat, descended the narrow stairs, and opened the front door. The landlady heard him, and screamed from the basement to know if he would be in to dinner.

"I shall not be in at all to-night," he answered, in a hard, dry voice that travelled along the dingy passage with a penetrating distinctness. The landlady murmured to the slatternly maidservant an ejaculatory diatribe on the dissipatedness of young literary gentlemen as the door banged. Trenchard disappeared in the gathering darkness, and soon left Smith's Square behind him.

It chanced that day that, in the theatre, Henley encountered some ladies who carried him home to tea after the performance. They lived in Chelsea, and in returning to Smith's Square afterwards Henley took his way along the Chelsea Embankment. He always walked near to the dingy river when he could. The contrast of its life to the town's life through which it flowed had a perpetual fascination for him. In the early evening, too, the river presents many Doré effects. It is dim, mysterious, sometimes meretricious, with its streaks of light close to the dense shadows that lie under the bridges, its wailful, small waves licking the wharves, and bearing up the inky barges that look like the ferryboat of the Styx. Henley loved to feel vivaciously despairing, and he hugged himself in the belief that the Thames at nightfall tinged his soul with a luxurious melancholy, the capacity for which was not far from rendering him a poet. So he took his way by the river. As he neared Cheyne Row, he saw in front of him the figure of a man leaning over the low stone wall, with his face buried in his hands. On hearing his approaching footsteps the man lifted himself up, turned round, and preceded him along the pavement with a sort of listless stride which seemed to Henley strangely familiar. He hastened his steps, and on coming closer recognised that the man was Trenchard; but, just as he was about to hail him, Trenchard crossed the road to one of the houses opposite, inserted a key in the door, and disappeared within, shutting the door behind him.

Henley paused a moment opposite to the house. It was of a dull red colour, and had a few creepers straggling helplessly about it, looking like a torn veil that can only partially conceal a dull, heavy face.

"Andrew seems at home here," he thought, gazing up at the blind, tall windows, which showed no ray of light. "I wonder—"

And then, still gazing at the windows, he recalled the description of the house where Olive Beauchamp lived in their book.

"He took it from this," Henley said to himself. Yes, that was obvious. Trenchard had described the prison-house of despair, where the two victims of a strange, desolating habit shut themselves up to sink, with a curious minuteness. He had even devoted a paragraph to the tall iron gate, whose round handle he had written of as "bald, and exposed to the wind from the river, the paint having long since been worn off it." In the twilight Henley bent down and examined the handle of the gate. The paint seemed to have been scraped from it.

"How curiously real that book has become to me!" he muttered. "I could almost believe that if I knocked upon that door, and was let in, I should find Olive Beauchamp stretched on a couch in the room that lies beyond those gaunt, shuttered windows."

He gave a last glance at the house, and as he did so he fancied that he heard a slight cry come from it to him. He listened attentively and heard nothing more. Then he walked away toward home.

When he reached his room, he found upon his table the envelope which Trenchard had directed to him. He opened it, and unwrapped the key from the inclosed sheet of note-paper, on which were written these words:

"Dear Jack,

"I am off again. And this time I can't say when I shall be back. In any case, I have completed my part of the book, and leave the finishing of it in your hands. This is the key of the drawer in which I have locked the manuscript. You have not seen most of the last volume. Read it, and judge for yourself whether the dénouement can be anything but utterly tragic. I will not outline to you what I have thought of for it. If you have any difficulty about the *finale*, I shall be able to help you with it even if you do not see me again for some time. By the way, what nonsense that saying is, 'Dead men tell no tales!' Half the best tales in the world are told, or at least completed, by dead men.

"Yours ever,
"A. T."

Henley laid this note down and turned cold all over. It was the concluding sentence which had struck a chill through his heart. He took the key in his hand, went down to Trenchard's room, unlocked the drawer in his writing table, and took out the manuscript. What did Andrew mean by that sinister sentence? A tale completed by a dead man! Henley sat down by the fire with the manuscript in his hands and began to read. He was called away to dinner; but immediately afterward he returned to his task, and till late into the night his glance travelled down the closely-written sheets one after the other, until the light from the candles grew blurred and indistinct, and his eyes ached. But still he read on. The power and gloom of Andrew's narrative held him in a vice, and then he was searching for a clue in the labyrinth of words. At last he came to the final paragraph, and then to the final sentence:

"But at length he laid his hand upon the door that divided him from Fate."

Henley put the sheet down carefully upon the table. It was three o'clock in the morning, and the room seemed full of a strange, breathless cold, the peculiar chilliness that precedes the dawn. The fire was burning brightly enough, yet the warmth it emitted scarcely seemed to combat the frosty air that penetrated from without, and Henley shivered as he rose from his seat. His brows were drawn together, and he was thinking deeply. A light seemed slowly struggling into his soul. That last sentence of Trenchard's connected itself with what he had seen in the afternoon on the Chelsea Embankment. "He laid his hand upon the door that divided him from Fate."

A strange idea dawned in Henley's mind, an idea which made many things clear to him. Yet he put it away, and sat down again to read the unfinished book once more. Andrew had carried on the story of the man's growing hatred of the woman whom he had tried to rescue, until it had developed into a deadly fury, threatening immediate action. Then he had left the *dénouement* in Henley's hands. He had left it ostensibly in Henley's hands, but the latter, reading the manuscript again with intense care, saw that matters had been so contrived that the knot of the novel could only be cut by murder. As it had been written, the man must inevitably murder the woman. And Andrew? All through the night Henley thought of him as he had last seen him, opening the door of the red house with the tattered creepers climbing over it.

At last, when it was dawn, he went up to bed tired out, after leaving a written direction to the servant not to call him in the morning. When he awoke and looked at his watch it was past two o'clock in the afternoon. He sprang out of bed, dressed, and after a hasty meal, half breakfast, half lunch, set out towards Chelsea. The day was bright and cold. The sun shone on the river and sparkled on the windows of the houses on the Embankment. Many people were about, and they looked cheerful. The weight of depression that had settled upon Henley was lifted. He thought of the strange, yet illuminating, idea that had occurred to him in the night, and now, in broad daylight, it seemed clothed in absurdity. He laughed at it. Yet he quickened his steps toward the red house with the tarnished iron gate and the tattered creepers.

But long before he reached it he met a boy sauntering along the thoroughfare and shouting newspapers. He sang out unflinchingly in the gay sunshine, "Murder! Murder!" and between his shouts he whistled a music hall song gaily in snatches. Henley stopped him and bought a paper. He opened the paper in the wind, which seemed striving to prevent him, and cast his eyes over the middle pages. Then suddenly he dropped it to the ground with a white face, and falteringly signed to a cabman. The *dénouement* was written. The previous night, in a house on the Chelsea Embankment, a woman had been done to death, and the murderer had crept out and thrown himself into the gray, hurrying river.

The woman's name was Olive Beauchamp.

The Man Who Intervened

I

The atmosphere of the room in which Sergius Blake was sitting seemed to him strange and cold. As he looked round it, he could imagine that a light mist invaded it stealthily, like miasma rising from some sinister marsh. There was surely a cloud about the electric light that gleamed in the ceiling, a cloud sweeping in feathery, white flakes across the faces of the pictures upon the wall. Even the familiar furniture seemed to loom out faintly, with a gaunt and grotesque aspect, from shadows less real, yet more fearful, than any living form could be.

Sergius stared round him slowly, pressing his strong lips together. When he concentrated his gaze upon any one thing—a table, a sofa, a chair—the cloud faded, and the object stood out clearly before his eyes. Yet always the rest of the room seemed to lie in mist and in shadows. He knew that this dim atmosphere did not really exist, that it was projected by his mind. Yet it troubled him, and added a dull horror to his thoughts, which moved again and again, in persistent promenade, round one idea.

The hour was seven o'clock of an autumn night. Darkness lay over London, and rain made a furtive music on roofs and pavements. Sergius Blake listened to the drops upon the panes of his windows. They seemed to beckon him forth, to tell him that it was time to exchange thought for action. He had come to a definite and tremendous resolution. He must now carry it out.

He got up slowly from his chair, and with the movement the mist seemed to gather itself together in the room and to disappear. It passed away, evaporating among the pictures and ornaments, the prayer rugs and divans. A clearness and an insight came to Sergius. He stood still by the piano, on which he rested one hand lightly, and listened. The raindrops pattered close by. Beyond them rose the dull music of the evening traffic of New Bond Street, in which thoroughfare he lived. As he stood thus at attention, his young and handsome face seemed carved in stone. His lips were set in a hard and straight line. His dark-grey eyes stared, like eyes in a photograph. The muscles of his long-fingered hands were tense and knotted. He was in evening dress, and had been engaged to dine in Curzon Street; but he had written a hasty note to say he was ill and could not come. Another appointment claimed him. He had made it for himself.

Presently, lifting his hand from the piano, he took up a small leather case from a table that stood near, opened it, and drew out a revolver. He examined it carefully. Two chambers were loaded. They would be enough. He put on his long overcoat, and slipped the revolver into his left breast pocket. His heart could beat against it there.

Each time his heart pulsed, Sergius seemed to hear the silence of another heart.

And now, though his mind was quite clear, and the mists and shadows had slunk away, his familiar room looked very peculiar to him. The very chair in which he generally sat wore the aspect of a stranger. Was the wall paper really blue? Sergius went close up to it and examined it narrowly, and then he drew back and laughed softly, like a child. In the sound of his laugh irresponsibility chimed. "What is the cab fare to Phillimore Place, Kensington?" he thought, searching in his waistcoat pocket. "Half a crown?" He put the coin carefully in the ticket pocket of his overcoat, buttoned the coat up slowly, took his hat and stick, and drew on a pair of lavender gloves. Just then a new thought seemed to strike him and he glanced down at his hands.

"Lavender gloves for such a deed!" he murmured. For a moment he paused irresolute, even partially unbuttoned them. But then he smiled and shook his head. In some way the gloves would not be wholly inappropriate. Sergius cast one final glance round the room.

"When I stand here again," he said aloud, "I shall be a criminal—a criminal!"

He repeated the last word, as if trying thoroughly to realise its meaning.

Then he opened the door swiftly and went out on to the staircase.

Just as he was putting a hasty foot upon the first stair, a man out in the street touched his electric bell. Its thin tingling cry made Sergius start and hesitate. In the semi-twilight he waited, his hands deep in his pockets, his silk hat tilted slightly over his eyes. The porter tramped along the passage below. The hall door opened, and a deep and strong voice asked, rather anxiously and breathlessly—

"Is Mr. Blake at home?"

"I rather think he's gone out, sir."

"No—surely—how long ago?"

"I don't know, sir. He may be in. I'll see."

"Do—do—quickly. If he's in, say I must see him—Mr. Endover. But you know my name."

"Yes, sir."

The porter, mounting the stone staircase, suddenly came upon Sergius standing there like a stone figure.

"Lord, sir!" he ejaculated. "You give me a start!" His voice was loud from astonishment.

"Hush!" Sergius whispered. "Go down at once and say that I've gone out!"

The man turned to obey, but Anthony Endover was half-way up the stairs.

"It's all right," he exclaimed, as he met the porter.

He had passed him in an instant and arrived at the place where Sergius was standing.

"Sergius," he cried, and there was a great music of relief in his voice. "Hulloa! Now you're not going out."

"Yes, I am, Anthony."

"But I want to talk to you tremendously. Where are you going?"

"To dine with the Venables in Curzon Street."

"I met young Venables just now, and he said you'd written that you were ill and couldn't come. He asked me to fill your place."

Sergius muttered a "Damn!" under his breath.

"Well, come in for a minute," he said, attempting no excuse.

He turned round slowly and re-entered his flat, followed by Endover.

II

For some years Endover had been Sergius Blake's close friend. They had left Eton at the same time; had been at Oxford together. Their intimacy, born in the playing fields, grew out of its cricket and football stage as their minds developed, and the world of thought opened like a holy of holies—beyond the world of action. They both passed behind the veil, but Anthony went farther than Sergius. Yet this slight separation did not lead to alienation, but merely caused the admiration of Sergius for his friend to be mingled with respect. He looked up to Anthony. Recognising that his friend's mind was more thoughtful than his own, while his passions were far stronger than Anthony's, he grew to lean upon Anthony, to claim his advice sometimes, to follow it often. Anthony was his mentor, and thought he knew instinctively all the workings of Sergius' mind and all the possibilities of his nature. The mother of Sergius was a Russian and a great heiress. Soon after he left Oxford, she died. His father had been killed by an accident when he was a child. So he was rich, free, young, in London, with no one to look after him, until Anthony Endover, who had meanwhile taken orders, was attached as fourth—or fifth—curate to a smart West End church, and came to live in lodgings in George Street, Hanover Square.

Then, as Sergius laughingly said, he had a father confessor on the premises. Yet to-night he had bidden his porter to tell a lie in order to keep his father confessor out. The lie had been vain. Sergius led the way morosely into his drawing room, and turned on the light. Anthony walked up to the fire, and stretched his tall athletic figure in its long ebon coat. His firm throat rose out of a jam-pot collar, but his thin, strongly-marked face rather suggested an intellectual Hercules than a Mayfair parson, and neither his voice nor his manner was tinged with what so many people consider the true clericalism.

For all that he was a splendid curate, as his rector very well knew.

Now he stood by the fire for a minute in silence, while Sergius moved uneasily about the room. Presently Anthony turned round.

"It's beastly wet," he said in a melodious ringing voice. "The black dog is on me to-night, Sergius."

"Oh!"

"You don't want to go out, really," Anthony continued, looking narrowly at his friend's curiously rigid face.

"Yes, I do."

"Not to Curzon Street. They've filled up your place. I told Venables to ask Hugh Graham. I knew he was disengaged to-night. Besides—you're seedy."

Sergius frowned.

"I'm all right again now," he said coldly, "and I particularly wished to go. You needn't have been so deuced anxious to make the number right."

"Well, it's done now. And I can't say I'm sorry, because I want to have a talk with you. I say, Serge, take off those lavender gloves, pull off your coat, let's send out for some dinner, and have a comfortable evening together in here. I've had a hard day's work, and I want a rest."

"I must go out presently."

"After dinner then."

"Before ten o'clock."

"Say eleven."

"No—that's too late."

A violent, though fleeting expression of anxiety crossed Endover's face. Then, with a smile, he said—

"All right. Shall I ring the bell and order some dinner to be sent in from Galton's?"

"If you like. I'm not hungry."

"I am."

Anthony summoned the servant and gave the order. Then he turned again to Sergius.

"Here, I'll help you off with your coat," he said.

But Sergius moved away.

"No thanks, I'll do it. There are some cigarettes on the mantelpiece."

Anthony went to get one. As he was taking it, he looked into the mirror over the fireplace, and saw Sergius—while removing his overcoat—transfer something from it to the left breast pocket of his evening coat.

He wanted still to feel his heart beat against that tiny weapon, still to hear—with each pulse of his own heart—the silence, not yet alive, but so soon to be alive, of that other heart.

And, as Anthony glanced into the mirror, he said to himself, "I was right!"

He withdrew his eyes from the glass and lit his cigarette. Sergius joined him.

"I'm in the blues to-night," Anthony said, puffing at his cigarette.

"Are you?"

"Yes—been down in the East End. The misery there is ghastly."

"It's just as bad in the West End, only different in kind. You're smoking your cigarette all down one side."

Anthony took it out of his mouth and threw it into the grate. He lit two or three matches, but held them so badly that they went out before he could ignite another cigarette. At last, inwardly cursing his nerves that made his hasty actions belie the determined calm of his face, he dropped the cigarette.

"I don't think I'll smoke before dinner," he said. "Ah, here it is. And wine—champagne—that's good for you!"

"I shan't drink it. I hate to drink alone."

"You shan't drink alone then."

"What d'you mean?"

"I'll drink with you."

"But you're a teetotaller."

"I don't care to-night."

Anthony spoke briefly and firmly. Sergius was amazed.

"What!" he said. "You're going to break your vow? You a parson!"

"Sometimes salvation lies in the breaking of a vow," Anthony answered as they sat down. "Have you never registered a silent vow?"

Sergius looked at him hard in the eyes.

"Yes," he said; and in his voice there was the hint of a thrilling note. "But I shan't—I shouldn't break it."

"I've known a soul saved alive by the breaking of a vow," Anthony answered. "Give me some champagne."

Sergius—wondering, as much as the condition of his mind, possessed by one idea, would allow—filled his friend's glass. Anthony began to eat, with a well-assumed hunger. Sergius scarcely touched food, but drank a good deal of wine. The hands of the big oaken-cased clock that stood in a far corner of the room crawled slowly upon their round, recurring tour. Anthony's eyes were often upon them, then moved with a swift directness that was akin to passion to the face of Sergius, which was always strangely rigid, like the painted face of a mask.

"I sat by a woman to-day," he said presently, "sat by her in an attic that looked on to a narrow street full of rain, and watched her die."

"This morning?"

"Yes."

"And now she's been out of the world seven or eight hours. Lucky woman!"

"Ah, Sergius, but the mischief, the horror of it was that she wasn't ready to go, not a bit ready."

Sergius suddenly smiled, a straight, glaring smile, over the sparkling champagne that he was lifting to his lips.

"Yes; it's devilish bad for a woman or a—man to be shot into another world before they're prepared," he said. "It must be—devilish bad."

"And how can we know that anyone is thoroughly prepared?"

Sergius' smile developed into a short laugh.

"It's easier to be certain who isn't than who is," he said.

The eyes of Anthony fled to the clock face mechanically and returned.

"Death terrified me to-day, Sergius," he said; "and it struck me that the most awful power that God has given to man is the power of setting death—like a dog—at another man."

Sergius swallowed all the wine in his glass at a gulp. He was no longer smiling. His hand went up to his left side.

"It may be awful," he rejoined; "but it's grand. By Heaven! it's magnificent."

He got up, as if excited, and moved about the room, while Anthony went on pretending to eat. After a minute or two Sergius sat down again.

"Power of any kind is a grand thing," he said.

"Only power for good."

"You're bound to say that; you're a parson."

"I only say what I really feel; you know that, Serge."

"Ah, you don't understand."

Anthony looked at him with a sudden, strong significance.

"Part of a parson's profession—the most important part—is to understand men who aren't parsons."

"You think you understand men?"

"Some men."

"Me, for instance?"

The question came abruptly, defiantly. Anthony seemed glad to answer it.

"Well, yes, Sergius; I think I do thoroughly understand you. My great friendship alone might well make me do that."

The face of Sergius grew a little softer in expression, but he did not assent.

"Perhaps it might blind you," he said.

"I don't think so."

"Well, then, now, if you understand me—tell me—"

Sergius broke off suddenly.

"This champagne is awfully good," he said, filling his glass again.

"What were you going to say?" Anthony asked.

"I don't know—nothing."

Anthony tried to conceal his disappointment. Sergius had seemed to be on the verge of overleaping the barrier which lay between them. Once that barrier was overleapt, or broken down, Anthony felt that the mission he had imposed upon himself would stand a chance of being accomplished, that his gnawing anxiety would be laid to rest. But once more Sergius diffused around him a strange and cold atmosphere of violent and knowing reserve. He went away from the table and sat down close to the fire. From there he threw over his shoulder the remark—

"No man or woman ever understands another—really."

III

Anthony did not reply for a moment and Sergius continued—

"You, for instance, could never guess what I should do in certain circumstances."

"Such as—"

"Oh, in a thousand things."

"I should have a shrewd idea."

"No."

Anthony didn't contradict him, but got up from the dinner table and joined him by the fire, glass in hand.

"I might not let you know how much I guessed, how much I knew."

Sergius laughed.

"Oh, ignorance always surrounds itself with mystery," he said.

"Knowledge need not go naked."

Again the eyes of the two friends met in the firelight, and over the face of Sergius there ran a new expression. There was an awakening of wonder in it, but no uneasiness. Anxiety was far away from him that night. When passion has gripped a man, passion strong enough, resolute enough, to override all the prejudices of civilisation, all the promptings of the coward within us, whose voice, whining, we name prudence, the semi-comprehension, the criticism of another man cannot move him. Sergius wondered for an instant whether Anthony suspected against what his heart was beating. That was all.

While he wondered, the clock chimed the half hour after nine. He heard it.

"I shall have to go very soon," he said.

"You can't. Just listen to the rain."

"Rain! What's that got to do with it?"

Sergius spoke with a sudden unutterable contempt.

"Ring for another bottle of champagne," Anthony replied. "This one is empty."

"Well—for a parson and a teetotaller, I must say!"

Sergius rang the bell. A second bottle was opened. The servant went out of the room. As he closed the door, the wind sighed harshly against the window panes, driving the rain before it.

"Rough at sea to-night," Anthony said.

The remark was an obvious one; but, as spoken, it sounded oddly furtive, and full of hidden meaning. Sergius evidently found it so, for he said:

"Why, whom d'you know that's going to sea to-night?"

Anthony was startled by the quick question, and replied almost nervously—

"Nobody in particular—why should I?"

"I don't know why, but I think you do."

"People one knows cross the channel every night almost."

"Of course," Sergius said indifferently.

He glanced towards the clock and again mechanically his hand went up, for a second, to his left breast. Anthony leaned forward in his chair quickly, and broke into speech. He had seen the stare at the clock face, the gesture.

"It's strange," he said, "how people go out of our lives, how friends go, and enemies!"

"Enemies!"

"Yes. I sometimes wonder which exit is the sadder. When a friend goes—with him goes, perhaps forever, the chance of saying 'I am your friend.' When an enemy goes—"

"Well, what then?"

"With him goes, perhaps forever, too, the chance of saying, 'I am not your enemy.'"

"Pshaw! Parson's talk, Anthony."

"No, Sergius, other men forgive besides parsons; and other men, and parsons too, pass by their chances of forgiving."

"You're a whole Englishman, I'm only half an Englishman. There's something untamed in my blood, and I say—damn forgiveness!"

"And yet you've forgiven."

"Whom?"

"Olga Mayne."

The face of Sergius did not change at the sound of this name, unless, perhaps, to a more fixed calm, a more still and pale coldness.

"Olga is punished," he said. "She is ruined."

"Her ruin may be repaired."

Sergius smiled quietly.

"You think so?"

"Yes. Tell me, Sergius"—Anthony spoke with a strong earnestness, a strong excitement that he strove to conceal and hold in check—"you loved her?"

"Yes, I loved her—certainly."

"You will always love her?"

"Since I'm not changeable, I daresay I shall."

Anthony's thin, eager face brightened. A glow of warmth burned in his eyes and on his cheeks.

"Then you would wish her ruin repaired."

"Should I?"

"If you love her, you must."

"How could it be repaired?"

"By her marriage with—Vernon."

Anthony's strong voice quivered before he pronounced the last word, and his eyes were alight with fervent anxiety. He was looking at Sergius like a man on the watch for a tremendous outbreak of emotion. The champagne he had drunk—a new experience for him since he had taken orders—put a sort of wild finishing touch to the intensity of the feelings, under the impulse of which he had forced himself upon Sergius to-night. He supposed that his inward excitement must be more than matched by the so different inward excitement of his friend. But he—who thought he understood!—had no true conception of the region of cold, frosty fury in which Sergius was living, like a being apart from all other men, ostracised by the immensity and peculiarity of his own power of emotion. Therefore he was astonished when Sergius, with undiminished quietude, replied:

"Oh, with Vernon, that charming man of fashion, whose very soul, they say, always wears lavender gloves? You think that would be a good thing?"

"Good! I don't say that. I say—as the world is now—the only thing. He is the author of her fall. He should be her husband."

"And I?"

Anthony stretched out his hand to grasp his friend's hand, but Sergius suddenly took up his champagne glass, and avoided the demonstration of sympathy.

"You can be nothing to her now, Serge," Anthony said, and his voice quivered with sympathy.

"You think so? I might be."

"What?"

"Oh, not her husband, not her lover, not her friend."

"What then?"

Sergius avoided answering.

"You would have her settle down with Vernon in Phillimore Place?" he said. "Play the wife to his noble husband? Well, I know there's been some idea of that, as I told you yesterday."

The clock chimed ten. Although Sergius seemed so calm, so self-possessed, Anthony observed that now he paid no heed to the little, devilish note of time. This new subject of conversation had been Anthony's weapon. Desperately he had used it, and not, it seemed, altogether in vain.

"Yes; as you told me yesterday."

"And it seems good to you?"

"It seems to me the only thing possible now."

"There are generally more possibilities than one in any given event, I fancy."

Again Anthony was surprised at the words of Sergius, who seemed to grow calmer as he grew more excited, who seemed, to-night, strangely powerful, not simply in temper, but even in intellect.

"For a woman there is sometimes only one possibility if she is to be saved from ignominy, Serge."

"So you think that Olga Mayne must become the wife of Vernon, who is a—"

"Coward. Yes."

At the word coward, Sergius seemed startled out of his hard calm. He looked swiftly and searchingly at Anthony.

"Why do you say coward?" he asked sharply. "I was not going to use that word."

Anthony was obviously disconcerted.

"It came to me," he said hurriedly.

"Why?"

"Any man that brings a girl to the dust is a coward."

"Ah—that's not what you meant," Sergius said.

Anthony stole a glance at the clock. The hand crawled slowly over the quarter of an hour past ten.

"No, it was not," he said slowly.

IV

Sergius got up from his chair and stood by the fire. He was obviously becoming engrossed by the conversation. Anthony could at least notice this with thankfulness.

"Anthony, I see you've got a fresh knowledge of Vernon since I was with you yesterday," Sergius continued; "some new knowledge of his nature."

"Perhaps I have."

"How did you get it?"

"Does that matter?"

"You have heard of something about him?"

"No."

"You have seen him, then; I say, you have seen him?"

Anthony hesitated. He pushed the champagne bottle over towards Sergius. It had been placed on a little table near the fireplace.

"No; I don't want to drink. Why on earth don't you answer me, Anthony?"

"I have always felt that Vernon was a coward. His conduct to you shows it. He was—or seemed—your friend. He saw you deeply in love with this—with Olga. He chose to ruin her after he knew of your love. Who but a coward could act in such a way?"

An expression of dark impatience came into the eyes of Sergius.

"You are confusing treachery and cowardice, and you are doing it untruthfully. You have seen Vernon."

Anthony thought for a moment, and then said:

"Yes, I have."

"By chance, of course. Why did you speak to him?"

"I thought I would."

Sergius was obviously disturbed and surprised. The deeply emotional, yet rigid calm in which he had been enveloped all the evening was broken at last. A slight excitement, a distinct surface irritation, woke in him. Anthony felt an odd sense of relief as he observed it. For the constraint of Sergius had begun to weigh upon him like a heavy burden and to move him to an indefinable dread.

"I wonder you didn't cut him," Sergius said. "You're my friend. And he's—he's—"

"He's done you a deadly injury. I know that. I am your friend, Serge; I would do anything for you."

"Yet you speak to that—devil."

"I spoke to him because I'm your friend."

Sergius sat down again, with a heavy look, the look of a man who has been thrashed, and means to return every blow with curious interest.

"You parsons are a riddle to me," he said in a low and dull voice. "You and your charity and your loving-kindness, and your turning the cheek to the smiter and all the rest of it. And as to your way of showing friendship—"

His voice died away in something that was almost a growl, and he stared at the carpet. Between it and his eyes once more the mist seemed rising stealthily. It began to curl upwards softly about him. As he watched it, he heard Anthony say—

"Sergius, you don't understand how well I understand you."

The big hand of the clock had left the half-hour after ten behind him. Anthony breathed more freely. At last he could be more explicit, more unreserved. He thought of a train rushing through the night, devouring the spaces of land that lie between London and the sea that speaks, moaning, to the South of England. He saw a ship glide out from the dreary docks. Her lights gleamed. He heard the bell struck and the harsh cry of the sailors, and then the dim sigh of a coward who had escaped what he had merited. Then he heard Sergius laugh.

"That again, Anthony!"

"Yes. I didn't meet Vernon by chance at all."

"What? You wrote to him, you fixed a meeting?"

"I went to Phillimore Place, to his house."

Sergius said nothing. Strange furrows ploughed themselves in his young face, which was growing dusky white. He remained in the attitude of one devoted entirely to listening.

"You hear, Sergius?"

"Go on—when?"

"To-day. I decided to go after I met you yesterday night—and after I had seen that woman die—unprepared."

"What could she have to do with it?"

"Much. Everything almost."

Anthony got up now, almost sprang up from his chair. His face was glowing and working with emotion. There was a choking sensation in his throat.

"You don't know what it is," he said hoarsely, "to a man with—with strong religious belief to see a human being's soul go out to blackness, to punishment—perhaps to punishment that will never end. It's abominable. It's unbearable. That woman will haunt me. Her despair will be with me always. I could not add to that horror."

His eyes once more sought the clock. Seeing the hour, he turned, with a kind of liberating relief, to Sergius.

"I couldn't add to it," he exclaimed, almost fiercely, "so I went to Vernon."

"Why?"

"Sergius—to warn him."

There was a dead silence. Even the rain was hushed against the window. Then Sergius said, in a voice that was cold as the sound of falling water in winter—

"I don't understand."

"Because you won't understand how I have learnt to know you, Sergius, to understand you, to read your soul."

"Mine too?"

"Yes; I've felt this awful blow that's come upon you—the loss of Olga, her ruin—as if I myself were you. We haven't said much about it till yesterday. Then, from the way you spoke, from the way you looked, from what you said, even what you wouldn't say, I guessed all that was in your heart."

"You guessed all that?"

Sergius was looking directly at Anthony and leaning against the mantelpiece, along which he stretched one arm. His fingers closed and unclosed, with a mechanical and rhythmical movement, round a China figure. The motion looked as if it were made in obedience to some fiercely monotonous music.

"Yes, more—I knew it."

Sergius nodded.

"I see," he said.

Anthony touched his arm, almost with an awestruck gesture.

"I knew then that you—that you intended to kill Vernon. And—God forgive me!—at first I was almost glad."

"Well—go on!"

Anthony shivered. The voice of Sergius was so strangely calm and level.

"I—I—" he stammered. "Serge, why do you look at me like that?"

Sergius looked away without a word.

"For I, too, hated Vernon, more for what he had done to you even than for what he had done to Olga. But, Sergius, after you had gone, in the night, and in the dawn too, I kept on thinking of it over and over. I couldn't get away from it—that you were going to commit such an awful crime. I never slept. When at last it was morning, I went down to my district; there are criminals there, you know."

"I know."

"I looked at them with new eyes, and in their eyes I saw you, always you; and then I said to myself could I bear that you should become a criminal?"

"You said that?"

The fingers of Sergius closed over the China figure, and did not unclose.

"Yes. I almost resolved then to go to Vernon at once and to tell him what I suspected—what I really knew."

The clock struck eleven. Anthony heard it; Sergius did not hear it.

"Then I went to sit with that wretched woman. Already I had resolved, as I believed, on the course to take. I had no thought for Vernon yet, only for you. It seemed to me that I did not care in the least to save him from death. I only cared to save you—my friend—from murder. But when the woman died I felt differently. My resolve was strengthened, my desire was just doubled. I had to save not only you, but also him. He was not ready to die."

Anthony trembled with a passion of emotion. Sergius remained always perfectly calm, the China figure prisoned in his hand.

"So—so I went to him, Sergius."

"Yes."

"I saw him. Almost as I entered he received your letter, saying that you forgave him, that you would call to-night after eight o'clock to tell him so, and to urge on his marriage with Olga. When he had read the letter—I interpreted it to him; and then I found out that he was a coward. His terror was abject—despicable; he implored my help; he started at every sound."

"To-night he'll sleep quietly, Anthony."

"To-night he has gone. Before morning he will be on the sea."

The sound of the wind came to them again, and Sergius understood why Anthony had said: "Rough at sea to-night."

Suddenly Sergius moved; he unclosed his fingers: the ruins of the China figure fell from them in a dust of blue and white upon the mantelpiece.

"No—it's too late, Sergius. He went at eleven."

Sergius stood quite still.

"You came here to-night to keep me here till he had gone?"

"Yes."

"That's why you—"

He stopped.

"That's why I came. That's why I broke my pledge. I thought wine—any weapon to keep you from this crime. And, Sergius, think. Vernon dead could never have restored Olga to the place she has lost. That, too, must have driven me to the right course, though I scarcely thought of it till now."

Sergius said, as if in reply: "So you have understood me!"

"Yes, Sergius. Friendship is something. Let us thank God, not even that he is safe, but that you—you are safe—and that Olga—"

"Hush! Has she gone with him?"

"She will meet him. He has sworn to marry her."

The hand of Sergius moved to his left breast. Anthony's glowing eyes were fixed upon him.

"Ah, yes, Sergius," Anthony cried. "Put that cursed, cursed thing down, put it away. Now it can never wreck your life and my peace."

Sergius drew out the revolver slowly and carefully. Again the mist rose around him. But it was no longer white; it was scarlet.

There was a report. Anthony fell, without a word, a cry.

Then Sergius bent down, and listened to the silence of his friend's heart—the long silence of the man who intervened.

A Tribute of Souls
(with Frederic Hamilton)

Prelude

The matter of Carlounie, the village of Perthshire in Scotland, is become notorious in the world. The name of its late owner, his remarkable transformation, his fortunate career, his married life, the brooding darkness that fell latterly upon his mind, the flaming deed that he consummated, its appalling outcome, and the finding of him by Mr. Mackenzie, the minister of the parish of Carlounie, sunk in a pool of the burn that runs through a "den" close to his house—all these things are fresh in the minds of many men. It has been supposed that he had discovered a common intrigue between his wife, Kate, formerly a hospital nurse, and his tenant, Hugh Fraser of Piccadilly, London. It has been universally thought that this discovery led to the last action of his life. The following pages, found among his papers, seem to put a very different complexion on the affair, although they suggest a mediæval legend rather than a history of modern days. It may be added that careful enquiries have been made among the inhabitants of Carlounie, and that no man, woman, or child has been discovered who ever saw, or heard of, the grey traveller mentioned in Alistair Ralston's narrative.

I

The Stranger by the Burn

Can a fever change a man's whole nature, giving him powers that he never had before? Can he go into it impotent, starved, naked, emerge from it potent, satisfied, clothed with possibilities that are wonders, that are miracles to him? It must be so; it is so. And yet—I must go back to that sad autumn day when I walked beside the burn. Can I write down my moods, my feelings of that day and of the following days? And if I can, does that power of pinning the butterfly of my soul down upon the board—does that power, too, bud, blossom from a soil mysteriously fertilised by illness? Formerly, I could as easily have flown in the air to the summit of cloud-capped Schiehallion as have set on paper even the smallest fragment of my mind. Now—well, let me see, let me still further know my new, my marvellous self.

Yes, that first day! It was Autumn, but only early Autumn. The leaves were changing colour upon the birch trees, upon the rowans. At dawn, mists stood round to shield the toilet of the rising sun. At evening, they thronged together like a pale troop of shadowy mutes to assist at his departure to the underworld. It was a misty season, through which the bracken upon the hillsides of my Carlounie glowed furtively in tints of brown and of orange; and my mind, my whole being, seemed to move in mists. I was just twenty-two, an orphan, master of my estate of Carlounie, a Scotch laird, and my own governor. And some idiots envied me then, as many begin to envy me now. I even remember one ghastly old man who clapped me on the shoulder, and, with the addition of an unnecessary oath, swore that I was "a lucky youngster." I, with my thin, chétif body, my burning, weakly, starved, and yet ambitious soul—lucky! I remember that I broke into a harsh laugh, and longed to kill the babbling beast.

And it was the next day, in the afternoon, that I took that book—my Bible—and went forth alone to the long den in which the burn hides and cries its presence. Yes, I took Goethe's *Faust*, and my own complaining spirit, and went out into the mist with my misty, clouded mind. My cousin Gavin wanted me to go out shooting. He laughed and rallied me upon my ill-luck on the previous day, when I had gone out and been the joke of my own keepers because I had missed every bird; and I turned and railed at him, and told him to leave me to myself. And, as I went, I heard him muttering, "That wretched little fellow! To think that he should be owner of Carlounie!" Now, he sings another tune.

With *Faust* in my hand, and hatred in my heart, I went out into the delicately chilly air, down the winding ways of the garden, through the creaking iron gateway. I emerged on to the wilder land, irregular, grass-covered ground, strewn with grey granite boulders, among which coarse, wiry ferns grew sturdily. The blackfaced sheep whisked their broad tails at me as I passed, then stooped their ever-greedy mouths to their damp and eternal meal again. I heard the thin and distant cry of a hawk, poised somewhere up in the mist. The hills, clothed in the death-like glory of the bracken, loomed around me, like some phantom, tricked-out procession passing through desolate places. And then I heard the voice of the burn—that voice which is even now forever in my ears. To me that day it was the voice of one alive; and it is the voice of one alive to me now. I descended the sloping hill with my lounging, weak-kneed gait, at which the creatures who called me master had so often looked contemptuously askance. (I was often tired at that time.) I descended, I say, until I reached the edge of the tree-fringed den, and the burn was noisy in my ears. I could see it now, leaping here and there out of its hiding place—ivory foam among the dripping larches, and the birches with their silver stems; ivory foam among the deep brown and flaming orange of the bracken, and in that foam a voice calling—calling me to come down into its hiding place, presided over by the mists—to come down into its hiding place, away from men: away from the living creatures whom I hated because I envied them, because they were stronger than I, because they could do what I could not do, say what I could not say. Gavin, Dr. Wedderburn, my tenants, the smallest farm boy, the grooms, the little leaping peasants—I hated, I hated them all. And then I obeyed the voice of the ivory foam, and I went down into the hiding place of the burn.

It ran through strange and secret places where the soft mists hung in wet wreaths. I seemed to be in another world when I was in its lair. On the sharply rising banks stood the sentinel trees like shadows, some of them with tortured and tormented shapes. As I turned and looked straight up the hill of the burn's descending course, the mountain from which it came closed in the prospect inexorably. A soft gloom hemmed us in—me and the burn which talked to me. We two were out of the world which I hated and longed to have at my feet. Yes, we were in another world, full of murmuring and of restful unrest; and now that I was right down at the waterside, the ivory face of my friend, the ivory lips that spoke to me, the ivory heart that beat against my heart—so sick and so weary—were varied and were changed. As thoughts streak a mind, the clear amber of the pools among the rocks streaked the continuous foam that marked the incessant leaps taken by the water towards the valley. The silence of those pools was brilliant, like the pauses for contemplation in a great career of action; and their silence spoke to me, mingling mysteriously with the voice of the foam. The course of the burn is broken up, and attended by rocks that have been modelled by the action of the running water into a hundred shapes. Some are dressed in mosses, yellow and green, like velvet to the touch, and all covered with drops of moisture; some are gaunt and naked and deplorable, with sharp edges and dry faces. The burn avoids some with a cunning and almost coquettish grace, dashes brutally against others, as if impelled by an internal violence of emotion. Others, again, it caresses quite gently, and would be glad to linger by, if Nature would allow the dalliance. And this army of rocks helps to give to the burn its charm of infinite variety, and to fill its voice with a whole gamut of expression; for the differing shape of each boulder, against which it rushes in its long career, gives it a different note. It flickers across the small and round stone with the purling cry of a child. From the stone curved inwards, and with a hollow bosom it gains a crooning, liquid melody. The pointed and narrow colony of rocks which break it into an intricate network of small water threads, toss it, chattering frivolously, towards the dark pool under the birches, where the trout play like sinister shadows and the insects dance in the sombre pomp of Autumn; and when it gains a great slab that serves it for a springboard, from which it takes a mighty leap, its voice is loud and defiant, and shrieks with a banshee of triumph—in which, too, there is surely an undercurrent of wailing woe. Oh, the burn has many voices among the rocks, under the ferns and the birch trees, in the brooding darkness of the mists and shadows, between the steep walls of the green banks that hem it in! Many voices which can sing, when they choose, one song, again and again and—monotonously—again!

So—now on this sad Autumn day—I was with the burn in its hiding place, cool, damp, fretful. Carlounie sank from my sight. My garden, the wilder land beyond, the moors on which yesterday my incompetence as a shot had roused the contempt of my cousin and of my hirelings—all were lost to view. I was away from all men in this narrow, tree-shrouded cleft of a world. I sat down on a rock, and, stretching out my legs, rested my heels on another rock. Beneath my legs the clear brown water glided swiftly. I sat and listened to its murmur. And, just then, it did not occur to me that water can utter words like men. The murmur was suggestive but definitely inarticulate. I had come down here to be away and to think. The murmur of my mind spoke to the murmur of the burn; and, as ever, in those days, it lamented and cursed and bitterly complained.

Why, why was I pursued by a malady of incompetence that clung to both mind and body? (So ran my thoughts.) Why was I bruised and beaten by Providence? Why had I been given a soul that could not express itself in the frame of a coward, a weakling, a thin, nervous, dwarfish, almost a deformed, creature? If my soul had corresponded exactly to my body, then all might have been well enough. I should have been more complete, although less, in some way, than I now was. For such a soul would have accepted cowardice, weakness, inferiority to others as suitable to it, as a right fate. Such a soul would never have known the meaning of the word rebellion, would never have been able to understand its own cancer of disease, to diagnose the symptoms of its villainous and creeping malady. It would never have aspired like a flame, and longed in vain to burn clearly and grandly or to flicker out forever. Rather would such a soul have guttered on like some cheap and ill-smelling candle, shedding shadows rather than any light, ignorant of its own obscurity, regardless of the possibilities that teem like waking children in the wondrous womb of life, oblivious of the contempt of the souls around it, heedless of ambition, of the trumpet call of success, of the lust to be something, to do something, of the magic, of the stinging magic of achievement. With such a soul in my hateful, pinched, meagre, pallid body—I thought, sitting thus by the burn—I might have been content, an utterly low, and perhaps an utterly satisfied product of the fiend creation.

But my soul was not of this kind, and so I was the most bitterly miserable of men. God—or the Devil—had made me ill-shaped, physically despicable, with the malign sort of countenance that so often accompanies and illustrates a bad poor body. My limbs, without being actually twisted, were shrunken and incompetent—they would not obey my desires as do the limbs of other men. My legs would not grip a horse. When I rode I was a laughing-stock. My arms had no swiftness, no agility, no delicate and subtle certainty. When I tried to box, to fence, I was one whirling, jigging incapacity. I had feeble sight, and objects presented themselves to my vision so strangely that I could not shoot straight. I, Alistair Ralston the young Laird of Carlounie! When I walked my limbs moved heavily and awkwardly. I had no grace, no lightness, no ordinary, quite usual competence of bodily power. And this was bitter, yet as nothing to the Marah that lay beyond. For my body was in a way complete. It was a wretch. But when you came to the mind you had the real tragedy. In many decrepit flesh temples there dwells a commanding spirit, as a great God might dwell—of mysterious choice—in a ruinous and decaying lodge in a wilderness. And such a spirit rules, disposes, presides, develops, has its own full and superb existence, triumphing not merely over, but actually through the contemptible body in which it resides, so that men even are led to worship the very ugliness and poverty of this body, to adore it for its power to retain such a mighty spirit within it. Such a spirit was not mine. Had it been, I might have been happy by the burn that Autumn day. Had it been, I might never— But I am anticipating, and I must not anticipate. I must sit with the brown water rushing beneath the arch of my limbs, and recall the horror of my musing.

In a manner, then, my soul matched my body. It was feeble and incompetent too. My brain was dull and clouded. My intellect was sluggish and inert. But—and this was the terror for me! —within the rank nest of my soul—my spirit—lay coiled two vipers that never ceased from biting me with their poisoned fangs—Self-consciousness and Ambition. I knew myself, and I longed to be other than I was. I watched my own incompetence as one who watches from a tower. I divined how others regarded me—precisely. The blatant and comfortable egoism of a dwarf mind in a dwarf body was never for one moment mine. I was that terrible anomaly, an utterly incomplete and incompetent thing that adored, with a curious wildness of passion, completeness, competence. Nor had I a soul that could ever be satisfied with a one-sided perfection. My desires were Gargantuan. When I was with my cousin Gavin, a fine all-round sportsman, I longed with fury to be a good shot, to throw a fly as he did, to have a perfect seat on a horse. I felt that I would give up years of life to beat him once in any of his pursuits. When I was with Dr. Wedderburn, my desires, equally intense, were utterly different. He represented in my neighbourhood Intellect—with a capital I. A man of about fifty, minister of the parish of Carlounie, he was astonishingly adroit as a controversialist, astonishingly eloquent as a divine. His voice was full of music. His eyes were full of light and of the most superb self-confidence. He rested upon his intellect as a man may rest upon a rock. The power of his personality was calm and immense. I felt it vehemently. I shook and trembled under it. I hated and loathed the man for it, because I wanted and could never possess it. So, too, I hated my cousin Gavin for his possessions, his long and sure-sighted eyes, great and strong arms, broad chest, lithe legs, bright agility. My body could do nothing. My soul could do nothing—except one great thing. It could fully observe and comprehend its own impotence. It could fully and desperately envy and pine to be what it could never be. Could never be, do I say? Wait! Remember that is only what I thought then as I sat upon the rock, and, with haggard young eyes, watched the clear brown water slipping furtively past between my knees.

My disease seemed to culminate that day, I remember. I was a sick invalid alone in the mist. Something—it might have been vitriol—was eating into me, eating, eating its way to my very heart, to the core of me. Oh, to be stunted and desire to be straight and tall, to be dwarf and wish to be giant, to be stupid and long to be a genius, to be ugly and yearn to be in face as one of the shining gods, to have no power over men, and to pine to fascinate, hold, dominate a world of men—this indeed is to be in hell! I was in hell that Autumn day. I clenched my thin, weak hands together. I clenched my teeth from which the pale lips were drawn back in a grin; and I realised all the spectral crowd of my shortcomings. They stood before me like demons of the Brocken—yes, yes, of the Brocken! —and I cursed God with the sound of the burn ringing and chattering in my ears. And I devoted Gavin, Doctor Wedderburn, every man highly placed, every lowest peasant, who could do even one of all the things I could not do, to damnation. The paroxysm that took hold of me was like a fit, a convulsion. I came out of it white and feeble. And, suddenly, the voice of the burn seemed to come from a long way off. I put out my hand, and took up from the rock on which I had laid it, "Faust." And, scarcely knowing what I did, I began mechanically to read—to the dim rapture of the burn—

"*Scene III.—The Study. Faust (entering, with the poodle).*" I began to read, do I say, mechanically? Yes, it is true, but soon, very soon, the spell of Goethe was laid upon me. I was in the lofty-arched, narrow Gothic chamber, with that living symbol of the weariness, broken ambition, learned despair of all the ages. I was engrossed. I heard the poodle snarling by the stove. I heard the spirits whispering in the corridor. Vapour rose—or was it indeed the mist from the mountains among the birch trees? —and out of the vapour came Mephistopheles in the garb of a travelling scholar. And then—and then the great bargain was struck. I heard—yes, I did, I actually, and most distinctly, heard a voice—Faust's—say, "*Let us the sensual deeps explore.... Plunge we in Time's tumultuous dance, In the rush and roll of circumstance.*" A pause; then the Student's grave and astonished tones came to me: *Eritis sicut Deus, scientes bonum et malum*. The cloak was spread, and on the burning air Faust was wafted to his new life—nay, not to his new life merely, but to life itself. He vanished with his guide in a coloured, flower-like mist. I dropped my hand holding the book down upon the cold rock by which the cold water splashed. It felt burning hot to my touch. My head fell upon my breast, and I had my dreams—dreams of the life of Faust and of its glories, gained by this bargain that he made. And then—yes, then it was!—the voice of the burn, as from leagues away in the bosom of this very mist, began to sing like a fairy voice, or a voice in dreams, and in visions of the night, "*If it was so then, it might be so now.*" At first I scarcely heeded it, for I was enrapt. But the song grew louder, more insistent. It was travelling to me from a far country. I heard it coming: "*If it was so then, it might be so now*"—"*If it was so then, it might be so now.*" How near it was at last, how loud in my ears! And yet always there was something vague, visionary about it, something of the mist, I think. At length I heard it with the attention that is of earth. I came to myself, out of the narrow Gothic chamber in which the genius of Goethe had prisoned me, and I stared into the mist, which was gathering thicker as the night began to fall. It seemed flower-like, and full of strange and mysterious colour. I trembled. I got up. Still I heard the voice of the burn singing that monotonous legend, on, and on, and on. Slowly I turned. I climbed the bank of the den. The sheep scattered lethargically at my approach. I passed through the creaking iron gate into the garden. Carlounie was before me. There was something altered, something triumphant about its aspect. The voice of the burn faded in a long diminuendo. Yet, even as I gained the door of my house, and, before entering it, paused in an attentive attitude, I heard the water chanting faintly from the den—*"If it was so then, it might be so now."* ... As I came into the hall, in which Gavin and Dr. Wedderburn stood together talking earnestly, I remember that I shivered. Yet my cheeks were glowing.

From that moment not a day passed without my visiting the burn. It summoned me. Always it sang those words persistently. The sound of the water can be very faintly heard from the windows of Carlounie. Each day, at dawn, I pushed open the lattice of my bedroom and hearkened to hear if the song had changed. Each night, at moonrise, or in the darkness through which the soft and small rain fell quietly, I leaned over the sill and listened. Sometimes the wind was loud among the mountains. Sometimes the silence was intense and awful. But in storm or in stillness the burn sang on, ever and ever the same words. At moments I fancied that the voice was as the voice of a man demented, repeating with mirthless frenzy through all his years one hollow sentence. At moments I deemed it the cry of a fair woman, a siren, a Lorelei among my rocks in my valley. Then again I said, "It is a spirit voice, a voice from the inner chamber of my own heart." And—why I know not—at that last fantasy I shuddered. Even in the midnight from my window ledge I leaned while the world slept and I heard the mystic message of the burn. My visits to its bed were not unobserved. One morning my cousin Gavin said to me roughly, "Why the devil are you always stealing off to that ditch"—so he called the den that was the home of my voice—"when you ought to be practising to conquer your infernal deficiencies? Why, the children of your own keepers laugh at you. Try to shoot straight, man, and be a real man instead of dreaming and idling." I stared at him and answered, "You don't understand everything." Once Dr. Wedderburn, who had been my tutor, said to me more kindly, "Alistair, action is better for you than thought. Leave the burn alone. You go there to brood. Try to work, for work is the best man-maker after all."

And to him I said, "Yes, I know!" and flew with a strong wing in the face of his advice. For the voice of the burn was more to me than the voice of Gavin, or of Wedderburn; and the mind of the burn meant more to me than the mind of any man. And so the Autumn died slowly, with a lingering decadence, and shrouded perpetually in mist. I often felt ill, even then. My body was dressed in weakness. Perhaps already the fever was upon me. I wish I could know. Was it crawling in my veins? Was it nestling about my heart and in my brain? Could it be that? ...

Certainly during this period life seemed alien to me, and I moved as one apart in a remote world, full of the music of the burn, and full, too, of vague clouds. That is so. Looking back, I know it. Still, I cannot be sure what is the truth. In the late Autumn I paid my last visit to the burn before my illness seized me. The cold of early Winter was in the air and a great stillness. It was afternoon when I left the house walking slowly with my awkward gait. My face, I know, was white and drawn, and I felt that my lips were twitching. I did not carry my volume of Goethe in my hand; but, in its place, held an old book on transcendental magic. The voice of the burn—yes, that alone—had led me to study this book. So now I took it down to the burn. Why? Had I the foolish fancy of introducing my live thing of the den to this strange writing on the black art? Who knows? Perhaps the fever in my veins put the book into my hand. I shivered in the damp cold as I descended the steep ground that lay about the water, which that day seemed to roar in my ears the sentence I had heard so many days and nights. And this time, as I hearkened, my heart and my brain echoed the last words—*"It might be so now."* Gaining the edge of the burn, then in heavy spate, I watched for a while the passage of the foam from rock to rock. I peered into the pools, clouded with flood water from the hills, and with whirling or sinking dead leaves. And all my meagre body seemed pulsing with those everlasting words: "Why not now?" I murmured to myself, with a sort of silent sneer, too, at my own absurdity. I remember I glanced furtively around as I spoke. Grey emptiness, grey loneliness, dripping bare trees through whose branches the mist curled silently, cold rocks, the cold flood of the swollen burn—such was the blank prospect that met my eyes.

There was no man near me. There was no one to look at me. I was remote, hidden in a secret place, and the early twilight was already beginning to fall. No one could see me. I opened my old and ragged book, or, rather, let it fall open at a certain page. Upon it I looked for the hundredth time, and read that he who would evoke the Devil must choose a solitary and condemned spot. The burn was solitary. The burn was condemned surely by the despair and by the endless incapacities of the wretched being who owned it. I had taken off my shoes and placed them upon a rock. My feet were bare. My head was covered. I now furtively proceeded to gather together a small heap of sticks and leaves, and to these I set fire, after several attempts. As the flames at last crept up, the mist gathered more closely round me and my fire, as if striving to warm itself at the blaze. The voice of the burn mingled with the uneasy crackle of the twigs, and a murmur of its words seemed to emanate also from the flames, two elements uniting to imitate the utterance of man to my brain, already surely tormented with fever. And now, with my eyes upon my book, I proceeded to trace with the sharp point of a stick in some sandy soil between two rocks a rough Goetic Circle of Black evocations and pacts. From time to time I paused in my work and glanced uneasily about me, but I saw only the mists and the waters.

At length my task was finished, and the time had arrived for the supreme effort of my insane and childish folly. Standing at Amasarac in the Circle, I said aloud the formula of Evocation of the Grand Grimoire, ending with the words "Jehosua, Evam, Zariat, natmik, Come, come, come."

My voice died away in the twilight, and I stood among the grey rocks waiting, mad creature that I surely was! But only the rippling voice of the burn answered my adjuration. Then I repeated the words in a louder tone, adding menaces and imprecations to my formula. And all the time the fire I had kindled sprang up into the mist; and the twilight of the heavy Autumn fell slowly round me. Again I paused, and again my madness received no satisfaction, no response. But it seemed to me that I heard the browsing sheep on the summit of the right bank of the gully scatter as if at the approach of someone. Yet there was no stir of footsteps. It must have been my fancy, or the animals were merely changing their feeding ground in a troop, as they sometimes will, for no assignable cause. And now I made one last effort, urged by the voice of the burn, which sang so loudly the words which had mingled with my dream of Faust. I cried aloud the supreme appellation, making an effort that brought out the sweat on my forehead, and set the pulses leaping in my thin and shivering body. "*Chavajoth! chavajoth! chavajoth! I command thee by the Key of Solomon and the great name Semhamphoras.*"

A little way up the course of the burn the dead wood cracked and shuffled under the pressure of descending feet. Again I heard a scattering of the sheep upon the hillside. My hair stirred on my head under my cap, and the noise of the falling water was intolerably loud to me. I wanted to hear plainly, to hear what was coming down to me in the mist. The brushwood sang nearer. In the heavy and damp air there was the small, sharp report of a branch snapped from a tree. I heard it drop among the ferns close to me. And then in the mist and in the twilight I saw a slim figure standing motionless. It was vague, but less vague than a shadow. It seemed to be a man, or a youth, clad in a grey suit that could scarcely be differentiated from the mist. The flames of my fire, bent by a light breeze that had sprung up, stretched themselves towards it, as if to salute it. And now I could not hear any movement of the sheep; evidently they had gone to a distance. At first, seized with a strange feeling of extreme, almost unutterable fear, I neither moved nor spoke. Then, making a strong effort to regain control of my ordinary faculties, I cried out in the twilight—

"What is that? What is it?"

"Only a stranger who has missed his way on the mountain, and wants to go on to Wester Denoon."

The voice that came to me from the figure beyond the fire sounded, I remember, quite young, like the voice of a boy. It was clear and level, and perhaps a little formal. So that was all. A tourist—that was all!

"Can you direct me on the way?" the voice said.

I gave the required direction slowly, for I was still confused, nervous, exhausted with my insane practices in the den. But the youth—as I supposed he was—did not move away at once.

"What are you doing by this fire?" he said. "I heard your voice calling by the torrent among the trees when I was a very long way off."

Strangely, I did not resent the question. Still more strangely, I was impelled to give him the true answer to it.

"Raising the Devil!" he said. "And did he come to you?"

"No; of course not. You must think me mad."

"And why do you call him?"

Suddenly a desire to confide in this stranger, whose face I could not see now, whose shadowy form I should, in all probability, never see again, came upon me. My usual nervousness deserted me. I let loose my heart in a turbulent crowd of words. I explained my impotence of body and of mind to this grey traveller in the twilight. I dwelt upon my misery. I repeated the cry of the burn and related my insane dream of imitating Faust, of making my poor pact with Lucifer, with the Sphinx of mediæval terrors. When I ceased, the boy's voice answered—

"They say that in these modern days Satan has grown exigent. It is not enough to dedicate to him your own soul; but you must also pay a tribute of souls to the Cæsar of hell."

"A tribute of souls?"

"Yes. You must bring, they say, the mystic number, three souls to Satan."

Suddenly I laughed.

"I could never do that," I said. "I have no power to seduce man or woman. I cannot win souls to heaven or to hell."

"But if you received new powers, such as you desire, would you use them to win souls, three souls, to Lucifer?"

"Yes," I said with passionate earnestness. "I swear to you that I would."

Suddenly the boy's voice laughed.

"*Quomodo cecidisti*, Lucifer!" he said. "When thou canst not contrive to capture souls for thyself! But," he added, as if addressing himself once more to me, after this strange ejaculation, "your words have, perhaps, sealed the bond. Who knows? Words that come from the very heart are often deeds. For, as we can never go back from things that we have done, it may be that, sometimes, we can never go back from things that we have said."

On the words he moved, and passed so swiftly by me into the twilight down the glen that I never saw his face. I turned instinctively to look after him; and, this was strange, it seemed that the wind at that very moment must have turned with me, blowing from, instead of towards, the mountain. This certainly was so; for the tongues of flame from my fire bent backward on a sudden and leaned after the grey traveller, whose steps died swiftly away among the rocks, and on the shuffling dead wood and leaves of the birches and the oaks.

And then there came a singing in my ears, a beating of many drums in my brain. I drooped and sank down by the fire in the mist. My fever came upon me like a giant, and presently Gavin and Doctor Wedderburn, searching in the night, found me in a delirium, and bore me back to Carlounie.

II

The Soul of Dr. Wedderburn

To emerge from a great illness is sometimes dreadful, sometimes divine. To one man the return from the gates of death is a progress of despair. He feels that he cannot face the wild contrasts of the surprising world again, that his courage has been broken upon the wheel, that energy is desolation, and sleep true beauty. To another this return is a marvellous and superb experience. It is like the vivid re-awakening of youth in one who is old, a rapture of the past committing an act of brigandage upon the weariness of the present, a glorious substitution of Eden for the outer courts where is weeping and gnashing of teeth. It will be supposed that I found myself in the first category, a terror-stricken and rebellious mortal when the fever gave me up to the world again. For the world had always been cruel to me, because I was afraid of it, and was a puny thing in it. Yet this was not so. My convalescence was like a beautiful dream of rest underneath which riot stirred. A simile will explain best exactly what I mean. Let me liken the calm of my convalescence to the calm of earth on the edge of Spring. What a riot of form, of scent, of colour, of movement, is preparing beneath that enigmatic, and apparently profound, repose. In the simile you have my exact state. And I alone felt that, within this womb of inaction, the child, action, lay hid, developing silently, but inexorably, day by day. This knowledge was my strange secret. It came upon me one night when I lay awake in the faint twilight, shed by a carefully shaded lamp over my bed. Rain drummed gently against the windows. There was no other sound. By the fire, in a great armchair, the trained nurse, Kate Walters, was sitting with a book—*Jane Eyre* it was—upon her knees. I had been sleeping and now awoke thirsty. I put out my hand to get at a tumbler of lemonade that stood on a table by my pillow. And suddenly a thought, a curious thought, was with me. My hand had grasped the tumbler and lifted it from the table; but, instead of bringing my hand to my mouth I kept my arm rigidly extended, the tumbler poised on my palm as upon the palm of a juggler.

"How long my arm is!" that was my thought, "and how strong!" Formerly it had been short, weak, awkward. Now, surely, after my illness, my arms would naturally be nerveless, useless things. The odd fact was that now, for the first time in my life, I felt joy in a physical act. An absurd and puny act, you will say, I daresay. What of that? With it came a sudden stirring of triumph. I lay there on my back and kept my arm extended for full five minutes by the watch that ticked by my bedhead. And with each second that passed joy blossomed more fully within my heart. I drank the lemonade as one who drinks a glad toast. Yet I was puzzled. "Is this—can this be a remnant of delirium?" I asked myself. And beneath the clothes drawn up to my chin I fingered my arm above the elbow. It was the limb of a big, strong man. Surprise, supreme astonishment forced an exclamation from my lips. Kate got up softly and came towards me; but I feigned to be asleep, and she returned to the fire. Yet, peering under my lowered eyelids, I noticed an expression of amazement upon her young and pretty face. I knew afterwards that it was the sound of my voice—my new voice—that drew it there. After that night my convalescence was more than a joy to me, it was a rapture, touched by, and mingled with something that was almost awe. Is not the earth awestruck when she considers that Spring and Summer nestle silently in her bosom? With each day the secret which I kept grew more mysterious, more profound. Soon I knew it could be a secret no longer. The fever—it must be that!—had wrought magic within my body, driving out weakness, impotence, lassitude, developing my physical powers to an extent that was nothing less than astounding. Lying there in my bed, I felt the dwarf expand into the giant. Think of it! Did ever living man know such an experience before? A bodily spring came about within me. And I was already twenty-two years old before the fever took me. My limbs grew large and strong; the muscles of my chest and back were tensely strung and knit as firmly as the muscles of an athlete. I lay still, it is true, and felt much of the peculiar vagueness that follows fever; but I was conscious of a supine, latent energy never known before. I was conscious that when I rose, and went out into the world again, it would be as a man, capable of holding his own against other strong, straight men. That was a wonder. But it was succeeded by a greater marvel yet.

One afternoon, while I was still in bed, Doctor Wedderburn came to see me and to sit with me. He had been away on a holiday, and, consequently, had not visited me before, except once when I had been delirious. The doctor was a short, spare man, with a sharply cut brick-red face, lively and daring dark eyes, and straight hair already on the road to grey. His self-possession bordered on self-satisfaction; and, despite his good heart and the real and anxious sanctity of his life, he could seldom entirely banish from his manner the contempt he felt for those less intellectual, less swift-minded than himself. Often had I experienced the stinging lash of his sarcasm. Often had I withered beneath one of his keen glances that dismissed me from an argument as a profound sage might kick an urchin from the study into the street. Often had I hated him with a sick hatred and ground my teeth because my mind was so clouded and so helpless, while his was so lucent and so adroit. So now, when I heard his tap on the door, his deep voice asking to come in, a rage of self-contempt seized me, as in the days before my illness. The doctor entered with an elaborate softness, and walked, flat-footed, to my bed, pursing his large lips gently as men do when filled with cautious thoughts. I could see he desired to moderate his habitual voice and manner; but, arrived close to me, he suddenly cried aloud, with a singularly full-throated amazement.

"Boy—boy, what's come to you?" he called. Then, abruptly putting his finger to his lips, he sank down in a chair, his bright eyes fixed upon me.

"It's a miracle," he said slowly.

"What is?" I asked with an invalid's pettishness.

"The voice, too—the voice!"

I grew angry easily, as men do when they are sick.

"Why do you say that? Of course I've been bad—of course I'm changed."

"Changed! Look at yourself—and praise God, Alistair."

He had caught up a hand mirror that lay on the dressing table and now put it into my hand. For the first time since the fever I saw my face. It was as it had been and yet it was utterly different, for now it was beautiful. The pinched features seemed to have been smoothed out. The mouth had become firm and masterful. The haggard eyes were alight as if torches burned behind them. My expression, too, was powerful, collected, alert. I scarcely recognised myself. But I pretended to see no change.

"Well—what is it?" I asked, dropping the glass.

The doctor was confused by my calm.

"Your look of health startled me," he answered, sitting down by the bed and examining me keenly.

All at once I was seized by a strange desire to get up an argument with this man, by whom I had so often been crushed in conversation. I leaned on my elbow in the bed, and fixing my eyes on him, I said—

"And why should I praise God?"

The doctor seemed in amazement at my tone.

"Because you are a Christian and have been brought back from death," he replied, but with none of his usual half-sarcastic self-confidence.

"You think God did that?"

"Alistair, do you dare to blaspheme the Almighty?"

I felt at that moment like a cat playing with a mouse. My lips, I know, curved in a smile of mockery, and yet I will swear—yes, even to my own heart—that all I said that day I said in pure mischief, with no evil intent. It seemed that I, Alistair Ralston, the dolt, the ignoramus, longed to try mental conclusions with this brilliant and opinionated divine. He bade me praise God. In reply I praised—the Devil, and I forced him to hear me. Absolutely I broke into a flood of words, and he sat silent. I compared the good and evil in the scheme of the world, balancing them in the scales, the one against the other. I took up the stock weapon of atheism, the deadly nature, the deadly outcome of free will. I used it with skill. The names of Strauss, Comte, Schopenhauer, Renan, a dozen others, sprang from my lips. The dreary doctrine of the illimitable triumph of sin, of the appalling mistake of the permission granted it to step into the scheme of creation, in order that its presence might create a *raison d'être* for the power of personal action one way or the other in mankind—such matters as these I treated with a vehement eloquence and command of words that laid a spell upon the doctor. Going very far, I dared to exclaim that since God had allowed his own scheme to get out of gear, the only hope of man lay in the direction of the opposing force, in frank and ardent Satanism.

When at length I ceased from speaking, I expected Dr. Wedderburn to rise up in his wrath and to annihilate me, but he sat still in his chair with a queer, and, as I thought, puzzled expression upon his face. At last he said, as if to himself:

"The miracle of Balaam; verily, the miracle of Balaam."

The ass had indeed spoken as never ass spoke before. I waited a moment, then I said—

"Well, why don't you rebuke me, or why don't you try to controvert me?"

Again he looked upon me, very uneasily I thought, and with something that was almost fear in his keen eyes.

"Ah!" he said, "I have praised the Lord many a morning and evening for his gift of words to me. It seems others bestow that gift too. Alistair"—and here his voice became deeply solemn—"where have you been visiting when you lay there, mad to all seeming? In what dark place have you been to gather destruction for men? With whom have you been talking?"

Suddenly, I know not why, I thought of the grey stranger, and, with a laugh, I cried—

"The grey traveller taught me all I have said to you."

"The grey traveller! Who may he be?"

But I lay back upon the pillows and refused to answer, and very soon the doctor went, still bending uneasy, nervous eyes upon me.

In those eyes I read the change that had stolen over my intellect, as in the hand mirror I had read the change that had stolen over my face. This strange fever had caused both soul and body to blossom. I trembled with an exquisite joy. Had Fate relented to me at last? Was it possible that I was to know the joys of the heroes? I longed for, yet feared my full recovery. In it alone should I discover how sincere was my transformation. Doctor Wedderburn did not come to me again. The days passed, my convalescence strengthened, watched over by the pretty nurse, Kate Walters, a fresh, pure, pious, innocent, beautiful soul, tender, temperate, and pitiful for all sorrow and evil. At length I was well. At length I knew, to some extent, my new, my marvellous self. For I had, indeed, been folded up in my fever like a vesture, and, like a vesture, changed. I had grown taller, expanded, put forth mighty muscles as a tree puts forth leaves. My cheeks and my eyes glowed with the radiance of strong health. I went out with my cousin Gavin, whose estate marched with mine, and I shot so well that he was filled with admiration, and forthwith conceived a sort of foolish worship for me—having a sportsman's soul but no real mind. For the first time in my life I felt absolutely at home on a horse, an unwonted skill came to my hands, and I actually schooled Gavin's horses over some fences he had had set up in a grass park at the Mains of Cossens. The keepers who had once secretly jeered at me were now at my very feet. Their children looked upon me as a young god. I rejoiced in my strength as a giant. But I asked myself then, as I ask myself now—what does it mean? The days of miracles are over. Yet, is this not a miracle? And in a miracle is there not a gleam of terror, as there is a gleam of stormy yellow in the fated opal? But here I leave my condition of body alone, and pass on to the episode of Doctor Wedderburn, partially related in the newspapers of the day and marvelled at, I believe, by all who ever knew, or even set eyes upon him.

The doctor, as I have said, did not come again to see me, but I felt an over-mastering desire to set forth and visit him. This was surprising, as hitherto I had rather avoided and hated him. Now something drew me to the Manse. At first I resisted my inclination, but a chance word led me to yield to it impulsively. Since my illness I had not once attended church. Moved by a violent distaste for the religious service, that was novel in me, I had frankly avowed my intention of keeping away. But, as I did not go to the kirk, I missed seeing Dr. Wedderburn; and I wanted to see him. One day, leaning by chance against a stone dyke in the Glen of Ogilvy, smoking a pipe and enjoying the soft air of Spring as it blew over the rolling moorland, I heard two ploughmen exchange a fragment of gossip that made excitement start up quick within me.

One said—

"The doctor's failin'. Man, he was fairly haverin' last Sabbath, on and on, wi'out logic or argeyment or sense."

The other answered—

"Ay; he's greatly changed. He's no the man he was. It fairly beats me; I canna mak' it out. Ye've heard that—" And here he lowered his voice and I could not catch his words.

I turned away from the wall, and walking swiftly, set out for the Manse with a busy mind. The afternoon was already late, and when I gained a view of the Manse, a cold grey house standing a little apart in a grove of weary-looking sycamores, one or two lights smiled on me from the small windows that stared upon the narrow and muddy road. The minister's study was on the right of the hall door; and, as I pulled the bell, I observed the shadow of his head to dance upon the drawn white blind, a thought fantastically, or with a palsied motion, I fancied. The yellow-headed maidservant admitted me with a shrunken grin, that suggested wild humour stifled by achieved respect, and I was soon in the minister's study. Then I saw that Doctor Wedderburn was moving up and down the room, and that his head was going this way and that, as he communed in a loud voice with himself. My entrance checked him as soon as he observed me, which was not instantly, as, at first, his back was set towards me and the mood-swept maid. When he turned about, his discomposure was evident. His gaze was troubled, and his manner, as he shook hands with me, had in it something of the tremulous, and was backward in geniality. We sat down on either side of the fire, the tea service and the hot cakes, loved of the doctor, between us. At first we talked warily of such things as my recovery, the weather, the condition of affairs in the parish and so forth. I noticed that though the doctor's eyes often rested with an almost glaring expression of scrutiny or of surprise upon me, he made no remark on the change of my appearance. Nor did I on the change of his, which was startling, and suggested I know not what of sorrow and of the attempt to kill it with evil weapons. The healthy brick-red of his complexion was now become scarlet and full of heat; his mouth worked loosely while he talked; the flesh of his cheeks was puffed and wrinkled; his eyes had the clouded and yet fierce aspect of the drunkard. But, absurdly enough, what most struck me in him was his abstinence from an accustomed act. He drank his tea, but he ate no hot cakes. This was a departure from an established, if trifling custom of many years' standing, and worked on my imaginative conception of what the doctor now was more than would, at the first blush, appear likely, or even possible. Instead of, as of old, feeling myself on the worm level in his presence, I was filled with a sense of pity, as I looked upon him and wondered what subtle process of mental or physical development or retrogression had wrought this dreary change. Presently, while I wondered, he put his cup down with an awkward and errant hand that set it swaying and clattering in the tray, and said abruptly—

"And what have you come for, Alistair, eh? what have you come for? To go on with what you've begun? Well, well, lad, I'm ready for you; I'm ready now."

His voice was full of timorous irritation, his manner of pitiable distress.

"I've thought it out, I've thought it all out," he continued; "and I can combat you, I can combat you, Alistair, wherever you've got your fever-mind from and your fever-tongue."

I knew what he meant, and suddenly I knew, too, why I had wanted so eagerly to come to the Manse. My instinct of pity and of sympathy died softly away. My new instinct of cruel rapture in the ruthless exercise of my—shall I call them fever-powers then?—woke, dawned to sunrise. And Doctor Wedderburn and I fell forthwith into an animated theological discussion. He was desperately nervous, desperately ill at ease. His argumentative struggles were those of a drowning man positively convinced—note this,—that he would drown, that no human or divine aid could save him. There was, too, a strong hint of personal anger in his manner, which was strictly undignified. He fought a losing battle with bludgeons, and had an obvious contempt for the bludgeons while in the act of using them in defence or in attack. And at last, with a sort of sharp cry, he threw up his hands, and exclaimed in a voice I hardly knew as his—

"God forgive you, Alistair, for what you're doing! God forgive you—murderer, murderer!"

This dolorous exclamation ran through me like cold water and chilled all the warmth of my intellectual excitement.

"Murderer!" I repeated inexpressively.

Doctor Wedderburn sat in his chair trembling, and looking upon me with despairing and menacing eyes, the eyes of a man who curses but cannot fight his enemy.

"Of a soul, of a soul," he said. "The poisoned dagger?—doubt, the poisoned dagger—you've plunged it into me, boy."

Then raising his voice harshly, he exclaimed:

"Curse you, curse you!"

I was thunderstruck. I declare it here, for it is true. I had defamed—and deliberately—the doctor's dearest idols. I had driven my lance into his convictions. I had blasphemed what he worshipped, and had denied all he affirmed. But that I had made so terrific an impression upon his mind, his soul—this astounded me. Yet what else could his passionate denunciation mean? Had I, a boy, unused to controversy, unskilled in dialectics, overthrown with my hasty words the faith of this strong and fervent man? The thought thrilled one side of my dual nature with triumph, pierced the other with grim horror. My emotions were divided and complex. As I sat silent, my face dogged yet ashamed, the doctor got up from his chair trembling like one with the palsy.

"Away from me—away," he cried in a hoarse voice, and pointing at the door. "I'll have no more talk with the Devil, no more—no more!"

I had not a word. I got up and went, bending a steady, fascinated look upon this old mentor of mine, who now proclaimed himself my victim. Arrived in the garden I found a thin moon riding above the sycamores, and soft airs of Spring playing round the doctor's habitation. Strangely, I had no mind to begone from it immediately. I crossed the garden bit and paced up and down the country lane that skirted it, keeping an eye upon the lighted window of the study. So I went back and forth for full an hour, I suppose. Then I heard a sound in the Spring night. The doctor's hall door banged, and, peering through the privet hedge that protected his meagre domain, I perceived him come out into the air bareheaded. He took his way to the small path that ran by the hedge parallel to the lane, coming close to the place by which I crouched, spying upon his privacy. And there he paced, bemoaning aloud the ill fate that had come upon him. I heard all the awful complaining of this soul in distress, besieged by doubts, deserted by the faith and hope of a lifetime. It was villainous to be his audience. Yet, I could not go. Sometimes the poor man prayed with a desolate voice, calling upon God for a sign, imploring against temptation. Sometimes—and this was terrible—he blasphemed, he imprecated. And then again he prayed—to the Devil, as do the Satanists. I heard him weeping in his garden in the night, alone under the sycamores. It was a new agony of the garden and it wrung my heart. Yet I watched it till the spectral moon waned, and the trees were black as sins against the faded sky.

About this time, as I have said, his parishioners began to mark the outward change of Dr Wedderburn that signified the inward change in him. The talking ploughmen had their fellows. All who sat under the doctor were conscious of a difference, at first vague, in his eloquent discourses, of a diminuendo in the full fervour of his delivery and manner. Gossip flowed about him, and presently there were whisperings of change in his bodily habits. He had been seen by night wandering about his garden in very unholy condition, he who had so often rebuked excess. Children, passing his gate in the dark of evening, had endured with terror his tipsy shoutings. A maidservant left him, and spread doleful reports of his conduct through the village. By degrees, rumours of our minister's shortcomings stole, like snakes, into the local papers, carefully shrouded by the wrappings that protect scandal-mongers against libel actions. The congregation beneath the doctor's pulpit dwindled. Women looked at him askance. Men were surly to him, or— and that was less kind—jocular. I, alone, followed with fascination the paling to dusk of a bright and useful career. I, alone, partially understood the hell this poor creature carried within him. For I often heard his dreary night-thoughts, and assisted, unperceived of him, at the vigils that he kept. The lamp within his study burned till dawn while he wrestled, but in vain, with the disease of his soul, the malady of his tortured heart.

One night in Summer time, towards midnight, I bent my steps furtively to the Manse. It was very dark and the weather was dumb and agitating. No leaf danced, no grass quivered. Breathless, dead, seemed the woods and fields, the ocean of moorland, the assemblage of the mountains. I heard no step upon the lonely road but my own, and life seemed to have left the world until I came upon the Manse. Then I saw the light in the doctor's window, and, drawing near, observed that the blind was up and the lattice thrust open among the climbing dog-roses. Craftily I stole up the narrow garden path, and, keeping to the side of the window, looked into the room.

Doctor Wedderburn lounged within at the table facing me. A pen was in his shaking hand. A shuffle of manuscript paper was before him, and a Bible, in which he thrust his fingers as if to keep texts already looked out. Beyond the Bible was a bottle, three-quarters full of whiskey, and a glass. His muttering lips and dull yet shining eyes betokened his condition. I saw before me a drunkard writing a sermon. The vision was sufficiently bizarre. A tragedy of infinite pathos mingled with a comedy of hideous yet undeniable humour in the live picture. I neither wept nor did I laugh. I only watched, shrouded by the inarticulate night. The doctor took a pull at the bottle, then swept the leaves of the Bible....

"Let me die the death of the righteous," he murmured thickly. "That's it—that's—that's—" He wrote on the paper before him with a wandering pen, then pushed the sheet from him. It fell on the floor by the window.

"And let my last end be like his—Ah—ah!"

He drank again, and again wrote with fury. How old and how wicked he looked, yet how sad! He crouched down over the table and the pen broke in his hand. A dull exclamation burst from him. Taking up the bottle, he poured by accident some of the whiskey over the open Bible.

"A baptism! A baptism!" he ejaculated, bursting into laughter. "Now—now—let's see—let's see."

Again he violently turned the sodden leaves and shook his head. He could not read the words, and that angered him. He drank again and again till the bottle was empty, then staggered out of the room. I heard his frantic footsteps echoing in the uncarpeted passage. Quickly I leaned in at the window and caught up the sheet of paper that had fallen to the floor. I held it up to the light. Only one sentence writhed up and down over it, repeated a dozen times; "There is no God!" While I read I heard the doctor returning, and I shrank back into the night. He came stumbling in, another whiskey bottle full in his hand. Falling down in the chair he applied his lips to it and drank—on and on. He was killing himself there and then. I knew it. I wanted to leap into the room, to stop him, yet I only watched him. Why?—I want to know why—

At last he fell forward across the Bible with a choking noise. His limbs struggled. His arms shot out wildly, the table broke under him—there was a crash of glass. The lamp was extinguished. Darkness crowded the little room—and silence.

The papers recorded the shocking death of a minister. They did not record this.

As I stole home that night, alone in my knowledge of the doctor's appalling end, I heard going before me light and tripping footsteps, those, apparently, of some youth, not above three yards or so from me. What wanderer thus preceded me, I asked myself, with a certain tingling of the nerves, shaken, perhaps, by what I had just seen? I paused. The steps also paused. The person was stopping too. I resumed my way. Again I heard the tripping footfalls. Their sound greatly disquieted me, yet I hurried, intending to catch up the wayfarer. Still the steps hastened along the highway, and always just before me. I ran, yet did not come up with any person. I called "Stop! Stop!" There was no reply. Again I waited. This man—or boy— (the steps seemed young) waited also. I started forward once more. So did he. Then a fury of fear ran over me, urging me at all hazards to see in whose train I travelled. We were now close to Carlounie. We entered the policies. Yes, this person turned from the public road through my gates into the drive, and the footfalls reached the very house. I stopped. I dared not approach quite close to the door. With trembling fingers I fumbled in my pocket, drew out my matchbox, and, in the airless night, struck a match. The tiny flame burned steadily. I stretched my hand out, approaching it, as I supposed, to the face of the stranger.

But I saw nothing. Only, on a sudden, I heard someone hasten from me across the sweep of gravel in the direction of the burn. And then, after an interval, I heard the rush of startled sheep through the night.

Just so had they scattered on the day I spoke with the grey traveller by the waterside.

III

The Soul of Kate Walters

It is more than two years since I wrote down any incident of my life. Two years ago I seemed to myself a stranger. To-day an intimacy has sprung up between myself and that observant, detached something within me—that little extra spirit which looks on at me, and yet is, somehow, me. I am at home with my own power. I am accustomed to my strength of personality. From my fever I rose like some giant. Long ago my world recognised the obedience it owed me. Long ago, by many signs, in many ways, it taught me the paramount quality of the emanation from my soul that is called my influence. Yet sometimes, even now, I seem to stare at myself aghast, to turn cold when I am alone with myself. I am seized with terrible fancies. I think of the voice of the burn. I think of that childish Autumn ceremony upon its bank among the mists and the flying leaves. I think of the grey youth who spoke with me in the twilight, and my soul is full of questions. I muse upon the Wandering Jew, upon Faust, upon Van Der Decken, upon the monstrous figures that are legends, yet sometimes realities to men. And then—and this is ghastly—I say to myself, can it be that I, too, shall become a legend? Can it be that my name will be whispered by the pale lips of good men long after I am dead? For, is there not a whirl of white faces attending my progress as the whirl of dead leaves attends the Autumn? Do I not hear a faint symphony of despairing cries like a dreadful music about my life? Is not my power upon men malign? Boys with their hopes shattered, men with their faiths broken, women with their love turned to gall—do they not crowd about my chariot wheels? Or is it my vain fancy that they do? Here and there from the sea of these beings one rises like a drowned creature whom the ocean will not hide, stark, stiff, corpse-like. Doctor Wedderburn was the first. Kate Walters is the second—Kate Walters.

When my convalescence was well advanced she left Carlounie and went back to Edinburgh. Some months afterwards I heard casually that she was working in a hospital there. But a year and a half went by before I saw this girl again. Her fresh, pure, ministering face had nearly faded from my memory. Yet, she had attended intimately upon my marvellous transformation from my death of weakness to the life of strength. She had lifted me in her girl's arms when I was nothing. Yes, I had been in her arms then. How strange, how close are the commonest relations between the invalid and his nurse! When I chanced to meet Kate again I had no thought of this. I had forgotten. I came to Edinburgh on some business connected with a mine discovered on my estate, which seemed likely to make a great fortune for me, and is already on the way to accomplishing this first duty of a mine. My business done, I stayed on at my hotel in Princes Street amusing myself, for I had a multitude of friends in Edinburgh. One of these friends was a medical student attached to the hospital there, and he chanced to invite me to go with him through the wards one day. In one of the wards I encountered Kate Walters, fresh, clear, calm as in the old Carlounie days of my illness. She did not know me till I recalled myself to her recollection; then she looked into my face with the frankest astonishment. My superb physique amazed her, although she had attended upon its beginnings. I asked after her life in the interval since our last meeting; and she told me, with a delightful blush, that her period of nursing was nearly concluded, as she was engaged to be married to one Hugh Fraser, a handsome, rich, and—strange thing this!

—most steadfast youth, who lived in England in the south, and who loved her tenderly. I congratulated her, and was on the point of moving away down the ward with my friend when my eyes were caught again by Kate's blushing cheeks and eyes alight with the fiery shames and joys of love. How beautiful is the human face when the torches of the heart are kindled thus. How beautiful! I paused, and, before I went, invited Kate to tea one afternoon at my hotel. She accepted the invitation. Why not? In our meeting the old chain of sympathy between patient and nurse seemed forged anew. We felt that we were indeed friends. As we left the ward, my student chum chaffed me—I let his words go by heedlessly. I was not in love with Kate, but I was half in love with her love for Hugh Fraser. It had such pretty features. She came to tea and told me all about him; and when she talked of him she was so fascinating that I was loath to let her go. It was a sweet evening, and, as Kate had not to be back at the hospital early, I suggested that we should go for a stroll on Carlton Hill, and talk a little more about Hugh Fraser. The bribe tempted her. I saw that. And she agreed after a moment's hesitation.

There is certainly an influence that lives only out of doors and can never enter a house, or exercise itself within four walls. There is a wandering spirit in the air of evening, a soul that walks with gathering shadows, speaks in the distant hum of a city, and gazes through its twinkling lights. *There is a grey traveller who journeys in the twilight.* (What am I saying? To-day, as I write, I am full of fancies.) I felt that, so soon as Kate and I were away from the hotel, out under the sky and amid the mysteries of Edinburgh, we were changed. In a flash our intimacy advanced, the sympathy already existing between us deepened. Leaving the streets, we mounted the flight of steps that leads to the hill, and joined the few couples who were walking, almost like gods on some Olympus, above the world. They were all obviously lovers. I pointed this fact out to Kate, saying, "Hugh Fraser should be here, not I."

She smiled, but scarcely, I thought, with much regret. For the moment it seemed that a confidant satisfied her; and this pleased me. I drew her arm within mine.

"We must not alarm the lovers," I said. "We must appear to be as they are, or we shall carry a fiery sword into their Eden."

"You seem to understand us very well," she answered with a smile. And she left her arm in mine.

The mention of "us" chilled me. It seemed to set me outside a magic circle within which she, Hugh Fraser, these people sauntering near us, like amorous ghosts in the dimness, moved. I pressed her arm ever so gently.

"Tell me how lovers feel at such a time as this," I whispered, looking into her eyes.

From Carlton Hill at night one sees a heaving ocean of yellow lights, gleaming like phosphorescence on ebon waves. Towards Arthur's Seat, towards the Castle, they rise; by Holyrood, by the old town, they fall. That night I could fancy that this sea of light spoke to me, murmured in my ear, urging me to prosecute my will, ruthlessly stirring a strange and, perhaps, evanescent romance in my heart. I know that when I parted from Kate that night I bent and kissed her. I know that she looked up at me startled, even terrified, yet found no voice to rebuke me. I know that I did not leave Edinburgh, as I had originally intended, upon the morrow. And I know this best of all—that I had no ill-intent in staying. I was caught in a net of impulse despite my own desire. I was held fast. There are—I believe it unalterably now—influences in life that are the very Tsars of the empires of men's souls. They must be obeyed. Possibly—is it so I wonder? —they only mount upon their thrones when they are urgently invoked by men who, as it were, say, "Come and rule over us!" But once that invocation has been made, once it has been responded to, there is never again free will for him who has rashly called upon the power he does not understand, and bowed before the tyrant whose face he has not seen. I tremble now, as I write; I tremble as does the bond slave. Yet I neither speak with, nor hear, nor have sight of, my master. Unless, indeed—but I will not give way to any madness of the brain. No, no; I do not hear, I do not see, although I am conscious of, my Tsar, whose unemancipated serf I am.

I need not tell all the story of my soul's impression that was stamped upon the soul of Kate Walters. Perhaps it is old. Certainly it is sad. I stamped deceit upon the nature which had not known it, knowledge of evil where only purity had been, satiety upon temperance. And, worst of all, I expelled from this girl's heart love for a good man who loved her, and planted, in its stead, passion for a—must I say a bad, or may I not cry, a driven man? And all this time Hugh Fraser knew nothing of his sorrow, growing up swiftly to meet him like a giant. Even now, while I write these words, he knows nothing of it. As I had carelessly taken possession of the mind, the very nature of Dr. Wedderburn, so now I took possession of the very nature of Kate Walters. My immense strength, my abounding physical glory drew her—who had known me a puny invalid—irresistibly. I won the doctor by my mind; this girl, in the main, I think, by my body. And when at length I tired of her slightly, the woman, the gentle woman, sprang up a tigress. I had said one night that, since I was obliged to go to London, we must part for a while. I had added that it was well Hugh Fraser lived in complete ignorance of his betrayal.

"Why?" Kate suddenly cried out.

"Because—because it is best so. He and you—someday."

I paused. She understood my meaning. Instantly the tigress had sprung upon me. The scene that followed was eloquent. I learned what lives and moves in the very depths of a nature, stirred by the inexhaustible greed of passion, twisted by passion's fulfilment, the ardent touched by the inert. But upon that hurricane has followed an immense and very strange calm. Kate is almost cold to me, though very sweet. She has acquiesced in my departure for town. She has come to one mind with me on the subject of Hugh Fraser. More, she has even written a letter to him asking him to come to her, pressing forward their marriage, and I am to be the bearer of it to him. This is only a woman's whim. She insists that I must see once the man who is to be her husband.

So, after all, the tragedy of Dr. Wedderburn is not to be repeated. I— I shall not hear, stealing along the steep and windy streets of Edinburgh, any—any strange footsteps.

What is the awful fate that pursues me? A year ago I left Edinburgh carrying with me the letter which I understood to contain the request of Kate Walters to her lover, Hugh Fraser, to hasten on their marriage. As the train roared southwards, I congratulated myself on my clever management of a woman. I had, it is true, stepped in between Kate and the calm happiness she had been anticipating when I first met her in the hospital ward. But now I had withdrawn. And, I told myself, in time, all would be well. This girl would marry the boy who loved her. She would deceive him. He would never know that the girl he married was not the girl he originally loved. He would never perceive that a human being had intervened between her and purity, truth, honour. In this letter—I touched it with my fingers, congratulating myself—Hugh Fraser would read the summons to the future he desired, the future with Kate Walters. His soul would rush to meet hers, and surely, after a little while, hers would cease to hold back. She would really once more be as she had been. I forgot that no human soul can ever retreat from knowledge to ignorance.

Hugh Fraser's rooms in London were in Piccadilly. Directly I arrived in town I wrote him a note, saying that I was from Edinburgh with a message from Kate Walters for him. I explained that she had nursed me through a severe illness, and hoped I might have the pleasure of making his acquaintance. In reply, I received a most friendly note, begging me to call at an hour on the evening of the following day.

That evening I drove in a hansom from the Grand Hotel to Piccadilly, taking Kate's note with me. I was conscious of a certain excitement, and also of a certain moral exultation. Ridiculously enough, I felt as if I were about to perform a sort of fine, almost paternal act, blessing these children with genuine, as opposed to stage, emotion. Yes; I glowed with a consciousness of personal merit. How incredible human beings are! Arrived at Hugh Fraser's rooms, I was at once shown in. How vividly I remember that first interview of ours, the exact condition of the room, Hugh's attitude of lively anticipation, the precise way in which he held his cigarette, the grim, short bark of the fox terrier that sprang up from a sofa when I came in. Hugh was almost twenty-four years old, rather tall, slim, with intense, large, dark eyes—full of shining cheerfulness just then—very short, curling black hair, and fine, straight features. His expression was boyish; so were his movements. As soon as he saw me, he sprang forward and gave me an enthusiastic welcome—for the sake of Kate, I knew. He led me to the fire and made me sit down. I at once handed him my credentials, Kate's letter. His face flushed with pleasure, and his fingers twitched with the desire to tear it open, but he refrained politely, and began to talk—about her, I confess. I understood in three minutes how deeply he was in love with her. I told him all about her that might please him, and hinted at the contents of the letter.

"What!" he exclaimed joyously. "She wants to hasten on our marriage at last. And she's kept me off—but you know what girls are! She couldn't leave the hospital immediately. She swore it. There were a thousand reasons for delay. But now—by Jove!"

His eyes were suddenly radiant, and he clutched hold of my hand like a schoolboy.

"You are a good chap to bring me such a letter," he cried.

"Read it," I said, again filled with moral self-satisfaction, vain, paltry egoist that I was.

"No, no—presently."

But I insisted; and at length he complied, enchanted to yield to my importunity. He opened the letter, and, as he broke the seal, his face was like morning. Never shall I forget the change that grew in it as he read. When he had finished his face was like starless night. He looked old, haggard, black, shrunken. I watched him with a sensation that something had gone wrong with my sight. Surely radiance was fully before me and my tricked vision saw it as despair. Raising his blank, bleak eyes from the letter, Hugh stared towards me and opened his lips. But no sound came from them. He frowned, as if in fury at his own

dumbness. Then at last, with a sharp shake of his head sideways, he said in a low and dry voice:
"You know what is in this letter, you say?"
"I—I thought so," I answered, growing cold and filled with anxiety.
"Well, read it, will you?"
I took the paper from his hand and read—

"Dear Hugh—Make the man who brings you this letter marry me. If you don't, I will kill myself; for I am ruined.
KATE."

I looked up at Hugh Fraser over the letter which my hand still mechanically held near my eyes. I wonder how long the silence through which we stared lasted.

A month later I was married to Kate Walters!

IV

The Soul of Hugh Fraser

It may seem strange that my influence upon the soul of Hugh Fraser should follow upon such a situation as I have just described; but everything connected with my life, since the day when I met the grey boy by the burn, has been utterly strange, utterly abnormal. My treachery, one would have thought, must have led Fraser to hate me. I had wrecked his happiness. I had done him the deepest injury one man can do to another, and at first he hated me. When he had wrung from me a promise to marry Kate, he left me, and I did not see him again until after the wedding. But then, it seemed, he could not keep away from her. For he forgave us the wrong we had done him; and, after a while, wrote a friendly letter in which he suggested that we should all forget the past.

"Why should I not see you sometimes?" he concluded. "I only wish you both good, there is no longer any evil in my heart."

Poor boy! It was to be, I suppose. The Tsar of the empire of my soul set forth his edict, and one winter day carriage wheels ground harshly upon the gravel sweep, and Hugh Fraser was my guest at Carlounie. I welcomed him upon the very spot where those light footsteps paused that black night of Doctor Wedderburn's dreary end. And the faint sound of the burn mingled with our voices in greeting and reply.

The boy was changed. He had aged, grown grave, heavier in

movement, fiercer in observation, less ready in speech. But his manner was friendly even to me, and it was plain to see that Kate still had his heart. They met quietly enough, but a flush ran from his cheek to hers as they touched hands. Their voices quivered when they spoke a commonplace of pleasure at the encounter. So the wheels of Fate began slowly to turn on this winter's day.

I must tell you that my fortunes had greatly changed before Hugh Fraser came to Carlounie. I was grown rich. My investments, my speculations had prospered almost miraculously. The mine I have spoken of was proving a gold mine to me. All worldly things went well with me—all worldly things, yes.

Now, I believe that all mighty circumstances are born tiny, like children, at some given moment. As a rule, they usually seem so insignificant, so puny at the birth, that we take no heed of the fact that they have come into being, and that, in process of time, they will grow to might, perhaps to horrible majesty. Only, when we trace events backwards do we know the exact moment when their first faint wail broke upon our mental hearing. Generally this is so. But I affirm that I felt, at the very time of its first coming, the presence of the shadow, the tiny shadow of the events which I am about to describe. I even said to myself, "This is a birthday."

Among many improvements on my estate I had built a new Manse, in which, of course, our new minister lived. The old habitation of Doctor Wedderburn stood empty and deserted among its sycamores. One winter's day Hugh Fraser, Kate, and I, in our walk, passed along the lane by the now ragged privet hedge through which I had so often observed the doctor's agonies. It was a black and white day of frost, which crawled along the dark trees and outlined twig and branch. The air was misty, and distant objects assumed a mysterious importance. Slight sounds, too, suggested infinite activities to the mind. As we neared the Manse, Hugh Fraser said to me—

"Who lives in that old house?"

"Nobody," I replied.

Hugh glanced at me very doubtfully.

"Nobody," I reiterated.

"Really," he rejoined. "But the garden?"

"Is deserted."

"Hardly," he exclaimed, pointing with his hand. "Look!"

"Yes," said Kate, as if in agreement.

And she grew duskily pale.

I looked over the privet hedge, seeing only the rank and frost-bitten grass, the wild bushes and narrow mossy paths. Then I stared at my two companions in silence. Their eyes appeared to follow the onward movement of some object invisible to me.

"The old man makes himself at home," Hugh said. "He has gone into the summer house now."

"Yes," Kate said again.

There was fear in her eyes.

I felt suddenly that the air was very chill.

"That house is unoccupied," I repeated shortly.

We all walked on in silence. But, through our silence, it certainly seemed to me that there came a sound of someone lamenting in the garden.

A day or two later Fraser said to me—

"Why is that old house shut up?"

"Who would occupy it?" I said. "Of course, if I could get a tenant—"

"I'll take it," he rejoined quickly. "You can let me some shooting with it, can't you?"

"But," I began; and then I stopped. I had an instinct to keep the old Manse empty, but I fought it, merely because it struck me as unreasonable. How seldom are our instincts unreasonable! God—how seldom!

"I've been looking out for a shooting-box," Hugh said. "That house would suit me admirably."

"All right," I answered. "I shall be very glad to have you for a tenant."

So it was arranged. When Kate heard of the arrangement, I observed her to go very pale; but she made no objection. Hugh Fraser rented the house, furnished it, engaged servants, a gardener, enlarged the stables, and took up his abode there. Doctor Wedderburn's old study was now his den. When I looked in at the window through which I had seen the doctor die, I saw Fraser smoking, or playing with his setters. I don't know why, but the sight turned me sick.

My relations with Kate, of which I have said nothing, were rather cold and distant. My passion, such as it was, had died before marriage. Hers seemed to languish afterwards. I believe that she had really loved me, but that the shame of being with me, after I had wedded her actually against my will, struck this sentiment to the dust. When one feeling that has been very strong dies, its place is generally filled by another. Sometimes I fancied that this was so with Kate, that the bitterness of shattered self-respect gradually transformed her nature, that a cruel frost bound the tendernesses, the warm vagaries of what had been a sweet woman's heart. But, to tell the truth, I did not trouble much about the matter. My affairs were prospering so greatly, my health was so abounding, I had so much beside the mere egotism of brilliant physical strength to occupy me, that I was heedless, reckless—at first. Yet, I had moments of a dull alarm connected with the dweller at the Manse.

If Hugh Fraser changed as he read that fateful letter in London, he changed far more after he came to live at the Manse. And it seemed to me that there were times when—how shall I put it? —when he bore a curious, and, to me, almost intolerable likeness to—someone who was dead. A certain old man's manner came upon him at moments. His body, in sitting or standing, assumed, to my eyes, elderly and damnable attitudes. Once, when I glanced in at the study window before entering the Manse, I perceived him lounging over a table facing me, a pen in his hand and paper before him, and the spectacle threw all my senses into a violent and most distressing disorder. Instead of going into the house, as I had intended, I struck sharply upon the glass at the window. Fraser looked up quickly.

"What—what are you writing?" I cried out.

He got up, came to the window, and opened it.

"Eh? What's the row, man?" he said. "Why don't you come in?"

I repeated my question, with an anxiety I strove to mask.

"Writing? Only a letter to town," he said, looking at me in wonder.

"Not a sermon?" I blurted forth.

"A sermon? Good heavens, no. Why should I write a sermon?"

"Oh," I replied, forcing an uneasy laugh. "You—you live in a Manse. Doctor Wedderburn used to write his sermons in that room."

That evening I remember that I said to Kate:

"Don't you think Fraser is getting to look very old at times?"

"I haven't observed it," she replied coldly.

Another curious thing. Very soon after he took up his abode in the Manse, Fraser, who had been a godly youth, became markedly averse to religion. He informed us, with some excitement, that he had changed his views, and seemed much inclined to carry on an atheistical propaganda among the devout people of the neighbourhood. He declared that much evil had been wrought by faith in Carlounie, and appeared to deem it as his special duty to preach some sort of a crusade against the accepted Christianity of the parish. I began to combat his views, and once sought the reason of his ardour and self-election to the post of teacher. His answer struck me exceedingly. He said—

"Why should I be the one to clear away these senseless beliefs in phantasms, you say? Why, because I suppose they were woven by my predecessor in the Manse. Didn't the minister live and die there? Do you know, Ralston, sometimes, as I sit in that study at night, I have a feeling that instead of turning to what is called repentance when he died, the minister turned the other way, recanted in his last hour the faith he had professed all through his life, and expired before he could give words to his new mind and heart. And then I feel as if his influence was left behind him in that room, and fell upon me and imposed on me this mission."

And as he spoke, he suddenly plucked at his face with an old, habitual action of Doctor Wedderburn's when excited. I scarcely restrained a cry, and with difficulty forced myself to go out slowly from his presence. Nevertheless, I felt strongly impelled to fight against the atheism of this boy, I who had formerly sown the seeds of destruction in the soul of Doctor Wedderburn. But it was as if my own act of the past rose and conquered me in the present. I declare solemnly it was so. Some emanation from the poor dead creature's soul clung round that cursed place of his doom, and, seizing upon the soul of Fraser, spread tyranny from its throne. And whom did it take first as its victim, think you? Kate, my wife.

Let our individual beliefs be what they may, one thing we must all—when we think—acknowledge, that the pulse which beats eternally in the heart of life is reparation.

Kate, as I have said, was originally finely pure and finely dowered with the blessings of faith in a divine Providence, trust in the eventual redemption of the world, hope that sin, sorrow, and sighing would, indeed, flee away, and all mankind find eternal and unutterable peace. In my worst moments I had never tried to destroy this beauty of her soul; and, in her fall, now repaired, she had never abandoned her religion. It was, I know, a haunting memory of the last moments of the doctor that held me back from ever attacking the faith of another. For myself, I did not think much of my future beyond death. Life filled my horizon then.

But now, after a short absence in England, during which I left Kate at Carlounie, I returned to find her infected with Fraser's pestilent notions. She declined to go to the kirk, declaring that it was better to act up to her real convictions than to set what is called a good example to her dependents. She and Fraser gloried openly in their new-found damnation. I say damnation, for this was actually how the matter struck me when I began carefully to consider it. Men often see only what irreligion really is and means when they find it existing in a woman. I was appalled at this deadly fire flaring up in the heart of Kate, and I set myself, at first feebly, at length determinedly, to quench it and stamp it out.

But I fought against my own former self. I fought against the influence of the spectre that surely haunted the Manse, and that spectre rose originally from the very bosom of the burn at my summons. Am I mad to think so? No, no. Oh, the eternal horror that may spring from one wild and lawless action, from the recital of one diabolic litany! This was surely the strangest, subtlest reparation that ever beat in the inexorable heart of Life. Hugh Fraser was enveloped by the influence, still retained mysteriously in his abode, of the soul that was gone to its account. Through him it seized upon Kate, and thus the mystic number was made up, three souls were bound and linked together. (I hear as I write the voice of the grey traveller by the burn in the twilight.) And in the first soul I had planted the seed of death, and so in the second and in the third. Now, thrusting as it were backward through Kate and Hugh Fraser, I fought with a dead man, long ago, perhaps, wrapped in pain unknown. But, as the influence of Doctor Wedderburn had formerly—before the fever—dominated my influence, so now it dominated my influence from the tomb. Indeed, this man whom I had destroyed had a drear revenge upon me. There had been an interregnum when the doctor wavered from Christianity to atheism. But that had ceased to be. He died undoubting, a blatant unbeliever. Hence, surely, his deadly power now. He returned, as it were, to slay me. The spectre at the Manse defied me.

Slowly I grew to feel, to know, all this. It did not come upon me in a moment; for sometimes my worldly affairs still occupied me. My glory of health and of strength still delighted me. I was as Faust—I was as Faust in his monstrous and damnable youth. But there came a time when the spectre at the Manse touched me with the hand of Hugh Fraser. And then I rose up to battle with it, trembling at the thought of the grey boy's words at the thought of the Cæsar of hell whose tribute was three human souls.

Kate and I were taking tea one evening with Fraser. We sat around the hearth, by which was placed the table with the tea service and the hot cakes. Fraser began, as was his habit now, to discuss religious subjects and to rail against the professors of faith. Kate listened to him eagerly—a filthy fire, so I thought, gleaming in her great eyes. I was silent, watching. And presently it seemed to me that Fraser's gestures in talking grew like the dead gestures of the doctor. He threw his hands abroad with the fingers divided in a manner of Wedderburn's. He struck his knees sharply, and simultaneously, with both his palms to emphasise his remarks, a frequent habit of the dead man's. So vehement was the similarity that I began presently to feel that the doctor himself declaimed in the firelight, and I was seized with a desire to combat effectively his wicked, but forcible arguments. I broke in, then, upon Fraser's tirade and cried the cause of religion. He turned upon me, dealt with my pleas, scattered my contentions—growing, I fancied, very old and with the rumbling voice of age—thrust at me with the lances of sarcasm, sore belaboured me into silence and mute fury. And all the time Kate sat by, and I seemed to see her soul, with fluttering outstretched wings, sinking down to hell, as a hawk drops out of sight into a dark cleft of the mountains. And then, in the last resort, Fraser struck his hand down on mine to clinch his defeat of me. And I, looking upon that poor Kate, cried out—

"God forgive you, Fraser, for what you're doing—murderer! murderer!"

Scarcely had my cry died away than I knew I had borrowed the very words of Wedderburn to me. A cold, like ice, came upon me. This reversal of the past in the present was too ironic. I heard the doctor chuckling drearily in Hades. I suddenly sprang up like one pursued, and got away into the night, leaving Kate and Fraser together by the fire. But the spectre of the Manse surely pursued me. I heard its soft but heavy footsteps coming in my wake. I heard its old laughter in the dark behind me; and I sickened and faltered, and was in fear beyond all human fear of an enemy.

The next day I told Fraser he must leave the Manse; I would build him a shooting-lodge on any part of my estate that he preferred.

"No," he said, "no; I have grown to love the old place; I never feel alone there."

I looked in his eyes, searching after his meaning.

"I would rather pull down the Manse," I said.

In reply, he touched with his forefinger the lease I had signed with him, which lay on his writing table.

"You cannot, my friend," he said.

I cannot do anything that I would. I am driven on a dark road by the creature with the whip that is surely after every man who once yields to his worst desires.

Just after this I received a visit from Mr. Mackenzie, the new minister, a young and fervent, but not very knowledgeable man, whose zeal was red-hot, but incompetent, and who would have died for the faith he could never properly expound, like many young ministers of our church. The little man was in a twisting turmoil of distress, and was moved, so he said, to deal very plainly with me. I bade him deal on. It seemed that his flock was becoming infected with atheism, which spread like the plague, from the old Manse. The young children lisped it to each other in the lanes; lovers talked it between their kisses; youths chattered perdition at the idle corner by the church wall. Even the old began to look askance at the Bible that had been their only book of age, and to shiver wantonly at the inevitable approach of death. The young minister cried denunciation upon Fraser, like a vague-minded, but angry Jonah before a provincial Nineveh.

"Turn him out, Mr. Ralston, drive him forth," he ejaculated. "What is his rent to you? What is his money in comparison with the immortal souls of men? Away with him, away with him."

I mentioned the small matter of the lease. The young minister, with a quivering scarlet face, replied stammering—

"A lease! But—but—your own wife—she is—is—"

"I do not discuss her," I said sternly.

"Well; they are deserting the services. You see that yourself. They will not come to hear me preach. They will not listen to me."

The man was tasting bitterness. He was almost crying. I was terribly sorry for him. Yet, all I could do was to think of the spectre at the Manse and answer—

"I can do nothing."

His words were true. Carlounie's soul was being devoured as by a plague. A colony of unbelievers was springing up in the midst of the beautiful woods and the mountains. Soon the evil fame of the place began to spread abroad, and men, in distant parts of Scotland, to speak of mad Carlounie. The matter weighed intolerably upon me, and at last became a fixed idea. I could think of nothing else but this devil's home in the hills, this haunted and harassed centre of doom and darkness which was my possession and in which I lived. I fell into silence. I ceased to stir abroad beyond my own land. It seemed to me that Carlounie should keep strict quarantine, should be isolated, and that each person who went over its borders carried a strange infection and was guilty of murder. I forbade Kate to drive beyond my estates.

"I never wish to," she said.

And I knew that where Fraser was she was happy. He had her soul fast by this; or, it would be truer to say, the spectre of the Manse had both him and her. And he aged apace and bore on his countenance the stamp of evil. And I brooded and brooded upon the whole matter. But, from whatever point I started, I came back to the Manse and to the spectre dwelling in it with Hugh Fraser. I had given death to Doctor Wedderburn, in return for the life so miraculously given to me, and now his spirit, retained in its ancient abiding-place, spread death about it in its turn. This was, and is, my conviction. The influence of the departed clings to roof, to walls, to floors, leans on the accustomed window-seat, trembles by the bed-head, sits by the hearthstone, stands invisible in the passage way. *To kill it one must destroy its home.* It was my duty to kill it, therefore it was my duty to destroy the Manse. This thought at length took complete possession of me, and, following it, I strove in every imaginable way to oust Fraser from the house among the sycamores. But he would not go. He loved the place, he said. He stood by his lease and I was powerless.

Oh, God, I have, surely I have, my excuse for what I have done! I meant to be a saviour, not a destroyer! I would have restored Fraser and my poor Kate to their freedom of heart. That was what I meant. Ay, but the grey traveller fought against me. Shut up here by night in my house, on the verge of—that which I cannot, dare not speak of, I declare that I am guiltless. Let him bear the burden, him alone! In these last moments, before my deed is known, I write the truth that men may exonerate me. This is the truth.

Overwhelmed with this idea that Carlounie must be rescued, that Hugh Fraser and Kate must be rescued from this damnation that was preying upon them, I determined, secretly, on the destruction of the Manse, in which the spectre of the doctor stayed to work such evil. But, to do this, I must first make sure that Hugh Fraser was at a distance, and that his small household—he only kept two servants, hired from the village—were away from the haunted dwelling. I, therefore, suggested to Fraser that he should come and spend a week with me, and give his maids a holiday. After a little demur, and drawn, I see now, by his hidden passion for Kate, he accepted my invitation. He dismissed the maids to their homes for a week, and moved over to us. When the minister knew of it, he, no doubt, fully included me in his prayers for the damnation of those who worked evil among his flock. Will he ever read these pages, I wonder? Kate was now an avowed atheist, and she and Fraser were continually together, glorying in their complete freedom from old prejudices, and their new outlook upon life. They had, I heard them say, broken through the ties that bound poor, terrified Christians; and, when they said this, they smiled, the one upon the other. I did not then know why. Meanwhile, I was preparing for my deed of redemption, as I called it, and meant it to be. I was resolved to go out by night to the empty Manse, and secretly to set it in flames. It stood alone. The country people slept sound at night. I calculated that if I chose midnight for my act none would see the flames, and, ere the peasants woke at dawn, the Manse and the spectre within it would be destroyed forever. Such was my belief—such the spirit in which I prepared myself for this strange work.

V

The Return of the Grey Traveller

I write these last words after the dead of night, towards the coming of the dawn. Ere the light is grey in the sky I shall be away to the burn to meet him, the grey traveller. He is there waiting for me. He has come back. I go to meet him, and I shall never return. Carlounie will know my face no more. All is done as he ordained. My words have been as deeds, have marched on inevitably to actual deeds. Long ago he said that sometimes, even as we can never go back from things that we have done, we can never go back from things that we have said. So, indeed, it is.

According to my fixed intention, I determined on a night for the destruction of the Manse. The house was old and would burn like tinder. I should break into it through the window of the study, which was never shuttered. I should set fire to the interior at several points, and escape in the darkness of the night. By dawn the accursed place would be a ruin, and then—then I looked for a new era. Fool! Fool! I looked to see the burden of the vile influence of the spectre lifted from the soul of Fraser, and so from the soul of Kate, which was infected by him. I looked to see my people sane and satisfied as of old, Carlounie no more a plague-spot in the land, that poor and zealous man, the minister, calm and at rest with his little faithful flock once more. All this I looked for confidently. And so, when the black and starless night of my deed came, I was happy and serene. That night Kate pleaded a headache, and went to bed very early, before nine. She begged me not to come to her room to bid her good-night, as she wanted perfect quiet and sleep. All unsuspecting, I agreed to her request. Soon after she had gone, Fraser, who had seemed heavy with unusual fatigue all through the evening, also went off to bed, and I was left alone. But it was not yet time for me to start on my errand of the darkness. The burning Manse would surely attract attention before midnight. People might be out and about in the village. A belated peasant might be on his way home by the lane that skirted the privet hedge. I must wait till all were sleeping. The time seemed very long. Once I fancied I heard a movement in the house—again I dreamed that soft and hurried footsteps upon the gravel outside broke on the silence. But I said to myself that I was nervous, highly strung because of my strange project, that my imagination tricked me. At last the hour came. Without going upstairs I drew on my thickest overcoat, took my hat and a heavy stick, opened the hall door, and passed out into the night. It was still and very cold, and the voice of the burn came loudly to my ears. Treading quietly, I made my way into the road, and set forth along it in the direction of the Manse. The ground was hard, and scarcely had I gone a few yards before I thought that someone was furtively following me. I stopped rather uneasily, and listened, but heard nothing. I went on, and again seemed aware of distant footsteps treading gently behind me. The sound made me suppose that some one of my household must be after me, moved by curiosity as to the reason of my present pilgrimage; but I was not minded to be watched, so I turned sharply, yet very softly, around and faced the way I had come. I encountered no one, nor did I any longer catch the patter of feet. So, reckoning that my nerves must be playing with me, I pursued my way. But the whole of the distance between my dwelling and the Manse I seemed vaguely to hear a noise of one treading behind me. And, although I said to myself that there was nobody out beside myself, I was filled with the stir of a shifting uneasiness. I entered the lonely and narrow lane that led beside the Manse, and presently arrived in front of the house; when, what was my astonishment to perceive a light gleaming in the study window. My hand was on the gate when it went out, and all the front of the house was black and eyeless. For so brief a moment had I seen the light that I was moved to think that it, too, existed, like the sound of steps, only in my excited brain. Nevertheless, I did not go up at once to the house, but paced the lane for a full half-hour, always—so it seemed to me—tracked by someone. But, since I kept turning about, and the footfalls were always at my back, I grew certain that they were nothing more nor less than a fantasy on my part. It must have been well after twelve when I summoned courage to enter the garden and to approach the Manse. The steps, I thought, followed me to the gate and then paused, as if a sentinel was posted there to keep watch. Arrived at the stone step which preceded the hall door, I, too, paused in my turn and listened. Did the spectre that inhabited this abode know of my coming, of my purpose? Was it crouching within, like some frantic shadow, fearful of its impending fate? Or was it, perhaps, preparing to attack, to repel me? Strangely, I had now no fear of it, or of anything. I was calm. I felt that my deed was one of rescue, even though, by performing it, I wrought destruction. I moved to the study window, and was about to smash in the glass with my heavy stick when a mad idea came to me to try the hall door. I put my hand upon it and found it not locked. This opening of the door sent a shiver through me, and a ghastly sense of the occupation of this deserted abode. I was filled again with an acute consciousness of the indwelling spectre, whom, in truth, I came to murder. But, I reasoned, this door has been left unbarred by the carelessness of Fraser's servants, that is all.

I stood on the lintel, struck a match and set it to a candle end which I drew from my coat pocket. The flame burned up, showing the narrow passage, the umbrella stand, the doors on either side. I entered the study softly, looking swiftly on all sides of me as I did so. Did I expect a vision of Doctor Wedderburn lounging at the table, his fingers thrust into a Bible? I scarcely know; but I saw nothing except the grimly standing furniture, the lamp on the table, the vacant chairs, the books in their shelves. I listened. There was no rustle of the spectre that I came to kill. Did it watch me? Did it see me there? I set fire to the room, passed quickly to the chamber on the other side of the passage, from thence to the kitchen and the dining parlour, leaving a track of dwarf flames behind me. The means of destruction I had prepared and carried with me. They availed. When I once more reached the garden, the ground floor of the Manse was in a blaze. But now came the incredible event which I must chronicle before I go down to the burn for the last time.

Having gained the garden, I waited there in the darkness to watch my work progress. I saw the light within the Manse, at first a twinkle, grow to a glare. I heard the faint crackle of the burning rooms increase to a soft and continuous roar. And, as I watched and listened, a mighty sense of relief ran through me. Thus did I burn up my past! thus did I sacrifice grandly and gladly the ill spirit my wild desires had evoked! Thus—thus! All the base of the Manse was red-hot, when, on a sudden, I heard a great shout that seemed to come from the sky. Light sprang in an upper window. There followed a sound like the smash of glass, and I saw two arms shoot out, the top part of a figure and a face framed in the glare. I deemed it the vision of the poor spectre that I destroyed. I looked upon it and fancied I could detect the tortured lineaments of the doctor, his accustomed gestures distorted by fear and fury. But then I seemed to see behind him another figure, struggling, and to hear the failing scream of a woman. But the flames from below leaped to the roof. The floors fell in with an uproar. The figure, or figures, disappeared.

Trembling I turned to go, my mind shuddering at the thought of the apparition I had seen. I got into the lane and hastened towards home. Soon the burning Manse was out of sight, and I was swallowed up in the intense darkness.

Now, as I went along, a terrible and very peculiar sensation came upon me. I heard no footsteps; all was silence. Yet I seemed to be aware that I was closely companioned, that at my very side something—I knew not what—walked, keeping pace with me. And so close did I believe this thing to be, that at moments I even felt it pressing against me like a slim figure in the night. Once, when it thus nestled to me, as if in affection, I could not refrain from crying out aloud. I stretched forth my arms to grasp this surely amorous horror of the darkness, but found nothing, and pursued my road in a sweat of apprehension. And still, the thing was certainly with me, and seemed, I thought, to praise me as I walked, as the good man is praised on his journey. My great horror was that this creature that I could not see, could not hear, could not feel, and yet was so sharply conscious of, was *well disposed towards me*. My heart craved its hatred—but it loved me I knew. My soul demanded its curses. I almost heard it bless me as I moved. My knees knocked together, my limbs were turned to wax, as it was borne in upon me that I had surely done this terror that walked in darkness a service of some kind. To be pursued in fury by one of the dreadful beings that dwell in the borderland beyond our sight is sad and dreary; but to be followed thus by one as by a dog, to be fawned upon and caressed—this is appalling. I longed to shriek aloud. I broke into a run, and, like one demented, gained the gate of Carlounie; but always the thing was with me—full of joy and laudation. At the house door I paused, facing round. I was moved to address this thing I could not see.

"Who is it that walks with me?" I cried, and my voice was high and strained.

A voice I knew, young, clear, level, a little formal, answered out of the darkness—

"It is I."

It was the voice of the grey traveller whom I had seen long ago by the burnside. I leaned back against the door and my shoulders shook against it.

"What do you want of me?"

"I come to thank you."

"What, then, have I done?"

"You have brought the tribute money."

I did not understand, and I answered—

"No. One soul I may have destroyed, but two I have saved to-night. For I have slain the spectre that preyed upon them and I have set them free from bondage."

The voice answered—

"*Go into the house and see.*"

Then again I was filled with apprehension. I turned to go in at my door, and, as I did so, I heard footsteps treading in the direction of the burn, and a fading voice which cried, like an echo—

"And then come to me."

And, as the voice died, I heard the rush of sheep in the night.

Filled with nameless fear and a cold apprehension, I entered the house, and, led by some cruel instinct, made my way to Kate's room. The lamp she always had at night burned dimly on the dressing table and cast a grave radiance upon an empty bed.

What could this mean?

I stole to the room of Fraser, bearing the lamp with me. His chamber was also untenanted; but, on the quilt of the bed, lay a piece of paper written over. I took it up and read—with the sound of the burn in my ears—

> "You stole her from me. I take back my own. To-night we stay at the old Manse. To-morrow we shall be far away.
> HUGH FRASER."

The paper dropped from my hand upon the quilt. A woman's scream rang in my ears above the roar of flames. I understood.

The tribute money has been paid. I go down to the burn. The grey traveller is waiting there for me.

The Spinster

I had arrived at Inley Abbey that afternoon, and was sitting at dinner with Inley and his pretty wife, whom I had not seen for five years, since the day I was his best man, when we all heard faintly the tolling of a church bell. Lady Inley shook her shoulders in a rather exaggerated shudder.

"Someone dead!" said her husband.

"It's a mistake to build a church in the grounds of a house," Lady Inley said in her clear, drawling soprano voice. "That noise gives me the blues."

"Whom can it be for?" asked Inley.

"Miss Bassett, probably," Lady Inley replied carelessly, helping herself to a bonbon from a little silver dish.

Inley started.

"Miss Sarah Bassett! What makes you think so?"

"Oh, while you were away in town she got ill. Didn't you know?"

"No," said Inley.

I could see that he was moved. His dark, short face had changed suddenly, and he stopped eating his fruit. Lady Inley went on crunching the bonbon between her little white teeth with all the enjoyment of a pretty marmoset.

"Influenza," she said airily. "And then pneumonia. Of course, at her age, you know— By the way, what is her age, Nino?"

"No idea," said Inley shortly.

He was listening to the dim and monotonous sound of the church bell.

Lady Inley turned to me with the childish, confidential movement which men considered one of her many charms.

"Miss Bassett is, or was, one of those funny old spinsters who always look the same and always ridiculous. Dry twigs, you know. One size all the way down. Very little hair, and no emotions. If it weren't for the sake of cats, one would wonder why such people are born. But they're always cat lovers. I suppose that's why they're so often called old cats."

She uttered a little high-pitched laugh, and got up.

"Don't be too long," she said to me carelessly as I opened the dining room door for her. "I want to sing 'Ohé Charmette' to you."

"I won't be long," I answered, thinking what exquisite eyes she had.

She turned, and went out in her delicious, thin way. No wonder she had made skeletons the rage in London. When I came back to the dinner table Inley was sitting with both his brown hands clenched on the cloth.

His black eyes—inherited from his dead mother, who had been one of the Neapolitan aristocracy—were glittering.

"What is it, Nino?" I asked as I sat down. We had been such intimate friends that even my five years' absence abroad had not built up a barrier between us.

"I wonder if it is Miss Bassett?" he said, looking at me earnestly.

"But was she a great friend of yours?" I said. "If Lady Inley's description of her is accurate, I can hardly imagine so."

"Vere doesn't know what she's saying."

"Then Miss Bassett—"

"Oh, she does look like that; dried up, unemotional, tame, English, even comic."

"The regular spinster, eh?"

"She looks it. But, damn it all, Vere has no business to say she has no emotions, to wonder why such people are born. But she doesn't know—Vere doesn't know."

His agitation grew, and was inexplicable to me. But I knew Inley, knew that he was bound to tell me what was on his mind. He could be reserved, but not with me. So I took a cigar, cut the end off it deliberately, struck a match, lighted it, and began to smoke in silence. He followed my example quickly, and then said:

"Vere talks like that, and, but for Miss Bassett, Vere would have been murdered two years ago."

I started, and dropped my cigar on the table.

"Murdered!"

"Yes; and I—"

He fixed his eyes on me, and put his hand up to his throat. Nino was half Neapolitan, and I saw a man being hanged. I picked up my cigar with a hand that slightly shook.

"But," I said, "I always thought Lady Inley and you were very happy together."

It sounded banal, even ridiculous, but I hardly knew what to say. I was startled. The tolling of the bell, too, was getting on my nerves.

"One doesn't write such things," he said. "You've been abroad for years."

"It's all right now?"

He nodded.

"I suppose so. Vere has never had the least suspicion."

He drew his chair closer to mine, and was about to go on speaking when the servants came in with the coffee.

"Who's the bell tolling for, Hurst?" he said to the butler.

"I couldn't say, my lord."

When the servants had gone Inley continued, at first in a calmer voice:

"Miss Bassett lived in the red cottage just beyond the gate of the South Lodge from time immemorial. You generally came to us in Scotland, I know, but I should think you must have seen her."

Suddenly a recollection flashed upon me—a recollection of a long, flat figure, a drab face, thin hair coming away from a wrinkled forehead under a mushroom hat, flapping, old-fashioned golden earrings.

"Not the person I used to call 'the Plank'?" I said.

"Did you?"

He thought for a moment.

"Yes; I believe you did. I'd forgotten."

"She was always in church twenty minutes before the service began, and always dropped her hymn book coming out if there were visitors in the Abbey pew!"

"Yes, yes; that's it. Miss Bassett is very nervous in little ways."

"I remember her now perfectly. And you say she—"

I looked at him, and hesitated.

"She saved Vere's life and, indirectly, mine. I'll tell you now we're together again at last. I shall never tell Vere."

He looked towards the windows, across which dark blue silk curtains were drawn, as if he could see the passing-bell swinging in the old square tower. Then he turned to me.

"You know how mad I was about Vere. It's always like that with me. Unless I'm stone I'm fire. After we were married I got even madder. Having her all to myself was like enchantment, and in Italy, too, my other native land."

I thought of Lady Inley's eyes.

"I can understand," I said.

"Of course, when we got back it had to be different. Friends came in, and she was run after and admired and written about. You know the publicity of life in modern London."

"City of public houses and society spies."

"I bore it, because it's supposed to be the thing. And Vere rather likes it, somehow. So I let her have her fun, as long as it was fun. I didn't intend it should ever be anything else."

He frowned. When he did that, and his thick eyebrows nearly met, he looked all Italian.

"We did the usual things—Paris, Ascot, Scotland, and so on—till Vere had to lie up."

"Your boy?"

"Yes; Hugo came along. I was glad when that was over. I thought she was going to die. You knew Seymour Glynd?"

"Life Guards? Killed hunting a year ago?"

Inley nodded.

"He was a great deal with us soon after Hugo's birth. I thought nothing of it. I'd known the fellow all my life. But then one nearly always has."

He laughed bitterly.

"To cut that part short, two years ago in autumn we had Glynd staying with us down here for shooting. There were some others, of course—Mrs. Jack, Bobbie Elphinton, and Lady Bobbie—but you know the lot."

"I did."

"Ah," he said, "you've been well out of it these years. Well, the shoot was to break up on a Friday, and I'd arranged to go to town that day with the rest. Vere didn't intend to come. She said she was feeling tired, and was going to have a Friday to Monday rest cure. That's the thing, you know, nowadays. You get a Swedish *masseuse* down to stay, and go to bed and drink milk. Vere had engaged a *masseuse* to come on the Friday night. On the Thursday, the day before we were all going to town, Glynd hurt his foot getting over a fence into a turnip field—at least I thought so."

He stopped.

"Everyone thought so, I believe—except, of course, Vere. I wonder if they did, though?" he added moodily. "Or whether I was the only— But what does it matter now? Glynd said he only wanted a couple of days' rest to be all right again, and asked me if he might stay on at the Abbey till the Monday. Of course I said 'Yes; if he wouldn't want a hostess.' Because Vere said to me, when she heard of it, that she must have her rest cure all the same. Glynd swore he'd be quite happy alone. So he stayed, and the rest of us came up to town on the Friday. Well, on the Saturday morning I was walking across the park when I met the Swedish *masseuse* who was to have gone down to Vere on the Friday night. I knew her, because Vere had often had her before in London. 'Hullo!' I said. 'You ought to be down at Inley Abbey with my wife.' 'No, my lord,' she said. 'Why not?' 'I've had a wire from Lady Inley not to go.' 'A wire!' I said. 'When did you get it?' 'On Thursday night, my lord.' 'You mean last night?' I said, thinking Vere must have changed her mind after we had left. 'No,' said the woman; 'on Thursday night, late.' Then I remembered that, after Glynd had hurt his foot and asked to stay, Vere had gone out alone for a drive in her cart, to get a last breath of air before the rest cure. She must have sent the telegram herself then. All of a sudden I seemed to understand a lot of things."

He had let his cigar out, and now he noticed that he had. He tossed it into the fire.

"I said 'Good-morning' to the woman quite quietly, went back to the house, and told my man I shouldn't be at home that night."

He put his hand on my arm.

"I felt perfectly calm. Wasn't that strange?"

I nodded. "There was a train from town reaching Ashdridge Station at nine o'clock at night. I took it. I didn't care to go to Inley Station, where everybody would know me, and wonder what I was up to. I didn't take any luggage. My man asked if he should pack, and I said 'No.' I didn't dine. I was at Paddington three-quarters of an hour before the train was due to start. At last it came in to the platform. Going down I read the evening papers just like any man going home from business. Soon after we got away from London I saw there was rain on the carriage windows. That seemed to me right. We were a little late at Ashdridge. It was still wet, and I had my coat collar turned up. I don't believe they recognised me there. I set out to walk to Inley."

"What did you mean to do?"

"I told you before."

I looked into his face, and believed him. Then I thought of Lady Inley's childish, delicate beauty, of her slightly affected manner, the manner of a woman who has always been spoilt, whose paths have been made very smooth. And here she was living, apparently happily, with a man who had deliberately travelled down in the night to kill her. How ignorant we are!

"You are condemning me," Inley said, with a touch of hot anger.

"I was only thinking—"

"Yes?"

"That we don't know each other much in the greatest intimacy."

"That's what I thought then."

He said that in a way which suddenly put me on his side. He must have seen the change in my feelings, for he went on, with his former unreserve:

"I walked fast in the dark. I didn't think very much, but I remember that all the trees—there's a lot of woodland, you know, between Ashdridge and Inley—seemed alive. Everything seemed to me to be alive that night. I've never had that sensation before or since."

I realised what the condition of the man had been when he said that, as if I were a doctor and a patient had told me the symptom which put me in possession of his malady.

"When I reached Inley it was late, and the long village street was deserted. There were lights in the inn and in the schoolmaster's house, but there were no people about. I got through without meeting a soul, and came on towards the gates of the Abbey."

"You meant to go into the house?"

"Yes. I was sure—somehow I was sure; but I intended to see before I acted, merely for my own justification. But I was quite sure, as if Vere herself had told me everything. Soon after I had got clear of the village I heard a sound of wheels behind me. I stood up against the hedge, and in a minute or two a fly passed me going slowly. I saw the driver's face. It wasn't a man from Inley. Evidently the fly had come from a distance. It was splashed with mud, and the horse looked tired. I followed it till it came to the turning just below Miss Bassett's cottage, where there's a narrow lane going to Charfield through the woods. It went a little way down this lane, and stopped. I waited at the turning. I could see the light from the lamps shining on the wet road, and in the circle of light the driver's breath. He bent down, and I saw him looking at a big silver watch. Then he put it back. But he didn't drive on. I knew what he was waiting for. Vere was going with—with Glynd. That was more than I had ever thought of, that she would go. I put my hand into my pocket, took out my revolver, and went on till I was close to the red cottage. By this time the rain had stopped. I came up to within a few yards of the Abbey gates, stood for a moment, and then returned till I was at the wicket of Miss Bassett's garden. It's bounded by a yew hedge, beyond which there is a path shaded by mulberry trees. The hedge is low. The path is dark. It was a blackguardly thing to do, but I thought of nothing except myself, my wrong, and how I was to wipe it out. I opened the wicket, came into the path, and stood there under the mulberry trees behind the hedge. Here I was in cover, and could see the road. I held my revolver in my hand, and waited. It never struck me that Miss Bassett might be up. I saw no light in the cottage, and I had a sort of idea that people like her went to bed at about eight. While I was standing there listening I felt something rub against my legs. It made me start. Then I heard a little low noise. I looked down, and there was a great cat holding up its tail and purring. Its pleasure was horrible to me. I pushed it away with my foot, but it came back, bending down its head, arching its back, and pressing against me. I was thinking what to do to get rid of it when I heard a shrill, husky voice call out:

"'Johnny—John-nee!'

"It was Miss Bassett. I held my breath, and pushed away the cat.

"'Johnny, Johnny—John-nee!' went the voice again.

"The cat wouldn't leave me. God knows why it wished to stay. I was determined to get rid of it, so I put the revolver down on the path, picked the cat up in my arms, and dropped it over the hedge into the road. Just as I had caught up the revolver again I was confronted by Miss Bassett.

She had come in slippers up the path in the dark to look for her cat."

I uttered a slight exclamation.

Inley went on: "She had a handkerchief tied over her cap and under her chin, and a small lantern in her hands, on which she wore black mittens. I can see her now. We stood there on the path for a minute staring at each other without a word. The light from the lantern flickered over the revolver, and I saw Miss Bassett look down at it."

He stopped, poured out a glass of water, and drank it off like a man who has been running.

"Didn't she show surprise—fear?" I asked.

"Not a bit. Women are so extraordinary, even old women who've never been in touch with life, that I'm certain now she understood directly her eyes fell on the revolver."

"What did she do?"

"After a minute she said: 'Lord Inley, I'm looking for my cat. Have you seen him?'

"'Yes, I said; 'he's run into the house.'

"It was a lie, but I wanted her to go in. I had slipped the revolver back into my pocket, and tried to assume a perfectly simple, natural air. I fancied it would be very easy to impose on Miss Bassett when I heard her question. It sounded so innocent, as if the old lady was full of her pet. I even thought, perhaps, she had not known what the revolver was when she looked at it.

"'Did he run into the house?' she said, still looking at me from under her wrinkled eyelids.

"'Yes; when you came out. He was here on the path with me. You called "Johnny!" and he ran off there between the mulberry trees.'

"All the time I was speaking to her I had an eye to the road, and my ears were listening like an Indian's when he puts his head to the ground to hear the pad of his enemy.

"Miss Bassett stood there quietly for a moment as if she were considering something. She looked prim. I remember that even now—prim as a caricature. It was only a moment, but it seemed to me an hour. 'If they should come,' I thought, 'while she is out here!' The sweat came out all over my face with impatience—an agony of impatience. I longed to take the old lady by the shoulders, push her into the cottage, lock her in, and be alone, able to watch the bit of road from the Abbey gates to the wicket. But I could do nothing. I was obliged to repress every sign of agitation. It was devilish."

He got up with a sudden jerk from his chair, and stood by the fire. Even the telling of that moment had set beads of moisture on his square, low forehead.

At last she spoke again.

"'I wonder if you'd mind coming in for a minute to help me see if Johnny really is in the house?' she said.

"I don't know what I should have done—refused, I believe, refused her with an oath, for I began to feel mad; but just at that instant up came the cat once more, purring like fury, and lifting up his tail. He made straight for me, and began to rub himself against my legs again.

"'Oh!' said Miss Bassett, 'there he is! Naughty Johnny, naughty boy! Lord Inley, perhaps you'd be so good as just to lift him up and put him inside the door for me. I always have such a job to get him to come in of a night. He likes hunting in the woods. Doesn't he, the naughty Johnny?'

"'Now's my chance to get rid of her!' I thought.

"I bent down, picked the cat up, and went along the path towards the cottage, Miss Bassett following close behind me. The cat was an immense beast, awfully heavy, and just as I turned out of the yew path to go up to the cottage door he began struggling to get away, and scratching. I held on to him, but it wasn't easy, and I got my hand torn before I dropped him down inside the little hall. Away he ran, towards the kitchen, I suppose. Miss Bassett was very grateful, but I cut her gratitude short.

"'Very glad to have been able to help you,' I said. 'Good-night.'

"'Good-night, Lord Inley,' she said.

"I thought her voice sounded a little bit odd when she said that, and I just glanced at her funny old face, lit up by the lantern she was holding in one mittened hand. She didn't look at me this time as she had in the garden. Then I went out, and she immediately shut the door.

"'Thank God!' I thought, and I hurried to the wicket. I didn't dare stay in the garden now. Seeing her had made me realise my blackguardism in coming in at all, considering my reason. I resolved to hide in the field at the corner where the road turns off to Charfield. As I opened the wicket, instinctively I put my hand into my pocket for my revolver."

He bent down, looking full into my eyes. "It wasn't there."

"Miss Bassett!" I exclaimed.

"In a moment I realised that Miss Bassett must have grasped the situation; that her asking me to carry in her cat was a ruse, and that while the beast was struggling between my hands she must have stolen the revolver from behind. I say I knew that, and yet even then, when I thought of her look, her manner, the sort of nervous old thing she was, I couldn't believe what I knew. Then I remembered her voice when she said 'Good-night' to me in the passage, her eyes looking down instead of at me, and that she was only holding the lantern in one hand, whereas in the garden she was using two. She must have had the revolver in her other hand concealed in the folds of her dress. I ran back to the cottage door, and knocked hard. Not that I thought she'd open. I knew she wouldn't, but she did directly. I could hardly speak. I was afraid of myself just then. At last I said:

"'Miss Bassett, you know what I want.'

"'You can't have it,' she said, looking straight at me.

"I kept quiet for a second, then I said:

"'Miss Bassett, I don't think you know that you're running into danger.' For I felt that there was danger for her then if she went against me. She knew it, too, perhaps better than I did. I saw her poor old hands, all blue veins, beginning to tremble.

"'You can't have it, Lord Inley,' she repeated.

"There wasn't the ghost of a quiver in her voice.

"'I must, I will!' I said, and I made a movement towards her—a violent movement I know it was.

"But the old thing stood her ground. Oh, she was a gallant old woman.

"'Do what you like to me,' she said. 'I'm old. What does it matter? She's young.'

"Then I knew she understood.

"'You've seen them together!' I said. 'Since I went!'

"She wouldn't say. Not a word. I was mad. I forgot decency, everything. I took her. I searched her for the revolver. I searched her roughly—God forgive me. She trembled horribly, but never said a word. It wasn't on her. She must have hidden it somewhere in that moment when she was alone in the cottage. That was another ruse to keep me searching in there while— But I saw it almost directly. I broke away, and rushed out and down the road. Something seemed to tell me they had passed. I got into the lane that leads to Charfield. The fly was gone. Then, all of a sudden, I felt perfectly calm. I turned, and went up to the Abbey gates. I knocked them up at the lodge. The keeper came out. When he saw me he said:

"'You, my lord! However did you know?'

"'Go on!' I said. 'Know what?'

"'About Master Hugo?'

"I didn't say one way or the other.

"'The doctor says it's a bitter bad quinsy, but there's just a chance. Her ladyship's nearly mad. It only came on a few hours ago quite sudden.'

"I went up to the Abbey, and found Vere by the child's bed. She looked flushed, and was breathing hard, as if she had just been running."

He stopped, and took out his cigar case.

"Running!" I said.

"She had parted finally from Glynd in front of Miss Bassett's cottage," he said. "He told me that afterwards."

There was a moment's silence. Then he spoke more calmly.

"I went up to town when the child was safe, and had it out with Glynd. They had meant to go that night. It was the boy who stopped her. She took it as a judgment. You know how women are. Glynd swore she was stopped in time. You understand?"

"Yes."

"He didn't lie to me."

"And your wife?"

"I never spoke of it to her. I saw her with the boy, and—well, I saw her with the boy, and what she was to him when he was close to death."

His voice went for a moment. Then he added:

"I told her I'd had a presentiment Hugo was ill. She believed me, I think. If not, she's kept her secret."

Just then the dining room door opened, and Lady Inley put in her pretty head.

"Are you never coming?" she said with her little childish drawl.

I got up, and went towards her.

"By the way, Nino," she added, "the bell was for poor, funny old Miss Bassett. What will her cat do, I wonder?"

As I followed her towards the drawing room I heard Inley's voice mutter behind me:

"*Requiescat in Pace.*"

The Lady and the Beggar

Nothing in life is more rare than the conversion of a person who is "close" about money into one generous, open-handed and lavish. The sparrow will sooner become the peacock than the miser the spendthrift. And if this is so, if such a transformation seldom occurs in life, it is even more unusual for a man or woman to leave behind in dying a manifesto which contradicts in set terms the obvious and universally recognised tendency of their whole existence. Naturally, therefore, the provisions of Mrs. Errington's will surprised the world. Old gentlemen in Clubs stared upon the number of the *Illustrated London News* which announced the disposal of her money as they might have stared upon the head of Medusa. The fidgety seemed turned to stone as they read. The thoughtless gaped. As for the thoughtful, this will drove them to deep meditation, and set them walking in a maze of surmises, from which they found no outlet. One or two, religiously inclined, recalled that saying concerning the rich individual and the passage of a camel through a needle's eye. Possibly it had come home to Mrs. Errington upon her deathbed. Possibly, as her end drew near she had perceived herself tower to camel size, the entrance to Paradise shrink to the circumference which refuses to receive a thread manipulated by an unsteady hand. Yes, yes; they began to expand in unctuous conjecture that merged into deliberate assertion, when someone remarked that Mrs. Errington had died in exactly three minutes of the rupture of a blood vessel on the brain. So this comfortable theory was exploded. And no other seemed tenable. No other explained the fact that this wealthy woman, notorious during her life for her miserly disposition, her neglect of charity, her curious hatred of the poor and complete emancipation from the tender shackles of philanthropy, bequeathed at death the greater part of her fortune to the destitute of London, and to the honest beggars whom fate persistently castigates, whom even Labour declines to accept as toilers at the meanest wage.

Only Horace Errington, the dead woman's sole child, and Captain Hindford, of the Life Guards, exactly knew the truth of the matter. And this truth was so strange, and must have seemed so definite a lie to the majority of mankind, that it was never given to the world. Not even the rescued poor who found themselves received into the Errington Home as into some heaven with four beautiful walls, knew why there had sprung up such a home and why they were in it. The whole affair was discussed ardently at the time, argued about, contested, and dropped. Mystery veiled it. Like many things that happen, it remained an inexplicable enigma to the world. And finally, the world forgot it. But Horace Errington remembered it, more especially when he heard lighthearted people merrily laughing at certain strange shadows of things unseen which will, at times, intrude into the most frivolous societies, turning the meditative to thoughts deep as dark and silent-flowing rivers, the careless to frisky sneers and the gibes which fly forth in flocks from the dense undergrowths of ignorance.

The Erringtons were magnets, and irresistibly attracted gold instead of steel. Mr. Errington died comparatively young, overwhelmed by the benefits showered upon him by Fortune, which continued to dog persistently the steps of his widow, whom he left with one child, Horace. This boy was destined by his father's will to be a millionaire, and had no need of any money from his mother, so that, eventually, Mrs. Errington did him no wrong by the bequest which so troubled the curious. She was a brilliant and an attractive woman, sparkling as a diamond, and apparently as hard. That she loved Horace there was no doubt, and he had adored her. Yet he could not influence her as most only sons can influence their mothers. She was liberally gifted with powers of resistance, and in all directions opposed impenetrable barriers to the mental or spiritual assaults of those with whom she came in contact. It seemed impossible for Mrs. Errington to receive, like a waxen tablet, a definite impression. She was so completely herself that she walked the world as one clad in armour which turned aside all weapons. This might have been partly the reason why men found her so attractive, partly, also, the reason why Horace considered her, even while he was not yet acquainted with trousers, as so very wonderful among women.

Among many indifferences, Mrs. Errington included a definite indifference to the sufferings of those less fortunate than herself. Legacies came to her as often as mendicants to Victor Hugo's Bishop of D—. She received them with a quiet greediness so prettily concealed at first that nobody called it vulgar. As time went on this greediness grew to gluttony. Mrs. Errington began to feel that fatal influence which came upon the man who built walls with his gold, and each day longed to see the walls rise higher round him. A passion for mere possession seized her and dominated her. Even, she permitted the world, always curiously nosing, like a dog, in people's gutters, to become aware of this passion. This beautifully dressed, gay and clever woman was known to be an eager miser by her acquaintance first, and last by her own son Horace. It is true that she spent money on the so-called "good things" of life, gave admirable dinners, and would as soon have gone without clothes as without her opera box. But she practised an intense economy in many secret and some public ways, and, more especially, she was completely deaf to those appeals of suffering, and sometimes of charlatanry, which besiege our ears in London, so full of wily outcasts and of those who are terribly in need. Mrs. Errington's name figured in no charitable lists. She seldom even gave her patronage to a bazaar, and, above all things, she positively abhorred the beggars who make the streets and parks their hunting grounds, who hover before doorsteps, and grow up from the ground, like mustard seeds, when a luggage-laden cab stops or a carriage unblessed with a groom pauses before a shop.

Horace knew this hatred very well, so well that, although his nature was as lavish as his mother's was mean, he seldom sought to rouse any pity in her pitiless heart, or to strike the rock from which experience had taught him that no water would gush out. Every habit of conduct, is, however, broken through now and then, when the moment is exceptional and the soul is deeply stirred. And this reticent mood of the boy when with his mother one day received a shock which drove him into a contest with her, and moved him to strive against the obedience which his love for her habitually imposed upon him.

It was springtime. Horace, now sixteen, and long established at Eton, was at home for the Easter vacation, which he was spending with Mrs. Errington, not at their country place, but in her town house in Park Lane. One morning, when the City was smiling with sunshine, and was so full of the breath of the sweet season that in quiet corners it seemed in some strange and indefinite way almost Countrified, Horace went into Mrs. Errington's boudoir and begged her to come out for a walk in the Park, where he had already been bicycling before breakfast. When there was no question of money she was always ready to accede to any request of the boy's, and she got up at once from her writing table—she was just sending a short note of refusal to subscribe to some charity pressed upon her attention by a hopeful clergyman—and went to her room to put on her hat. Five minutes later she and Horace set forth.

Weather may have a softening or a hardening influence on the average person. On Mrs. Errington it had neither. She felt much the same essentially in a thunderstorm or in midsummer moonlight, on a black, frost-bound winter's day, or on such a perfect and tender spring morning as that on which she now passed through the park gate with her son. She never drew weather into her soul, but calmly recognised it as a fact suitable for illustration on the first page of the *Daily Graphic*. Now she walked gaily into the Row with Horace, looking about her for acquaintances. She found some, and would not have been sorry to linger with them. But Horace wanted her to go further afield, and accordingly they soon moved on towards the Serpentine. It was when they were just in sight of the water that they met Captain Hindford, already alluded to as a man who had eventually more knowledge than other people of the events which led to the drawing-up of Mrs. Errington's strange will. He was one of the many men who admired Mrs. Errington while wondering at her narrow and excommunicative disposition. And he stopped to speak to her with the eager readiness which is so flattering to a woman. The spring, so much discussed, was lightly discussed again, and, by some inadvertence, no doubt, Captain Hindford, who was almost as genial as if he had lived in the days of Dickens, was led to exclaim—

"By Jove, Mrs. Errington, this first sunshine's as seductive as a pretty child—makes one ready to do anything! Why, I saw an old crossing-sweeper just now sweeping nothing at all—for it's as dry as a bone, you see—and I had to fork out a sixpence; encouraged useless industry just because of the change in the weather, 'pon my word, eh?"

Mrs. Errington's lips tightened ever so little.

"A great mistake, Captain Hindford," she said drily.

Horace looked at his mother with a sort of bright, boyish curiosity. Although he knew so well what her nature was like, it did not cease to surprise him.

"You think so?" said the Captain. "Well, perhaps, you're right; I don't know. Daresay I've been a fool. Still, you know a fool in sunshine is better than a wise man in a fog; 'pon my word, yes, eh?"

Mrs. Errington did not verbally agree, and they parted after the Captain had accepted an invitation to dine quietly in Park Lane that evening.

"Devilish odd woman, devilish odd!" was Hindford's comment. And he watched the mother's and son's retreating figures with a certain astonishment.

"Wonder what the boy thinks of her?" he muttered. "Jove, if there isn't a beggar going after them! She'll soon settle him!"

And he remained standing to watch the encounter. From where he stood he had seen the beggar, who had been half-sitting, half-lying, on a bench facing the water, glance up at Mrs. Errington and her son as they passed, partially raise himself up, gaze after them, and finally rise to his feet and follow their footsteps. Hindford could only see the man's back. It was long, slightly bending, and apparently youngish. A thin but scrupulously neat coat of some poor shiny and black material covered it, and hung from the man's shoulders loosely, forming two folds which were almost like two gently rounded hills with a shallow valley running between them up to the blades of the shoulders. Certainly the coat didn't fit very well. The Captain watched, expecting to see this beggar address an appeal to Mrs. Errington or Horace. But apparently the man was nervous or half-hearted, for he followed them slowly, without catching them up, until the trio vanished from view on the bank of the Serpentine.

When this disappearance took place the Captain was conscious of an absurd feeling of disappointment. He could not understand why he felt any anxiety to see Mrs. Errington refuse a beggar alms. Yet he would gladly have followed, like a spy, to behold a commonplace and dingy event. Despite the apparent reluctance of the beggar to ply his trade, Hindford felt convinced that presently the man would approach Mrs. Errington and be promptly sent about his business. Her negative would, no doubt, be eager enough even upon this exquisite and charitable morning. Wishing devoutly that, being a gentleman, he had not to conform to an unwritten code of manners, Hindford walked away. And, as he walked, he saw continually the back of the beggar with that black coat of the two hills and the valley between the shoulder blades.

Meanwhile, Mrs. Errington and Horace, quite unaware that they were being followed, pursued their way. There were a few boats out on the water, occupied by inexpert oarsmen whose frantic efforts to seem natural and serene in this to them new and complicated art drew the undivided attention of the boy, a celebrated "wet Bob." Mrs. Errington was thinking about her latest investments and watching the golden walls grow higher about her. Mother and son were engrossed, and did not hear a low voice say, "I beg your pardon!" until it had uttered the words more than once. Then Horace looked round. He saw a tall and very pale young man, neatly though poorly dressed in dark trousers and a thin loose black coat that might have been made of alpaca, and fitted badly. This man's face was gaunt and meagre, the features were pointed, the mouth was piteous. His eyes blazed with some terrible emotion, it seemed, and when Horace looked round a sudden patch of scarlet burned on his white and bony cheeks. Horace's attention was pinned by his appearance, which was at the same time dull and piercing, as the human aspect becomes in the tremendous moment of an existence. This man's soul seemed silently screaming out in his glance, his posture, his chalk-white cheeks starred with scarlet spots, his long-fingered hands drooping down in the shadow of his ill-fitting coat, which fluttered in the breeze. Horace turned, looked, and stood still. The man also stood still. Mrs. Errington looked sharply round.

"What is it, Horace?" she said.

She glanced at the man, and her lips tightened.

"Come along, Horace," she said. "Come!"

But Horace, who seemed fascinated by the spectre that had claimed their attention, still hesitated, and the man, noticing this, half held out one hand and murmured in a husky voice—

"I am starving."

With the words, the scarlet spots in his cheeks deepened to a fiercer hue, and he hung his head like one abruptly overwhelmed with shame.

"For God's sake give me something!" he muttered. "I've—I've never done this before."

Horace's hand went to his waistcoat pocket, but before he could take out a coin Mrs. Errington had decisively intervened.

"Horace, I forbid you," she said.

"Mater!"

"Understand—I forbid you."

She took his arm and they walked on, leaving the man standing by the waterside. He did not follow them or repeat his dismal statement, only let his head drop forward on his bosom, while his fingers twisted themselves convulsively together.

Meanwhile a hot argument was proceeding between Mrs. Errington and Horace. For once it seemed that the boy was inclined to defy his mother.

"Let me give him something—only a few coppers," he said.

"No; beggars ought not to be encouraged."

"That chap isn't a regular beggar. I'll wager anything it's true. He is starving."

"Nonsense! They always say so."

"Mater—stop! I must—"

Horace paused resolutely and looked round. In the distance the man could still be seen standing where they had left him, his head drooped, his narrow shoulders hunched slightly forward.

"Let me run back," the boy went on; "I won't be a minute."

But Mrs. Errington's curious parsimony was roused now to full activity.

"I will not allow it," she said; "the man is probably a thief and a drunkard. Hyde Park swarms with bad characters."

"Bad character or not, he's starving. Anyone can see that."

"Then let him starve. It's his own fault. Let him starve! Nobody need unless they have committed some folly, or, worse, some crime. There's bread enough for all who deserve to live. I have no sympathy with all this preposterous pauperising which goes by the name of charity. It's a fad, a fashion—nothing more."

She forced her son to walk on. As they went he cast a last glance back at the beggar.

"Mater, you're cruel!" he said, moved by a strength of emotion that was unusual in him—"hard and cruel!"

Mrs. Errington made no reply. She had gained her point, and cared for little else.

"You'll repent this someday," Horace continued.

He was in a passion, and scarcely knew what he was saying. Strings seemed drawn tightly round his heart, and angry tears rose to his eyes.

"You'll repent it, I bet!" he added.

Then he relapsed into silence, feeling that if he spoke again he would lose all the self-control that a boy of sixteen thinks so much of.

All that day Horace thought incessantly of the beggar, and felt an increasing sense of anger against his mother. He found himself looking furtively at her, as one looks at a stranger, and thinking her face hard and pitiless. She seemed to him as someone whom he had never really known till now, as someone whom, now that he knew her, he feared. Why his mind dwelt so perpetually upon a casual beggar he couldn't understand. But so it was. He saw perpetually the man's white face, fierce and ashamed eyes, the gesture at once hungry and abashed with which he asked for charity. All day the vision haunted the boy in the sunshine.

Mrs. Errington, on her part, calmly ignored the incident of the morning and appeared not to notice any change in her son's demeanour. In the evening Captain Hindford came to dine. He was struck by Horace's glumness, and in his frank way openly chaffed the boy about it.

"What's up with this young scoundrel?" he said to Mrs. Errington.

Horace grew very red.

"Horace is not very well to-day," said his mother.

"Mater, that's not true—I'm all right."

"I think it more charitable to suppose you seedy," she replied.

"Charitable!" Horace cried. "Well, Mater, what on earth do you know about charity?"

Captain Hindford began to look embarrassed, and endeavoured to change the subject, but Horace suddenly burst out into the story of the beggar.

"It was just after you left us," he said to the Captain.

"I saw the fellow following you," the Captain said. Then he turned to Mrs. Errington. "These chaps are the plague of the Park," he added.

"Exactly. That is what I tell Horace."

"I don't care!" the boy said stoutly. "He *was* starving, and we were brutes not to give him something. The Mater'll be sorry for it someday. I know it. I can feel it."

Captain Hindford began to talk about French plays rather hastily. When Mrs. Errington went up to the drawing room, Horace suddenly said to the Captain—

"I say, Hindford, do me a good turn to-night, will you?"

"Well, old chap, what is it, eh?"

"When you say 'good-night,' don't really go."

The Captain looked astonished.

"But—" he began.

"Wait outside a second for me. When the Mater's gone to bed I want you to come into the Park with me."

"The Park? What for?"

"To find that beggar chap. I bet he's there. Lots of his sort sleep there, you know. I want to give him something. And—somehow—I'd like you to come with me. Besides, it doesn't do to go looking for anyone in the Park alone at night."

"That's true," the Captain said. "All right, Errington; I'll come."

And, after bidding Mrs. Errington good-night, he lingered in Park Lane till he was joined by Horace. They turned at once into the Park and began to make their way in the direction of the Serpentine. It was a soft night, full of the fine and minute rain that belongs especially to spring weather. The clocks of the town had struck eleven, and most of the legitimate sweethearts who make the Park their lover's walk had gone home, leaving this realm of lawns and trees and waters to the night-birds, the pickpockets, the soldiers, and the unhealthily curious persons over whom it exercises such a continual and gloomy fascination. Hindford and Horace could have seen many piteous sights had they cared to as they walked down the long path by the Row. The boy peered at each seat as they passed, and once or twice hesitated by some thin and tragic figure, stretched in uneasy slumber or bowed in staring reverie face to face with the rainy night. But from each in turn he drew back, occasionally followed by a muttered oath or a sharp ejaculation.

"I bet he'll be somewhere by the Serpentine," the boy said to Hindford.

And they walked on till at length they reached the black sheet of water closely muffled in the night.

"We met him somewhere just here," Horace said.

"I know," Hindford rejoined. "He got up from this seat. But he may be a dozen miles off by now."

"No," Horace said, with a curious pertinacity; "I'm sure he's about here still. He looked like a man with no home. Ugh! how dreary it is! Come along, Hindford."

The good-natured Captain obeyed, and they went on by the cheerless water, which was only partially revealed in the blackness. Suddenly they both stopped.

"What's that?" Horace exclaimed.

A shrill whistle, followed by shouts, came to them, apparently from the water. Then there was an answering whistle from somewhere in the Park.

"It's the police," said Hindford. "There's something up."

They hurried on, and in a moment saw what looked like a great black shadow, rising out of the water, lifting in his arms another shadow, which drooped and hung down with the little waves curling round it. As they drew close they saw that the first shadow was a policeman, up to his waist in the water, and the second shadow was a man whom he held in his arms, as he waded with difficulty to the shore.

"Lend a hand, mates," he shouted as he saw them.

Just then a light shone out over the black lake from the bull's-eye of a second policeman who had hurried up in answer to his comrade's whistle. Between them they quickly got the man on shore, and laid him down on the path on his back. The bull's-eye lantern, turned full on him, lit up a face that seemed all bony structure, staring eyes, a mouth out of which the water dripped. He had no coat on and his thin arms were like those of a skeleton.

"Dead as a doornail," said the first policeman. "A case of suicide."

"God! Hindford, it's he! It's the chap who asked me for money this morning!" whispered Horace. "Is he really dead?"

The Captain, who had been examining the body and feeling the heart, nodded. Horace gazed upon the white face with a sort of awful curiosity. He had never before looked at a corpse.

"Look here, Errington," Hindford said to the boy that night as he parted from him in Park Lane, "don't tell your mother anything of this."

"But—but, Hindford—"

"Come, now, you take my advice. Keep a quiet tongue in your head."

"But perhaps it was her fault; it was—if we'd given the poor chap something he'd—"

"Probably. That's just the reason I don't want you to tell Mrs. Errington anything of it. Come, promise me on your honour."

"All right, Hindford, I'll promise. How horrible it's all been!"

"Don't think about it, lad. Good-night."

Horace trembled as he stole up the black staircase to bed. He meant to keep his promise, of course, but he wondered whether the Mater would have owned that she was in the wrong that morning if she had heard his dreary tale of the beggar's death in the night.

The next day it was Mrs. Errington who asked Horace to go out walking. She looked rather pale and fatigued at breakfast, but declared her intention of taking a constitutional.

"Come with me, Horace," she said.

"Very well," he answered, with a curious and almost shy boyish coldness.

"Not into the Park, Mater," he said, as they were starting.

"Why not? We always walk there. Where else should we go?"

"Anywhere—shopping—Regent Street."

"No, Horace, I've got a headache to-day. I want a quiet place."

He didn't say more. They set out, and Mrs. Errington took the precise route they had followed the day before. She glanced rather sharply about her as they walked. Presently they reached the seat on which the beggar had been sitting just before he got up to follow them. Mrs. Errington paused beside it.

"I'm tired. Let us sit down here," she said.

"No, Mater, not here."

"Really, Horace," Mrs. Errington said, "you are in an extraordinary mood to-day. You have no regard for me. What is the matter with you?"

And she sat down on the seat. Horace remained standing.

"I shan't sit here," he said obstinately.

"Very well," Mrs. Errington replied.

She really began to look ill, but Horace was too much preoccupied with his own feelings to notice it. There was something abominable to him in his mother sitting calmly down to rest in the very place occupied a few hours ago by the wretched creature who had, so Horace believed, been driven to death by her refusal of charity. He felt sick with horror in that neighbourhood, and he moved away, and stood staring across the Serpentine. Presently Mrs. Errington called to him in a faint voice—

"Horace, come and give me your hand."

He turned, noticed her extreme pallor, and ran up.

"What's the row? Are you ill, Mater?"

"No. Help me up." He put out his hand. She got up slowly.

"We'll go home," he said. "You look awfully seedy."

"No; let us walk on."

In spite of his remonstrances she insisted on walking up and down at the edge of the Serpentine for quite an hour. She appeared to be on the look-out for somebody. Over and over again they passed the spot where the beggar had drowned himself. Their feet trod over the ground on which his dead body had been laid. Each time they reached it Horace felt himself grow cold. Death is so terrible to the young. At last Mrs. Errington stopped.

"I can't walk much more," she said.

"Then do let's go home now," Horace said.

She stood looking round her, searching the Park with her eyes.

"I suppose we must," she said slowly. Then she added, "We can come here again to-morrow."

Horace was puzzled.

"What for? Why should we?" he asked.

But his mother made no reply, and they walked home.

Next day she insisted on going again to the same place, and again she was obviously on the look-out. Horace grew more and more puzzled by her demeanour. And when the third day came, and once more Mrs. Errington called him to set forth to the Serpentine, he said to her, with a boy's bluntness—

"D'you want to meet someone there?"

Mrs. Errington looked at him strangely.

"Yes," she said, after a minute's silence.

"Why, who is it?"

"That beggar I wouldn't let you give money to."

Horace turned scarlet with the shock of surprise and the knowledge—which he absurdly felt as guilty knowledge—that the man was dead, perhaps even buried by now.

"Oh, nonsense, Mater!" he began, stammering. "He won't come there again. Besides, you never give to beggars."

"I mean to give this man something."

Horace was more and more surprised.

"Why?" he exclaimed. "Why now? You wouldn't when I wanted you to, and now—now it's too late. What do you wish to give to him for now?"

But all she would say was, "I feel that I should like to, that—that his perhaps really was a deserving case. Come, Horace, let us go and try to find him."

And the boy, bound by his word to Captain Hindford, was forced to go out in search of a dead man. He felt the horror of this quest. To-day Mrs. Errington carried her purse in her hand, and looked eagerly out for the beggar. Once she fancied she saw him in the distance.

"There he is!" she cried to Horace. "Run and fetch him."

The boy turned pale, and stared.

"Where, Mater?"

"Among those trees."

"It can't be! Nonsense!"

"No," she said; "you are right. I made a mistake. It's only somebody like him. Why, Horace, what's the matter?"

"Nothing," he answered.

But he was shaking. The business was too ghastly. He felt he couldn't stand it much longer, and he resolved to go to Captain Hindford and persuade the Captain to absolve him from his promise. In the afternoon of the same day, accordingly, he went off to Knightsbridge. He rang, and was told that Captain Hindford had gone to Paris and was afterwards going for a tour on the Continent. His heart sank at the news. Was he to go on day after day searching with his mother for this corpse, which was rotting in the grave? He asked for Hindford's address. It was Poste Restante, Monte Carlo. But the servant added that letters sent there might have to wait for two or three days, as his master's immediate plans were unsettled. Horace, however, went to the nearest telegraph office and wired to Hindford—

"Let me off promise; urgent. —Horace Errington."

Then, having done all he could, he went back to Park Lane. He found his mother in a curiously restless state, and directly he came in she began to talk about the beggar.

"I must and will find that man," she said.

"Mater, why?"

"Because I shall never be well till I do," she said. "I don't know what it is, but I cannot be still by day, and I cannot rest by night, for thinking of him. Why did I not let you give him something?"

"Mater, I wish to God you had!" the boy said solemnly.

Mrs. Errington did not seem to notice his unusual manner. She was self-engrossed.

"However, we shall see him again, no doubt," she went on. "And then I shall give him something handsome. I know he needs it."

Horace went hastily out of the room. He longed for a wire from Captain Hindford. Next day he "shammed ill," as he called it to himself, so as to get out of going into the Park. So Mrs. Errington went off by herself in a condition of almost feverish anticipation.

"I know I shall see him to-day," she said, as she left Horace.

She returned at lunchtime, and came up at once to his room.

"I have seen him," she said.

Horace sat up, staring at her in blank amazement.

"What, Mater? What d'you say?"

"I have seen him."

"No?"

"Yes. I went to the place where he asked you for money, and walked up and down for ages. But he wasn't there. At last I gave it up and crossed the bridge. I took it into my head to come home on the other side of the water. Well, when I was half-way along it, I looked across, and there I saw him."

"Rot, Mater!"

"He was standing alone by the water, staring straight across at me, just as if he saw me and was trying to attract my attention."

"No, no!"

"Horace, don't be silly! Why do you contradict me? He looked just the same as when we saw him first, only he had no coat on."

Horace gave a sort of gasp.

"I suppose his poverty had compelled him to pawn it," Mrs. Errington continued. "Don't you think so, Horace? People can pawn clothes, can't they?"

The boy nodded. His eyes were fixed on her.

"I looked across at him," Mrs. Errington continued, "and made a sign to him to come round to meet me by the other end, near the Row. I held up my purse so that he might understand me."

"What did he do?"

"He turned away and hurried off among the trees."

"Ah!"

"Do you know, Horace," Mrs. Errington continued rather excitedly, "I think if you had beckoned to him he would have come. He's afraid of me, perhaps, because—because I wouldn't let you give to him. To-morrow you must come out with me. Till I've relieved that man's wants I shall have no peace."

She hastened out of the room, apparently in a quiver of unusual agitation. Horace sat petrified. If only Hindford would telegraph! That cursed promise!

On the following day it rained. Nevertheless, Mrs. Errington almost violently insisted upon Horace accompanying her to search for the beggar.

"We shall go to the far side of the water," she said. "I believe when we go to the other side he sees us coming and avoids us. But if we can catch sight of him, as I did yesterday, you can beckon to him, and I am certain when he sees you he will come."

Horace said nothing. He felt cold about the heart, not so much with fear as with awe and wonder. They went to the far bank, and almost directly Mrs. Errington cried out—

"There he is, and without his coat again! How wet he must be getting!"

Horace looked across the dull water, through the driving rain. He saw no one on the opposite bank.

"He sees us," Mrs. Errington added. "Horace, you beckon to him. Here, take my purse. Hold it up, and then point to him to come round and meet us."

Mechanically the boy obeyed.

"Ah, I knew it! This time he is coming," said Mrs. Errington.

"He is coming, Mater?"

"Yes; come along."

She hurried towards the end of the Serpentine. Horace walked by her side, staring in horror through the rain.

"Poor man!" Mrs. Errington said presently. "How ghastly he looks!"

"Mater—I say—"

"Well?"

"Is he near?"

"Near?"

Mrs. Errington stopped in amazement.

"Why, what do you mean, Horace?"

"What I say. Is he near now?"

"Near? He's just coming up."

Suddenly the boy fainted.

When he came to he was lying in the shelter of the Rescue Society.

"Ah, Horace," his mother said, "you ought to have stayed in bed another day."

"Yes, Mater."

"You frightened that poor man. He made off when you fainted."

That evening Horace received a telegram from Monte Carlo—

"Very well but better say nothing. —HINDFORD."

He read it, laid it down, and told Mrs. Errington the truth.

As already stated, she died very suddenly not long afterwards, leaving behind her the will which so astonished London.

The Lost Faith

I

When Lord Sandring returned from America he was in high spirits. His visit had been more interesting, more delightful, even than he had anticipated. He had been warmly welcomed in various centres of culture, had met many fascinating personalities, and to crown his satisfaction, which, indeed, almost amounted to complacency, had brought off a coup; yes, really a *coup*. He had persuaded, induced, got—he finally settled on that strong, virile little word *got*—Olivia Traill, the most remarkable woman in New York (if he knew anything of women), to promise that she would cross the ocean in February and pay a visit to London to show them all how well founded his theories were. His peers might call him a crank, a fellow with a bee in his bonnet, a victim of charlatans, even a bit of a charlatan himself. Pioneers, the hewers of new paths through the forest of ignorance towards the clear light of true understanding, were always girded at, sneered at. Olivia—it had already come to that, merely Olivia—Olivia would show them! Lord Sandring went about almost chuckling under his bristling brown moustache, as he repeated to himself again and again that Olivia would show them!

Lord Sandring was unmarried, rich, and just at the right age. He was thirty-eight; old enough to know, young enough to exult. The follies of youth lay behind him, the dreary regrets of old age perhaps before, but far ahead in the distance. Meanwhile, there he was—mature, like an excellent bottle of wine. And he had got Olivia to do it. He was indeed a happy man when he walked into the Bureau of Psychic Healing, which he had established at his own expense in a quiet street not far from Piccadilly. He was going to make Harley Street "sit up," by Jove, he was. The doctors laughed at his pretensions, but wait till Olivia arrived!

She came by the Yellow Star Liner, the *Hiawatha*, and Lord Sandring and his ardent coadjutor, Miss Averil Jones, met her on the quay at Liverpool. It was a day such as might have been described in the *Inferno*, but Lord Sandring was in a state of properly controlled ecstasy, and Miss Jones, in a coat and skirt of heather mixture, boots the shape of the foot, and a hat that would have looked well on the head of a statesman of sporting tendencies, beamed over her pince-nez as who should say "Hallelujah!"

"Are you quite alone?" said Lord Sandring, as he grasped Olivia's firm hand and looked into her steady, unworldly grey eyes.

"Oh, yes," she said, in a strong mezzo-soprano voice.

"No maid?"

"I don't need a maid on a journey. Do you?" she turned her cordial eyes on Averil Jones.

"No, of course not," said Averil. "But then, I never wear anything that fastens behind!"

"Now you're treading on the verge of the mysteries," laughed Lord Sandring. "Hullo!"

At this moment a tall, well-dressed young man, apparently almost a boy, with light, straight hair, a short upper lip, and ardent, indeed almost fanatical, blue eyes, suddenly interposed his athletic figure between Olivia and her welcomers.

"I've got all your luggage together," he said to Olivia. "Your porter's number is fifty-three, a short man with a nose—well, I mean, with an unusually large nose. Shall I?"

"Let me introduce you to Lord Sandring," interrupted Olivia.

The young man swung round with an eager, searching look.

"Lord Sandring, this is a friend of mine, Fernol West. Fernol, this is Miss Averil Jones."

"Glad to meet you," said the young man. "You may possibly have heard of me. Not that I am famous! But she cured me. I'm just one of her marvellous cures. My father is Garstin Allerton West, the financier. I had a bad accident in Central Park, fell from my horse. She pulled me out of hell."

Lord Sandring glowed.

"Of course I've heard of you. I was hoping to meet you in New York, but you were in Chicago with your father when I was there. You are one of the greatest proofs of our dear friend's powers. Miss Jones, you remember my telling you—"

"The case is tabulated at the Bureau," said Averil. She gazed at the young man with profound interest. "You're tabulated," she assured him.

"Sounds cosy!" he rejoined. "Seems to give me a sort of niche over here, makes one feel at home. I shall think of that at the Savoy to-night. I owe it to her. I owe everything to her."

There was something striking in the tone of his manly voice, something that suggested worship, a hidden thing absorbed, living by, and in, some atmosphere, deprived of which it must fail and fall away and be as nothing. Lord Sandring's thin, eager face suddenly became grave, intense. A piercing curiosity shone in his small, dark eyes. He lowered his head and gazed at Olivia.

"I was enabled to do him good," she said simply, without the least trace of conceit or egoism. "He had faith in me and that made it inevitable. Now, good-bye, Fernol. I'll remember—number fifty-three, with a nose. I'll write to you when I'm settled."

The young man took off his soft hat. But Lord Sandring had a word to say to him, more than a word.

"You'll be at the Savoy!" he said. "I shall be certain to find you there if I call?"

"Oh, yes. It's good of you to say—"

"Good! I'm deeply interested in your case. You are a living wonder, Mr. West."

"That's what my people over there say."

"You are a great proof that my theories are founded on the impregnable rock of truth. Lunch with me to-morrow in the restaurant at half-past one, will you? We must be friends."

"So—you didn't come alone!" said Lord Sandring to Olivia, as they went towards the customs, jostled by the crowd in the gathering darkness of winter. "You brought one of your 'cures' with you. A very sensible thing to do. It will help us greatly with London."

"But I didn't bring Fernol," she said. "He turned up on the boat. I knew nothing of his intention. But I'm very glad he came over. I love him."

Miss Jones jumped in her heather mixture under the statesman's hat.

"One loves those whom one has healed," said Olivia. "They are witnesses to the Divine Power, and one can't look at them without joy. And joy and love are twins, I think."

"I know! I know!" said Lord Sandring.

"Oh, in that way! I quite understand!" said Miss Jones, with a little air of evaporation.

She took a long and very feminine survey of the Faith healer, and then added: "I think you are very universal, Miss Traill."

"But very personal, too," said Lord Sandring. "Intensely personal."

"There's the nose!" exclaimed Olivia. "I'm certain that's number fifty-three."

"How quick you are!" said Lord Sandring. "Nothing escapes you! You are really wonderful!"

And he made for her porter.

Within half an hour they were all in the London express, rushing through the darkness towards the great city.

They had agreed not to talk at the request of Olivia. She had said very simply that she wanted to "get ready" for London. She had never yet been there. She was going there not as the ordinary person goes on business, or pleasure, or family affairs, but to bring to London her great power of healing, a new force, almost a new gospel. Although absolutely free from pose, Olivia took herself and her powers seriously. She could not do otherwise, for she believed herself to be the repository of a noble force, and she had to be careful of it, to guard it, to cherish it, lest it might diminish or die out altogether. So she "gathered herself together" while the train ran on, while Lord Sandring read the *Hibbert Journal*, and Miss Averil Jones turned the pages of *Country Life* and meditated on the respective beauties of Tudor and Georgian homesteads.

Olivia was only just twenty-eight, but she had had already a remarkable career. The daughter of a Boston bookseller, she had been an unusually earnest and meditative child, though crammed full of vitality, and not without the saving grace of a robust sense of humour. She had worked hard at college and had done well. But her teachers, and even many of her schoolmates, had felt rather than noticed in her something that set her apart from the typical "bright" student, who is good at passing examinations and carrying off prizes. Sometimes she had seemed to fall into waking dreams, to become abruptly remote, and at these moments there was about her, as if emanating from her, an atmosphere heavy, indeed almost sullen, which suggested a caged power softly struggling to spread itself over large spaces. Many were disturbed by this atmosphere, and asked Olivia why she was so "odd" at times. She had no satisfactory answer to give them. For it was no satisfactory answer to tell them that she felt "odd" in these moments. She herself did not know why she was seized with a strange sensation as if someone were thwarting her, as if she possessed something—some power—which she ought to give out, to exercise, but which she was obliged to keep shut up within herself, useless, till it lay like a burden upon both her body and soul. Sometimes, giving herself up to introspection, she asked herself what this power was. But she could not identify it. She did not feel that she was superior to her college mates in intellect. She had fairly good brains, but there were many others who had brains as good as hers, or much better. Her imagination was not remarkable. She was not conscious of possessing the peculiar gifts of one destined to be creative. Nevertheless, she often felt that she possessed some hidden force which set her apart from all those about her, and at times it seemed almost to rend her. Then she became melancholy, brooding, perhaps sullen, and was beset by a numbing misery half spiritual, half physical. This continued till she was seventeen.

Then enlightenment came.

A young and pretty girl who was afflicted with St. Vitus's dance arrived at the school. At times she was like the other girls, but in moments of excitement, or if she were startled by any unexpected happening, she would twitch, jump, turn her poor head awry, jerk her hands and arms, almost rattle in the throes of her piteous complaint. Some of the girls laughed at her till they were rebuked by the mistresses; others were afraid of her. Nearly all the pupils wondered at and finally pitied her. And the poor child pitied herself, and was deeply ashamed of the exhibitions she gave.

Olivia, who had a great deal of stillness and calm, despite her abounding vitality, had never before witnessed such a nervous complaint, and at first she looked on it with an amazement which she tried to conceal. Her amazement was succeeded by a shrinking of disgust for which she blamed herself severely. But her blame of herself did not drive the disgust away until the appointed time.

One day when Olivia had fallen into one of her "moods," as her college mates called her peculiar fits of depression and uneasiness, Lily happened to be in the room with her reading. Lily was deeply interested in her book, and was sitting quite still, immersed, self-forgetful and happy. Olivia was brooding in a corner. A dog outside gave vent to a piercing and prolonged howl.

Instantly Lily fell into a sort of convulsion. The hand which was holding the book shot up from her lap, hurling the book into the air. Her head jerked frantically. Her whole body was in violent movement. Even her teeth snapped. Olivia sat watching for a moment. Then, as if ordered, she got up, came over to the child, stood in front of her, gazed steadily at her, and said in a firm, rather loud voice:

"Lily, you need not do that."

"I—can't—help—it!" gasped the child.

Olivia stretched out her hands.

"Yes, you can. Take hold of me."

The child mechanically snatched at Olivia's hands and clutched them.

"That's right. Now believe that I can stop you from shaking like that and I shall be able to stop you."

There was authority in her voice, authority in her whole bearing, and in her steady and shining eyes. Lily looked at her, and was quieter.

"Now lift your hands with mine and press them against your forehead."

Lily did so, and in a few minutes was perfectly calm.

"I can cure you of your trouble," said Olivia.

"But the doctors can't."

"That's no matter. Just tell me—do you believe that I can cure you?"

After a pause, and a long look, the child replied simply:

"Yes."

That was the beginning of Olivia's career. She had discovered what the power was which she had long suspected she possessed, which she had long sought for. She was a natural "healer."

An extraordinary feeling of relief, of emancipation, came to her. She seemed to float into peace. Strength thrilled in her, tingled all through her. A great oppression was removed. The burden dropped from her— the burden of ignorance. She had not known what she was, now she knew. And she was wonderfully happy, and worshipped. She worshipped what was within her, and Him who had put it there. But she did not worship herself. For, even in that first moment of illumination, she regarded herself as a vessel into which something precious had been poured, and she was humble in spirit.

She was humble, but she was exalted with faith. Faith made her feel strong like a lion and prodigiously independent, as if the world belonged to her, was suddenly enclosed in her hand.

So—Olivia began her career, a career which was to bring her into extraordinary prominence, even into fame.

She cured Lily of St. Vitus's dance—not immediately, but within a few months. The nervous accesses became less violent, less prolonged; the intervals between them widened; finally they yielded instantaneously to treatment by Olivia, and at last ceased altogether.

Lily's parents were enraptured, and Lily herself regarded Olivia as a giver of life. The cure, having been made in a big school, was carried abroad by many tongues of mistresses and pupils.

Olivia was soon on the way.

At first her parents were inclined to be alarmed by the new and startling development in the family circle, but they quickly "came round" when they realised Olivia's quiet determination, and noticed the respect in which she began to be held by many of their neighbours. Mr. Traill had an important and prosperous bookseller's business, and as his daughter's fame spread abroad he found that it did him no harm. Certainly the doctors showed a strongly antagonistic spirit, and were contemptuous of his daughter's "cure," but, on the other hand, the newspaper men took her up. She was written about, interviewed. People thronged to the store to inquire about her, and often bought books when their curiosity was partially satisfied. Olivia's peculiar gift, if gift it were, certainly made things hum in the store. And then Olivia herself was greatly improved since that first strange episode with Lily. A sunny cheerfulness radiated from her. Her vitality of mind and her vigour of body were strengthened. It was impossible not to feel the power which emanated from her, difficult not to believe that it was wholly beneficent.

Her parents would never submit themselves to Olivia when they were unwell, which happened now and then. They stuck to the family doctor, who, by the way, was a good customer to the store. But they soon began to be rather proud of her "cures" in the town, and acknowledged that there was "something in it all." America is the home of strange "cults." By degrees a sort of "cult" for Olivia grew up. She took it all very quietly and reasonably. Her head was never in any danger of being turned by the noise made about her. She was full of robust common sense, and never encouraged folly in others. But side by side with the strain of common sense in her there was another strain. When she had discovered her power of healing she had discovered the source from which it flowed. That source was faith. When she stood before her convulsed schoolmate she had felt that she was resting on a rock, the rock of a great faith; faith in her power to heal, faith in Him who had given it to her. At that moment she had realised a mighty truth, that faith can move the mountains. And she knew that she had moved her first mountain on the day when Lily was cured.

From that day onward she strove to live by faith. She boldly called herself a faith healer, and declared that, though no doubt she possessed some peculiar physical gift, without faith she would be powerless to employ it beneficially.

She spoke quite frankly to those who cared to listen about the necessity of this strange and mysterious aid, and demanded cooperation from those who consulted her.

"I don't believe I can bring about a complete cure of any malady if I fail to convey my own faith in myself to the patient," she said. "I need reciprocal faith."

And often she would say to the sick: "I believe that I can cure you, and you must believe it too. Then we shall work together, and all must go well."

Very seldom she failed to pour faith into those who came to her. The mere sight of her often swept away scepticism.

Olivia was not beautiful. She was fairly tall, with a rather large frame and robust shoulders. Her features were blunt and rough-hewn, lacking in fineness and delicacy, but powerful and indicative of will. Her brow was broad and intellectual, and her grey eyes were large and lustrous. She had splendid brown hair, full of life and warm colour, which she wore parted in the middle and gathered into a big roll behind. Her whole appearance suggested honesty, fixity of purpose, energy and kindliness. There was never a trace of self-consciousness in her look or manner. Her bearing was fearless and simple. She always dressed plainly, with extraordinary neatness, and never wore anything that was eccentric or likely to draw attention to her. Most people were instinctively attracted to her at first sight. There were some who declared that she possessed hypnotic powers and used them without acknowledging them.

Her fame gradually spread from her native city to distant parts of America. She was discussed, written about, praised and abused. The Christian Scientists soon heard of her, and tried hard to persuade her to declare herself one of their body. But she told them plainly that she found grave errors in their teaching. She thought the denial of disease either insincere or ridiculous. She considered that to tell people that disease exists only in mortal mind was to tell them a flat lie. She held that disease does exist, that it ravages the tissues of the body, that it causes often agonies of pain, that it may devour the organs by which men live, and bring about the cessation of life, but that it may be arrested and finally expelled by the mysterious curative influence of another body helped by the mind and soul within it.

"I have such a body," she would boldly declare, "and by it, using it as a vehicle, I convey the healing force which is mysteriously connected with the soul." She never tried to cure people without touching them. "I don't believe I could do it," she said. "I have no faith in what the Christian Scientists call 'absent treatment.' Perhaps I am wrong in my scepticism. I can't help that. My beliefs and my disbeliefs are given to me, I suppose, like my hands and feet. I find myself unable to change them. I think it honest to acknowledge them. Christ used the body in healing, and I cannot do less than He did."

She firmly believed, and always upheld, that the so-called miracles of Christ were performed within the natural Law, were not arbitrary violations of it. Perhaps she forgot the raising of Lazarus.

The incident which made Olivia famous throughout the whole of the States was her cure of Fernol West....

Fernol West was the only child of one of the greatest financiers in America, and was adored by both his parents. He was a particularly strong, healthy and joyous boy, very athletic and devoted to sports and games, crammed full of life and hope and promise. When he was eighteen he was the victim of a terrible accident. While out riding in Central Park his horse, a very difficult one, bolted and dashed the rider against a tree. He was picked up senseless, and remained unconscious for three days. Then he opened his eyes, moved, spoke, took nourishment readily. His delighted parents thought that all danger was over. There was a wound in the head, but it gradually healed. No limbs were broken. The boy was soon able to sit up, to walk. He remembered his accident clearly. He knew what was going on around him. The doctors, the most famous in New York, said that he would soon be all right. He had had a tremendous shock, but boys as strong as he was got over such things, got over almost anything.

"It will be all right with him soon."

That was the verdict. And presently there was the rider—"He is all right."

But time passed and it wasn't all right with Fernol.

His accident had left him mysteriously and horribly changed.

He regained all the former strength of his body, but he had lost all his zest for life. He was haunted day and night by the black dog of an intense nervous misery. He tried to take up his old occupations, to study, to play games, to ride and shoot. His old companions sought him out. His devoted parents did everything they could think of to make existence bright and cheery for him. Love surrounded him. Money was lavished upon him. But it was all in vain. He got up in the morning dreading the day that lay before him. He went to bed at night secretly fearing the dark hours. Nobody was able to be of any real good to him. No amusements really distracted him. Formerly he had been devoted to music. Now the sound of music deepened, put an edge to his wretchedness, drove him lower down in his nightmare. Sometimes, carried by his malady beyond the restraining sense of shame, he would put his head down on his mother's knees and cry till he was exhausted. As he said himself, he felt "damned." It was inconceivable by him that he had once enjoyed almost every moment of life, had enjoyed getting up, bathing, eating, studying, talking, playing games, shooting, dancing, reading a book over the fire, meeting other fellows and knocking about with them, sitting in a corner with a pretty girl. He moved as one encompassed by a hideous black cloud dreading everything, above all dreading himself.

Nerve doctors were called in to him. They said he was the victim of acute neurasthenia, no doubt brought on by his accident. They prescribed all sorts of things: massage, physical exercises, tonics, sleeping in the open air, rest cures, moving about, hypnotism, cold douches, travel, hard mental work, no work at all, gaieties, complete solitude. Their followed advice did Fernol no good. Even the hypnotists failed entirely with him. He was not mad; he was just profoundly and unalterably miserable. The brain specialists said that there must be some obscure pressure on the brain. An operation was suggested, but as the surgeons evidently did not know exactly what they would operate for, Fernol's parents would not allow it.

The boy began to be haunted by a longing for suicide. But as he was sane he fought against it. Nevertheless he wished with all his might that he could die painlessly and have done with his misery, which was almost unbearable.

At last his parents tried a Christian Science healer, who treated their son for a long period with absolutely no result. This had seemed to them the last chance for Fernol. Its failure left them and him in despair. The boy said to his mother:

"Mum, I shan't be able to stick it out very much longer. You don't know what it is. Nobody who hasn't had this sort of thing can know what it is. I tell you it's like going about and knowing you are damned for all eternity. I'm sane, though you mightn't think it. I swear I'm sane. But I can't stick it out much longer. When I hear anyone laugh or see a happy face it just—"

He broke off, and again had one of his dreadful fits of weeping.

That night the mother said to his father:

"Garstin, what are we to do?"

"There's nothing more we can do," said her husband.

"But if Fernol should—"

She did not dare to finish the sentence. They looked into each other's faces for an instant in silence.

Then Mrs. West said:

"There's only one more thing I can think of—that woman in Boston."

"What woman?"

"Olivia Traill."

"Another doctor! But—"

"No; she's a healer."

"That's what the doctors call themselves," said Mr. West bitterly.

"She lays her hands on people."

"Much good that'll do! No; we've tried everything. The boy'll never be right again."

"Let us try that Miss Traill," said Mrs. West. "It will be useless, of course, but—she has made wonderful cures, they say."

"Who say?"

"Well, the newspapers."

"The papers! Good God—if that's all!"

"I can't help it. I shall take Fernol to Boston."

"But we've tried the Christian Scientists."

"She isn't one. She doesn't believe in their theories."

"Then what does she believe in?"

"Herself, I suppose. She contends that it's done partly by faith."

"Money-making humbug."

"Do you mean that you would grudge any money—"

"No, no! Take Fernol to Boston, my dear, if you can get him to go."

"I think he would try anything, poor child. It's—it's heart-rending, and one feels so impotent."

"One feels what one is," said Mr. West drearily.

At first Fernol refused to go to Boston.

"It's no good, Mum," he said. "It's no good. I thought that hypnotist fellow might put me right. I believed in him. Even after sixteen goes of it I still hoped. But—"

"Come, for my sake."

"No, Mum! Don't ask me anymore. Faith healing! And I've no more faith in any damned thing. Don't drag me to Boston."

"Go by yourself then!"

"No, Mum. Don't ask me."

She gave it up. But, to her great surprise, after a few days, Fernol said to her desperately:

"I am going to Boston. I can't stand another week of this. What's that woman's name?"

"Olivia Traill."

"Where does she live?"

"I don't know. But her father's a well-known bookseller. Ask for—"

"I'll find her."

There was an almost frantic look on his grey face; a frantic light shone in his sunken blue eyes.

"She'll be no earthly good, but I'll try her."

Afterwards Fernol often told the story of that visit to Boston, told it as a man might tell how out of darkness he was caught up into heaven.

He sought out the bookseller's store, and went in among the stacks of books and asked for the address of the bookseller's daughter.

A clerk looked at him curiously and gave it.

"When does she see people?" asked Fernol.

"Any time, I believe," said the clerk. "If she's in."

"I'll go now."

And he was out of the store in an instant. Not many minutes later he stood at the door of a modest apartment on the western outskirts of the city. A maidservant answered his ring. He asked for Miss Traill.

"She's out at a meeting," was the reply.

Fernol felt a sickness run all over him till it seemed to find its way to his soul and make its home there.

"When will she be back?" he said.

"I couldn't quite say."

"May I wait? Please let me wait. I don't care how long she is. I'll just sit till she comes."

"You need her, I can see," said the girl. "You can come right in. She'd wish it."

"Would she?" said Fernol.

"She'd wish it."

He often said afterwards that something in those last words of the girl, and in the way they were said, gave him "a sort of lift."

"She'd wish it."

He stepped in, put his hat down, and was shown into a plain little living room, without any pictures or ornaments. On the wall hung a scroll showing the words: "*Thy faith hath saved thee.*" A few books were lying about. They were all by the great optimists of the world: Emerson, Browning, etc. Fernol sat down in a small, but very comfortable easy chair, rested his head on the back and looked at the scroll. Presently he shut his eyes. He didn't feel sleepy, but he did feel inclined to be passive. As he sat there life somehow seemed just bearable. For many months, though he had borne it, it had seemed unbearable. He laid his hands on his knees and let his muscles relax.

"There seemed to be something in the room," he afterwards said, "that quieted a fellow down."

He sat like this for over an hour without taking count of time. Then he heard steps in the passage, the opening and shutting of a door and a voice speaking. It said:

"I'm rather late, Annie. Has anyone called for me?"

Another voice—the girl's—answered in a long and careful murmur. Then the first voice said:

"That's quite right. Never turn anyone away who seems really to need me. I'm here for that. Just take my hat and cloak and I'll go right in to him."

Fernol sat up. His misery was still upon him, that almost unbearable misery, at the same time vague and terrific. But he felt a sense of expectation which was new to him since his accident. Then the door opened and Olivia came into the room. He got up. She looked straight at him with a smile, held out her strong hand cordially, and said:

"Good evening. I'm sorry I've kept you waiting. I've been out to a lecture. What's your trouble?"

"Don't you—don't you want to know my name?" Fernol stammered.

"If you'd like me to know it."

"Fernol West."

Olivia sat down very near to him.

"Thank you. Now sit right down and I'll try to help you."

He obeyed.

"I've come from New York. My mother heard of you. She wished— I thought I would come."

"I'm glad. You're all wrong. I can see that. You're just chock-full of what Metchnikoff calls 'disharmonies.' You know what I mean by that, don't you? You keep striking discords inside, and they make life hideous to you."

"Yes, that's just it. Life is hideous. How did you know?"

"Your face shows it. You want to get back to the harmonies."

"I do; oh, I do! It seems so unmanly—but I can't help it."

"Of course you can't. It isn't your fault. How did it begin?"

He told her the story of his accident and of his apparent recovery from it. Olivia listened with concentrated attention without interrupting him by a word.

"The doctors said I was all right," he concluded at last. "Until I had to go to the nerve men."

"And what did they say and do?"

"Well, some of them said I was all right, too, if I would only use my will and look on the bright side of things."

"In your condition that's easier said than done. Tell me everything they tried on you. Don't miss anything."

He told her about everything, including the suggested operation, the efforts of the hypnotists, and of the Christian Scientist.

"He told me there was no such thing as disease, that my trouble only existed in mortal mind."

"I sometimes wish it was so," said Olivia. "But, you see, the trouble is that it isn't."

"Then you think I am really ill?"

"You're very bad," said Olivia. "You're right down in Hell, and you've got to be pulled out. I know how you feel."

"Yes?" he said. "I—I thought I would come to you."

"Very well. Now, then, the first thing is to get quite clear between ourselves. I'm not a doctor, I'm a healer."

She spoke without the least trace of irony.

"I can heal," she said, quietly in her full voice. "I can heal you. That's as sure as that we're sitting here. But you've got to help me. Let's have a little talk about faith. Goethe says some fine things about Faith."

She paused, seemed quietly to collect herself, and then, leaning forward, quoted:

"In Faith everything depends on the fact of believing. Faith is a profound sense of security. The strength of this confidence is the main thing. Faith is a holy vessel, into which every man may pour his feelings, his understanding, and his imagination, as entirely as he can."

Again she paused.

"That's what Goethe says about Faith. And someone greater than Goethe said, 'If thou canst believe, all things are possible to him that believeth.'"

"Yes—I remember that," said Fernol.

"And I dare say it seemed to you just an improbable assertion, as it does to a great many people. Now, when you set out for Boston, had you any hope at all that I might cure you?"

"I don't think I had," said Fernol.

"Well, you took a ticket all the same. And when you got right here where I live?"

"I don't think I had any real hope."

"And when you sat in this room?"

"I—I seemed to feel something in this room."

"What?"

"I could hardly say. I felt quiet here, in a way."

"Did you hear me outside?"

"Yes."

"I meant you to. Get anything from my voice?"

"I—I don't know. But—yes—perhaps I did. I do believe I did."

"And then I came in, and here I am. D'you get anything from me?"

Her large grey eyes were fixed upon him, but tranquilly. There was no effort in their gaze. They just rested upon him, like the eyes of a good friend.

"Yes, I do," Fernol said at last, after a long silence.

"What do you get?"

"I feel more of a man with you than I have felt since I had the accident."

"You'd given up all hope of being cured, hadn't you?"

"Yes."

"And what do you say now?"

"I feel that if anyone on earth could put me right it would be you."

She smiled, almost tenderly and quite happily.

"That's just what I want you to feel. You're coming my way. And I'm just all faith; I haven't a doubt in me about my power to put you right. But I've got to fill you right up with faith too. Reach out your hands."

Fernol obeyed, and Olivia took hold of them, and kept them in hers resting on her knees while she went on talking about faith, and quoting what great men had written and said about it. She filled the little room with faith, till it almost seemed to the boy that he could see faith hovering there about the two of them like something tangible. Then at last she was silent and just sat holding his hands. Perhaps ten minutes went by; then she released his hands.

"You're better," she said.

Fernol started. Suddenly, when she spoke, he realised that for ten minutes he had been feeling contented—interested for the first time since his accident. That was very wonderful.

"You—you want me to go now?" he said.

He did not want to go; he dreaded to leave that room.

"I don't want you to go at all," said Olivia; "but I've got to get some tea, and then I have one or two others to see."

Fernol got up.

"Shall I see you again?" he asked.

A horrible anxiety pulled at his heart.

"Why, of course! I may have to see you a good few times. I can't tell yet how long it will take. But it's going to be quite all right. Where are you putting up?"

He told her the name of his hotel.

"Go there and keep quiet. Don't see a lot of people. Keep yourself for me. Read—" she went over to a table and selected a book—"Read some Walt Whitman. I love old Walt. And come here again to-morrow at the same hour. I feel very happy about you."

Her strong face lighted up with a splendid smile.

"There's a lot of faith in you already. But I want it to fill you right up. Faith makes men, and women too."

Fernol stood for a moment gazing at her. Then, with a slight awkwardness and with a flush on his face, he said:

"May I—will you please tell me what the fee is?"

"Oh, I never charge anything. See here, this is how it is. My father's a bookseller—"

"I know. I went to his store to get your address."

"Well, he's a good father to me. He knows how I feel, that to sell what comes out of the spirit into the body and goes out to those who need it badly wouldn't help me any in what I am trying to do. I never could hold with that, somehow. It would seem to get in the way. So he just keeps me going like this. It's good of him, but he's a good man though he runs a prosperous business. There's nothing to pay. And now before you go, just lay hold of this. You're not cured yet. So don't think it. Maybe before you get back to where you're staying, you'll feel almost as bad as ever, perhaps quite as bad. If you do, just say to yourself: 'But I was well for ten minutes. And to-morrow I shall be well for half an hour.' I tell you that. Do you believe it?"

"Yes," said Fernol.

"That means you're on the way to be perfectly well. You've got your two feet on the path that's to lead you right into the blessed sunshine. I do feel happy about you. Come again to-morrow at the same hour, and write to your mother to-night that you're better. I guess that will ease her mind."

"Thank you," he said. "She will be glad; my father too. But you give me all this and I—"

"I like giving out. That's how I get in strength."

"That's funny."

"You'll try it someday and find it answers."

And she went with him to the door. As she opened it she said:

"Don't forget that letter to your mother."

"No, I won't."

"And if you feel very bad to-night, you'll write it just the same? You'll tell her you're better?"

"Yes."

"And you'll mean it, won't you? Then just put a good thick line under the words. Score them under. What time will you write?"

"Any time."

"No, that won't do. Tell me the time."

"Just before I go to bed—ten o'clock."

At ten o'clock I'll sit and think of you scoring a line under 'I'm better.'"

She shook his hand and let him out....

Just before ten o'clock that same night Fernol sat in his room in the hotel and felt terribly miserable. The influence of Olivia Traill seemed to him to be operative only for so long as he was with her, to be limited to her close neighbourhood. It was great. He knew that. He had felt it like something one can grasp and lean on. But when her door had shut her out from him, when he was alone, could no longer see her steady eyes and hear her reliant voice, he had fallen again into the blackness. And awful doubts had assailed him. If she could only act upon him when he sat with her, felt the clasp of her hands, he could never be healed by her. For he could not live always in her presence. Was she like a doctor whose treatment was only efficacious while he was sitting by the patient's bedside? Fernol was almost terrified. For he had mounted, and now felt like one fallen from a height and lying bruised and bleeding in some hideous ravine. Nevertheless, as the hour of ten drew near he remembered his promise, went to the writing table and sat down. He did not like to break his promise. That would be dishonourable. And yet how could he write to his mother a lie? It would make her happy, fill her with hope, and then, when she saw him again, her old distress would return upon her intensified. Had he the right thus to deceive her, to lay up for her such a burden of grief?

Yet he took paper and pen. He began to write. The clock struck ten.

He thought of Olivia. He knew she was doing what she had said she would do. She was sitting in her little room thinking of him. She would take nothing from him. She was a splendid woman anyhow. A sense of pure chivalry came to the boy, guided his pen in the words: "*I am better.*" Then he hesitated. Could he score a line under them? "Yes, damn it, I will!" he said to himself with a sort of defiance. And he drew a thick line. As he did so the cloud lifted from him—for just a moment, and he thought Olivia was smiling in her room....

Three weeks later he wrote to his mother:

"*I am cured. Olivia Traill is the greatest woman I have ever met. I am happy. I enjoy everything I do. And it is all owing to her.*"

He returned to New York a changed being. His parents saw once more the gay energetic youth, full of the zest for life, whom they had rejoiced in and mourned almost as we mourn for the dead. They could not contain their delight. Their gratitude to the woman who had wrought the marvel was unbounded. Her absolute disinterestedness in the matter astonished them almost as much as her extraordinary powers. Mr. West, especially, who was one of the shrewdest and hardest men of business in the States, found it almost impossible to believe that Olivia wanted no reward for all the time she had given up to his son.

"But no one does anything for nothing!" he said. "You must have made a mistake, boy. She'll send in the bill to me."

"I tell you, Father, she never takes money for her cures."

"Then she must take something else."

"She doesn't!" asserted Fernol, almost indignantly. "She works for the sake of humanity. There's no other woman like her. If you could only see her you'd understand."

"Does she know who I am?" said Mr. West.

"Of course she does."

"Then she's certainly a right down extraordinary woman."

When he was alone with his wife Mr. West said:

"I feel like going over to Boston to see this Miss Traill. I can't quite understand things."

"How d'you mean, dear?" asked his wife.

"Doesn't it strike you that Fernol may be in love with her?"

"I had thought of that," Mrs. West said, reflectively.

"Fernol will have big money someday."

He glanced at his wife.

"She might be playing for the big money, eh?"

"If she were I'd forgive her. I'd forgive her anything for what she has done."

"Well, Kate, I think I'll just run over to Boston and have a look at her.

I can judge women as well as most men, I guess. That's why I married you."

Mrs. West found it difficult to combat this proof of her husband's astuteness. Moreover, she was intensely anxious about the Faith healer. So she encouraged him to go. He returned from Boston almost as enthusiastic as his son.

"The boy's right!" he said. "There's no other woman like Olivia Traill. And she's no more designs on Fernol than I have on the Presidency. What's more she won't take a cent. She's a grand woman. I only hope Fernol isn't in love with her. For she'd never look at the boy. I'm as certain of that as I am that I shall carry through the amalgamation of Chicago Automatics with—but you take no stock in such facts, though you don't mind playing with the interest. A woman like Olivia Traill wouldn't fall in love easily, and if she ever did she'd choose a man among men. She's strong, she's bully strong, she'd look for strength."

"But our boy is strong, Garstin!" said Mrs. West, with a slight sound of huffiness in her gentle voice.

"Not in the way such a woman would want. Besides, she's seen him very sick, remember."

"And what has that to do with it?"

"You'd jump to it if you knew her. Watch it, Kate, for the boy."

And Mrs. West watched it, with that gentle, terrible cleverness of the adoring mother, and came to a not too unhappy conclusion.

Fernol adored Olivia Traill, but not in the way of a hopeful or even of a longing lover. He looked up to her as a lover never quite looks up. There was a peculiar moral admiration in his worship which somehow excluded the possibility of physical passion. Mrs. West soon found that out, and was perfectly at ease in the matter.

"Fernol could no more imagine Miss Traill belonging to him than I could imagine belonging to Mercury," she said. "He sees her with wings, Garstin."

"So you've figured it out that I haven't got any wings."

She stroked his hand.

"I should never have fallen in love with Mercury. We needn't worry."

And they didn't. But they made a tremendous propaganda for Olivia. And the papers were full of her marvellous cure of the millionaire's son. Fernol had no sort of shyness in alluding to his former condition of misery and contrasting it with the glory and wonder of his now abounding health. He tried to pay part of his great debt to Olivia by singing her praises. He interested himself in the progress of her fame. He was furious with those who attacked her, resented all criticism of her almost fanatically. There was indeed a hint of fanaticism in him since his return to health which had been absent from, or at any rate had lain dormant in, him before his accident. This marked a slight, but definite, change in the boy. But few people noticed it as anything strange. And his father and mother thought it quite natural, and even fine, a proof that their boy had in him chivalrous feeling and an almost fierce sense of gratitude. Fernol's great desire was to persuade Olivia to come to New York, and, at last, with the help of his parents, he achieved it.

She stayed with them for a week in Fifth Avenue.

From the first moment of her arrival she conquered Fernol's mother. And she conquered many others in New York. She wished to have a quiet visit and the Wests wished her to have it, but it was impossible to keep everyone out. There were many who were anxious for her to try her healing powers on them, and who clamoured to be received by her. She was firm in refusal of these, however, and saw only the Wests' most intimate friends. She had come to have a little holiday because she needed it. She knew when rest was necessary for her, and she was resolved to have it. So she went about with Fernol and his mother to see beautiful things, pictures, statues, antiquities, and she let them take her to hear fine music.

"I'll come here again someday to work," she said. "There's a new field for me here, and I feel like tilling it and putting in some seed. But not just now."

It was when they were at a concert one afternoon that Fernol realised, with a sort of almost cutting sharpness, what Olivia had done for him. Music, once his delight, had been a torture to him when he was ill. Now, once more, it led him into those pure regions of joy to which no other art gives the soul of man entrance.

"When I hear music I know what you have done for me," he whispered to Olivia, during a pause. "And music makes me almost ache to do something tremendous for you. Why can't I? It hurts."

"You do all I want by being healthy in body and mind and soul," she said. "By being clean and bright right through."

After the concert he returned to this "ache," as he called it.

"That's the worst of music," he said. "It makes one feel one ought to do wonderful things, that one might do them if—something. But what is the 'something'? Music never seems to tell me."

"Perhaps someday you'll find some wonderful thing to do lying close to your hand, Fernol," said Olivia. "And then you'll do it, without music. I believe in doing things without anything from outside helping. All that is necessary to prompt us to the finest actions we are capable of lies in ourselves. I'm certain of that."

"You must be right. You always are," he said. "I hope if I ever can do anything wonderful I shall do it for you."

Olivia carried out her intention of putting in some seed in New York later on. She left Boston, rented a modest apartment which the Wests found for her in a quiet street not far from them, and settled down there to carry on her strange profession. She still refused to take fees, and continued to live on the very moderate allowance she received from her father. And people of all classes thronged to the little room where she saw patients, and read, as they came in at the door, the words Fernol had seen on the scroll at Boston, "Thy faith hath saved thee."

It was there that Lord Sandring found her when she had been in New York for over three years.

II

Lord Sandring was an enthusiast about what he called "Psychic Healing," and proclaimed his enthusiasm in season and out of season. He was an amiable man, with a good deal of energy and some cleverness, but he was easily carried away, and on more than one occasion had been taken in by charlatans. Society was inclined to laugh at him, and the medical profession sniffed in a superior manner when his name was mentioned. But he was delightfully imperturbable and revelled in controversy. He was always keen to have "a slash at the doctors," and frequently appeared on the platform in support of his bureau. He possessed large estates in Northamptonshire and Wiltshire, and, when they would allow it, tried his powers of psychic healing on his tenants and villagers. He asserted that he had made several "cures," and had published a beautifully-bound volume dealing with them in detail. His claims and assertions had been received, alas, with polite incredulity by a sceptical world, but opposition only nerved him to renewed efforts. He was of those who doubt the value of any new theory unless it is attacked, and often said: "If the doctors didn't go for me I should be afraid I was on the wrong road." Such a man is difficult to knock out, and hitherto, even after the most violent bouts, Lord Sandring had always gone smiling out of the ring. But, as his "Psychic Healing Bureau" did not make much headway, he had gone to America to seek for "new blood." Olivia Traill's arrival in London was a triumph for him. He had persuaded her to come over for a short time merely in order to show people that he had preached a true gospel, that the healing power, backed by faith, could accomplish marvels, that spirit could sometimes do for the body something that medicine could not do. His psychic healers had not been altogether lucky in their well-meant endeavours to get the better of physical troubles. His instinct told him that the time had arrived to "make a big splash." He meant to make this big splash with Olivia.

She had come to London simply to put some seed in new ground. She had accepted from Lord Sandring the money for her passage over, not a penny more. He had prepared for her a room at the Psychic Healing Bureau, where she would receive patients, and he had given it out that the famous Miss Traill would not make any money out of her visit to England, but came to put her extraordinary powers gratuitously at the service of suffering humanity. He had also arranged for her to deliver a short course of lectures on "Faith," "The Power of Spirit over Matter," and kindred subjects.

Olivia's first lecture at the small Queen's Hall was not largely attended, but several well-known people were present. Among them, to the great surprise of Lord Sandring, was the celebrated soldier, General Sir Hector Burnington.

What Sir Hector was doing in that *galère* Lord Sandring could not imagine. He came in two or three minutes late alone, sat down at the back of the room, stayed till the end of Olivia's speech, and then got up and went out. Lord Sandring saw the General's towering figure on its way to the door, as he rose to "say a few words" of comment on the lecture and of thanks to the lecturer. He was almost stupefied, but recovered his aplomb in a moment, and spoke with his usual energy and effectiveness. Afterwards he said to Olivia:

"You had one of our greatest men to hear you."

Fernol West, who was with them, said eagerly, "Who was that? Was it the immensely tall fellow who sat at the back?"

"To be sure it was," said Lord Sandring.

"I saw him," said Olivia. "Who is he?"

"Sir Hector Burnington, the only man we've got with a genius for organisation and a supreme power of managing men."

"Burnington!" exclaimed Fernol. "You don't say!"

He flushed with pride for Olivia.

"We must get that in the Press."

"I shouldn't," said Lord Sandring, with unusual self-restraint. "Burnington's a wonderful fellow, but he's an odd fellow, and wants careful handling, if he can be handled at all. Some of the politicians say he can't. As to women—well, Miss Traill, I dare say you know his reputed views about them!"

"They say in the States that he thinks we are not helps but hindrances to any big man who's got big work to do in the world. Is it true?"

"True as gospel. Burnington has no use for women, but they worship him from afar."

"I wonder why he came to hear a woman speak," Olivia said thoughtfully.

"That beats me!" said Lord Sandring. "You spoke grandly to-night. I wonder what he thought of you."

Olivia did not show any anxiety to know the great man's verdict, but even she, who was almost entirely free from personal vanity, was secretly impressed by the fact that Burnington had sat and listened to her—a woman—for over an hour.

A few days later she received the following note:

2a, Cadogan Square, S.W.
Feb'y 17th.

Madam, —I have not the honour of knowing you, but I heard your first lecture the other night at the small Queen's Hall. You are evidently a genuine believer in the power you claim to possess. I should like to have a few words with you if you have no objection. As I prefer not to set foot in the Psychic Healing Bureau—not that I have anything against it—I should be glad to know whether you could appoint a time to see me somewhere else. I should not detain you for more than a few moments.

Believe me, Madam,

Yours faithfully,
HECTOR BURNINGTON.

Olivia laid down this letter, after she had read it carefully twice, and sat wondering for a moment. She felt both surprised and interested; she also felt flattered. The General's reputation was enormous. He was regarded by his countrymen as their supreme efficient, a man who had the strength and the intelligence to pull whole countries out of messes, to quiet rebellions by his mere presence on the scene of them, to set staggering protectorates firmly on their feet. He had transformed a war. What had he not done? But Olivia's peculiar interest in him sprang from report of his personality and from her remembrance of his many adventures, which had been recounted in the newspapers of the world. The mysteries of the East hung about him like heavy odours. Far away he had built up his reputation in regions whose mere names suggested romance. He had ruled over peoples whose wild eyes had never looked on our complicated civilisation, and had inspired them with reverence and awe. He spoke strange dialects of the East, and, a master of travesty, had travelled as a blood comrade with men who would have slain him had they known who he was. And he was reputed to be strangely selfless and heroic, and threaded through with a strain of fatalistic mysticism. He stood out from his nation as something portentously invulnerable; a soul of bronze in a body of bronze; supremely successful but cold and indifferent in his success, alive not to love, not to pity, not to fear, not to enjoy, but to get things done.

"Why does this man want to see me?" Olivia asked herself.

And the quiet firmness of her was slightly shaken. A hidden string vibrated for just a moment. She sat down and answered the letter, suggesting that the General should come to the little furnished flat which she had taken in Buckingham Palace Mansions on the following evening at six o'clock. She was usually at the Bureau till after five. In reply to her note she received on the following day a telephone message. The message was:

"The gentleman Miss Olivia Traill kindly wrote to will call on her at six o'clock."

When she had read it—she only did so at a quarter to six—she sent down a message asking the porter to bring up anyone who called at six. She was not expecting any visitor but Sir Hector. After her day's work she usually rested, unless she had to deliver a lecture. Lord Sandring would have gladly "run" her in his social circle, but she had resisted his kind importunities.

At five minutes to six when she was in her small sitting room awaiting Sir Hector there was a ring at the bell. She went to answer the door, and found Fernol West with some flowers for her, and a new book by Rabindranath Tagore, which he knew she wanted to read.

"I didn't wait for the lift. I just ran up," he said. "May I sit with you for a bit?"

He saw that she hesitated.

"You're busy."

"No; come in, Fernol."

She shut the door.

"I'm waiting for someone who is coming to see me at six. It is Sir Hector Burnington."

"Burnington coming here!" exclaimed Fernol. "Do you know him?"

"No. He wrote to me."

"Is he ill?"

His eyes shone.

"If he's ill and you cure him the whole of England will believe in you. It will silence even those beastly doctors. They've begun to attack you furiously already. Have you seen to-night's *Messenger?*"

"No."

"There's an article by Sir Mervyn Butler called 'Human Credulity and the Charlatans,' warning people against you. Oh, it's made me so mad. These wretched fellows who can't—"

"Don't abuse people. That only does you harm."

"I know. But it's difficult when I know what you are, when I'm a breathing proof of your powers. Is he ill? Is Burnington ill?"

"Not that I know of."

"It may seem inhuman, but I would give anything for him to be downright sick, real bad, so that you might cure him. Ah, it would go all over the world in a moment—such a cure as that!"

"Fernol," Olivia said, looking at him steadily. "I hope you will never be fanatical about me. I don't like fanaticism at all. I think it is unhealthy. And I want to feel that there's nothing unhealthy in you."

Before he could answer the front doorbell rang.

"There he is!" said the boy, with an eager start. "Oh, I oughtn't to be here."

"You need not speak of his coming. I should be sorry to have a great name used. Now you might let him in."

As Fernol turned to go down the little hall, he whispered, with a sort of laughing worship:

"I can't help it. I want him to be ill, desperately ill!"

A minute later he opened the sitting room door, showed a strongly flushed, excited face, and said,

"Miss Traill, Sir Hector Burnington has come to see you."

Then he stood against the wall, rather like a soldier at attention, and gave room for the famous general to pass.

Seen close in the bright light from electric burners Sir Hector looked almost gigantic in height. As a matter of fact, he was just over six foot three. His face was unusually dark in complexion for an Englishman, his dark brown smooth hair was parted in the middle above a very broad and very low forehead; his nose was straight and short, his chin firm but not aggressive, his mouth determined with tightly closed full lips. His ears were large, were set close to his head and indicated power. His figure was lean, and his tread was firm and striding. But in that first moment of meeting Olivia looked at his eyes. They were very peculiar eyes, set far apart, long, in colour green and brown—some people called them "greeny brown"—with unusually small pupils. And there was a curious glazed look in them, which suggested not dullness of intellect but secrecy, a remoteness that somehow was watchful. Impossible to look into them! Yet they seemed to look into you as well as beyond you. On his upper lip the general wore a thick brown moustache with a marked curve in it. His eyebrows were almost straight.

He strode in, looking imperturbable, grave and quite unself-conscious, and held out a long brown hand.

"Good evening, Miss Traill. Very good of you to see me. What's your friend's name?"

"Fernol West," said Olivia.

The general shook hands with Fernol, neither cordially nor coldly.

"I'll be off now," said Fernol to Olivia.

She knew he was simply longing to stay, but she did not like to keep him as an appointment had been made with her visitor, so she said good-bye.

"Good-bye—sir," said Fernol to Sir Hector.

"Good-bye."

Fernol turned to go, took two steps towards the door, hesitated, then abruptly swung round.

"If you'll allow me I should like to tell you that when I was broken to pieces she put me together again. They attack her. They've attacked her to-day in a paper called the *Messenger*. But I was in hell and she's made life worth living for me. I swear it."

He paused. There was something almost violent in his look and manner. He covered Sir Hector with an eager, searching glance.

"Ah!" said Sir Hector.

And he turned his strange glazed eyes on the lad.

Fernol waited an instant more, then went out, shutting the door rather sharply behind him.

"I did him good, so, as he's a chivalrous lad, he sings up in praise of me," said Olivia simply. "Please sit down."

Sir Hector sat down without any comment.

"Allow me to tell you the reason of my visit," he said. "I heard of you some two years ago. I know the States pretty well and I see American papers. As I happen to be interested in various things which most English people deride, and as I believe in a great deal which untravelled islanders, profoundly ignorant and proud of being so, deny, I attended your first lecture—as I mentioned in my note. I wished rather to obtain an impression of you than to listen to what you had to say. The impression I obtained was that you thoroughly believe in yourself."

"Yes, I do," said Olivia, looking steadily up at him from her chair. "I have absolute faith in my power of healing."

"Without it you could probably not heal even a slight nervous complaint," returned Sir Hector.

"I don't think I could, though I am sure I have some exceptional physical gift. It may be a gift of conveyance, which most people lack."

"Ah!" said the general.

He stared either at her, or beyond her—she was not quite sure which—for a moment, then he continued, in his deep and steady voice:

"I am not married, and I live at present—I'm looking into the condition of our artillery at the moment—with my only near relative, my unmarried sister. She is four years older than I am—sixty. She was, in my opinion, the finest horsewoman in the British Isles, but eight years ago, when I was in Afghanistan, she had an accident in the hunting-field. Her horse, a big Irish hunter, fell at a wall and rolled over on her. She was kicked on the back of the head. Since then she has suffered from agonising headaches. They come on about once in ten days. The pain at first is slight, gradually increases—she often keeps about for some hours after the premonitory symptoms—and finally becomes terrific. Then she goes to bed and stays there, usually from twenty-four to thirty-six hours. After that the pain subsides and ceases. Of course, she has had all the big doctors. And she's got one—a pleasant fellow, Mervyn Butler by name—who attends her regularly. He doesn't do her any good and she knows it. But he does something, and I suppose, when one's in such a condition, it's a sort of relief to know something's being done. (I've never been ill in my life, so I'm no judge.) It isn't pleasant to me to see my sister under these perpetual attacks. And they'll certainly break her up in time if they aren't stopped. I should like you to try to stop them."

"I will gladly do so."

"Ah!" said Sir Hector, with his peculiar stare, which suggested to Olivia that he was looking out over some vast expanse, in the foreground of which she was set, an almost infinitesimal figure.

"That is very kind of you. Thank you," he answered, after the pause which was characteristic of him. "But there's a drawback."

"What is it? Her doctor would—"

"Her doctor doesn't matter. He doesn't cure her and I shall have no consideration for him. He fails in his job. And no consideration should be shown to failures; otherwise you create a sort of forcing-house for the cultivation of inefficients. My sister is the drawback."

"Why is that?"

"She's the most sceptical woman in England about anything mysterious. She likes hard facts, things ascertained by science."

"Hard facts. And you?" said Olivia.

"I've travelled widely, and she hasn't," returned the general. "I judge by results. My sister's doctor knows a great many medical facts and is totally unable to cure her headaches. He and his facts are, therefore, quite useless to my sister. But, as women are remarkably unreasonable, she pays him heavy fees to go on not curing her. Multitudes of women in England do exactly the same. My sister will probably be entirely sceptical of your power to do her any good if you come to her as a healer … because she is ill. And her scepticism might frustrate your attempt to heal, I dare say."

"Perhaps it might," said Olivia. "But, then, what is your plan?"

"How do you know I have a plan?"

"I don't think you would have come here without one."

"Ah!"

Again the stare and the pause—a long pause this time. Then the general said:

"I told you that these headaches return every ten days or so with remarkable regularity. One knows when they are due. What I wish to do is this. I intend to arrange for a dinner party at my house on a certain evening. I shall know pretty well when to fix it. Even if my sister's headache has started she'll be down. She never gives in till she's obliged to. I want you, if you will, to come in the evening after dinner. (I hope another time you will honour me by dining.) My sister will meet you socially, will be able to observe you and see what you are, without connecting you with herself. It is possible that you may be able to impress her with confidence in your *bona fides*. If so, the ground will be prepared for the attempt at a cure. Then the cure might be attempted under favourable conditions."

"I am quite ready to come," said Olivia. "But please tell me one thing. Do you believe I can make such a cure?"

"I think it quite possible."

He stared into the distance.

"People are often sceptical from sheer colossal ignorance, or they are afraid of seeming superstitious. Both superstition and scepticism may grow from the same root—the root, by the way, of nearly all evil. I may write to you then?"

"Certainly."

"Do you object to cigarette smoke in your drawing room?"

"Dear no!"

The general lighted up, after offering Olivia a cigarette, which she refused.

"Now," he said, "I wish to say a word or two in confidence. I shall probably be offered almost immediately one of the highest posts a man of British birth can fill. For years it has been the ambition of my life to get this particular post, because I know I am peculiarly fitted for it. It's a job I could do better than any other man I can think of. But it would be necessary for me to have a woman at my side if I accepted it. My sister is at present far too ill to undertake the position. She must be made sound."

In saying the last sentence the general seemed to be giving an order to someone.

"The doctors can't do it," he added.

"And if I fail in my job?" asked Olivia.

"H'm!" said the general.

A faint smile flickered over his face.

"You'll kick me out of your consideration into the limbo where the charlatans dwell, I suppose?" said Olivia.

"I shall be deeply obliged to you if you succeed," he replied.

He got up.

"The matter's quite clear now, I think."

"Quite clear. But may I ask you something?"

"Please do."

"Why, when I spoke just now about hard facts, did you say, 'I've travelled widely and she hasn't'?"

"I merely meant to convey that in travelling one comes up against many people with peculiar gifts, and that, therefore, one is not so disposed to deny possibilities as those who seldom move out of the region in which they were born. The English have some remarkable gifts as a nation; but their limitations are also remarkable. My sister is very English. She hates humbug. Having only just come over here, you may not know yet that in an English mouth the word humbug often covers just those very things which are most worthy of minute investigation. Ah!"

He stared down at her and, for a moment, there seemed to Olivia to be something piercing in the expression of his strangely detached eyes. He held out his hand. She got up and took it.

"If your friend, Mr. Fernol West, would care to come to my house with you when you come, I should be very glad to see him," said the general. "Goodbye."

He turned and went out of the room, striding with long loose limbs which looked as if they were made to grip a great war horse.

Six days later Olivia received a note from her visitor asking her if she would come to his house the following evening at half-past nine; in a postscript was added:

"PS.—*I shall be very glad to see Mr. West, too.*"

Olivia wrote to say she would come and would give Fernol the message. She believed that she knew why Fernol was invited. Miss Burnington was sceptical; Fernol was an almost fanatical believer. The general knew that. Olivia had already realised that he was a man who usually had a purpose behind what he did.

Fernol was overjoyed when she gave him the invitation, and on the way to Cadogan Square on the following evening he expressed his feelings with animation. His chivalry had been hurt by Olivia's reception in London. So far her visit had not been a great success. Not many people had consulted her, and the attacks upon her, led by Sir Mervyn Butler, had been fierce. In a certain very well-known weekly paper it had been roundly asserted that American charlatans ought not to be allowed to prey upon the gullible English public, and that the powers of the police ought to be extended if they were not already sufficient to deal with such people in a fitting manner. Olivia's name had not been mentioned in the article, but it was obvious at whom the arrows were aimed. And a sentence in which "Pernicious busy-bodies whose brain power is as low as their rank is high" were gibbeted was undoubtedly meant for Lord Sandring.

"I like Lord Sandring," said the boy to Olivia in the taxicab. "And he's worth all these beastly journalists and doctors put together. But I rather wish you hadn't come over under his auspices. I've found out that they laugh at him and the Bureau in London."

"I dare say they do," said Olivia's calm voice.

"Yes, but I mean he's really made some bad mistakes. He's made claims without proving them. He's had some rank failures connected with his Bureau. I can't bear to see all that come back upon you. Besides, it sets up a regular wave of unbelief."

He broke off, then said in an excited voice:

"I count a lot on this evening. If Sandring has done you harm—of course without meaning to—I count on Burnington to set you where you ought to be. I don't ask you to tell me why he called on you, or why he asked us to-night, but, of course, I know it must be something to do with your lecture. You must have made a fine impression on him. And he's a thundering great man. It's grand of him to ask me, and I can't think why he's done it. Can you?"

"He didn't say," was Olivia's quiet answer.

"If only he could fall sick and you could cure him! I would give anything for that."

"I don't like to hear you wish sickness for anyone, Fernol. That's the wrong sort of mind action. Sir Hector Burnington has never been ill in his life. My wish for him is that he never may be."

"I know it's all wrong of me, but don't you see—"

"I never want anyone to wish an unclean thing because of me."

"Unclean!" cried Fernol, as if stung.

"Yes, Fernol. I call it unclean to wish evil to anyone for any reason."

"I shall never be selfless like you," he said almost sulkily.

And he did not speak again till they reached the general's house.

As a footman opened the door of a large drawing room on the first floor Olivia heard a murmur of conversation and was conscious of a very unusual feeling. Perhaps she was not quite sincere with herself in mentally calling it "excitement"; perhaps nervousness would have been the right name for it. She knew that it was caused by something in Sir Hector's personality, by the expectation of a great man who had impressed her with the sense of his ruthless bigness. Since she had met him she quite understood why he managed to make the men under him work up to the very limit of their capacity. She felt that she was about to be tested as she had not been tested hitherto. And a slight anxiety crept through her. She did not like it, and instinctively she put her head a little back, sticking forward her chin, as she walked into the room, followed closely by Fernol.

"Miss Olivia Traill—Mr. Fernol West," said the footman.

And immediately there was a silence in the drawing room.

Sir Hector met them, shook them by the hand, and took them to a tall woman, with thickly waving white hair, who was getting up from a sofa by the fire.

"Let me introduce my sister."

Olivia looked at the pale, lined but handsome face of her hostess, a face marked with the impress of suffering, and at once lost her feeling of anxiety. Miss Burnington said a kind word or two, in a cordial, yet strictly non-committal manner, then turned to make the newcomers known to her other guests, Mrs. Harford, Lady Pangbourne, Colonel Lumley, and Sir Mervyn Butler.

At the mention of the last name Fernol's young face was flooded with indignant blood. This was the famous doctor who had attacked Olivia in the *Messenger*. Of course, the Burningtons were not aware of that or they would never have arranged a meeting between the two. Making a strong effort at self-control Fernol stared at the enemy, and saw a good-looking, clean-shaven man, with a massive head covered with snow-white hair, deep-set yellow eyes, and a smiling sarcastic mouth. Then he found himself—he scarcely knew how—in a corner near a grand piano, talking with Mrs. Harford, a pretty woman, with a worn-out face, bright, quickly glancing eyes, and a pathetic smile, the wife of a well-known politician. She got him in less than five minutes on to the subject of Olivia.

"The general sprang her on us as a surprise," she said. "Do tell me about her. She's had quite a bad Press over here."

Fernol took up the cudgels. Mrs. Harford listened, at first with indulgence, then with swiftly growing interest.

"It's a great pity she's let Lord Sandring nobble her," she said presently.

"He's got so hopelessly wrong with the doctors."

She glanced at Sir Mervyn, who at the moment was sitting with Colonel Lumley, a handsome man of not more than thirty-six, with a sharply intelligent soldier's face, and was taking very deliberate stock of the woman he had so recently thrashed in an article.

"I hate doctors," said Fernol, in a very low, very fierce voice. "Oh, I'm sorry!"

"Millie Pangbourne seems interested," said Mrs. Harford. "But she's interested in everybody who makes a noise."

"A noise?" said Fernol.

"In the world! If you don't make a noise she physically can't trouble about you. Her eyes mechanically refuse to see you. She's trained them to it, I suppose."

Lady Pangbourne, a dark, smart, pale and puffy woman, with self-conscious eyes, was engaged in a rattling conversation with Olivia. She did all the rattling. It was plain to see that Sir Hector's "surprise" had given her impetus. The general and his sister were in the group, and Fernol saw that Miss Burnington was watching Olivia with close attention, and that, while doing so, occasionally she winced, as if flicked sharply by whipcord, shut her eyes for an instant, and compressed her pale lips.

"She's got one of her horrible headaches coming on," observed Mrs. Harford. "She oughtn't to be up. But she's almost as iron in resolution as her brother. Fortunately for him he's got iron health too—never been ill in his life."

"Oh, does Miss Burnington suffer from headaches?"

"She's a martyr to them, a real martyr. Sir Mervyn is her doctor."

"Then why doesn't he cure her of them?" said Fernol. She caught his boyish sneer on the wing, as it were, and gave it a faint smile.

"For the best of reasons," she murmured. "Because he doesn't know how to."

"She could!" said Fernol.

"Can that be why she's here?" said Mrs. Harford. "The general always has a purpose." She broke off. "It would be just like him," she concluded after an instant.

At this moment Miss Burnington shivered and, losing her self-control for a second, put a thin hand to the back of her head. Sir Mervyn got up.

"Forgive me," he said, in a weighty agreeable voice, "I see you are suffering. Now do forget about us. Go up to bed and just do what I advised you with the—"

Before he had finished she had put her hand down and was smiling.

"No, no! What's that, Lady Pangbourne?"

"But, dear, you really look—"

"What were you saying?"

"I forget—something about Boston. Miss Traill, why don't you show us what you can do with poor Miss Burnington?"

As Lady Pangbourne said this she looked as alert as a weasel, and put her head on one side.

"Sir Mervyn won't mind. Will you, Sir Mervyn?"

The sarcastic lips smiled.

"I should be very much interested to see an exhibition of Miss Traill's healing force."

Olivia sat quite still for a moment looking at Miss Burnington. It seemed to her just then that she was back at her old school. She shut her eyes and saw Lily convulsed. And there came upon her that irresistible feeling of power to heal, of necessity to exercise it, that had long ago revealed to her what she was intended to do in the world. She remembered what Sir Hector had said about the scepticism of his sister, about the importance of preparing the ground. But something within her swept away caution. She felt too strong, too certain of herself just then to be cautious. She opened her eyes, and they rested on the face of Sir Mervyn Butler, who was looking at her with an expression of half amused, half contemptuous satire. No doubt he thought that her silence, her closing of the eyes, were calculated effects, tricks of the Sibyl designed to create an impression on the foolish. His face said so plainly. Sir Hector was watching her, too, with his remote and yet penetrating gaze. She looked at Miss Burnington.

"I never try to heal people in public," she said quietly.

"Very wise of you, Miss Traill," said Sir Mervyn.

"But—" She paused. Then she said to Miss Burnington, whose face was twisted with agony:

"I know I could do you good if you were able to believe in me. Can you believe in me?"

Miss Burnington evidently made a great effort to control herself. Her thin tall body stiffened under the influence of the mind.

"It's very kind of you to care," she said. "I'm sorry I am making such a fool of myself. But I'm really afraid there's nothing to be done for these tiresome headaches."

"I can cure you entirely in time," said Olivia, "if you will only help me by believing I can."

Miss Burnington forced a smile.

"I should be only too thankful to anyone—" she began.

She broke off and got up from her sofa.

"I'm very sorry, but I must go up to bed," she said. "The pain's too severe. Do forgive me for making such a fuss. Hector, I'm quite ashamed of myself."

"Let me take you up," said Sir Mervyn.

"No, no—I don't want to break up the party. Good night. Good night."

She went towards the door. The general looked at Olivia. She rose and followed Miss Burnington.

"Please let me come with you."

"It's too kind of you, but—"

She turned towards Olivia.

"Well," she said. "If you really ... just to my bedroom door."

They went out together.

"Oh, but I wanted to see it done!" said Lady Pangbourne in a frustrated voice. "I thought they just put their hands on people and the pain fled away."

"You are mixing Miss Traill up with your recollections of the New Testament, Lady Pangbourne," said Sir Mervyn. "These good ladies from the United States are not all direct descendants of the Apostles."

"May I please tell you what Miss Traill did for me?" said Fernol.

His cheeks were burning and he clenched his hands. He came and stood before the doctor....

Meanwhile Olivia had accompanied Miss Burnington into her bedroom and shut the door. A fire was burning in the grate. Miss Burnington felt vaguely for the electric light switch.

"No; don't turn it on," said Olivia. "Let us sit by the fire."

She drew Miss Burnington down gently into a chair and took both her hands.

"I will make you believe in me."

The firelight flickered over her strong face. Miss Burnington looked at her with eyes full of pain.

"I'm a fearful sceptic," she said. "I can't help it."

"Do you believe Sir Mervyn Butler can cure you?"

"Sir Mervyn—oh, no!"

"Yet you call him in, don't you?"

"Yes. I suppose I've a faint hope—"

"Have a little hope in me. That's all I ask of you—yet."

"Well, I do believe you're a very kind woman."

"I never take any money. I only wish to do what I was intended to do when I was sent into the world. We are only at ease with ourselves when we do that. Now sit quite still. Don't say anything and I shall very soon make you much better."

Miss Burnington leaned back in her chair and shut her eyes.

"The touch of your hands is certainly very strong and very soothing," she murmured.

It was half-past eleven when Olivia returned to the drawing room. She found Sir Hector alone with Fernol West. He looked at her with, she thought, a sort of severe enquiry when she came into the room.

"Your sister is asleep," she said.

"That's very unusual. Did she take a sleeping draught?"

"No. I got her to bed. No one must disturb her. I will call and see her to-morrow. Now, Fernol, we must be going."

"I'll have a taxicab sent for," said the general, ringing the bell.

While the servant was getting it, they stood by the fire, and Olivia told them what had happened in the bedroom.

"Your sister was in such acute pain," she said, "that I think it undermined her scepticism. She clung to me as I suppose she has clung to her doctor. That seemed to be enough—her longing to be helped. Anyhow, I was able to diminish the pain, and finally she fell asleep. That is a step on the way to a cure."

"I am immensely obliged to you," said the general.

"You've done a lot for your country," said Olivia. "I shall be very glad to do something for you."

"If you cure my sister you will have done a great deal."

When he said that, Olivia wondered whether he was thinking of his sister or of himself. His words, "She's got to be made sound," were still in her memory.

"I'm sure you are very fond of her," she said, almost appealingly. "She's a very brave woman, I should think."

"It would be odd if she were a coward," he returned.

The footman came in.

"The taxicab is at the door, sir."

"I'll take you down," said the general.

He came out bareheaded on to the pavement and helped Olivia into the cab.

"Good night," he said.

His large hand grasped hers.

"If you get my sister right Sir Mervyn will hate you."

"Isn't he fond of your sister?"

"Very, I believe; but fonder of himself as a sacred repository of medical science. Good night, Mr. West. Sir Mervyn considers you a neurotic, but you are an excellent fighter."

He turned away and disappeared into the house, leaving the footman to shut the door behind him.

"I—a neurotic!" said Fernol indignantly as they drove away. "Sir

Mervyn said that because he won't have it that you can cure anyone, and I told him, I told them all, how you had cured me. I'm glad Sir Hector thinks I can fight. He's a glorious fellow. All England looks up to him. He could do anything for you."

"I don't want him to do anything for me," said Olivia.

"No; but others may wish for you more than you wish for yourself."

And then he fell into silence. But in the cab Olivia could feel the excitement of his atmosphere, and the doctor's verdict "neurotic" on Fernol stayed somehow disagreeably in her mind. When Fernol had first come to her in Boston he had certainly been suffering acutely from what the nerve doctors generally call neurosis. Did any trace of that old malady still show in him, perceptible to the trained observer? Or was Sir Mervyn merely malicious? She wondered a little. Surely she had made a complete cure of Fernol? She had never really doubted it till this moment. She was not sure that she doubted it now. But since they had been in London she had noticed once or twice ...

The taxicab stopped at the door of Buckingham Palace Mansions, and Olivia said good-bye to Fernol.

After a hard fight, one of the hardest of her career, Olivia conquered Miss Burnington's headaches. Her difficulty in doing this came, she believed, from the peculiar mind of her patient, for Sir Hector's diagnosis of his sister's nature had proved to be right. She found it almost impossible to believe thoroughly in any power which partook of the mysterious, any power to which she could not attach hard facts of which she could make a list for the benefit of herself and those about her. When Olivia had once in the course of argument with her quoted Sir Hector as an example of partially mysterious powers, Miss Burnington had disagreed with her.

"My brother rules men because he knows more about their jobs than they do themselves," she said. "He is a storehouse of knowledge."

Olivia could not gainsay that. But she tried to make Miss Burnington acknowledge that the extraordinary influence which the general exercised over men was partially due to something totally independent of knowledge, to a force born in him, not acquired by him, a force felt by everyone but not to be explained by anyone.

"Oh, Hector is no hypnotist," said Miss Burnington, with a touch of sarcasm. "He is just a wonderfully able man with a remarkably strong character. He does big things because he knows. There you have the secret of his power over men."

"Then it isn't a secret," said Olivia, with her pleasant, strong smile.

And she set herself again to the struggle with Miss Burnington's malady; and she won, almost in despite of Miss Burnington—almost, but not quite, for Miss Burnington was longing to be cured, and had lost all faith in the doctors. Perhaps her longing helped Olivia, was the weapon which put her scepticism out of action. Olivia believed so, and was thankful. For she had never before wished so ardently to triumph over any ill-health as over those headaches of Miss Burnington. Sir Hector's influence was potent upon her, that influence which she felt to be mysterious. Like the men who worked under him, and were often afraid of him, she wished, even longed, to satisfy him, to wring from him a "well done." Hitherto she had never worked to win the approval of anyone. Her efforts had been made because they were necessary to herself. She had healed as an artist creates to satisfy an imperious need. But now a change had been wrought in her.

"My sister must be made sound."

As upon the scroll in her room at the Bureau her patients saw "Thy faith hath saved thee" so, during her fight with Miss Burnington's scepticism and ill-health, Olivia saw gleaming before her mind's eyes those words of Sir Hector. She had received her order from this strange man. She was determined to carry it out. And at last she did carry it out. The headaches came more rarely, lasted a shorter time when they did come, became less and less painful, and finally ceased. Two months went by without any headache at all. Miss Burnington looked, as all her friends declared, "a different creature." The dread which, despite her almost Spartan courage, had haunted her eyes and been seen of men, faded from them. A day came when she ventured to say:

"It really seems as if I might consider myself cured."

She was, of course, deeply grateful to Olivia for the extraordinary kindness and assiduity which had been shown without any hope of a reward. She had indeed come almost to love Olivia. Nevertheless, so strong was her ingrained habit of mind, she could not be fully persuaded that the cure was entirely owing to Olivia's power of healing. It might be so. The facts seemed to point that way. And yet—might it not be a mere strange coincidence that she began to get better only when Olivia came into her life? Might not some physical change have been at work which happened to begin manifesting itself just after she was brought into contact with Olivia? Miss Burnington did not express these characteristic doubts of hers to anyone except her brother. But they prevented her from coming out into the open as a whole-hearted champion of Olivia's powers. She was a very sincere woman. Had she been positive that Olivia, and Olivia only, had cured her, she would certainly not have hesitated to proclaim the faith that was in her. As it was she showed, hand in hand with her frank and freely spoken of gratitude to Olivia, a certain reserve. She could not help it. She was one of those rare women who have to be true to themselves. She was not sure, and so she would not say she was sure.

This slight but definite holding back on her part infuriated Fernol West. And he spoke hotly about it to Olivia.

"After what you've done it's unfair," he said. "I believe it's because you're a woman."

"I'm quite certain it isn't," said Olivia. "Miss Burnington has been extraordinarily kind about me."

"If Sir Mervyn Butler had done for her what you have done she would have told everyone in London what a marvellous doctor he was. But women hate to give credit to a woman. I can't think why. Now, if it had been the general he would have said straight out that you had cured him, although they call him a despiser of women. He's great enough to do that."

"I'm quite sufficiently rewarded for what I have been able to do," said Olivia.

"How are you rewarded? People still write against you over here. You have never been accepted as you were in America."

"If I tell you, will you give me your word of honour not to repeat it?"

"Yes."

"Sir Hector has told me that he is convinced his sister's restored health is entirely owing to me. And not only that. He said to me only yesterday that if he were ever ill he would call me in and would not summon a doctor."

Fernol was silent for a moment.

"Did he say that?" he said at last.

There was something so peculiar in the tone of his voice that Olivia wondered.

"Yes," she said. "And I know he meant it. That is reward enough for me."

"Did he give you his word?"

"What do you mean?"

"Did he give you his word he would call you in?"

"I have just told you what he said. Why should he give his word? He never is ill, thank God."

"That's just it!" said Fernol slowly. "He never is. So what's the good of such a promise?"

He paused, like one thinking deeply, brooding almost. Then he said:

"The English are fearfully slow in catching on to big things that they're unaccustomed to, aren't they? We are more open-minded in America. Look at the way you've been ignored here, except when you've been libelled. It makes me sick. I should like to give them a lesson."

"Them?" said Olivia. "Whom?"

"The people over here, the doctors and the whole lot of them. They want it badly."

"Oh, I shall soon be going back to America. And it's high time you went. Your father wants you to help him, and you ought to be at work."

As she spoke she looked at him rather narrowly.

"I don't like to see you idle, Fernol."

"Do you want to get rid of me?" he said.

"No. But I want to see you busy and happy in the best way. I don't think you're quite yourself here in London."

"That's because of the way they have treated you."

"I am quite satisfied," said Olivia, smiling.

"Because Sir Hector said that?"

"Coming from him it did please me very much."

"Well, I only wish he could have the chance to fulfil his promise," said Fernol. "Then the English would catch on to you at last. For everything Burnington stands for is gospel to them. They say he'll be the next Viceroy of India."

"I shouldn't wonder if he were," said Olivia.

"Would you be glad?" he asked her.

"Yes. I think he would be the very man for such a great post."

"You are wonderfully unselfish, Olivia!" he said.

There was a sort of break in his voice. His expression was oddly emotional. He gazed at her, and she saw an affection in his eyes which stirred a faint anxiety in her.

"You do everything for others, and no one does anything for you. Sometimes I hate the world."

"Fernol, dear, if you talk like that —"

"Well?"

"I shall think I didn't really cure you," she said soberly, almost sadly.

"You did cure me!" he exclaimed passionately. "And I shall never forget it, never."

And he flung out of the room.

When he had gone Olivia sat for a long while quite still. She was more disturbed in mind than she had ever been before, disturbed about Fernol and herself. She was almost sure that Fernol had guessed her secret. How? Had his curious devotion to her made him clairvoyant? or—did perhaps others know? For some time she had been deeply in love with Sir Hector, but hitherto she had believed that she had hidden her love from everyone. She was possessed by it, but she did not wish anyone to suspect that possession. For she felt sure that Sir Hector felt nothing for her. She could not imagine him loving a woman in that way.

He seemed to stand entirely aloof from the ordinary human passions, isolated from them by an almost cold intensity, the intensity of the tremendous worker, concentrated on the doing of big things for his country. Perhaps—probably even—he was abnormally ambitious, but she did not feel his ambition as she felt his greed for work, his lust for the job he was fitted to carry through in the world.

Only a great man could be like that; no woman could ever care for accomplishment in just that way. In a woman's life, work could never shoulder love out of the path. Did Fernol know her secret? She feared so. He had looked at her strangely when he said, "You are wonderfully unselfish." There had surely been knowledge in his eyes. She was touched by Fernol's devotion to her; she was grateful for it. She knew he was not in love with her, never had been. And yet to-day she felt as if there were something almost dangerous, almost menacing, in his affection; she felt almost afraid of—or was it for—Fernol.

She had known for some time that the post Sir Hector was hoping for was the viceroyalty of India. That was why he had been so anxious for his sister to be well. There must be a woman out there to be the handmaid to his glory.

Was he not less, or more, than human?

There was a good deal of disquiet in India. A woman had been active in stirring it up. So rumour said.

He would soon crush it, that man of bronze.

It was tragic to love such a man. Yet she knew that she clung to her love. A word from him meant more to her than all the deeds of others. She had satisfied him, had come up to his expectation of her in what she had tried to do for him. That was enough reward. The attacks, the contempt or indifference of others, were as nothing to her.

It did not occur to Olivia that, for the first time since she had found out her power as a healer, she had used that power for a partially selfish reason; that, for the first time, she had been instigated to a healing effort by something akin to egoism. Her love had made her think of, act for, her own advantage; and her love now prevented her from being quite sincere with herself.

A week later it became known that the Viceroy of India had sent in his resignation, and Sir Hector's name was mentioned in *The Times* as his probable successor.

Two days after this piece of news had been read by Olivia, Sir Hector telephoned asking if he could see her at a certain hour. She had never received him in her flat since his first visit there, but she had seen him many times in Cadogan Square. She answered saying she would be at home at the hour he mentioned, and, punctually to the moment, he strode into the room.

She thought him looking rather worn, even a little weary. But he smiled as he gripped her hand.

"Is it true what they say in the papers?" she asked. "I hope it is true."

He shrugged his big shoulders.

"We shall know presently. I've got a word or two to say to you about my sister. Let me sit down and light up, may I?"

"Yes, do."

When his cigarette was alight and he had crossed his long legs comfortably, he said:

"Now, tell me. Do you believe that my sister is really cured—finally cured?"

"Yes, I do," said Olivia, without hesitation. "Do you doubt it?"

She looked at him with a sudden keen anxiety which transformed her strong face.

"I wanted to hear your opinion. I know it is an absolutely honest one. I am not given to trusting women, but I trust you thoroughly. I am not speaking of your intellect; anyone can make a bad mistake. I am speaking of your *bona fides*."

"Thank you," said Olivia. "But I wish you would tell me your opinion."

"I don't know that it would be worth much on a matter of this kind. She certainly seems to me to be cured. Since her accident she has never looked, never seemed, as she looks and seems now. The change is extraordinary."

He pulled his moustache and looked straight before him. After a pause he continued:

"Fernol West is a strange young fellow."

"What made you think of him just then?"

"Well, he's the only 'cure' of yours whom I happen to know. He dined with my sister and me last night. I ran across him in Whitehall and asked him."

"I didn't know," said Olivia. "I haven't seen Fernol to-day."

As the general said nothing she added, after a silence:

"Why do you think Fernol strange?"

"Well, I've had a great deal to do with men of all classes and a good many nationalities, and it strikes me that there's something decidedly unusual about young West. Last night I noticed it."

"Did Fernol do or say—

"You know my sister. She's abominably truthful, eh?"

"She's thoroughly sincere. I love it in her."

"Like answers to like. Last night you were spoken of. West stuck up for you, as he always does, and was very bitter about the way you've been treated over here. (By the way, that's a good deal Sandring's fault. Between you and me he's more than a bit of a fool.) Finally, he asked my sister if she wouldn't, in some public way, acknowledge that you had cured her of her torturing headaches."

"I am very sorry Fernol did that."

"Then, of course, my sister's drastic sincerity came into play. She said she couldn't do that because she was not positively certain that her cure had been owing to you. She spoke of nervous headaches, of how nerves and the imagination seem to be connected sometimes, implied that, possibly, she had been mentally influenced rather than physically. You know how women run on, messing things all up together. I saw West was getting more and more excited. Finally, my sister said that if she had had some perfectly definite disease, such as cancer, or diabetes, and had been treated by you and recovered, she would have told the whole world what you were. As it was, she could only be tremendously grateful to you, and say that it was quite possible that you had had a great deal to do with getting rid of her headaches. Ah!"

"And then—was that all?"

"Well—no. West just managed to contain himself. But I never saw a pair of eyes look more menacing than his did."

"Menacing!" said Olivia, sitting forward in her chair.

"Yes," returned the general with quiet force. "He turned to me and asked me if I were cured by you of ill health whether I would publicly acknowledge it. I said I would—and let them laugh at me as much as they liked. Then he became calmer. I took my sister upstairs. We'd just finished dinner and I had to go to the telephone. When I came back to the dining room I found West standing by the window with the curtain pulled back."

"What was he doing?"

"Getting some air. He looked odd—deucedly odd."

"In what way?"

"White. However, we finished our wine together and he seemed to calm down. But all the rest of the evening I felt that he was keeping something under. In India I've seen two or three native soldiers run amuck. H'm!"

He was silent and seemed to be thinking profoundly.

"What did you cure West of exactly?" he asked presently.

Olivia told him.

"It was like acute neurasthenia. Some of the doctors thought there was some pressure on the brain. He was desperately miserable and haunted by a desire to kill himself."

"Ah!"

He lit another cigarette and uncrossed his legs.

"The brain!" he said, as if to himself. "My sister fell from a horse, too," he added, speaking to Olivia.

"Yes, I know."

"There might be something akin in the two cases?"

"I—perhaps there might."

After a minute of silence Olivia said:

"I'm afraid you doubt my cure of your sister."

"Well—no; I don't."

"Not even—after last night?"

"You follow me, I see."

He looked full at her. And this time she did not feel like a tiny figure in the foreground of some vast space over which he was gazing. Her heart began to beat fast.

"My instincts guide me more than you might suppose," he observed. "I believe you have made a cure of my sister. But I wanted to taste your mind. I might sacrifice a good many people if I thought their sacrifice would advance things. But I shouldn't care to sacrifice my sister. She is an unselfish woman where I am concerned. I don't wish to take too great advantage of that weakness in her. Well, I must leave you."

He got up. So did Olivia.

"I'm—I'm almost sure now that you wouldn't call me in if you were ill," she said.

Her lips were trembling. She could not keep them still.

"Would you wish me to?" he asked.

"Yes, I should."

"Then I would give you the chance to put me right. It would be my way of paying the debt I owe you. I always settle my debts. Some men have reason to wish I didn't, I believe. Good-bye."

He stood for a moment looking towards her. And again Olivia noticed, this time more definitely, some subtle change in his appearance. She could not have defined it, but she was strongly aware of it.

He shook her hand and went out.

When he had gone Olivia sat for a long while thinking about him, about Miss Burnington, about Fernol, and about herself, and she was conscious that her usually steady and strong mind was troubled. Events seemed to be stealthily grouping themselves together to make an ugliness, some shape that she would not care to look upon. Presently she even began to feel as if that shape were looming over her, although she could not see it yet.

She did not meet Fernol that day. A week went past, and she neither saw him nor heard from him. This surprised her, as he generally looked in on her at the flat three or four times a week. Saturday came. She went as usual to the Bureau. She had been there about an hour when a messenger arrived with a note for her. It was marked "Private and urgent." She opened it and read:

"Strictly private."

2A, CADOGAN SQUARE.
"Saturday."
"MY DEAR MISS TRAILL,
"Can you possibly come at once? My brother is very unwell and wishes to see you. Please do not say a word to anyone about this. I know I can rely on you to keep the matter a secret.
"Yours sincerely,
"HONORIA BURNINGTON."

III

Olivia burnt Miss Burnington's note, had a taxicab called, got into it and was on the way to Cadogan Square within five minutes of the receipt of this message. As the cab moved out into the stream of traffic she leaned back and shut her eyes. The great moment of her life had surely come. She was trying to collect all her forces to meet it. But for the moment she felt frightened, horribly frightened, almost like a child struck for the first time and shuddering not merely in body but in soul. Fernol's desire had been fulfilled. That was strange. She thought of ill-wishing, of the old superstition connected with the burning of a waxen image of your enemy, of the more modern belief that by the force of his thought a man may cause to happen that which he longs for. Was Fernol's thought-power very strong? Could he have set himself to an evil use of it? She saw before her Sir Hector and Fernol, the great man and the excitable boy. It was fantastic to suppose that such a man could be influenced by such a boy. Yet there was force in Fernol. His concentrated devotion to her had proved that to Olivia long ago. And more than once he had almost passionately expressed a wish that Sir Hector could have the chance of redeeming his promise. And now the chance had come. Sir Hector was going to redeem it. She did not doubt that. Directly she had read Miss Burnington's note she had understood.

She strove to gather her forces together; she called upon her faith as if it were distant and needed a summons.

When the cab stopped she opened her eyes.

She rang the bell. A footman came to the door.

"Can I see Miss Burnington?" she asked.

As she spoke her eyes searched the young man's face and found only a stolid indifference.

"Yes, Ma'am," he replied. "Miss Burnington is expecting you."

He shut the door and preceded her up the staircase.

She waited for a moment in the familiar drawing room which to-day seemed unfamiliar. Then Miss Burnington came in looking anxious and—Olivia thought—almost stern.

"Thank you for coming," she said quickly, holding out her hand. "Had you gone to the Bureau?"

"Yes. I got your message there."

"I sent to your flat too. Miss Traill, you know my real regard for you, don't you?"

"Yes."

"And my great gratitude to you. But I'm afraid you may doubt both when—"

She broke off, then resumed:

"Hector made me send for you. And, of course, his word is law in this house. But I want him to have a doctor at once. I want him to have Sir Mervyn. If you will only refuse to go to him then the road will be clear, and he must give way. Don't you see? It isn't that I doubt you. I know you are thoroughly sincere. But Hector's life is so precious and science—"

"Sir Hector wished for me," said Olivia. "Doesn't that show—"

But Miss Burnington interrupted her.

"He insisted. He said he had a debt to pay and he meant to pay it."

"That was like him!"

"But I know you will feel yourself that it is madness not to send for a doctor. He has never been ill before, so he can't understand. My headaches—they were nothing. Anyone may have—but—I'm asking a great deal, I know. It is almost like an insult, but indeed I don't mean it so."

Suddenly, with an almost violent gesture, she took both Olivia's hands in hers.

"I don't know how to make you understand, but I can't help it. I have no real faith in any healing power outside medical or surgical science. If you will only refuse to go to Hector I can call in a doctor. May I? May I?"

"Your brother trusts me. If I refuse he will think I don't trust myself, that I am a humbug. He has asked for me, and I must go to him. Remember how ill you were."

"And now I'm well. Yes, I know, I know. But I'm nothing."

"You were everything to me when I was treating you. And now he will be everything to me. Dear Miss Burnington, please take me to him."

Miss Burnington's thin figure stiffened.

"Well, if I must," she said, with a beaten intonation. "But just one thing. Hector doesn't wish anyone to know he's ill. He's ashamed of being ill, I believe. At any rate—unless we can't help it—we are not to say a word."

"But the servants?"

"Only Sidney, his valet, knows. The others think he's got a slight chill and is keeping his room."

She stood quite still, then threw back her head.

"Please come up," she said.

But now a strange hesitation seized Olivia. She was afraid to go to that room upstairs, to see the man who was ill.

"Miss Burnington—wait a moment!" she said.

"Yes? What is it?"

"What is the matter?"

"I don't know."

"Is he very ill?"

"You will see for yourself, Miss Traill. Do you believe you can cure anything?"

Her dark eyes looked piercing, as if she would read the soul of her visitor. Olivia did not answer her. There was a moment of silence. Then Miss Burnington said:

"He has never been ill before. I cannot understand it. I can only suppose that he has eaten, or drunk, something which has made him ill. His constitution is marvellous. But no one is safe from a chance of that kind."

"No, of course not. Well, let us go up."

And she followed Miss Burnington out of the room.

Sir Hector lived on the second storey, in a set of three rooms at the back of the house—bedroom, bathroom, and writing room. Olivia had expected to be taken into a bedroom, but when Miss Burnington softly opened a door she saw a small chamber full of books, and containing a large flat writing table, a settee and some armchairs. Sitting with his back to her, close to the fire, towards which he was leaning, was Sir Hector.

So he was up! She felt a strong sense of relief. But it died away as he looked round.

"Here is Miss Traill, Hector," said Miss Burnington.

And she went out of the room.

Sir Hector sat with his head turned towards the door and his eyes fixed on Olivia.

"Very good of you to come," he said. "There's something wrong with me."

"Yes."

She came up to the fire.

"What do you feel?"

"As if I were going to be very much worse than I am now. It's been coming on for days—stealthily—creeping on me. I kept about till I was afraid of people noticing it. To-day, when the light came, I knew I couldn't do a thing. So here I am—useless. If you don't stop it I shall soon be pretty bad."

"Yes, I can see that."

She sat down. Now that she was close to him it seemed to her that the pupils of his strange eyes had altered. When she had met him first she had been struck by their abnormal smallness. Now they were larger, or, at any rate, looked larger.

"What are you staring at?" Sir Hector said, with a touch of almost sharp suspicion.

But she did not answer him.

"Just tell me what you feel," she said, in a practical voice.

"Well, I should say it's all very much like the beginning of enteric."

"Enteric fever! That's the same as typhoid fever, isn't it?"

"Yes; intestinal fever. I've never had it, but I've seen chaps sickening for it by the dozen. They were all as useless as I am. I feel tired all the time—without doing anything. It's abominable. The thought of food turns me sick. My head aches like the devil. And it's all getting worse. I'm on the road to something infernally bad, Miss Traill, and the pace is quickening every hour. I'm certain of that."

He lay back with a heavy sigh.

"I thought you didn't look quite as usual the day you called on me," said Olivia.

"The day after young West dined with us. It was just beginning then, I believe."

There was a moment of silence, during which Olivia looked at the man whom she loved, noticing the almost sinister change in him. He was pale, a bad colour. A sort of crust of weariness lay over his strength, like moss on a wall of stone. There was something hopeless, broken, in his whole aspect. Even his great limbs looked hopeless. Near his eyes fever seemed lurking eager to light up her torches. Olivia knew—something that was not medical knowledge told her—that this man who had never been ill in his life was on the verge of a dangerous, perhaps a deadly, illness. And an agony of pity and fear swept through her, pity and fear for him and for herself. At that moment she felt very helpless. The fact that he had sent for her, that he had held to his word, given when probably he had felt, like most healthy and very strong men, that illness could never come to his powerful body, touched her too much, almost unnerved her. Had she really any force within her that could operate on a human being whom she felt to be far above her, on one whom she loved? To believe so seemed to her at that moment to be almost an insolence. Yet, if her faith in herself deserted her, she must surely be useless. She must believe in herself more strongly than she had ever done before. The supreme chance had been offered to her by fate. She must seize it. She must triumph over her own weakness—that of a woman who loved, and who, because she loved, feared.

She strove to recover by force the sensation of mysterious power which had filled her when she went up to Lily and said: "I can cure you."

... She got up and stood before Sir Hector, looking down upon him.

"If you hadn't made me a promise," she said, "would you have sent for me?"

Sir Hector opened his eyes.

"I have sent for you," he replied, with a touch of his old commanding brusqueness. "That's enough. But please keep it quiet. I hate people to know I am ill. If you put me right—that's another matter."

"If I do I will ask you to give me another promise—never to tell anyone, either that you were ill or that I was able to help you."

"And—young West?" he said, faintly, but with a strange half smile on his lips.

"Fernol? Why should Fernol ever know? Now, please give me your hands."

That evening Olivia telephoned to the Savoy Hotel and asked for Fernol West. She feared that he might not be in, but almost directly she was put through to him.

"It is Olivia speaking," she said.

"Oh!" said Fernol's voice at the other end. "Are you all right?"

"Yes. Have you anything to do this evening?"

After a perceptible pause Fernol's voice answered:

"No."

"Will you come round and have a talk, then? I'm all alone."

Again a pause, then the voice: "All right. I'll come."

Olivia put the receiver up and looked at her watch. It was half-past eight. If Fernol started at once he would be with her in ten minutes. She wondered whether he would start at once. She had received through the telephone an impression of reluctance. But, of course, he would come. She sat down, took up the book of Tagore, which he had given her, and tried to read. It was essential that she should be serene, complete mistress of herself, to-night. Any turmoil of spirit must weaken her. She must banish anxiety, suspicion, and, above all, fear. She must control thought.

"He will be better to-morrow," she said to herself. "I know that. He's getting better now. Tonight he's going to sleep calmly. He will wake refreshed, free from headache, free from malaise. The headache will have left him. He will be much better."

She put down her book and insisted on these strong and hopeful thoughts. Fear disintegrates. Suspicion does harm to her who suspects. Doubt is destructive. Faith can move the mountains. Presently she sent her mind to Palestine, to dwell in imagination by the delicate shores of Galilee. When she had read the Bible, very often she had wondered at the lack of faith shown by many of those among whom Christ wrought his miracles. "If I had been alive then," she had said to herself, "I should have been one of the first to believe, and I should never have wavered in my faith." Now she wished to think herself back into that mood of robust and glorious confidence. She looked into the fire and trod the ways of the Holy Land with Christ. "Only believe!" What is impossible to God? And God works through men and women, sends His spirit—a double portion of it—into those who wait for it, and are eager to receive it. He had helped her to heal, and He would help her to heal again. Through Him she could walk on the waters. But if once she let fear invade her, complete trust desert her, she would sink in them. They would sweep over her. She would drown...."

Presently she moved and looked up. She had made a strong effort of mind and will and she felt almost tired. She glanced again at her watch. It was twenty minutes past nine. And Fernol had not come yet. She was beginning to wonder whether he would come, in spite of his "All right!" when the door bell sounded. She got up, but she did not go at once to the door. Something held her back. She waited, looking towards the passage. The doorbell sounded again. Then she turned out the electric light with the exception of one lamp in a corner, walked down the passage and opened the door.

Fernol West was standing outside. The night was cold, and he was wrapped up in a big fur coat with the collar raised to his ears.

"Well, Olivia!" he said.

His blue eyes were fixed upon her, and she noticed that instead of moving he stood quite still where he was, almost like a man who doubted whether he would be let in.

"Good evening, Fernol. Come in. How late you are. I'd almost given you up."

"Am I late?" he said.

He stepped in and she shut the door
"Take off your coat. I've got a good big fire."
"That's splendid. It's horribly cold. I walked."
He went to hang up his coat.
"Why didn't you take a cab?"
"I wanted air."
The words recalled to Olivia Sir Hector's description of Fernol standing by the dining room window in Cadogan Square with the curtain pulled back.
"Don't you get enough in the day?" she asked.
"Not always."
He had hung up his coat. As he turned round from the hook he shivered.
"It is cold!" he exclaimed. "Let's get to the fire."
"Yes. You'll soon be splendidly warm.... Sit down here close to it."
She drew forward an armchair. For the first time with Fernol she felt embarrassed. She knew why, but she did not wish him to notice it. He sank down in the chair with a boyish sort of flop, and stared into the flames. She sat on the sofa and took up a piece of work.
"Smoke if you like."
"No, thank you, Olivia. I'm off smoking."
"Why's that?"
"I don't know."
"Nothing wrong with you, I hope?"
"Wrong!"
He shot a side glance at her.
"Why should there be?"
"I don't know. But you haven't been near me for quite a long time."
"Just over a week."
"Well, that's quite a long time—for us."
"Yes, I suppose it is."
There was a pause. Then Fernol shifted his chair round towards her.
"Since I've seen you I've dined with Sir Hector and his sister," he said.
"I know."
"Oh! You've seen them, then?"
"Sir Hector called here the next day."
"Did he? And he told you, of course? It was good of him to ask me. But I can't stand Miss Burnington."
"I like her very much."
"You like everyone. It's your creed. But I can't. I'd give my life for a friend, but some people—"
He broke off and moved his hands nervously.

"I think I will smoke," he said. "D'you mind a cigar?"

"No; anything you like."

He drew out and lit a cigar. She noticed that his left hand was trembling.

"Are you still cold?" she asked.

"No; why?"

"Your hand is shaking."

He started.

"Give it to me for a moment."

"It's all right. I'll hold it to the fire."

He stretched his right hand out towards the flames.

"It's your other hand," said Olivia.

"Oh," he said brusquely. "Don't bother about me."

"Fernol, what is the matter with you? Why haven't you been near me all these days? What's troubling you?"

"Who's been talking to you about me?" he retorted almost savagely.

"Nobody has mentioned you, except Sir Hector."

"And what did he say?" said Fernol, with an ugly glance at her.

"Don't you like Sir Hector?"

"Yes. He's a real live man."

"Well, you may be sure he has never said anything against you."

"Have you seen him again since he called on you?"

"Yes. I saw him to-day."

Fernol was staring at her. Was it the light of the fire which set two gleams in his eyes?

"To-day! Here?"

"No; I called at Cadogan Square."

Fernol said nothing, but continued to stare at her like one who was fiercely expectant of something. Olivia realised that he was in an acute state of nervous excitement, was quivering with anxiety, or under the lash of some intense desire. Could he have got wind of Sir Hector's illness? That seemed impossible since even the servants in the Burningtons' house did not know the truth. She was not a curious woman, but Fernol's look, his whole manner, woke in her a strong curiosity mingled with an under reluctance which was akin to apprehension. Everything to-day seemed fighting against her, fighting to beat down the strength which had made her what she was, a woman who was of use in the suffering world, one to whom the afflicted came, and from whom they went away renewed. Even Fernol was, perhaps unconsciously, attacking her, Fernol, who had been one of her greatest joys, a piece of her handiwork of which she had been humbly proud. She no longer felt proud of him. To-night something in him forced upon her a knowledge that was a deadly foe to her soul. A voice within her said clearly again and again, "Fernol is not cured. You thought him cured, but you were wrong. Look at him, listen to him, and be sincere with yourself. You know that you have not cured him."

At this moment, while Fernol was staring at her, the voice was louder than before, the silent voice which nothing can drown, not even the roar of Niagara. It drove Olivia to greater frankness. She could not be really frank to-night, because she had to keep the secret of another, but she could surely clear away some of the debris which divided her from Fernol.

"Fernol," she said, in a resolute voice. "You know I believe very much in the force of thought, don't you?"

"Yes."

"I look upon thought as a weapon for good or evil. A wicked thought, I believe, does harm to the thinker. But that's not all. It may harm another too. It often does. I am sure of that. Some of us are much stronger in thinking than others. We can put much more force into a thought than they can. I believe you and I are strong in that way. I know you are. You can concentrate tremendously. I feel it. And I feel it specially to-night."

"I don't know why you should," said Fernol uneasily.

"You and I are good friends. That links our minds together perhaps. It helps me to feel your mind easily. But to-night, though, I feel I don't know. I wish you would help me to know. I've been afraid for some time."

"Afraid! What of?"

"That you might be led to think in a wrong way."

"What way, then?"

Suddenly Olivia resolved to tell Fernol the secret which perhaps he had divined. An obscure instinct, of which she was scarcely conscious, but to which she yielded without a battle, a woman's instinct, drove her to do this. But her cheeks flushed as she spoke.

"Fernol, I'm going to give you a proof of my friendship for you, and I know I can trust to your honour never to speak of what I am going to tell you."

An expression that was like an expression of fear changed Fernol's face.

"Don't you want me to tell you?" she asked, startled.

Fernol passed his tongue over his lips and clenched his hands together.

"Yes—yes. Go on! Go on!" he said, roughly.

"Perhaps you know it already," she said, seized with hesitation.

His look and manner were so strange that they checked the impulse within her. At her last words the boy's face seemed to her to go white in the light from the fire. But perhaps that was an effect of the flames.

"Know it!" he exclaimed. "How should I know it? Of course I don't.... Well, what is it? Tell me—please!"

"I care very much for Sir Hector Burnington."

She stopped. He said nothing, and seemed to be waiting for something else.

"Do you understand what I mean?" she said.

"You love him!" said Fernol.

"Yes. No one knows that but you."

"Is that all?"

"All!"

"Yes, or have you something more to tell me?"

"Isn't that enough?"

"Why do you tell me?"

"I thought I would."

"But why? I know you have a reason. What is it, please?"

He spoke with a sort of dogged obstinacy which surely was the child of apprehension.

"I am not sure."

She stopped and searched her mind.

"It was something—there seemed something to clear away from between us. And I want you to know how anything which affects Sir Hector must affect me, because of my feeling for him. I know very well that you care for my happiness. I don't seek it in any selfish way. Sir Hector only looks on me as a sincere sort of woman trying to do her best with any powers she has. I look for nothing more from him than that. He is made for big work, not to love any woman. I have no illusions about him—none. Such happiness as I can ever have in connection with him must lie in seeing him strong and happy and able to carry forward the great things he is meant to do for his country. Now, Fernol, I have bared my heart to you. It hasn't been easy, but I have done it. Do something for me in return."

"What is it you want me to do, Olivia?" he asked, in a voice that for a moment was husky, as if he were moved by some strong emotion.

"Promise me that you will never—of course, I mean in thought—try to do harm to Sir Hector!"

"Why—why should you suppose?"

He stopped. He was no longer looking at her.

"We don't know exactly what a concentrated desire may be able to accomplish. Lots of people would probably say nothing, unless it were aided by some definite action. But my own experience tells me it may accomplish a great deal—wonders even—good things—horrible things.

What is faith but a great concentration; a sort of gathering together of the best forces of the soul? When you came to me in Boston, and we were together so many times in my little room there, and I saw how dreadfully wretched you were, my one desire was to get you right. It was so strong that it was almost like an enormous physical effort which I made. I felt as if I were standing up and fighting against the powers of darkness for you. And I—I thought I won."

"Thought!" Fernol exclaimed. "You did win!"

"Thank God if I did."

"Do you mean you have ever doubted it?" he said passionately. His cheeks were flaming, and he looked straight into her eyes.

"I never doubted it in America."

"And here! What do you mean? How can you say that—what is there the matter with me? I'm perfectly well. Anyone can see that."

"Don't be angry, Fernol. But just answer me one question. Two or three times you have said to me that you wished Sir Hector could have a chance to carry out his promise to me. You know that could only happen if he were ill. Have you gone on wishing him to be ill? Have you concentrated on that?"

"You always come first with me," he said obstinately, looking down. "That's my idea of gratitude. You condemn it, I know. But I can't help it. I can't be like you."

"Then you have concentrated on an evil desire?"

"Why do you go into all this to-night? Is—is there anything the matter with Sir Hector?"

Something in Fernol's expression as he asked this question startled Olivia. She felt at that moment almost certain that Fernol did know something of what had happened in Cadogan Square. But her promise to Miss Burnington prevented her from touching on the subject. If she did touch on it, if she allowed Fernol to pursue it any further, she would be unable to keep Sir Hector's illness secret from Fernol. She was forced to be something less than sincere.

"What I wish to say to you, Fernol, is this," she said, ignoring his question. "If you care for me really at all, if you wish to show gratitude to me, there is only one way in which you can do it. Turn your mind from evil desires. Put good desires in their place. Use your strength only in a fine way. Wish well to Sir Hector. I know you will now I have told you what—was very difficult to tell. I cannot bear that for me you should become evil. It makes me feel that it would be better if you had never seen me. If I produce evil in you I must be an evil influence. I—I hate to think that of myself."

She was deeply moved as she spoke. Something that had been firm seemed to be crumbling beneath her feet.

"Good night, Fernol," she said, after a pause. "I want to be alone now."

He stood looking at her in silence, but he did not move.

"Please go," she said.

"Yes. But say that you know you did cure me first."

"You could not be fanatical about me if you were thoroughly normal," she answered, looking at him with steady, sad eyes. "The sane mind in the sane body is never fanatical."

"Then you think I am mad?" he exclaimed bitterly.

"Oh, Fernol, it's no use—perhaps we are both exaggerating things to-night. Don't let us talk anymore. Now, good night."

She took his reluctant hand.

"Give yourself to good thoughts and all will be well, dear Fernol. Send good thoughts to me and—to him too. Perhaps we both need them."

"It would be no use," he said, almost in a whisper. "But, anyhow, I would die for you."

He wrung her hand, hurting her. But she did not wince.

"Do you believe it?"

"I don't want you to die. I want you to live and be fine."

"Perhaps someday you'll—"

He did not finish his sentence but left her. She heard him in the passage taking his heavy coat down from the hook. Then there was a long silence. No doubt he was putting his coat on. But the silence lasted till she was surprised at it and wondered what could be happening.

"What are you doing, Fernol?" she called out, without going to the door.

Instantly she heard a movement. Then the outer door was opened and shut. He had gone.

"He's sick—he's sick!" said the voice within her. "The man you love is ill in body, and the boy you thought you had healed is ill in mind and soul. You never healed him. You can't heal. You haven't the healing power. Perhaps you had it once, but it's left you. It came to you, it stayed with you a little while, and now it has deserted you. You're an empty vessel. You're worse—you're a humbug. You know you haven't got what you claim to possess, and so you're a living lie."

As she listened to the voice, the faith within her was shaken. It seemed to grow pale, to be fading away, to be dying. And a sensation of despair seized her. But she fought it. She recalled the many cures she had made—or was it had seemed to make?—in America, the deep confidence she had inspired in women and men, the gratitude which had been showered upon her. And then she recalled the attacks which had been made upon her, the cruel names she had been called, charlatan, humbug, crank, self-deceiver. Self-deceiver! Had she been really that all through her career as a healer? Had she been, as it were, self-hypnotised, and, because of that, had she hypnotised others—Lily first of all, and then many suffering human beings? She saw, as in a vision, a long procession of those who had sought her out, headed by Lily. Presently Fernol went by with his eyes bent down to the ground, as if he dared not let her see what was in them; and long after him Miss Burington with a sceptical smile on her lips. She had not believed. Perhaps her brain was too strong, too penetrating, to be tricked. And last of all strode Sir Hector, with his mien of bronze, and his strange glazed eyes. And he looked at her, and his motionless lips seemed to be saying: "I am the great test. Cure me and all will believe. But if you fail, death is waiting for me, and you will have been my murderer."

Then, in her fight to bring back red life to the fading faith, she told herself that the reason of this hideous collapse was that she had been less, or more, than a woman, and that now she was just a woman. She had loved, or thought she loved, humanity, the mass of created beings, with their affections, their sorrows, their terrors, their yearning desires; now she loved one man. And he blotted out humanity from her view; he expelled humanity from her heart. She knew the narrowness of a great love. Her widely diffused power of sympathy had shrunk. She saw it as a burning spark, minute but fierce with the terrible fierceness of fire. She would let the world go for one man.

But she would not let him go. She would not fail in the job he had set her, the greatest job a woman who loves can have. Exactly how much he believed in her power she did not know. He was a difficult man to read. He had never been ill before, and perhaps even now, in spite of his assertion that the pace was quickening, could not realise that at the end of the path he was treading death might be waiting. Such a man is apt to have the illusion that he is invulnerable, until old age leads him by almost imperceptible degrees to cessation. He was paying a debt. But if he got worse? If the knowledge were forced on him that he was in the hands of a loud-mouthed impotence? She would give it all up before that moment came. She herself would proclaim herself helpless.

But she shivered when she thought of making such an acknowledgment to such a man. What a contempt he would have for her. If she was not what she claimed to be, she was far less than the unknown millions who had made no claim to be other, or more, than their brethren. She was only an assertive nothingness. Her cheeks burned at the thought of being found out to be that by the man whom she loved. She could not bear it. Women can bear so much, but there is the impossible—the one thing that cannot be endured. And that would be the impossible for her.

Suddenly she wished she had medical knowledge. She could have used it to back up her mysterious power. (She was trying to smother the voice.) Sir Hector's words recurred to her mind. "I should say it's all very much like the beginning of enteric." Possibly, if a doctor—Sir Mervyn—had been summoned he would have diagnosed the case as one of enteric fever. And then he would have done certain things. What things? She wished she had a medical book handy. That would tell her a good deal of what she needed to know. Her eyes fell on a bookcase against the wall of the little room near the door. It was not likely that— She went over to the bookcase.

Sir Walter Scott's Novels; *Shakespeare's Works*; *The Mill on the Floss*; *The Sorrows of Satan*; *Shelley's Poems*; *Wuthering Heights*; *The Life of Goethe—*

She read on and on till she came to the bottom shelf, which was larger than any of the others.

Chambers's Encyclopaedia.

There were many volumes. She sought eagerly for the letter E, found it, and drew out the heavy book.

"Enteric Fever—*see* Typhoid Fever."

She sought again, and found what she wanted.

Presently she laid the book she had been reading down upon her knees. What was the matter with Sir Hector? Was he sickening for typhoid? From what she had just read she judged that possibly, even perhaps probably, he was. Yet the disease was rarely met with after middle life. He was between fifty and sixty, and tremendously strong. It seemed very unlikely that, living as he did in excellent hygienic conditions, he would be stricken by such a disease. Since she had read about typhoid, her former preoccupation about Fernol's state of mind seemed almost absurd to her. Ill-wishing could not produce an illness which science had long ago proved to be caused by an organism. And yet she could not get rid of the feeling that somehow Fernol's peculiar concentration on her was harmful, or might be harmful, to Sir Hector. Whenever she thought of either, the other came up in her mind immediately. The great man and the excitable boy were inexorably linked together. Her instincts were at work in the matter. She knew that, and she had long ago learned that instinct is greater than reason. The fact that Fernol's openly and vehemently proclaimed wish that Sir Hector might fall ill had been so quickly followed by his illness was a very strange coincidence, and Fernol's behaviour troubled her terribly. He was certainly concealing something from her. His eyes were furtive. His whole manner suggested acute uneasiness. All his former frankness and joyousness had left him. What was the matter with him? What did he know about Sir Hector? What was he expecting? He seemed to be quivering with some secret expectation.

She looked down again on the book and her eyes fell on the words: "The pupils are generally somewhat larger than normal." A little lower down she saw the brief statement: "Death may take place by coma, by exhaustion, in consequence of severe hemorrhage of the bowels or of perforation of their coats, or from pneumonia or some other complication; rarely from any cause before the second week."

Perhaps the second week of the illness had begun. Sir Hector had told her that he thought "it" was just beginning the day after Fernol had dined with him.

Suddenly Olivia turned white and cold. A horrible thought had come upon her like an enemy. She hated it. She was indignant with herself for being able to hold it in her mind. Quickly she shut up the encyclopaedia, put it back on the shelf, turned out the lamp, and went to her bedroom. But the horrible thought went with her, poisoning her mind, doing harm surely to her soul. She did not know how to get rid of it. She undressed, wrapped herself in a dressing gown and knelt down by her bed. She wanted to pray, but though for years she had practised thought-control and had achieved an unusual mastery of the mind, tonight she was like a city invaded by a horde of brutal enemies. It was as if she heard the tramp of their feet in the night, saw the glare of their incendiary fires. She knew the impotence of the conquered. In vain she tried to concentrate on God and her close connection with Him. Fernol rose up before her. She saw a glass of wine set on a white cloth; Fernol standing by a window holding back a curtain; Sir Hector entering the room. But it was impossible. Such a thing was impossible. She crushed her face down in her hands. How could such a punishment come upon her when she had always exerted herself for good? Always she had aimed at helping people and not at self-advancement. She could not accuse herself of trying to become rich, or of the more subtle endeavour—the attempt to win notoriety or glory. A certain fame had been hers in America; but, honestly, she could say that she had not sought it. She was not conscious of being an egoist. Then, surely, such a fearful punishment as she had just conceived of could not be meted out to her. When she looked around her she certainly saw much apparent injustice in the fates of men and women; nevertheless, she had always believed in the Divine justice, and it would be a refinement of injustice that could bring about, or even allow to be, what she had just thought of, was thinking of now in spite of all her efforts to drive it out of her mind. Something unhealthy in Fernol must have infected her to-night. But her mind was not reading his when it had formed that hideous surmise.

A something disturbed her. She did not know what it was, but she lifted her head from her hands and listened. It was surely some sound in the flat. Presently she felt, rather than heard it again. She wondered what it could be. She had an odd feeling that there was someone near her, either attending to her in some peculiar way, or trying to tell her something. Sir Hector! She sprang up and stood still. Perhaps he had suddenly become worse; was wishing her to be with him. Perhaps Miss Burnington was sending for her. She thought first of dressing quickly, and went to her wardrobe. But just as she was opening its door she was again aware of some muffled and yet near sound. This time she went out into the passage. And immediately she heard distinctly the telephone bell in the drawing room. It must be that Sir Hector was worse. She ran down the passage, went into the drawing room, and took down the receiver.

"Yes—yes? What is it? Is he worse? Shall I come?" she said.

She was so obsessed by the idea that the message was from Cadogan Square that she did not think of imprudence till she heard Fernol's voice saying:

"It's I—Fernol. What's the matter?"

"Fernol!" she said.

"Yes. Is who worse?"

"What, Fernol?"

"Is who worse?"

"I—I thought it might be someone of those I have been treating. What is it you want? I was going to bed."

"Sorry I disturbed you. I just wanted to tell you I know very well what you were thinking about me to-night."

She fancied that there was a sinister sound in the voice that was speaking.

"I—I don't think I understand," she said.

"Oh, yes, you do. You were thinking I was wrong in the head—mad, in fact. But you're mistaken. I'm as sane as you are. Good night."

"Fernol," she said. "Fernol!"

But she was cut off.

After this she made no further attempt to pray. She no longer even tried to control her thoughts. She let herself go to thought and to emotion as heedlessly as a terrified girl. There was no longer firm ground beneath her feet. Fernol's reiterated allusion to madness, his uncalled-for assertion of sanity, drew her on to the contemplation of a possibility so awful that it banished sleep. And she lay awake all night, companioned by fear. Towards dawn she got up, went to the drawing room, took down the volume of the encyclopaedia which contained the article on typhoid fever, and, returning to bed, studied it minutely till the murky daylight of London filtered into the room. She even committed a great part of it to memory, learning with a feverish intensity of concentration which she had never been able to summon up when studying for an examination in the days of her youth. And all the time that she was learning the silent voice kept repeating: "You hypocrite! You hypocrite!" The words ticked in her brain as a clock ticks in a lonely room. But she defied them. A great life, perhaps, was at stake, and the whole of her happiness. One sentence which she read—she knew she could never forget it, even if she lived to be very old—was as follows:

"No drug is known to cut short the disease; and in many cases none is required."

She clung to that sentence; she cherished it in her mind. As she dressed, while she breakfasted—she forced herself to eat as usual—she repeated it over and over; to her it meant this: "A doctor would be of no use to him; I can do all that a doctor could do." She thanked God for that sentence.

After breakfast she walked to Cadogan Square. She had sent a message to the Bureau to say she could not go there either in the morning or afternoon. She had resolved to give all her strength, all her powers, to Sir Hector. She knew she had nothing to give to anyone else.

The day was brilliantly clear, but intensely cold. She welcomed the sharpness of the air as a tonic. Although she had had no sleep, she felt violently alive. As she walked, by way of the Park, and then down Sloan Street, she strove to gather her forces together. She had resolved what to do. She meant to remain in the house all day, to spend the night there if necessary, to take charge of the case like a doctor as well as like a healer. She would fill Miss Burington with confidence in her. She was bracing herself for the fight of her life. There was no longer any question in her mind of giving in, of acknowledging that she was doubtful, of yielding her place to Sir Mervyn or anyone else. A change in her had come with the sleepless night. The fibre of her nature seemed to have hardened under the stress of the agony she had gone through. There are crises in which the human being either breaks down or becomes fierce and almost brutally defiant. Olivia had not broken down. But something tender and beautiful in her, something sincere and very delicate, seemed to have snapped like a string drawn too tight. Fernol's visit had made her for the moment unscrupulous. He had put fear in her, and in fighting down fear she had caught something of the brutality of the soldier in battle.

When she reached the house in Cadogan Square, and was waiting for the door to be opened, she said to herself:

"He has slept well. He is better to-day. The illness is leaving him." And when the footman came she was smiling.

She wished him "good morning," and went upstairs. Miss Burnington met her on the first landing.

"He's better, isn't he?" said Olivia.

"Please come in here before you go up to him," said Miss Burnington in a low voice.

She shut the drawing room door carefully. Then she said:

"Miss Traill, why did you tell Mr. West my brother was ill?"

"But I haven't told him."

"Haven't you seen him since you were here yesterday?"

"Yes. I saw him last night."

"He called early this morning to ask how my brother was. I didn't see him. The footman said as far as he knew there was nothing the matter but a slight cold. You must have said something."

Olivia explained how she was startled by hearing the telephone, and what she had said exactly before she knew Fernol was speaking.

"I am very sorry," she said. "But I never mentioned your brother's name."

"But he guessed who it was. Why was that?" asked Miss Burnington.

As she spoke she looked at Olivia with suspicion in her eyes. There was something of half-veiled hostility in her look and manner.

"How can I tell? I never even hinted to Fernol that there was anything wrong with your brother."

"Then it's very strange."

Miss Burnington paused.

"I don't like Mr. West," she said, after a moment of silence. "I know he's your friend, but there's something in him I shrink from. I think he's abnormal in some way. If people like him find out that Hector is ill, I can't answer for what I might do."

"I don't understand you."

"Hector is worse this morning. He's had a very bad night. I shan't be able to allow this sort of thing to go on much longer."

Olivia knew now she was speaking to an enemy.

"You visit my brother," continued Miss Burnington. "You keep the doctors out by doing so. But have you any idea what is the matter with him?"

"Yes," said Olivia firmly.

"Then, what is it?"

"I shall be more certain to-day. You must not think that because I am only a healer I know nothing about illness."

"Have you ever studied either medicine or surgery?"

"Not as doctors do, but—"

"Exactly!" interrupted Miss Burnington. "You haven't. You know nothing of the science. And yet you dare to take chances with such a life as my brother's! I speak strongly, but I can't help it. I feel strongly. I must tell you this, Miss Traill: if anything should happen to Hector you will be held responsible by public opinion—and by me."

"I will take the risk. He trusts me. That is enough for me."

"I suppose you realise that, if Hector doesn't get better, it will soon be impossible to keep his illness from the public. It will get into the papers. It will go all over the world. And the fact of your presence by his bedside—"

"Isn't he up?" Olivia interrupted sharply.

"No—not to-day.... The fact of your presence by his bedside will be a public scandal. It will make my brother ridiculous in the eyes of the world, and I'm afraid it will make you—odious."

"You are trying to frighten me, but I am not to be frightened. I have too much faith in myself."

"Do you really believe in yourself?" said Miss Burnington. And she looked at Olivia as if she would probe into the depths of her, would drag into the light her sincerity or insincerity.

"I have always believed in myself. And your brother must believe in me or he would call in the doctors."

"He has always hated doctors. And he's tremendously obstinate. But you can bring him to reason. Refuse to treat him. Tell him you think it is very serious and he ought to call in a doctor, and I'm sure he will do it."

"Yes, and put me down as the humbug I am not! No, Miss Burnington, I will not do that."

"Well, if it all becomes known the whole world will laugh at my brother. I know what people are. A great soldier, a great public man in the hands of the faith healers! It would ruin Hector. No man's reputation can survive that sort of thing. If you are ready to gamble with his life, at least pause and think before you gamble with his reputation."

"I am sorry," said Olivia, with a sort of cold obstinacy which concealed a turmoil of emotion. "I understand your anxiety. It makes you rather cruel to me, but I suppose that is natural. So I won't resent it. No one can care more for your brother's safety, for his future, for his honour and fame than I do—"

"Are you of his blood, then?" interrupted Miss Burnington, with uncontrollable bitterness.

"No, but I—" Olivia broke off, startled by the wildness of her own imprudence.

"Yes, Miss Traill?"

"I have his interests and his safety at heart. Indeed—indeed I have."

"Well, I will say no more. But I warn you that, in certain eventualities, I shall act on my own responsibility. I shall defy my brother's wishes, even his orders. Although I am only a woman, I have something of his obstinacy, and I shall not let him die without showing that obstinacy."

"Die!" said Olivia, struck by the word as by a blow in the heart.

"Yes—die."

The two women gazed at each other for a moment, and in that moment Miss Burnington read Olivia's secret.

"He is going to recover," said Olivia, with a strong effort to control herself. "I know it. I am not afraid either for him or myself."

"Very well!" said Miss Burnington, with icy coldness. "Please go to him. Shall I take you up?"

"No, don't trouble. Is it the door next to the sitting room?"

"Yes."

"Then I know it."

And she left the room.

As she ascended the stairs she felt as if the devil went with her. Never before had she been conscious in this sharp way of the evil within her. Perhaps, blinded by self-conceit, she had thought that she was one of the exceptional people who are naturally good. But now—she could not help it, she thought—she was deliberately giving herself to evil. The strange thing was that her love drove her down the broad path. It was her love which had waked in her defiance, insincerity, fear, selfishness, even hardness. It was her love which had changed her into a humbug. She felt at that moment that she would do anything, risk anything, rather than acknowledge that she had no more real faith in herself. She knew that she ought to say to Sir Hector, "I thought I had cured Fernol West, but I was wrong. I know that now, and it has shaken my belief in my healing power. Your health is more precious than his. I have no right to try to do for you what I have failed to do for him." When she reached the door of his bedroom she stood outside for a moment. For a moment there was a struggle between the good and evil within her. For a moment she was uncertain what she would do when she entered the room. But her hesitation was short-lived. She remembered Sir Hector's quiet remark: "No consideration should be shown to failures." And when she opened the door she had made up her mind to go on, even to the edge of the precipice, even perhaps into the gulf.

Sir Hector was stretched on a narrow, very long bed in a plainly furnished room. His face was turned towards her as she came in. She had set her face in an expression of calm self-confidence. And as she looked at him this expression did not change, though she saw at once that he was much worse. His colour was ghastly; his features had sharpened; the torches of fever were alight in his eyes. But he was apparently normal in mind. The first thing he said to her was:

"It hasn't acted yet."

"The power? You must give it time. Miracles are not worked in a moment."

She sat down by the bedside.

"In a case like yours, we must make use of every means that can help."

"Means?" he said, moving restlessly on the pillow.

"Yes. You mustn't suppose that because I heal people without medicine or surgery I neglect elementary precautions. That would be foolish, even wicked. Don't you think so?"

"I can't think clearly," he said. "My head's too infernally bad."

"Don't bother about anything."

She laid her hand on his broad forehead.

"Just give yourself up to me and all will be well with you."

"It seems deucedly odd to come to this," he murmured through a sigh.

"Shut your eyes. I am going to try to get you to sleep."

He shut his eyes obediently. When he did that she was conscious of the child in him and knew her love better. And the obedience of this man whom so many had obeyed revived for a moment her belief in her power. Surely such a man could not yield himself to her if she were really impotent. He was a judge of men. Could he be utterly deceived in a woman? She was suddenly strengthened. Still keeping one hand on his forehead she tried to pour all her soothing strength and her love into it. And presently she saw he was sleeping.

Meanwhile Miss Burington was in her bedroom putting on a hat and a warm fur coat. She had not intended to go out that morning while she waited for the faith healer, but the scene with Olivia had driven her to a resolve. She was, like her brother, decisive. Hesitation, prolonged mental debate, were foreign to her nature. Before she came up to her bedroom she had ordered her car to come round as soon as possible. Within a very few minutes she was on her way to Harley Street. Sir Mervyn Butler had never done her any real good; Olivia, it seemed, had cured her. Yet now she was hurrying to Sir Mervyn to ask his advice. Such a proceeding might be unreasonable. Perhaps it was. She did not trouble about that. For years she had been accustomed to consult Sir Mervyn. He looked strong. She liked him and she knew he liked her. And, besides, he was a doctor and celebrated. After the painful scene with Olivia, she felt she must see him. She knew that the fact of her brother's illness must shortly get out. Such a thing could not be kept secret for long. Sir Mervyn was the model of professional discretion. She knew of no one else to whom she could entrust her anxieties.

When she arrived at the doctor's house his waiting room was thronged with visitors. Of course, she had no appointment, but the manservant was certain that Sir Mervyn would see her, although he was, as always, "very much taken up." While she sat in the large handsomely furnished room among the silent, or softly whispering, strangers, Miss Burnington felt a little less miserable. Sir Mervyn hadn't cured her, but he must have cured multitudes of others, or else why should he be so famous? The sight of the crowd renewed her natural woman's faith in doctors. There was something substantial to rest upon. Olivia Traill—what status had she? And she dared to love Hector! Miss Burnington was jealous of her brother. His long indifference to women had given her a delicious sense of security. Often she had thought to herself, "Hector only cares for one woman—for me." The knowledge that another woman was in possession of him made her heart burn with something that was very like hatred. And yet, through it all, she could not help being grateful to Olivia. That day she held in her many emotions.

Twice the manservant appeared and mysteriously summoned an anxious being to the august medical presence. A third time he opened the door, swept Miss Burnington with a sympathetic glance, raised his blond eyebrows, and formed some cabalistic word with his large and respectable lips. A moment later she was in Sir Mervyn's sanctum.

He welcomed her cordially, yet with a definite touch of friendly sarcasm.

"In spite of the descendant of the Apostles!" he said.

Miss Burnington blushed slightly.

"It's very good of you," she said, rather nervously. "You might very well have refused to receive me, especially without an appointment. But—"

"I knew the headaches would come back," he interrupted, with a sort of bland pity.

"But they haven't," she acknowledged, almost like one ashamed.

He looked largely taken aback, but quickly recovered himself.

"That's well! That's well! Then what is it? The nervous affliction has reappeared in some other part of the organism?"

"Well—no."

"Dear me!"

He cleverly hid his disapprobation and drowned his face in intelligent inquiry.

"It's Hector."

"Sir Hector! But he's never ill," said Sir Mervyn, with a touch of not wholly ungenerous regret.

"He is very ill."

The great doctor leaned back in his chair with an expression of almost fatalistic resignation, as one who bows to the inscrutable decree of a doubtless benign Providence.

And Miss Burnington developed her story.

He listened in silence till the end.

"And what do you wish me to do?" he then said, in a very detached voice.

"How can we let this go on? It is madness."

"Of course it is. But you must remember you set the example."

"I know and I blame myself bitterly."

"Don't distress yourself. The young woman has colossal determination and push, like all these successful frauds. Their stock in trade is small but effective; complete ignorance, unbounded self-confidence, a plausible tongue, and a hide of brass. I'm afraid I can't consent to meet her in consultation."

"You surely can't suppose—"

She stopped, as if unable to make mention of such an outrage.

"No," she went on. "But couldn't you come to the house this evening—she's sure to be there still—and see her, and try to bring her to a sense of the danger of the position? Do, Sir Mervyn, if you still have any friendship for me. She might listen to you. She might be afraid of you."

Sir Mervyn pursed his full lips meditatively.

"If she went on attending Hector and he were to die, what would happen?"

"It would be a serious business for the young woman."

"Make her understand it. Frighten her."

"The matter requires thinking over."

"If you will only come, I will make Hector see you. His illness is sure to get out in a day or two, and if it gets into the papers that he's called in a faith healer, what will people say?"

"I fear they might say—mind you, I don't pledge myself that they will—they might say that your brother was not the most suitable choice that could be made for the viceroyalty of India."

"Exactly! We can't risk that. If you have any friendship for me you will come."

"Very well!" said Sir Mervyn, after a suitable pause.

She took his large soft hand impulsively.

"That's good of you. But I knew you would. I knew your generous nature. And, of course, you won't say a word."

"Good Heavens, Miss Burnington!"

She left him feeling thoroughly rebuked but burning with gratitude. That afternoon, just after four, he arrived at Sir Hector's house.

His mouth was set in a grim expression as he mounted the stairs to the drawing room. He had a profound veneration for science, and an active hatred of quacks. He genuinely believed that Olivia was a conscious impostor, and that Fernol West was a neurotic young millionaire, whom she had probably hypnotised into the delusion that she had cured him of some nervous disease, and who doubtless supplied her with money. He had come there that day determined to give her no quarter. He had already struck hard at her in the Press. Now he had the chance of finishing her off in a personal encounter. It was a great opportunity and it should not find him wanting.

Miss Burnington joined him almost immediately, looking nervous, but determined.

"It is good of you!" she said. "You are a true friend in need."

"I have the highest regard for you both. Is she still here?"

"Oh, yes. Do sit down for a moment. Take this chair. I want to tell you something."

"What is it?"

"You know that young man, Mr. West?"

"The neurotic boy she claims as a cure. I saw him that once."

"Well, it's most extraordinary; he's been here again."

"Again?"

"Oh, I don't think I told you! He called early this morning to ask how Hector was."

"Then he knows of this illness?"

"Evidently. Yet Miss Traill swears she never mentioned my brother's name to him in connection with illness."

Sir Mervyn smiled.

"You don't believe her?"

He smiled again, as if he considered that was quite a sufficient answer.

"If she hasn't he must have guessed it somehow."

"That would be rather remarkable, wouldn't it?"

"It's all inexplicable to me. Anyhow he called again just now and made the most minute inquiries of the footman. He wanted to know what was the matter and whether any doctor had been called in."

"And what was he told?"

"The footman said, according to his own account of the interview, that he only knew that my brother was keeping his room and that Miss Traill had been in the house all day. Then, he said, the young gentleman seemed quite satisfied and gave him a sovereign."

"Most extraordinary!"

"Isn't it? John has been with us since he was a boy and would tell me everything. What do you think of it all?"

"What can one think except that Miss Traill and this neurotic young man are acting together? She must have told him something. I shall be very much surprised if it isn't all in the papers to-morrow morning."

"Oh, Sir Mervyn! I must tell you one thing more. Just before Hector was taken ill, Mr. West dined alone with me and my brother. At dinner there was a discussion about Miss Traill. Mr. West got very excited because I said I couldn't be sure she had really cured me of my headaches. (He had wanted me to acknowledge publicly that she had cured me.) Finally he asked my brother whether if *he* were ill and Miss Traill seemed to cure him—Mr. West didn't say seemed—Hector would let the world know it."

"And what did Sir Hector say?"

"My brother said he would, and let them laugh at him as much as they liked."

"Was your brother quite well at the time?"

"Perfectly well."

"And you say he became ill—when?"

"I thought he didn't look quite himself the very next day. And from then on he grew gradually worse."

Sir Mervyn looked very grave. He sat in silence for a moment while Miss Burnington watched him.

At last he said:

"Had your brother ever said, or implied, that he might possibly trust himself to Miss Traill if he ever were ill?"

"He never said so to me, not in so many words. But I think he believed Miss Traill had cured me, and when he felt ill he told me he would have Miss Traill, and that he had a debt to pay and was determined to pay it."

"He might have told her before he was ill that if he ever were ill he would send for her," said Sir Mervyn.

"I suppose so."

"And that young man—"

He paused.

"It's all very strange, isn't it?" said Miss Burnington.

"Yes."

"What do you think?"

The doctor, who seemed sunk in deep thought, shifted slowly in his armchair.

"When Mr. West dined with you, were you in the room all the time?"

"Naturally—that is, till I left him with my brother to finish their wine."

"And then, of course, Sir Hector was with him."

"Hector came upstairs with me and went to the telephone for a minute."

"While Mr. West remained alone in the dining room?"

"Yes."

There was a silence.

"Why do you ask me all this, Sir Mervyn?" Miss Burnington said at last.

"Oh—well! Put it down to professional curiosity."

"Professional!"

"Ah! And now, can I see the young woman?"

"I'll make her come down to you."

She got up.

"One moment! Suppose she refuses?"

"Surely she can't!"

"She might."

"Then what do you advise?"

"If you'll allow me, I'll write her a note."

He got up, went to the writing table, sat down, took pen and paper, and wrote a few lines, which he enclosed in an envelope.

"If she refuses you might give her that."

Miss Burnington took the note.

"I'll do everything you tell me. Oh, I'm so thankful you are here!"

And she hurried out of the room, while the doctor left the writing table and went to stand by the fire. The expression of grim sarcasm had left his powerful face. As he gazed into the flames he looked profoundly thoughtful and stern.

IV

It seemed a long time to Sir Mervyn before the door opened and Olivia came in. She held his note in her left hand and her face was white. When he turned from the fire and saw her, he bowed grimly.

"I see you've read my note, Miss Traill," he said.

"Yes."

"So much the better. I'm here at the urgent request, I might say on the insistence, of Miss Burnington."

"I know. She told me."

"Hadn't we better sit down? We've got to come to an understanding."

"Yes."

Olivia sat down, and the doctor followed her example.

"What does this note mean?" she asked. "You say in it, 'If you do not see me I shall be compelled to seek information as to Sir Hector's condition elsewhere. I shall be compelled to seek out your friend, Mr. Fernol West.' What has Fernol West to do with Sir Hector's illness? Sir Hector sent for me and I came. I have a right to be here as he wishes it. I have never told Fernol West about his illness."

"And yet he knows. He has just been here for the second time to inquire about Sir Hector."

Olivia looked startled.

"Didn't Miss Burnington tell you about it?" said Sir Mervyn.

"No."

"Then—let me do so."

He repeated Miss Burnington's account of the interview with the footman and the giving of the tip. While he was speaking he kept his eyes fixed on Olivia, and it seemed to him that beneath her rigid expression he detected the shadow of a great fear. She sat without moving till he had finished. Then she said:

"I can only repeat, I never told Mr. West that Sir Hector was ill."

"Who did, do you think?"

"I don't know."

"Perhaps it was unnecessary that anyone should tell him," said Sir Mervyn, significantly.

After a moment of hesitation she said, slowly, and with a sort of dull heaviness,

"How could that be? Please tell me what you mean."

But he did not answer her question.

"Miss Traill," he said, with stern coldness, "don't you think it would be wise to turn over this case to me? It is all very well to play about with neurotics. Nerve cases may possibly be susceptible sometimes to suggestion. Wild, inconsequent boys may be influenced, for a time, by a determined woman. But what can you hope to achieve with a man of iron like Sir Hector? You may perhaps kill him ..."

"Oh, how dare you—how dare you?" she interrupted, with sudden passion.

"... by not treating him properly," pursued Sir Mervyn inflexibly. "And even if you don't do that, you may easily destroy his reputation as a man of common sense, a man with a great brain, in the eyes of the world. For once a man is laughed at he is diminished to the size of the ordinary fool in the sight of all those who laugh at him. But cure Sir Hector of a dangerous illness you can't. And you know that as well as I do. All this faith healing bluff is perfectly useless. You have nothing to gain in this house, and everything to lose. For your own sake I advise you to go. If you do this and if, when I examine the patient, I find no reason to take any other course, I promise to let you alone."

"No reason!" she said, in a low voice. "How could there be a—"

Her voice died away. She was looking at him, and now he saw distinctly fear in her eyes.

"You think ... you imagine that—"

Again her voice failed, as if smothered by emotion. A deep flush spread over her face and even down to her neck. She bent her head like one moved almost beyond endurance, clasped her hands tightly together, and remained still for two or three minutes. And there was something so terribly sincere in her look and attitude that Sir Mervyn was taken aback in spite of himself, and was conscious of pity mingled with a sudden perplexity. As Olivia said nothing more, and the silence at last became intolerable to him, he broke it by saying, in a voice which he tried to make as hard and unemotional as possible,

"Now you have my promise, will you leave Sir Hector in my hands?"

Then Olivia looked up.

"Tell me why you think I am here," she said, in a low voice.

"To carry on your faith healing imposture, I suppose," returned the doctor, trying to fight against the sudden change which—he scarcely knew why—had taken place in his feeling towards her within the last few minutes.

"I have not been a humbug in my life," she said, with intense earnestness. "I have believed in my power to heal. I have believed that it was a gift made to me by God."

"In that case you have been self-deceived. But that doesn't make you any the less a public danger."

"I—I will never bring danger to him," she said. Tears stood in her eyes.

"You don't understand me at all," she added.

"Indeed?"

"No; not at all. But how should you? Why should I expect—"

She got up.

"Please go up to him. You can tell him I asked you to, because I was afraid, perhaps, I wasn't capable of—"

She stopped. Sir Mervyn looked away from her.

"Very well," he said. "You have done the right thing at last, Miss Traill."

He made a movement to go but she stopped him.

"I'll stay here. But you must come back and tell me exactly what you think. I must know. I have a special reason. I've got to know what is the matter with Sir Hector."

"Wait here then. I will come back presently."

He saw a sort of agony of inquiry in her eyes.

"You promise to tell me—whatever it is?"

The doctor hesitated. But something in her eyes overcame any reluctance which he felt.

"I will tell you," he said.

"Very well."

He left the room. As he went upstairs he wondered at himself. This woman had made an impression of sincerity even upon him. He found himself pitying her; he even found himself liking her.

When he had gone Olivia walked about the room for a few minutes, then stood at the window and looked out into the square.

The twilight was falling over London. The darkness of night was at hand. To-day, for the first time in her life, she realised imaginatively the horror of darkness, and she knew that she did this because there was darkness in her own soul. As she gazed out of the window, she understood that the human being carries everything within those mysterious recesses which can never be fully explored—heaven and hell, light and darkness.

"What a mystery I am!" she thought. "And I used to think I understood, even that I knew. I understand nothing. I know nothing."

How incalculable are the human impulses! She had entered that room a few minutes ago with the intention of fighting Sir Mervyn, in spite of the words he had written, words which conveyed a scarcely veiled threat. And now she had capitulated. And Sir Hector would know it; would know that she had no faith in herself, that she could not carry out her job, that she acknowledged herself to be a fraud. And yet she was not a fraud, but a sincere and deeply loving woman.

There seemed to be no continuity in her anymore. Her purposes were divided, antagonistic. A hideous uncertainty replaced her old firmness and strength. She had become the dwelling place of warring emotions. Fear had entered into her, the malady which carries disease through every part of the soul.

Sir Mervyn's revelation of Fernol's second visit to the house had changed a horrible suspicion into something more definite, into a tremendous apprehension. Very soon, no doubt, she would know the truth. Sir Mervyn would tell her. She knew that an abominable thought about her had entered his mind; she knew, or believed she knew, when it had died there. He was no longer the enemy he had been. But if he discovered something terrible, what would he do? Would his foul suspicion revive? It might. And then—

She saw herself plunged in the mud of a hideous scandal.

At last she came away from the window and sat down near the fire. And there she remained for over an hour. No one came to her. The house was silent, save for an occasional footstep overhead. She had time and opportunity for what seemed a lifetime of thought and feeling. And all the time, through it all, she was waiting strung up like one accused of a crime for the verdict. She knew herself innocent, and yet she was weighed down by a sensation of acute apprehension, almost of guilt. At that moment she realised, as never before, the responsibility she had assumed when she undertook to heal others. She had become answerable for Fernol.

Would Sir Mervyn never come down? What could be happening upstairs? What could he be doing? She thought of Sir Hector sleeping with her hand on his forehead. He had only slept for a very short time, but he had yielded to her influence. A painful jealousy invaded her as the time went on, tingled all through her. She began almost to regret that she had abdicated. Perhaps all her fear and suspicion were ridiculous. Suddenly it occurred to her that Sir Mervyn might have come to the house that day with a deliberate policy. He might have made up his mind to frighten her in order to get her away from the patient. The medical profession was notoriously prejudiced, and Sir Mervyn had shown a special animosity against her ever since her arrival in England, and even before he knew her. Besides, she had perhaps cured the patient whom he had been unable to cure. That fact alone was enough to make him hate her. And as he had failed with Miss Burnington, he might fail with Sir Hector.

She got up, threw his note into the fire, and went towards the door. She felt at that moment driven, and capable almost of an act of violence. This prolonged delay was unendurable. She felt she must put an end to it. She would go up to the sick man's room and find out for herself what was happening. But as she opened the door she saw Sir Mervyn coming down the stairs with Miss Burnington. At that moment she hated them both. Her jealousy made her hate them.

She stopped. Miss Burnington came up to her.

"Thank you, Miss Traill," she said. "You have done the right thing and I am grateful to you."

Olivia said nothing. She did not dare to speak lest she should say something violent or horrible, something unforgivable, which would oblige her to leave that house and render her return to it impossible. Miss Burnington looked at her in surprise, as if expecting some words from her, and then added,

"I am going downstairs to give some directions. I believe Sir Mervyn wishes to speak to you."

"Very well," Olivia forced herself to say.

Still looking surprised, Miss Burnington went on down the stairs and Olivia returned to the drawing room, followed by Sir Mervyn, who shut the door carefully behind him.

"What is it?" asked Olivia, as he came towards her.

"I am not certain yet, but I think he is probably in the first stage of typhoid fever."

Olivia was conscious of a strange sense of deep relief, as if a burden fell from her. But there mingled with it a feeling of outrage.

"I thought it might be typhoid," she said.

"You didn't say so."

"What would have been the good? What am I to say anything to a doctor? But now, haven't you anything to say to me?"

The sense of outrage was growing in her. She felt it burning her.

"To say? Well, I suppose you realise now what would have happened if a doctor had not been called in?"

"I didn't mean that at all."

"Please tell me what you did mean."

"Did you come here intending to frighten me?"

"I came here because I was asked—begged to come."

"I dare say. But wasn't it your policy to frighten me?"

"What makes you think so?"

"That note of yours for one thing."

"Why should my note have frightened you?"

"What did you intend to convey by it?"

"Exactly what I wrote. If you had not come to see me, I should certainly have gone to see Mr. West."

"Why? What did you—"

She paused. She felt like one on the edge of danger. Yet something drove her to take the onward step.

"What did you suspect?"

The doctor hesitated. At last he said:

"Under the present circumstances I don't think it is necessary to say."

"That means that you acknowledge how erroneous, how—how monstrous your suspicion was."

"You can interpret my meaning as you like," he replied coldly.

"Is that your idea of honesty? Is that the English idea?" she said bitterly.

"I am not in the least ashamed of anything I have done," he said, inflexibly.

"But that wasn't all. When I came down to see you, you hinted ... you implied that ... that ... I can't say it!"

"Miss Traill, as you have brought up this very painful subject, I am willing to say to you that I believe I have made a mistake about you, though I consider it a not wholly unnatural one. Since I have seen you to-day I do believe in your *bona fides*. I thought you a conscious charlatan. Now I think you merely a self-deceived woman."

"I made him sleep only this very day when the fever was on him."

"Indeed! For how long?"

"Not for long. But doesn't that show—"

"It really is useless for us to argue about it. I consider all faith healing an absolute imposture."

"And Miss Burnington's cure?"

He replied to her question by another.

"And Mr. Fernol West's cure?" he retorted.

Olivia winced. Sir Mervyn saw it and mercilessly pressed his advantage.

"What of that?" he said. "I have just told you that I have come—I scarcely know how or why—to believe in your honesty. Tell me—do you honestly believe you have made that young fellow sound?"

"I—I thought I had. His parents, his friends, everyone thought I had."

"And do you think so still?"

"I don't know."

"That is honest," he said, almost with heartiness.

"You only met Fernol once. How can you—"

"Miss Traill," he said. "I will match your honesty with mine. To see a man like Mr. West once is enough for anyone trained as I am, fortified as I am by a long medical experience. Shall I tell you exactly what I think about him?"

"Tell me."

"I think he's acutely neurotic. I'll go further. I shouldn't be surprised if he has the seeds of madness in him."

"Madness! Fernol!" she whispered.

He had put her fear into words, and by doing so had given it a vehement life such as it had not had before.

"Why—what has he done to make you think he is mad?"

"I don't say he has done anything. I have no actual proof of his madness. But have you never had the same suspicion as I have?"

Olivia tried to say "no," but her lips made no sound.

"Such an accident as I understand he had, might easily have an effect on the brain from which it could never recover," said Sir Mervyn.

"Then do you still think—but you say you believe it is typhoid?"

"I think it probably is."

"Then—" she paused, looking at him.

At this moment the drawing room door opened and Miss Burnington came in hurriedly, with a newspaper in her hand. She looked greatly agitated.

"I've telephoned as you told me to," she said to Sir Mervyn. "But oh, the worst that I feared has happened."

"What is it?"

"Look at this! In the evening paper! And I hear they telephoned from the office some time ago to have it confirmed before putting it in. Sidney answered and told them it was nonsense, that my brother only had a slight cold, but they have put it in all the same."

"Our Yellow Press!" said Sir Mervyn, taking the paper from her. "Where is it?" he asked.

Miss Burnington pointed to a paragraph. He read it.

"This must be contradicted at once—to-night," he exclaimed. "Miss Traill—read it. I shall want you to authorise a contradiction."

As he spoke he handed the paper to Olivia, and she read the following words:

SIR HECTOR BURNINGTON AND THE FAITH-HEALER.

As we go to press we learn that the famous general, Sir Hector Burnington, who has been mentioned as the probable future Viceroy of India, has been seized with sudden and severe illness. We are informed that he has refused to call in a doctor and has placed himself unreservedly in the hands of the American faith healer, Miss Olivia Traill, whose name has been so much before the public of late, and whose methods have brought forth such severe condemnation from the medical profession. This will be a hard blow for the doctors. It will also probably come as a surprise to the public, who, hitherto, have been under the impression that Sir Hector Burnington did not estimate the capacity of women too highly. In our late edition we hope to be able to state the exact nature of the great general's illness. Our informant was unable to satisfy our curiosity on this point. But that Miss Olivia Traill is in charge of the case, there is no doubt whatever.

As Olivia looked up from the paper she met Miss Burnington's eyes.

"If this isn't contradicted at once it will ruin Hector!" said Miss Burnington bitterly. "What can we do?"

Before either Sir Mervyn or Olivia could answer the footman opened the door. Miss Burnington turned with nervous abruptness.

"What is it, John?"

"A gentleman has called, Ma'am. He says he is a representative of the *Evening Dispatch* and begs to see you for a moment. He also asked for Miss Traill, Ma'am."

"For Miss Traill? Did you tell him Miss Traill was in the house?"

"He knew it, Ma'am. He said: 'I know Miss Olivia Traill is in the house. Please ask her to give me a moment. I shall only keep her a moment.'"

"Oh, Sir Mervyn! What shall we—"

"May I settle the matter?" said the doctor.

"Oh, yes. Please do what you think best."

"Very well."

He turned to the footman.

"Please show the gentleman into the library, and say that Sir Mervyn Butler, of Harley Street, will be down to see him in a moment."

"Yes, sir."

The footman went out.

"This visit is providential," said Sir Mervyn. "We shall be able to get a *démenti* out at once and knock this rumour on the head before the papers have time to turn it into a sensation. But you must help us, Miss Traill."

"What do you wish me to do?" asked Olivia.

"I shall ask you to give me a written statement to take to that man downstairs. Of course you realise who the informant mentioned here"—he struck the paper with his forefinger—"must be?"

"I? How should I know? I have nothing to do with it. When Sir Hector called me in I told him that if I was able to cure him I should like him to promise me never to tell anyone either that he was ill or that I had been able to help him. If you don't believe me, ask him."

Sir Mervyn and Miss Burnington exchanged glances.

"You really told him that!" said the doctor.

"Yes."

"That was, I must say, very fine of you," he said. "Very disinterested indeed."

"I only wanted to cure him, nothing but that."

"Thank you, my dear," said Miss Burnington. "I'm afraid I—"

"Oh, please—never mind!" said Olivia. "You have both of you misunderstood me utterly."

There was an awkward silence, which the doctor broke by saying,

"Surely you realise that the informant who gave this story to the Press must have been Mr. West."

"Perhaps it was."

"Of course it was."

"How could I help it?"

"You couldn't. But only you can kill this rumour."

"But it was true."

"It isn't true now," said Miss Burnington.

"We must give out a statement which must go into the paper to-night if possible," said Sir Mervyn, going over to the writing table. "The only question is how to word it."

He sat down, took a pen and drew a sheet of notepaper towards him.

"If you will allow me, Miss Traill, I'll write down what I think will do, read it out to you and then ask you to copy and sign it."

"Very well," she said, in a dull voice.

Suddenly she felt tired. She longed to lie down, shut her eyes and forget everything; forget her old enthusiasms, forget her lost faith, forget Fernol West and the devotion to her which had brought about this horrible situation, forget even Sir Hector and her great love for him. She knew that Sir Mervyn was right. She knew that it must be Fernol who was responsible for the dreadful paragraph which, perhaps, hundreds of people were reading, and repeating to other hundreds at that very moment. And she was scarcely able to doubt any longer that Fernol was also responsible for something else—for something so terrible that the mere thought of it would surely make her life hideous to her forever. For the first time she felt the burden of existence as a loathsome load which she longed to cast away from her. For the first time she thoroughly understood the temptation of suicide.

"Let me see!" said a meditative voice.

She looked across the room. Sir Mervyn had drawn out a pair of spectacles rimmed with tortoise-shell and perched them on his broad nose. Miss Burnington had gone to stand near him and was looking over his shoulder. She stared at them both, and they both seemed remote from her. It was difficult for her to believe that this man and this woman had anything to do with her. Sir Mervyn moved his lips, as if silently forming some words, and frowned, wrinkling his ample forehead. Then he bent over the paper and wrote, slowly, occasionally stopping for a moment to consider. Presently he paused and turned towards Miss Burnington.

"Do you think that will do?" he said, in a low voice.

Miss Burnington bent nearer to the paper.

"Admirable!" she said, after a moment. "The very thing."

"I think so. ... I think so!"

He looked across to Olivia over his spectacles.

"Miss Traill!"
Olivia heard a voice say "Yes."
"I'll just read out what I have written."
The voice paused.
"You are listening, Miss Traill?"
Again the voice said, "Yes."
This is it."
He cleared his throat, and leaning back in his chair read in a loud and important voice:

> "A paragraph in the 'Evening Dispatch' has just been brought to my notice containing the statement that, seized with sudden illness, General Sir Hector Burnington has refused to call in a doctor, and has placed himself unreservedly in my hands. I wish to deny emphatically that there is any truth in this statement. I am not attending Sir Hector Burnington, who is being treated by Sir Mervyn Butler, of Harley Street. I must ask you to give this denial publicity. The fact that I have been to Sir Hector Burnington's house merely as a friend to inquire after his health has doubtless given rise to this ridiculous rumour."

Sir Mervyn looked across again at Olivia.
"And then your signature," he said.
"You want me to sign that?" said Olivia.
"If you kindly will. And I shall ask you to copy it out first. ... It must be in your own handwriting."
Olivia crossed the room slowly. Sir Mervyn got up from the table.
"Here is the pen."
"Thank you."
She took it and sat down. For a moment the written words swam before her eyes. Then they grew clear. She began to copy them slowly and carefully. Sir Mervyn and Miss Burnington, who at first had stood behind her, left her and went softly over to the fireplace. She heard them whispering together as she wrote. And she felt as if she were writing her own condemnation. Presently she came to the last sentence, to the final words: "this ridiculous rumour." There she stopped. She still kept the pen in her hand; she still leaned over the paper. Her eyes stared at the word "ridiculous." This was what she had become—ridiculous; ridiculous in her own eyes, and in the eyes of the man she loved. How had he taken that confession of hers? She did not know that yet. She looked across the room to those two figures by the fire. They were no longer whispering together. They were silent now, watching her.

"Is anything the matter, Miss Traill?" said Sir Mervyn's voice. "Is there anything in the wording you object to?"

"Oh—no! I have no right—none—to object to anything now. It is not true, of course, but how can I object?"

"I don't understand. What is it then?"

And he came towards the writing table, looking curiously at her.

"What did he say when you told him?" she asked.

"He?"

"What did Sir Hector say?"

"He was too ill to say much."

"But what did he say?"

"As far as I remember, he said, 'very well—if she can't manage it, do the best you can.'"

"That was all?"

"He added, 'I was willing to pay my debt.' I think his mind was beginning to wander."

"Thank you."

She leaned down over the paper, copied out the last sentence, and signed her name at the bottom.

"Here it is!" she said, getting up.

Sir Mervyn took the paper and read it carefully.

"That's quite right. Thank you, Miss Traill. Now I'll go down."

He turned to Miss Burington.

"I shall only be a few minutes."

And he left the two women together.

"Won't you come to the fire?" said Miss Burington, after a silence.

The voice was gentle, almost pleading.

"I am not cold, thank you."

"But do come and sit down. You must wait and just hear the result of Sir Mervyn's interview with this man."

"Yes."

Olivia went over to the fire and sat down.

"I'm very sorry about all this—very," said Miss Burington in a quick, anxious voice. "I know you must think me a most ungrateful woman. I am really distressed. But—but I love my brother very much. And he is of such inestimable value to his country that I felt obliged to do what I did. Can you understand? Can you try to forgive me?"

"I understand," said Olivia.

"Anything I can do to show you how I feel about you I will gladly do. If you think—if it would be any good—I will say that I—that I owe my own cure to you."

"You don't! " said Olivia.

"But surely—"

"You don't. I can't heal anyone. I have no faith in myself."

"But you don't mean to say—"

"I say that I have deceived myself. I thought I possessed a power which I didn't possess. You were quite right not to believe in me. You saw what I didn't see, what Fernol and the others didn't see. You needn't reproach yourself. I didn't cure you. I didn't cure Fernol. And I could never have cured your brother. I shall never again attempt to heal anyone."

"I—I am sorry!" said Miss Burnington, almost helplessly.

Again the silence fell between them. It lasted a long time. Olivia broke it at length by saying:

"Is he very ill?"

"I'm afraid he is. We've sent for a trained nurse. Meanwhile, Sidney, his valet, a most devoted man, is with him. I shall go up directly Sir Mervyn comes back."

"Many people recover from typhoid, don't they?"

"Yes. We—we hope for the best."

Again the silence fell. And this time it lasted till Sir Mervyn came back.

"It's all right," he said. "I found the young man quite amenable. Your denial will appear in the late edition to-night, Miss Traill."

"I am glad."

"And I've written and signed a bulletin which will be affixed to the front door. That is necessary. There have been several inquiries since I went downstairs. Mr. West has been again."

"Mr. West!" said Miss Burnington. "Did you see him?"

"No. John told me. He came just as I was about to go into the library. I forbade John to let him in, or to trouble you about it."

"Does he know you are here?"

"Yes. I understand John had some difficulty in getting rid of him. But he's gone now."

Sir Mervyn looked at Olivia, who had sat in silence during this short conversation with her eyes fixed upon him.

"I think," he said, addressing Miss Burnington, "that it would be well if you returned to your brother."

"Yes, yes, I'll go!" she said, getting up quickly.

"I'll follow you almost directly. I expect Nurse Swann will be here in a moment."

Miss Burnington turned to Olivia.

"If I don't see you again to-night—" she said.

She held out her hand.

Olivia took it.

"Thank you for all you have done."

And she left the room. Then Sir Mervyn turned very gravely to Olivia.

"I didn't wish to say anything about it to Miss Burington. She has enough to trouble her already. And I'm afraid undue excitement might make her ill again. But I must tell you. John informed me that Mr. West was in a very excited state when he called just now."

"Excited!" said Olivia. "How—how did he show it?"

"When he heard I was in attendance on Sir Hector, he became violent and wished to force his way into the house. He demanded to see you. John was obliged to get rid of him by telling him a lie."

"What lie?"

"John said you weren't here, that you had gone home."

"And then—"

"He went away muttering angrily to himself. I'm afraid we shall have trouble with him. There's no doubt in my mind that a doctor ought to see him."

"Poor Fernol!" she said. "Poor Fernol!"

"It's a grievous business. Is he living quite alone?"

"Yes."

"Where?"

"At the Savoy Hotel."

"It's difficult to know what to do. It would be worse than useless for me to come into contact with him. He has conceived a violent hatred against me, no doubt. He said as much to the footman. And I saw it that evening I met him here. I think the best thing I can do is to give you the address of a first-rate man in such cases."

He took out a card and wrote on it a name and address in pencil.

"You might communicate with him. He will advise you better than I can."

"Who is he?" said Olivia.

"The best specialist we have for—for mental cases. And now I must go to Sir Hector!"

"Good night," said Olivia.

She took the card.

He stretched out his hand and grasped hers, almost with cordiality.

"One word more!"

"Yes?"

"I must warn you against seeing Mr. West alone for the present. Don't communicate with him. Don't let him in. Have you any servants?"

"No; I'm quite alone."

"On no account let him in."

"Thank you."

The footman opened the door.

"Nurse Swann has just come, sir."

"Good! Send her up to Miss Burington."

"Yes, sir."

The footman went out. Sir Mervyn hesitated, although there was surely nothing more to be said between him and Olivia.

"I don't quite like your going away alone," he said.

"I am accustomed to being alone."

"Yes—but to-night!"

Suddenly he went to the door, opened it, and called down the staircase.

"John! John!"

"Yes, sir?" came the footman's voice from below.

"Please call a cab for Miss Traill."

"Yes, sir."

The doctor came back.

"Drive home. I would rather you didn't walk."

"Very well."

"Do you live in a flat?"

"Yes."

"There's a hall porter?"

"Yes."

"Will you promise me to take him up with you as far as your flat door?"

"I'm not afraid of anything."

"No, no; of course not. But will you do as I say?"

"If you wish it."

"And on no account allow Mr. West to be shown up if he should call. He probably won't. But he might. Good night."

Again he took her hand and pressed it. Then they parted. Olivia went downstairs and he went up to his patient.

Olivia had to wait a few minutes in the hall while the footman stood on the pavement with his whistle at his lips. She looked into the darkness, searching for the figure of a man. She saw no one. At last a cab glided up.

As she drove away in the darkness she knew what it was to feel lonely. Everything that had meant life to her seemed to have fallen away from her suddenly. She had failed in her job; or, rather, she had thrown it up because she feared failure. The main purpose of her existence had been withdrawn put of her reach. For with the abrupt fading of her faith had vanished forever any power of healing she—perhaps—had once possessed. She knew quite well that she would never dare to try to heal anyone again. She could never be such a humbug as to attempt without faith that which she believed could only be accomplished by faith. Her career, therefore, was at an end. The man whom she loved might die. If he lived it could surely be only to despise her. Her chief friend in London had become to her a reason for apprehension, almost for horror. To think of him was to feel a cold breath from the abyss, to know the shuddering of nightmare.

Yes, she knew loneliness that night.

Sir Mervyn's reiterated warnings had not brought to the birth in her any physical fear. The fear that companioned her was wholly of the imagination and of—she fancied—the most intimate region of the heart.

"Poor Fernol!" she thought. "Poor Fernol!"

So the tragic grip had taken hold of him. The sharp fangs of an evil fate had fastened themselves in him. And all her energy, her will, her faith, her long effort had been wholly in vain. She thought of his mother and father far away in America, and the tears rose in her eyes. It was almost incredibly sad.

When the cab drew up before Buckingham Palace Mansions she looked quickly out through the window. There was no one waiting before the entrance. She got out, paid the fare, and went in. The porter in uniform stood by the lift.

"Has anyone been here for me?" she asked.

"Yes, Ma'am."

"Mr. West?"

"No, Ma'am. Lord Sandring."

And he gave her a card with Lord Sandring's name on it and some words pencilled on the back. Without reading them, she stepped into the lift and was taken up to her floor.

"You might just open the door for me," she said to the porter.

"Certainly, Ma'am."

He inserted his key and opened the door. She went into the little hall. As he was about to close the door she said:

"Just a moment!"

"Ma'am?"

Sir Mervyn's last warning was present in her mind: "On no account allow Mr. West to be shown up if he should call." She had made no promise to obey it, but now, as she recalled the look in the doctor's face, the sound of his voice, she resolved that she would.

"If Mr. Fernol West should call to-night, please don't show him up," she said.

"Very well, Ma'am. I'm to say you are out?"

"Yes, please. Wait! You are sure to be in the hall?"

"Oh, yes, Ma'am. I shall be there."

"Thank you."

He left her and shut the door, leaving her to her immense loneliness. She went into the bedroom, took off her jacket and hat, then walked to the little drawing room and turned on the electric light. Lord Sandring's card was still in her hand, with the card given to her by Sir Mervyn. She turned the former over and read:

> "Just seen the 'Evening Dispatch.' This is grand. That HE should be among the believers! Ecco un trionfo!— S."

Ecco un trionfo! Poor Lord Sandring! His joy would soon be turned into bitterness. She laid down the two cards, and looked round the familiar little room, which she had actually been able to think of as home since she had been in London. Now it was the cage of her loneliness. She was confined in it with the hours. The night lay before her, and then—all the future. She thought of beasts in captivity, going to and fro behind the bars with their wild eyes fixed on the other side of the world. What had she to look to?

The two armchairs by the fire, with their suggestion of repose, of mediation, or of happy talks, made her shiver when she looked at them. She glanced again at Lord Sandring's card. She would write to him. It would be something to do and it was absolutely necessary that he should know the exact position of affairs in regard to herself. She owed him an immediate explanation. She tore up his card, sat down, and began to write to him her confession of impotence. As she wrote a sort of brutal desire to hurt herself woke up in her. In the strongest words at her command she described her complete disbelief in her own powers, her absolute determination never again to attempt to heal any living creature.

> "You will never see me again at the Bureau. I know I shall cause you great pain by this letter, but anything is better than pretence. I cannot play the humbug with you, or with anyone. I know my own impotence, and I wish everyone who has heard of me to know it too. I am not more than others; I am less, because I have made claims which have no basis of fact. I can do no good to anyone. I may have even done harm to many. I don't know. But I do know that, from to-night, I will never set myself up as the superior of others. As to Sir Hector Burnington, I am not attending him. He knows I consider myself quite incapable of curing him of his illness. Sir Mervyn Butler is with him. Forgive me the disappointment and pain this letter will cause you, and, with

gratitude for all your kindness,

"Believe me,
"Your sincere friend,
"OLIVIA TRAILL."

She put this letter into an envelope, addressed it, stamped it, and laid it on the table. It could go by the morning's post. She did not want to go outside the flat door, or to ring and call the porter up to her. Yet, perhaps, it would be best if Lord Sandring got it by the first post on the morrow with the newspapers containing her statement. (She had little doubt that many of the papers would copy the announcement in the late edition of the *Evening Dispatch*.) Perhaps she ought to send away the letter that night. After some hesitation—she seemed to be made up of hesitation now—she rang the bell for the porter. In a few minutes he came up, let himself in with his key, and opened the door.

"You rang for me, Ma'am?"

"Yes."

She took up the letter.

"Could you put this in the post for me?"

"Certainly, Ma'am."

She gave him the letter and he turned to go. But when he was just going out of the room she called him back.

"One moment!"

"Ma'am?"

"If Mr. West should call I—I think I will see him."

"Very well, Ma'am."

She saw a faint look of surprise on his stolid face.

"I am to show him up then, Ma'am?"

"Well—yes. Yes, show him up. But perhaps he won't call."

"I couldn't say, Ma'am."

The expression of surprise grew more definite. He stood for a moment, then walked heavily out.

Had she really summoned him, not because of the letter, but on account of Fernol? She was not sure. She was sure of nothing to-night. But she now felt that to follow the advice of Sir Mervyn would be the act of a moral coward. Fernol had come to England only because of her. He had implicitly trusted her; had given himself to her in a peculiar, a touching way. His father and mother had an almost childlike confidence in her; admiration for her. Could she fail their boy in what was, perhaps, the supreme hour of his fate? That would be an act of almost loathsome weakness on her part. Her natural unselfishness rose up again in her, asserted itself almost violently. After all, did it matter now what happened to her? She had still a duty to carry out, at whatever cost to herself. If she deserted Fernol now, because of the horror which had attacked her imagination, no shred of self-respect would be left to her. She knew that she would have to condemn herself utterly.

Suddenly the battle was over. She felt a slight sense of relief. Whatever Fernol was, whatever he had done, she would recognise her responsibility towards him, would try to fulfil it to the uttermost.

"I don't matter anymore," she said to herself. "But I won't be afraid. I won't be afraid. If I am afraid I am the most contemptible of all creatures."

Usually she went out at about half-past seven to have her dinner at a small Italian restaurant close to Victoria Station. But to-night she had resolved not to go. She went into the kitchen of the flat, made herself some strong tea on the gas stove, drank it, and ate some bread and butter. Then she sat down to wait for Fernol. She now felt quite certain that he would come.

Soon after nine she heard the ring of the doorbell. He had come. Again that horror of the imagination seized her and shook her. But she strove to overcome it, to summon up all her courage. Nevertheless, as she got up and went down the passage, she was trembling. She opened the door and saw Fernol.

"So you're here!" he said.

His angry eyes searched her face. He looked excited, hostile. His face was as the face of a stranger.

"Of course I am here," she said, in a level voice. "Come along in."

He frowned as he came in.

"Leave your coat."

He said nothing more, but quickly pulled off his coat and threw it down on the floor of the hall.

"Please pick up your coat and hang it up properly," she said.

He shot a glance at her sideways, hesitated, then obeyed her.

"And now come right in."

Her instinct was to make him go in front of her, but she did not give way to it. She walked on and heard his step close behind her. She was glad when they were in the drawing room, and she could face him again.

"Sit down, Fernol."

"No, thank you."

"Anyhow, I will."

And she sat down, retaining an air of calm self-possession. He stood on the hearthrug and put his hands in his pockets. Then he took his right hand out and fidgeted with his watch chain. His eyes roved all over the room, avoiding hers.

"What's that?" he exclaimed in a loud voice.

"What? Where?"

"There! On the table!"

She looked and saw the card Sir Mervyn had given her with the name of the specialist in mental diseases written upon it.

"That! Oh, it's only—"

Before she could prevent him, he had gone to the table and picked up the card.

"Sir Mervyn Butler!" he exclaimed. "Do you mean to tell me—"

He turned the card over and read what was written on the back.

"What's this?" he demanded, still in a loud voice. "What's the meaning of this doctor's name?"

He came back to the fire with the card in his hand.

"What do you want with these cursed doctors? Why aren't you with Burnington?"

"Try to behave properly and I will tell you."

"You'd better!" he retorted.

"Put that card down."

"Why should I?"

"Because it's mine and I tell you to do so."

He dropped it on the floor.

"I've made a nice mistake," he said, with intense bitterness. "I believed in you and you're as treacherous as all the rest of them. What have you done? Why aren't you with Burnington? What's Mervyn Butler doing there? Why is he there, I say?"

"I'm going to tell you if you'll only listen and be quiet."

"Go on!"

"Fernol, did you go to the *Evening Dispatch?*"

"Of course I did."

"How did you know Sir Hector was ill?"

"Never mind. That's my business."

"How could you have known?"

"Didn't he swear he would send for you? Didn't he? Or did you tell me a damned lie?"

"Hush! He did send for me."

"Then—then you're going back to-morrow? You're going to throw that old humbug into the street?"

"Sir Mervyn is not a humbug, Fernol."

"He is. He pretends to cure disease and he can't. He takes money for what he can't do. All the doctors do that. And you, who can cure, don't take a farthing. And the world howls against you and sticks to the humbugs. But now they'll know. All London will know. I'll take care of that. But you must back me up. I'll bring it off. I'll work it all. That's why I'm here. You need a man to run you, one that knows the ropes. See how I worked the *Evening Dispatch?*"

He broke into a laugh.

"That was a surprise for the doctors, wasn't it? That was one from the shoulder, eh? When are you going back to throw old Butler out? I'll go with you. I want to see the fun. You owe that to me, Olivia, for if it wasn't for me—"

He stopped short and put his hand to his mouth, and a crafty look came into his face.

"Fernol, what have you done?"

"Never mind. When are you going back?"

"I am not going back."

"Not—"

He bent down and stared into her eyes.

"I'm not going back. Sir Hector is dangerously ill."

"Why not? All the better for you! Now's your chance to show what you can do."

"I am not going back."

The boy's face, which had been flushed, went suddenly white.

"You're going to let me down! After all I've done for you!"

After a moment of painful hesitation Olivia said, in a gentle voice, which sickened her as she heard it, because it sounded so false:

"Dear Fernol, if you don't tell me what you have done, how can I know what I owe you? You leave me in the dark. Is that friendship? How can two friends work together when one of them is left in ignorance of what the other is doing? Put me wise and then—"

"Yes—then?" he said eagerly.

"Then I shall be able to understand thoroughly what it is my part to do."

"That's horse sense, Olivia! Now you're talking!"

Again one hand went to his watch chain.

"You will do your part if I tell you?"

"Fernol, have I ever let you down?"

She felt like a traitor to friendship as she spoke. But the time for sincerity was past. At all cost she had to know.

"No, never. But, if I tell you, will you go back to-morrow?"

"I'll go to Cadogan Square to-morrow."

"You swear that?"

"I promise you."

His face was transfigured.

"Olivia, old girl, I've done the wonderful thing I've always wanted to do for you. I've given you the great chance of your life."

"How, Fernol?"

"It was I who made Sir Hector get ill."

Somehow—she never knew how—Olivia forced herself to meet the triumph in his eyes with a look of gratitude. She even held out her hand to him. He grasped it.

"How did you do it?"

"Don't tell! ... I've got a friend in Guy's Hospital. I made up to him for you, though I hate all the doctors. I managed to get hold of a culture of typhoid bacillus one day, when I was with him in the laboratory. (He was injecting typhoid into a rat.) That night I dined with Sir Hector I put some of it into his wine."

"Thank you, Fernol," she said, by a fierce effort concealing her horror.

"I gave you your chance."

"Yes, you gave me my chance."

"And you won't let it slip?"

His eyes were on her; his hand was always at his watch chain, twisting it to and fro.

"You'll put that old humbug into the street? You'll go there to-morrow and stay there till you've cured Burnington?"

After a moment of silence Olivia said slowly:

"What if I went to-night?"

The boy's face shone with enthusiasm.

"That's the way! Tackle old Butler to-night! But you've never told me how he got in?"

"Miss Burnington went and fetched him."

"Just like her! But why did you let him go near Sir Hector? Why did you leave the house and let him stay in it?"

"I didn't know what to do. Miss Burnington insisted."

"Isn't Burnington master in that house?"

"Yes, of course. But he's ill. And that makes it all difficult. I was there all day."

"Go back now and throw Butler out. I've done my part as a friend. Go and do yours now I've told you."

"Yes, I'll go and do mine," she said, faintly in spite of the effort she made.

She got up.

"I'll come with you!" he cried excitedly.

"No; I want you to stay here."

"Here? Why?"

"I'll just go and get things quite clear, and then I'll come back and tell you. If you come, there'll be trouble with Miss Burnington. She doesn't like you. Nor does Sir Mervyn."

"I'll wring his neck if I get at him!" he said savagely.

"Let me go alone. Promise me to stay here—promise me!"

"Very well. I don't so much mind now you know."

His air of triumph returned.

"You know me now, Olivia," he said. "And you know whether I care or not."

"Yes, I know now."

As she left him to go to her bedroom, she bent quickly and picked up the card from the floor. Instantly a suspicious look came into his face.

"What do you want with that?" he said, fiercely.

"Only to throw it into the fire," she replied.

As she turned to the flames she managed to read, the specialist's name and address. She dropped the card into the fire. Less than five minutes later she was out of the flat. In the hall she found the porter.

"Mr. West is staying on in the flat," she said. "I have to go out, but I shall soon be back."

"Very well, Ma'am."

She looked hard at the man. He was an old soldier, sturdy and strong, with a powerful, unemotional face.

"Look here!" she said. "I am going to say something to you which I beg you not to repeat."

"Honour bright, Ma'am."

"My friend, Mr. West, isn't quite himself tonight."

The porter looked much more intelligent.

"I'm going to fetch someone to see him. He's promised to wait for me. But, if I'm delayed, he might try to go. If he does, will you do your very best to detain him?"

"I will, Ma'am."

"Persuade him—don't let him go."

"I'll see to it, Ma'am."

"I shan't forget you."

He smiled slightly, and she hurried away. She found a cab and drove to the specialist's house. Luckily he was at home. He received her in his consulting room. He was a big, burly man, with enormous shoulders, a kind, strong face, and fearless and honest brown eyes. Olivia took a fancy to him at once. As briefly as she could, she laid the case of Fernol before him, after telling him that Sir Mervyn had given her his address. She did not tell him Fernol's terrible secret. She was resolved, if possible, to keep that hidden forever. But she told him quickly the history of the boy's accident, his condition afterwards, his apparent cure by her, his coming to London, her increasing anxiety about his state of health while in London, shown by his fanatical devotion to her interests, and his fanatical hatred of those whom he deemed her enemies. When she came to the Burningtons she found her task difficult. But she told as much as she dared, not sparing herself.

"My poor friend longed for Sir Hector to fall ill, so that I might cure him," she said. "And by an evil chance he fell ill."

Then she described Fernol's visits to the house in Cadogan Square, his tipping of the footman, and the scene he had made when he discovered Sir Mervyn's presence in the house. She also told about the newspaper paragraph.

"Sir Mervyn urged me not to see Mr. West tonight," she said. "But I did. I felt it my duty to see him. I—I can't tell you quite all that happened, but I'm absolutely sure the poor boy is mad. I know it. I have reason to know it. I dare not let him go. He is quite alone in London. To-morrow—even late to-night—the papers will publish a statement from me saying that I am not attending Sir Hector and that Sir Mervyn Butler is. If Mr. West sees it I am sure something terrible will happen. He is not sane. He might do anything. He is waiting in my flat now. He thinks I have gone to Sir Hector to turn Sir Mervyn out. Think of it! Can you help me?"

"Not a doubt of it!" said the doctor, after a moment of thought. "I suppose," he added, "you have told me everything of importance bearing on your friend's mental condition?"

As he said this, the honest brown eyes looked remarkably penetrating.

"I have told you all I can tell," she answered. "He is fanatical about me, because, poor boy, he thinks I have cured him. It's—it's very tragic for me."

"Yes; I can understand that. Well, the first thing to be done is for me to see him. I'll go at once. If, when I have seen him, I find clear indications of mental trouble, I can arrange for him to be under proper supervision."

"You won't … I couldn't bear for him to be put in a madhouse," said Olivia. "His father is a millionaire. I can cable to him. I'm sure he will come over."

"I have a home of my own at Hampstead for mental cases. I could take him there and watch him."

"Yes—yes. Oh, that would be the best thing possible for him."

"But I must tell you that, if I don't satisfy myself that his mind is astray, I can do nothing."

"I'm sure you will see that I am right about him."

"Very well."

The doctor got up.

"One moment! I must go to the telephone," he said.

He left the room and was away for nearly ten minutes. When he came back he had an overcoat on and his hat and gloves in his hand.

"Shall we go?" he said.

"I'm ready. You wish me to take you into the flat?"

"I wish you to drive me there. On the way I'll tell you what I propose to do."

They went out and got into the waiting taxicab.

When they arrived at Buckingham Palace Mansions, a big motor-car was standing before the entrance.

"Now," said the doctor, "you'll remain in the cab as I suggested. Have you your key? "

"Yes. Here it is."

She gave it to him. He got out, walked to the motor and stood by it for a moment, evidently speaking to someone inside. Then the door of it was opened, and a short, strongly built man emerged and joined the doctor on the pavement. After a short colloquy the doctor returned to Olivia.

"I'm going to tell your man to go a little farther on," he said. "It may be better, in certain eventualities, for you not to be just here, in front of the entrance. I may be some time. Try not to be anxious. I will return to you as soon as I can."

"I'll wait," said Olivia. "But hadn't I better just speak to the porter?"

"To be sure. I'll find him."

He went into the building and came out almost immediately with the porter.

"Is Mr. West still here?" asked Olivia.

"Yes, Ma'am."

"He hasn't tried to leave?"

"I haven't seen him, Ma'am. I've been here all the time. He must be still upstairs."

"Then please take this gentleman up."

"Yes, Ma'am."

The doctor spoke to the taxi-driver. As he turned to go into the house, followed by the porter and the man who had got out of the motor, Olivia's cabman drove on for, perhaps, a hundred yards, and then stopped. Olivia looked at her watch. It was half-past ten. She sat back in the cab and waited. For a few minutes she sat perfectly still, and then abruptly something within her, some barrier, seemed to break, and she was shaken by a passion of tears. She had controlled herself for too long, and now Nature took revenge upon her. The effort she had made when she took Fernol's hand after his hideous revelation, the hand of one who would perhaps prove to be the murderer of the man whom she loved, was the cause of this sudden and tremendous reaction. She felt now a sort of rage against Fernol. She hated him as she wept. Her pity for him was swept away. Whatever his fate he deserved it. Let him pay for what he had done; pay to the uttermost farthing! He had attacked the man whom she loved. And Sir Hector would die. All hope of his conquering the disease which was beginning to ravage him failed in Olivia at that moment. She saw nothing but blackness. She was drowned in blackness; submerged with the Furies. Her body trembled from head to foot. She clenched her hands. And she hated with her whole soul; hated the boy who had done this deed for her sake.

"Let him pay!" her brain kept crying out. "Let him pay!"

The cabman stirred on his seat. Presently he half turned. Then he slowly got down. The window of the cab was drawn up. He approached it. Then he laid his hand on the door. Olivia saw him and instinctively shrank into the corner farthest from the door. The man turned the handle and looked in.

"Did you call out, lady?" he said. "Did you want somethin'?"

Olivia managed to say "No."

The man muttered some words, and shut the door. Then he lit a pipe and walked up and down on the pavement. His interruption, the sight of his homely and moving figure, recalled Olivia to a cold sense of the present realities. She heard a clock strike eleven. The tears still streamed over her face, but now she began to wipe them away; and presently she was able to stop crying. But she kept on shivering like a child and her teeth chattered convulsively.

Half an hour passed. A sort of numb calm enfolded her. She felt frigid, detached and hard. The cabman reopened the door.

"How long are you goin' to be, lady?" he said, in a hoarse voice.

"I don't know."

"Because I don't want to be out all night. We aren't made of brick nor of stone neither, whatever some people think. There's some—" he broke off, and stared down the road in the direction of the Mansions.

"What is it?" said Olivia.

"There's someone comin' out, lady. I'm sure I do 'ope it's them, that I do."

He still stared into the night.

"There's that car—" he paused. "I do b'lieve it's the gentleman comin' at last. Yes, it is!"

A couple of minutes later Dr. Soames appeared at the window. He looked very grave. His face was slightly flushed and there was a glint of something like excitement, or unusual energy, in his eyes. His coat was buttoned up to the chin, and the collar was turned up to his ears.

"You can drive back to the Mansions," he said to the driver.

Then he opened the door.

"Shall we walk there?" he said to Olivia. "It's only a step."

"I'll get out," she said.

When she was out the driver turned the taxicab and drove off. They followed on foot.

"He's gone," said the doctor.

"Gone! Where?"

"I had two men there with the car. He'll be all right with them, poor fellow. They've taken him away."

"Then?"

"You were quite right. He's not fit to be at large."

"Was he violent?" she asked, without interest.

"Yes, at the end. But I know how to deal with such cases. He's being taken to the home I told you of at Hampstead. He'll have every care."

"Oh!"

"You mustn't see him for some time."

His tone was decisive. They were now in front of the Mansions.

"Will you come in?" she said, indifferently.

"I'll come in for five minutes. Then I should advise you to get to bed."

"I shan't sleep."

"Yes, you will. I'll take care of that. I'll only be a minute," he added to the taxi-driver.

The man began to grumble, but the doctor silenced him with money.

When they were upstairs, Olivia led the way mechanically to the drawing room. But she paused at the door. The room was in great disorder. An armchair was overturned, a small table had been broken, and the books which had been on it were strewn about the floor.

"What has happened?" she said.

She turned to the doctor.

"What did he do?"

"Nevermind."

Quietly and swiftly he put the room to rights.

"Now sit down."

She obeyed.

"Won't you take off your coat?" she said.

"No, thank you."

She noticed that he still kept the collar up. He saw her eyes on it, and said very simply,

"I'm not quite presentable."

"He attacked you?"

She spoke without any real interest, mechanically.

"He isn't himself. But we'll get him better in time, no doubt. I should cable to his father to-morrow."

"Very well."

"You didn't tell me that he suffers from hallucinations," said the doctor, looking her straight in the face.

"I didn't know it."

"Well, he does," said the doctor firmly. "He thought I was Mervyn Butler."

She was silent.

"No doubt he hasn't shown that side of his malady to you. He has also acute ego-mania. He imagines that he's done something very great, very wonderful. He has no conception whatever of right and wrong. He's in the condition when he might commit a crime and boast of it to anybody."

"It's just as well I fetched you," she said.

"Yes. Now we won't talk anymore to-night. I'll see you some time to-morrow. By the way, the reason you mustn't see him is a painful one, but I'd better tell you it. He has conceived a violent hatred for you."

"Has he?"

"Yes. He realises that you fetched me, a doctor, to him. That has turned him against you. He thinks you his greatest enemy."

"Perhaps I am," she said, coldly.

The doctor glanced at her, then took a small box from his overcoat pocket.

"Can you get me a glass of water?"

"Why?"

"I'm going to give you a couple of these and see you take them before I go. You've got to have a night's sleep."

She got up heavily, went out and came back with a glass of water.

When she had taken the pills he grasped her hand.

"Go straight to bed. You promise me?"

"Yes, I promise. But I know I shan't sleep."

He smiled.

"And I know you will. Good night."

He shook her hand and went to the door.

"Give a kind thought to the doctors," he said, and went out.

"Does he know?" Olivia thought vaguely. "Has Fernol told him? Does he know?"

Then she obeyed his direction, went to her room, undressed, and got into bed.

She felt tremendously tired, even exhausted. Her brain became dull and sluggish. It seemed to her that her body was heavy like a mass of lead.

"If only I could sleep!" she thought. "But I know I shan't."

That was her last thought before she slept....

A month had passed, and Olivia was still in London living in the little flat which had seen Fernol's tragedy. Her life, which had been so active, so full of that putting forth by which, as she had once said to Fernol, she drew in strength, had become lonely and monotonous. She saw very few people, went out very seldom. Her name, once the subject of discussion and of polemics in the Press, was now never mentioned in print, and seldom in any conversation. There had been a brief outburst when her statement had appeared in the papers denying that she was in attendance by the bedside of Sir Hector, but it had soon died down. Lord Sandring was bitterly disappointed in her. Her defection had given the final blow to his ambitions. After a painful interview, in which he had brought all his vitality to bear in an effort to persuade her to reconsider the decision so almost brutally put forth in her letter to him, he had acknowledged himself beaten by closing his Bureau of Psychic Healing. He had played his trump card, and fate had overtrumped him. There was nothing more to be done. The most remarkable woman in New York had laid him out. He retired to his estates, and began to breed Herefordshire cattle and to go in for Müller's exercises. Why Miss Traill—she was no longer Olivia to him—remained in England he could not imagine—unless it were on account of that poor chap, Fernol West, who was still in the doctors' hands, and who, of course, in such a situation, must not be expected to get better.

But it was not on Fernol's account that Olivia stayed on, laughed at and despised when she was remembered, a practically self-confessed failure. She could do nothing more for Fernol. She dared not even go to see him. His mother and father had arrived from New York, and therefore her responsibility was ended. And Fernol's maniacal hatred for her persisted. It was a fixed idea with him that she was his enemy and had deliberately ruined his life by giving him into the hands of the doctors. He had fought the doctors for her, and this was her reward to him.

Mr. and Mrs. West, in their misery, had shown the greatest delicacy, the greatest kindness to Olivia.

They knew that she had done her very best for their son, and they were still generous in their gratitude. Nevertheless, it was not possible for them to feel towards her as they had formerly felt. They had regarded her as the saviour of their adored son. Now they could only look upon her as a well-meaning and warm-hearted woman who had done her utmost, and who had failed in her endeavour. She felt pity concealed in their gentle courtesy to her, and she could scarcely bear to be with them. The look in their eyes reminded her of the belief in herself which was gone forever; the pressure of their hands intensified her regret for the faith which was lost.

And Fernol, their son, hated her. She had become part of his madness. She stayed on in London because of Sir Hector.

He was still dangerously ill with typhoid fever, hovering between life and death. She could not leave England till she knew whether he would live or die. She never went to the house in Cadogan Square. Although Miss Burnington and Sir Mervyn Butler had never said a word on the matter, she knew that, after the statement which had appeared in the *Evening Dispatch*, any visit from her might revive the rumour that she had gone as a faith-healer, anxious to interfere with the doctors, or summoned as a last hope because they could do nothing more.

She had made up her mind to complete self-sacrifice. And she was not a woman who believed in half measures. But she was kept informed of the state of the man whom she loved by Sir Mervyn Butler. The almost impossible had come about; her former antagonist and she were now staunch friends. Sir Mervyn had recognised the stark sincerity of the woman whom he had despised and done his best to ruin when she first came to London, and he had told her so in words which had kindled in her generous nature a warm response. Strangely, she now looked upon him as perhaps her best friend in England.

Sir Hector was too ill to be the friend or the enemy of anyone. And Miss Burnington, who had called on Olivia more than once, and tried to show her the greatest kindness, was obviously never quite at ease when with her. Between the two women lay dividing memories, and also the knowledge of a shared secret, which had never been spoken of by them, and so set them apart from each other.

The fifth week of the illness was nearly over when one evening Sir Mervyn Butler called on Olivia, just as she was about to leave the house for the Italian restaurant where she dined modestly alone every day. He came in with his usual rather ponderous dignity, but there was an unusually kind look in his eyes.

"He's better!" he said, immediately, without even greeting her. "The crisis is past."

"You think—will he recover?"

"I don't see why he shouldn't now. But, of course, it will be a long business, and I don't know whether he will ever be the man he was. In fact, at his age I doubt it."

Olivia said nothing. At that moment she did not dare to speak. She was rejoicing, and yet she felt stricken. For if that man had no great future what would his life be worth to him?

"I have two things I must tell you," continued Sir Mervyn, knitting his brows and looking straight before him. "Another man has got the viceroyalty of India."

"Oh!" said Olivia.

It was a little cry, and all the pity of woman was in it.

"My dear, he couldn't be fit for such a post for a long time, if ever. I should be against his returning to a strenuous life in the East."

"But his great ambition wrecked! Oh, what will he do when he knows?"

"He's a strong character. He'll take the blow standing."

She was silent, trying to control her emotion.

"The other thing I must tell you is this. He has asked for you."

"For me!" she said. "Oh, no!"

"He wants you."

"He doesn't know! He doesn't know!"

"Doesn't know what? I don't understand you."

"How can I—after all that has happened—Miss Burnington would be afraid to have me in the house."

"I consider it necessary for you to go there. His mind must not be troubled. He is insistent to see you."

"But is he quite himself?"

"Yes. He's terribly weak, of course, like a child almost. But his mind is quite clear. Surely you won't refuse to go to him?"

He was beginning to look surprised.

"I thought you had a strong regard for him."

"I have."

"Then what holds you back? Miss Burnington perhaps? But she wishes you to come."

"She asked you to tell me?"

"No. I should have done that in any case. My duty is towards my patient. But, of course, I spoke to her about it."

"What did she say?"

"She said, 'Beg Miss Traill to come. Tell her from me that I hope she will let bygones be bygones.' I don't think it would be like you to—"

"Oh, no, no! It isn't that!"

Her intense agitation was obvious. She seemed to be torn by some interior conflict.

"What will you do?" he asked.

"I'll go. If he wants me I must go. But tomorrow—I can't go to-night. Don't ask me to—please."

"Very well. But I have, your promise for tomorrow?"

"Yes, yes. But if the newspapers—"

"They won't, I dare say. But even if they do, it doesn't much matter now."

"No; it doesn't much matter now," she said.

"She loves him!" Sir Mervyn said to himself as he descended the stairs. "What an old fool I have been not to see it before."

And during his drive back to Cadogan Square he pondered over women, and came to the remarkable conclusion that possibly Miss Burnington had known for some time what had just come within the grasp of his admirable intelligence.

"Women are quick," he said to himself. "They're very unreasonable, but they're damned quick."

He knew something about them after all!

Three weeks later Sir Hector was treading slowly and feebly on the road to recovery. His natural strength was beginning at last to assert itself, and though he was still very weak he was gaining every day. Olivia was often at the house, sitting by him, talking to him, reading aloud to him, generally books of travel or memoirs of military men. One day he asked for Omar Khayyam, and she read to him for an hour.

When she had just read the lines:

> "One moment in annihilation's waste,
> One moment, of the well of Life to taste—
> The stars are setting, and the Caravan
> Draws to the Dawn of Nothing—oh, make haste!"

he stopped her.

"That's enough," he said, in the voice that was growing stronger every day.

Olivia shut up the book.

"The old chap thought pretty much what I've been thinking—when I could think at all—as I lay here," he said. "One moment of the well of Life to taste. It isn't very much, is it?"

"No," she said.

"I've sometimes wondered whether I've made the most of the part of the moment I've had till now."

"I'm sure you have," she said, wondering.

"I'm not."

"But think of the work you've done!"

"Work isn't everything after all. What about yours?"

"Mine is over," she said.

She and he had never yet spoken of her abdication. He had never alluded to it in any way since they had met again.

"I heard that," he said. "And I reckon mine is over too."

"Oh, no!" she said earnestly.

"Perhaps you think I don't know about the viceroyalty?"

"I—I—I had no idea. Your sister thinks—"

"I don't! Yes, and so does the doctor. They've kept the newspapers from me."

He smiled grimly.

"No doubt they meant to ... what is called 'break it to me' when I got better. But Sidney told me over a week ago."

She felt shaken with pity for him.

"I'm sorry," she said. "I'm sorry."

There was nothing else she could say just then.

"It's all right. I shouldn't be fit for the job now," he said, calmly.

She was silent.

"I've always lived to do jobs," he went on, without any emotion. "Perhaps I've made a mistake. How old are you?"

"Nearly twenty-nine," she answered.

"And I'm hard on the way to sixty. Do you think of me as an old man?"

"No!" she said, with a sudden gust of passion.

He looked at her hard from his pillow.

"Could you bring yourself to marry me?" he asked.

All the blood in her body—so it seemed to Olivia—rushed to her face, then retreated from it.

"I!" she said. "You—you don't know what you owe to me."

"Yes, I do."

"You don't! You don't! I never meant to tell you or anyone. But now I must. It is owing to me that you will never be Viceroy of India."

"How do you figure that out?" he asked, with a look of keen astonishment.

Then, in plain, simple words she told him all about Fernol.

"Poor boy!" she said. "He did it for me, because he thought I had healed him. I have been wicked enough to hate him for doing it. But he thought he was working for me."

Sir Hector lay for a while in silence. Then he said:

"Does anyone else know?"

"I don't think so; unless in his madness he told the doctor. And the doctor would probably not believe it."

"Wasn't West mad when he told you?"

"I know it is true. I know he did it."

Sir Hector stretched out his thin hand.

"You've done the right thing by me," he said, "but you're a woman of courage. I knew that directly I clapped eyes on you. When I get well, shall you and I keep West's secret together?"

Fernol West has been taken back to New York by his parents. A great surgeon out there, who has recently examined him, thinks it possible that a certain operation on the brain may eventually cure him. That lies in the future.

Sir Hector Burnington and Olivia were married not long ago.

To the great astonishment of Lord Sandring and of London, Sir Mervyn Butler gave her away.

THE END

Robert Hichens Bibliography

(1864-1950)

Novels
The Coast Guard's Secret (1886)
The Green Carnation (published anonymously, 1894; republished as by Hitchens, 1948)
An Imaginative Man (1895)
Flames (1897)
The Londoners (1898)
The Daughters of Babylon (1899; with Wilson Barrett)
The Slave (1899)
The Prophet of Berkeley Square (1901)
Felix (1902)
The Garden of Allah (1904)
The Woman With the Fan (1904)
Call of the Blood (1905)
Barbary Sheep (1907)
A Spirit in Prison (1908)
Bella Donna (1909; reprinted as *Temptation*, 1946)
The Dweller on the Threshold (1911)
The Fruitful Vine (1911)
The Way of Ambition (1913)
In the Wilderness (1917)
Mrs. Marden (1919)
The Spirit of the Time (1921)
December Love (1922)
After The Verdict (1924)
The Unearthly (1925; UK as *The God Within Him*)
The Bacchante and the Nun (1926; US as *The Bacchante*)
The First Lady Brendon (1927)
Dr. Artz (1928)
On the Screen (1929)
The Bracelet (1930)
The Gates of Paradise (1930)
The First Lady Brendon (1931)
Mortimer Brice (1932)
The Paradine Case (1933)
The Power to Kill (1934)
Susie's Career (1935)
The Pyramid (1936)
The Sixth of October (1936)
Daniel Airlie (1937)
Secret Information (1938)
The Journey Up (1938)
That Which Is Hidden (1939)
The Million (1940)
Married or Unmarried (1941)
A New Way of Life (1941)
Veils (1943)
Young Mrs. Brand (1944)
Harps in the Wind (1945; U.S. as *The Woman in the House*)
Incognito (1945; Hutchinson)
Too Much Love of Living (1947)
Beneath the Magic (1950; U.S. as *Strange Lady*)
The Mask (1951)
Night Bound (1951)

Collections
The Folly of Eustace and Other Stories (1896)
Bye-Ways (1897)
Tongues of Conscience (1898, 1900)
The Black Spaniel and Other Stories (1905)
Snake-Bite and Other Stories (1919)
The Last Time (1924)
The Streets and Other Stories (1928)
The Gardenia and Other Stories (1934)
The Man in the Mirror and Other Stories (1950)
The Return of the Soul and Other Stories (2001; ed. S. T. Joshi)

Nonfiction
Old Cairo (1908; article)
Egypt and Its Monuments (1908)
The Holy Land (1910)
The Spell of Egypt (1910; orig. published as *Egypt and Its Monuments*, 1908)
The Near East (1913)
Yesterday (1947)

Plays
The Law of the Sands (1916)
Black Magic (1917)
The Voice from the Minaret (1919)

Filmography [based on the novel unless otherwise noted]

Bella Donna (directed by Edwin S. Porter and Hugh Ford; 1915)
The Garden of Allah (directed by Colin Campbell; 1916)
Barbary Sheep (directed by Maurice Tourneur; 1917)
Flames (directed by Maurice Elvey; UK, 1917)
The Slave (directed by Arrigo Bocchi; UK, 1918)
Hidden Lives (directed by Maurits Binger and B. E. Doxat-Pratt; Netherlands, 1920, based on a play by Robert Hichens and John Knittel)
The Call of the Blood (directed by Louis Mercanton; France, 1920)
The Woman with the Fan (directed by René Plaissetty; UK, 1921)
The Fruitful Vine (directed by Maurice Elvey; UK, 1921)
The Voice from the Minaret (directed by Frank Lloyd; 1923, based on the play)
Bella Donna (directed by George Fitzmaurice; 1923)
The Lady Who Lied (directed by Edwin Carewe; 1925, based on the story)
The Garden of Allah (directed by Rex Ingram; 1927)
After the Verdict (directed by Henrik Galeen; UK, 1929)
Bella Donna (directed by Robert Milton; UK, 1934)
The Garden of Allah (directed by Richard Boleslawski; 1936)
Temptation (directed by Irving Pichel; 1946, based on the novel *Bella Donna*)
The Paradine Case (directed by Alfred Hitchcock; 1947)
Call of the Blood (directed by John Clements and Ladislao Vajda; UK, 1948)

www.ingramcontent.com/pod-product-compliance
Lightning Source LLC
LaVergne TN
LVHW021808060526
838201LV00058B/3288